THE
ORPHAN WITCH

THE
ORPHAN
WITCH

PAIGE CRUTCHER

ST. MARTIN'S GRIFFIN
NEW YORK

For three goddesses in my life,
Isla, Brinley, and Ava

First published in the United States by St. Martin's Griffin,
an imprint of St. Martin's Publishing Group

THE ORPHAN WITCH. Copyright © 2021 by Paige Crutcher.
All rights reserved. Printed in the United States of America.
For information, address St. Martin's Publishing Group,
120 Broadway, New York, NY 10271.

www.stmartins.com

Designed by Jonathan Bennett

Library of Congress Cataloging-in-Publication Data

Names: Crutcher, Paige, author.
Title: The orphan witch / Paige Crutcher.
Description: First edition. | New York : St. Martin's Griffin, 2021. |
    Identifiers: LCCN 2021016069 | ISBN 9781250797377
    (trade paperback) | ISBN 9781250823632 (hardcover) |
    ISBN 9781250797384 (ebook)
Subjects: GSAFD: Fantasy fiction.
Classification: LCC PS3603.R876 O77 2021 | DDC 813/.6—dc23
LC record available at https://lccn.loc.gov/2021016069

Our books may be purchased in bulk for promotional, educational,
or business use. Please contact your local bookseller or the Macmillan
Corporate and Premium Sales Department at 1-800-221-7945, extension
5442, or by email at MacmillanSpecialMarkets@macmillan.com.

First Edition: 2021

10 9 8 7 6 5 4 3 2 1

For there is no friend like a sister
In calm or stormy weather;
To cheer one on the tedious way,
To fetch one if one goes astray,
To lift one if one totters down,
To strengthen whilst one stands.

—CHRISTINA ROSSETTI, *Goblin Market*

one

THE ISLE OF WILE

1919

A s Amara Mayfair stood on the cliffs of Wile Isle, she wasn't thinking about power, not at first, though power was certainly in play. She wasn't thinking about magic either, though the sky was filled with it. As light danced around her, and electricity sparked in the palms of her hands, she was thinking about family. Lost family, like her ancestors sunken into the ocean, and those people we love but who end up lost to us even when they're only a few miles away.

After all, Amara had written the poem about goblins in the market for her lost sister. Amara had penned and published it through the name of a girl she met reading in a field in London, England. It had been easy to bespell the Rossetti girl when Amara was off island on her travels abroad. Amara hoped the poem would grant the girl a better life and a clear path. She doubted it, though. Magic had a cost, and Amara had learned you could never escape paying its price.

Still, she hoped the poem would prove worth the effort. That one day, it would lead to redemption. It was a road map after all, and all it needed was the right person looking for a guide.

Amara turned her head to the east and studied the ancient ash tree that was spelled into a carnival tent. The tent was lit from the inside, the light expanding out and casting shadows against the earth. The shadows undulated, and from where Amara stood, they looked like beings rather than reflections.

Under her the ground shook as above the night sky shifted from a deep purple to a furious violet. Time was running forward, and the show was nothing if not theatrical.

One hundred years ago Amara's ancestor had made a bargain for power. The islands, and Amara's people, had paid dearly for it. Tonight, she feared another bargain—of a sort—could cost the rest of her family everything they had left.

The island's heart pulsed in Amara's veins, because the magic was there. It was always there, waiting. Made of neither power nor loss, magic was like the Goddess. Secretive, all-knowing, and unwilling to bow down to the whims of man.

Amara closed her eyes and looked inward, to the women who had come before her. To the ones who craved magic so deeply they could not see when it went dark. Amara whispered the words she had written, the ones that sprang up when she closed her eyes and saw the truth, when she looked to the vision of the corrupted magic reflected on her lost ancestors' faces.

> "*One had a cat's face,*
> *one whisked a tail,*
> *one tramped at a rat's pace,*
> *one crawled like a snail,*
> *one like a wombat prowled obtuse and furry,*
> *one like a ratel tumbled hurry skurry,*
> *she heard a voice like voice of doves, cooing all together:*
> *they sounded kind and full of loves in the pleasant weather.*"

This was never about women betraying women or women betraying men or men betraying women. It was about magic and power, and the two coming together to take down anyone who stood in their path. And this night, this night with its wind blowing in from the wrong direction and the green lightning emblazing the skies, well, Amara had little doubt it was only the beginning.

"Come buy, come buy," she whispered.

Then Amara Mayfair turned and walked down the cliff and into the billowing flap of the carnival tent.

▸ ▸ ▸

Off Island
2019

BEING LOST WAS a thing Persephone May knew quite a lot about, being that lost was where she'd always been. She supposed if she had been born musical she'd know rather a lot about guitars and pan flutes, drums and trombones. As it was, she couldn't hold a note and had little patience for harmonies and sotto voce. But from the moment she'd been left on the doorstep of a firehouse at age six weeks, Persephone had been misplaced.

"She's a bit like Paddington, if the bear had claws for teeth and knives for paws. It's hard to embrace *that*," Persephone had once heard a social worker say of her when she was nine, while trying to place her in yet another group home. "Too bad about that last family, though."

The last family, the Millers, had almost been the ones: the people to claim Persephone, to finally give her a family and home. In their house, Persephone had a room of her own with an antique white desk and a twin bed with a lavender down comforter as soft as silk, pillows that cradled her head, and a lamp with a silver shade and the kind of light that made the room glow instead of burning her eyes. Persephone knew from the moment she sat on that bed it would be more than enough . . . if only it could last.

"You look so sad, honey," kind Mary Miller would say to the little girl who sat on a dead tree stump in her backyard staring up at the sky. "Why don't we try and find your smile?"

Mary Miller smiled with her whole face. When her lips curved, her eyes crinkled and friendly lines creased around her lips.

Persephone had been desperate to pocket that smile the first time she saw it.

The smiles didn't last, though. Mary would soon learn that Persephone, while lost, was powerful in ways no person should be.

Persephone had abilities she'd never understood. At the age of five, she had stirred the wind when she'd sent a diminutive tornado after a particularly nasty boy who tugged on her auburn pigtails and called her Pippi Longstocking. The tornado had carried the boy two fields over, and deposited him in Lockland Pond.

When she was seven, Persephone had made her foster sister disappear for six hours after the girl tried to flush Persephone's beloved copy of *Anne of Green Gables* down the toilet, and then blamed Persephone for the clog. At eight and three-quarters, Persephone had accidentally poisoned her depressed teacher by stirring her tea for her and thinking "laughter." The teacher spent three days giggling tears and had to be admitted into the local hospital's psychiatric wing.

But it was at age nine, when Mary Miller stared too long into Persephone's eyes and then hacked off her own hair with kitchen shears while shrieking, that Persephone finally, truly understood.

She was made wrong, she was evil, and she was cursed to be alone.

Things didn't improve from there. Gone was the room at the Millers' with linens that smelled like sunshine, and thick, home-made oatmeal with fresh fruit for breakfast. Replacing it were group homes with blankets that itched, processed food, floors that stuck under her shoes, and people who would never mistake Persephone as *family*. For the rest of her adolescence, anytime anyone made eye contact with Persephone for too long, a change would inevitably come over them. One minute, they were smiling, pleasant as a sunrise, the next . . . pure unfiltered rage.

She couldn't understand *why*. Over the years Persephone would spend her limited free time tucked in various libraries reading. When she wasn't escaping into worlds where mothers and daughters were best friends, families gathered around the kitchen table for dinner, and happily-ever-afters were guaranteed, she was studying. Persephone studied books on the occult, watched every online documentary, movie, and television series on magic she could get her hands on, and always came up empty.

Whatever power she had, it was wicked and it was *mean*.

Without meaning to, Persephone made one girl punch a wall, another boy kick a dog, and one supervisor at her group home slam her own face into a locker. After a girl threw Persephone off the second-floor balcony in a fit of rage (Persephone landed like a cat on her feet), she made the decision to keep her eyes to herself so no one else would get hurt.

Persephone kept her head down, and let go of her greatest dream of finding family and friends. The foster care system was an impossible one, but Persephone fought to make her lack of community—or distractions of any kind—work to her advantage. She finished her education online with a focus that bordered on obsessive, and defied the odds in a system that strove to forget people who should be unforgettable. Persephone secured admittance into an online university, where she went on to complete her bachelor's degree in English while working a series of odd jobs in forgettable towns and earning just enough to make fraying ends meet. Her love of learning and libraries (and her fascination with her own unruly power) would eventually lead Persephone to write her own book, *The Upside of Down Magicks*, which explored the use of magic in literature, and was published by a small press.

But the book would be forgettable and a failure, much like Persephone's ability to control her power. So even as she remained steadfast in her search for answers, Persephone May stayed lost.

And a lost thing is always waiting to be found.

▸ ▸ ▸

ON AN ASHEN gray late September morning, the clouds hovered so low to the horizon that Persephone's fingers twitched to reach out and catch them. While standing behind the counter at Gone Wired—the third coffee shop she'd worked in the third town that year—she felt someone watching her.

It was a tingle against her spine, the awareness of being studied. The first time Persephone felt that tingle she was four, and she was standing alone in a library in Asheville, North Carolina. One minute she was running down the aisle as fast as her feet could carry her, racing to find her foster sister and tag her in hopes the girl would finally be her friend. In the next moment, Persephone felt what at the time she could only describe as a *giggle* run down her spine. She stopped running, climbed up the two-foot stepping stool in front of a section of books on travel, and found herself face-to-face with a very stubborn-looking librarian. Persephone stared at his cheek and the thick stubble there, and watched his lips twitch into a smile.

"Hello there," he said. "Lost, are you?"

"No. Why, are you?"

He laughed, and shook his head. "Best be on your way then."

Something about his smile had made her hesitate, but then her foster sister's laugh rang out and Persephone had jumped down from the stool and taken off in her direction, desperate to try and win the game and the other little girl's affection.

Now the tingle was back, and thirty-two-year-old Persephone was wary. She turned her head, dipping her chin enough to see behind her as she worked to build the mocha latte for the waiting customer.

The man stood only inches from her station. A regular in the coffee shop, he was a professor at a nearby college who liked graphic novels and vintage novelty pins. The one he'd stuck to the pocket of his light flannel today advertised: *I like Ike*. His name was Thom and he'd been asking Persephone innocuous questions like, "Did you get certified to make those complicated frappuccinos?" and "Which do you prefer, movies or books or movies based on books?" for weeks now.

Thom wouldn't be the first man to find Persephone interesting. There was something inside her, whatever it was that made her wrong, that drew people to her. She'd noticed it when she was thirteen, and her hormones were misfiring like faulty fireworks.

For a girl who craved love like a drought craves rain, crushes had hit Persephone especially hard.

It started with Devon McEntire, the boy with caramel eyes and swooping black hair. The loner nephew of one of the guardians at the group home Persephone was residing in, Devon was beautiful in a clumsy way, and spent most of the afternoons on the creaking brown sofa drawing in a battered gray notebook. She watched him for weeks, lingering in doorways, taking twice as long sweeping the floor so she could study how his shoulders curved and his mouth compressed into a fine line while he worked. Eventually, Devon called Persephone out on it, asking her name and inviting her to join him on the sofa. She knew better than to look at him, so she brought her library books for the online home school program she was enrolled in and they sat side by side, not talking, but being there. Together.

In the evening, when the light faded, Persephone felt safer. Devon would look at her, his gaze drawing a blush hot across her chest, and she learned to crave the times when she could study the mole over his right eyebrow.

At dusk, the room grew warmer, the dragon of desire Persephone discovered living in her belly unfurling its wings and flapping each time Devon smiled her way. It wasn't love, but it was something—sitting with Devon, not talking but smiling . . . a lot. When the snowstorm came that January, and Devon had to stay the night, Persephone took it as a sign.

That night, he snuck into her closet-sized room. As the snow escaped the sky, he trailed kisses along her cheeks, and awkwardly bumped her nose with his chin before his mouth captured hers. Devon tasted of spearmint gum and smelled like Irish soap. In the morning, he snuck back into her room, crawling into her bed and kissing Persephone awake. It was like a dream. A normal, beautiful dream. That's why Persephone didn't think. That's why she looked into his eyes.

Persephone was lonely, living in the group home. Most kids in the system cycle in and out of any given home within eight months to a year. A few of them would arrive with an edge so sharp if you brushed past them too quickly, you'd bleed. It made it hard to make friends, even without Persephone's . . . problem.

Sometimes the kids came in with trauma too thick to unpack. The year before Devon came, a girl went into the bathroom with a razor blade and didn't come back out. So no one said much, after the snowstorm. After Devon looked into Persephone's eyes for too long, he jerked away from her, crossed to the window, yanked it up, and jumped out.

Devon, Persephone heard months later, made a full recovery. His aunt transferred homes and life, or something like it, went on. Though it was hard for Persephone to believe in romance after that.

From then on, when the dragon of desire would foolishly wake, Persephone would distract it with library books about fictional boyfriends. It was too painful, otherwise. Persephone ended up losing her virginity to a summer library intern with piercing blue eyes and a Scottish accent in a darkened microfilm room that smelled of Febreze. She learned that with the lights out, anyone could be a fictional boyfriend, and as long as she didn't let her heart become involved, her basest needs could be met.

Her life had been a journey of seeking satisfaction in the basics, knowing anything beyond it was impossible. Wishing for more touches, more connection, more . . . everything.

When Thom stepped up to rest his arm on the counter, and Persephone glanced down at the cuff of his sleeve, his long fingers inches from her own, yearning spread into her fingertips.

Persephone read a study once that said people crave being hugged at least fifteen times a day, and the number of seconds necessary to satisfy the need for affection was twenty seconds, which was surprising because when watching people hug—and Persephone knew this because she had timed them—an embrace typically only lasted five to seven seconds.

Persephone would gladly settle for a single moment.

"Morning, Pea," Thom said, using the nickname she'd written on her application that was now typed across her name tag. Persephone had hoped that in moving to the small town of Greenville two months ago, she might become Sweet Pea. She'd stopped inventing new backstories for herself, and knew even the name change was a halfhearted attempt, but she couldn't help it. Hope was a strong drug to quit.

"How's it going today, Thom?"

"Today's poetry workshop featured three poems written about body parts and one about an amorous dog," he said, laughter in his voice. "But there's coffee coming and a clever redhead to talk to, so it could be worse."

Persephone watched the young professor's pinky tap against the counter, a nervous tic. Yes, Thom either really liked her coffee or he really liked her. She tugged at the back of her apron strings, debating. It had been months since her last random hookup with a bartender at a swanky jazz bar. It had been a quick and forgettable encounter. Persephone long ago discovered the men she had fast and sweaty sex with lacked the knowledge and finesse female authoresses imbued their fictional love interests with.

She passed over his Americano, and his hand brushed her arm, a slight squeeze of warmth that lingered after he'd moved back. She breathed in deep, the spice of his aftershave tickling her nose.

"Perhaps tomorrow will prove better," she said, and smiled.

Thom laughed, and the sound slipped inside, past her carefully erected barriers. Persephone was so tired of meaningless. She was exhausted by trying so hard not to care. Why couldn't something have changed? Wasn't that how the world was supposed to work? Change was the constant and everyone else was the variable. Once again Persephone wished for something more, something real, and as Thom shifted his weight from foot to foot, she was suddenly overcome with the urge of: *Why not?*

Persephone tilted her chin and *looked*.

Thom's eyes were a deep chocolate brown, with tiny flecks of cinnamon. He blinked, and Persephone held her breath.

Just this once, she thought, *please let someone see me*. Her lips curved in a promise, and then it happened.

The smile dropped from his face. His eyes narrowed.

"I . . . I . . ." he stammered.

Thom shook his head like he was waking from a trance. He picked up the piping hot Americano and walked out the door.

Persephone's heart raced at how he didn't pause. He didn't look left or right. She was out from behind the counter and running for the door when Thom walked directly into traffic. Horns honked, tires squealed. A blue Jeep barely missed barreling into him. A young man in a green backpack shouted Thom's name, his student perhaps, and ran from the curb to pull the professor back onto the sidewalk.

Looking dazed, Thom stared at the young man, before trying to cross into the street again.

Persephone swallowed the tears as she stepped back inside the shop. She waited until the young man and his two friends had Thom firmly in hand, ushering him to safety, before she turned from the wide windows.

Running her hands over her apron one, two, three times, she tried to force a calm she did not feel back into her body. She had done that. Nearly killed the man because she was lonely. Just like what she'd done to Devon. Because she needed so badly to be seen. Hands shaking, Persephone walked past the counter, ready to break into a run for the bathroom.

"What a dumbass," said her co-worker, Deandra Bishop, as she set out large coffees on the to-go station.

Deandra rarely spoke to Persephone. At first Persephone had clumsily tried to befriend the girl, but she quickly learned Deandra had little time for talking at work—unless it was to argue with their other co-worker, Larkin.

Persephone nodded her agreement, pausing to take a gulp of air, and look back to the large windows and the crowd outdoors that was dispersing. The front door opened and a gangly young man charged in.

"Did you *see* that?" Larkin asked, hurrying in his lateness for his shift. "Professor Thom either had *way* too much or not enough coffee this morning."

"Funny," Deandra deadpanned. "Let me guess, his near-death experience inspired another bad poem for your Depressed Poets Society?"

"It's my poetry *workshop*, Deandra, and damn." He scratched his nose and looked over at Persephone, whose stomach was doing complicated flips as she listened to their conversation. "I hope it won't be canceled today. Do you think they'll cancel class for . . ."

Persephone blinked, staring into Larkin's eyes. She'd been so intent on listening, so shaken up from watching Thom try to kill himself that she hadn't looked away in time.

Oh. No.

Larkin stared at her, his eyes growing perceptibly wider, the pupils dilating as his mouth formed a perfect O.

"Larkin?" Persephone said his name softly, fear crawling along her skin. She rubbed at her arms, trying to brush it away.

Suddenly, his lips were moving and Larkin was speaking, the words coming out in a melodic rush.

> *"Her hips*
> *were a*
> *pendulum*
> *luring*
> *me in*
> *Swish swish*
> *A siren's wish*
> *Come*
> *come*
> *They beckon*
> *me on."*

Larkin took a step toward her like a puppet possessed. She held her breath, prepared to react when he grabbed for her, but instead he stepped past her to the large coffees resting on the to-go station.

He fisted one in each hand, looked at Persephone, and

squeezed. Hot coffee spurted out of both cups as he raised and dumped the steaming contents onto his face.

Persephone screamed. Deandra shouted. The commotion, riding on the coattails of the excitement from the morning, sent people on the sidewalk outside rushing in. Larkin, dripping with scalding hot coffee, his skin molten red, turned to go behind the counter— straight for the espresso machine.

Persephone dove after him. For a moment, the light in the room changed. It sparkled and shimmered. She thought she saw cobblestones and a spire on a church, then she tackled Larkin to the floor, whispering the only word she could think clearly: *release*.

Larkin's whole body relaxed beneath her. His head hit the floor, his eyes fluttered shut, and his limbs went limp. The hivelike buzz of the coffee shop was suddenly silent. Persephone turned her head.

Every single person in the room lay on the floor, their eyes closed.

Persephone gulped. She raised one shaky hand to her brow and wiped. Were they . . .

A seated woman in a brown sweater whose face was pressed into the table snored loudly and Persephone let out a shock of laughter. Beside her Larkin gave a wheezy exhale. Asleep. Not dead. They were all *asleep*.

A rustling to her left had Persephone pushing up to her feet, reaching for the table to steady herself.

Deandra Bishop stood five feet away, very much not asleep, tapping her bright yellow nails on the counter.

"But—" Persephone gave her head a shake. "How are you not . . ."

Deandra stepped into Persephone's sight line and gave her a long look. Deandra didn't flinch, didn't react like people usually did, turning ghost white from Persephone's sustained eye contact and trying to harm herself or someone else. Instead, her amber eyes flashed with irritation and she sidestepped over the small river of pooling coffee.

She rolled her shoulders back and stood with her chin raised, her voice dropping an octave. "What the hell *are you*?"

▸ ▸ ▸

PERSEPHONE DIDN'T PAUSE to take off her apron or close out her station. She babbled for ten seconds, then pushed past Deandra and ran for the door.

What the hell *are you*?

Inside the safety of her ancient Volvo sedan, Persephone tried to come up with a viable answer. But nothing could explain away how today she had driven two people to try and destroy themselves, and then knocked out a room of others. Nothing aside from one word: *monster*.

Persephone turned the A/C on full blast, took deep gulps of air, and tried to keep her hands steady on the wheel. She thought of how the other woman had looked in her eyes, and nothing happened, and quickly decided she'd imagined it. Deandra must have been out of earshot, perhaps in the bathroom, when Persephone spoke to Larkin, must have somehow escaped whatever Persephone had done.

She must have been terrified.

Persephone pulled into the long drive that led to her room in the aging Victorian house with cracked shutters. It was a month-to-month rental, and with every step she took into the house and then into her room, her nerves jumped.

This wasn't the first, second, or even tenth time something like this had happened. But it was the worst time. Whatever was wrong with her was amplifying and the gods only knew what would happen if she stayed a minute longer. She could imagine the confused faces of the customers as they awoke, and Deandra's fear and revulsion. Persephone couldn't explain herself. She'd sound crazy if she tried, and get hauled away to a psychiatric facility. Or, if someone *did* believe her, what then? She'd end up in an experiment locked in a crazy scientist's basement? No, thank you.

Persephone tugged her three-piece luggage set from under the bed. She kept one bag packed, so it was fairly easy to empty the dresser and dump the contents from her vanity and toiletry set into the other two. She paused long enough to fire off an email to the landlady, leaving the last of the rent in an envelope on the bed. She considered sending a second message to her boss at Gone Wired and giving her notice, but she couldn't know what Deandra would tell him about the day's events.

So Persephone left. She got back into her car with what felt like her whole world tucked in the backseat, and drove down the main road, onto the highway, and onto the interstate. She didn't look back. She never looked back.

Not anymore.

The tremble from her hands moved into her thighs, and she jimmied her legs as she drove. At a red light she checked her phone for a missed call from her boss—or the police—and blew out a breath of relief when she saw no one had called. She tried to sing along with the radio, but her voice cracked when it came out. The people debating on talk radio made her head buzz. Her mouth was as dry as a salt lick, and she was terrified to stop. It wasn't until the gas light came on over an hour into her drive to anywhere else, that she exited the interstate and stopped at a Gas n' Go.

Persephone was quick to pay for the bottles of water and granola bars while her tank filled. When she was back in the driver's seat, she heard the phone vibrate insistently from inside her bag.

Her heart gave a thump until she saw the name on the email. Hyacinth Ever.

Persephone had met Hyacinth one year ago, when working as a research assistant for a nondescript job in a nondescript town. Hyacinth had been emailing Persephone off and on ever since. Her messages were always upbeat and full of the colorful goings-on in her small town of Wile Isle. Over the past twelve months, they'd formed a long-distance friendship, or something like it. It was a first for Persephone, as precious as her early edition copy of *Rebecca*, and she still didn't know how to navigate it.

P,

Okay, I know the last time I asked you blew me off, but you have to come visit. Pretty, pretty please with whipped cream and sprinkles and cherries and all the tastiest things on top?

Come to Wile Isle, off the coast of North Carolina. Our front porch is teeming with books, there's a fresh pot of mint tea waiting, and the breeze from the ocean promises to blow all your troubles away.

I'm attaching a map.

—H

Persephone stared at the screen. Hyacinth *had* asked her to visit before, but Persephone couldn't tell if it was a piecrust invitation (easily made and easily broken) or if she'd meant it. It had been her first invitation of its sort.

She reread the email, and a strange sense of calm spread through her. If only her troubles *could* be blown away. If only there were a place she could not just escape into, but where she might belong. It was the oldest of all her dreams, and she tried to swat it away, but this time it scooted closer, pressed its way into her heart.

She downloaded the map and tugged on her lip as she studied it. It felt incredibly risky to go, especially on the heels of the episodes at the coffee shop. But what if change *could* happen, what if it simply didn't show up the way you expected?

What were the odds of receiving this particular email at this particular moment? Persephone was four hours away from Hyacinth and her island. Four hours and 240 miles from Wile Isle with nowhere else to go, and she didn't have to stay there if once she arrived, it felt wrong. Persephone considered her bags in the backseat. If there was anything Persephone was good at, it was leaving.

Combing a hand through her hair, she inhaled a deep breath. Salt, the sea, a tang of honey and wine. She tasted all four on her tongue and closed her eyes.

Wile Isle.

It sounded like forgotten words to a once beloved song. It sounded like a place to belong.

HYACINTH EVER'S JOURNAL

Twelve months prior

The stars are low in the sky tonight. I've been standing here all afternoon in this new town, my toes dug deep into this unfamiliar earth, waiting for dusk to bring the moon out. My face has stayed turned toward the clouds, my eyes closed.

Night-calling. That's what Moira would call it and maybe she's right. I know my sister wouldn't approve of my being here, but what she doesn't know can't hurt her.

I've been calling the night to me because lately I see better in the dark. It's important to see clearly, now more than ever, and today I think I saw her— the one to break the island's curse. She was walking down the street, coming toward me. Her red hair billowed behind her like a cape, power crackling off her in waves. She was singing softly under her breath. The song reached me first, and I knew her voice. Persephone May. She kept her eyes down, so she's not yet found her freedom. I can help her with that.

Because tonight, for the first time in a long time, I see the way forward.

The stars are low in the sky, but my toes are dug into the earth and this . . . if Moira were here, I'd tell her this is what not giving up hope feels like.

TWO

The night fog crept along the ground like a veil trailing after a bride. The earth beneath it was a damp bed of sanctuary, the grass so green it would hurt your eyes if the fog weren't covering it up. The ghost air, what Hyacinth had told Persephone people on Wile Isle called the incoming water vapor, stopped at five feet. The contrast made the crop of live oaks circling out from the dock feel like something in a storybook.

Persephone was a tangle of nerves and excitement. Nerves because she would get to see her friend in person again, which was a risk. And excitement over the possibility of what it could mean to finally have a true friend.

She watched the ripples in the water spread out as the boat tugged closer and closer to the island, and thought of the day she met Hyacinth. It was over a year ago, when Persephone worked a short stint as a research assistant. Hyacinth, while on vacation, had come into the office looking for someone, and ended up staying to get to know Persephone. It was the first time anyone had looked at Persephone and stayed. That in itself had seemed a miracle.

"What's your name?" Hyacinth asked the day they met. "I

don't think I've seen you before, and I've been in town a few times."

"Persephone. Persephone May."

"Sea goddess, right? Persephone?"

"Spring." Persephone said, flicking her eyes up for the briefest of moments. "Queen of the Underworld."

Hyacinth rubbed her chin, and Persephone was struck by how familiar the sight was. As though she'd seen her do it before—once or a thousand times. "Abducted Queen of the Underworld," said Hyacinth, her voice softer than velvet. "Hades stole her, didn't he?"

"He tried," Persephone said, looking down at the pages on her desk. "I like to think she stole herself. Women are always so much stronger than myths can convey."

Hyacinth laughed. "True."

Persephone decided Hyacinth Ever, whose name *she'd* stolen from the application she handed back, was someone she wished she could befriend. A name once stolen is hard to release, and Persephone expected Hyacinth to fade away, like a Polaroid developing in reverse. Instead Hyacinth emailed one week later.

"My island is waking up this week. There are flower carts in the street, bicycles with baskets full of books from the little free library set up by the beach, and a farmer's market where the misfits of Wile sell their wares," Hyacinth's email read. "You should come visit. Come see my corner of the world."

Hope is a dangerous thing, and as the boat pulled into the dock, Persephone leaned all the way into optimism. She imagined once more the moment of being reunited with her friend, and in the next instant a line of static started with a tingle in her toes and shot up the backs of her legs. It prickled along her scalp, ran down her forearms, and pulsed into her fingertips.

Oh.

The island was charged with power. It snapped into her, and Persephone's hands shook. She didn't look down for fear she'd see sparks. Instead she tucked her hands in her pockets and took a slow, deep breath.

Did *Hyacinth* know her island was so charged?

"It draws you in, doesn't it?"

Persephone jumped. She had been so caught up in daydreaming she hadn't realized there was another passenger on what the captain had called a ferry and any other person would call a tugboat.

"Didn't mean to startle you." The woman's voice was musical, high and crisp. It swelled like the sea on the final notes.

"The island is beautiful," Persephone said, her blood quickening. It felt like her whole system was waking up. The waves lapped against the dock Persephone faced, and it wasn't until the woman stood beside her that Persephone pulled her gaze from the sea. She cautiously studied the passenger's profile: the woman's sharp chin, deep-set eyes, and gorgeous linen suit the color of stormy skies.

Lightning split the sky, and the hairs on Persephone's arms stood at attention.

"It's worth the fuss," the stranger said. "And the muss."

Persephone ran her hands over her arms, unable to rid herself of the sudden chill. She assumed the stranger meant accepting the limitations the island came with, such as poor Wi-Fi, or how she couldn't board her car because the road that ran to the island was washed out. But then the woman grinned and Persephone's fingers tingled like the tips were conducting electricity.

"Do you know where you're going?" the passenger asked.

"I'm . . . staying with a friend," Persephone said, testing the word out loud, shaking out her fingers, hoping the woman didn't find her too odd.

Her thoughts shifted again to Hyacinth. Her *friend*. Speaking that word felt wonderful. Persephone imagined she was the protagonist in a buddy comedy, going to be reunited with her bosom friend, ready to have a montage of adventures that ended in laughter and exuberant hugs. She couldn't hold back the smile.

Persephone noted the beginnings of a town off the dock. In the distance she saw lights and a road and a series of stone shops with slate roofs. The town appeared charming, though the world around it was silent.

Thunder rumbled, and the stranger took a step back.

"A *friend* you say," the woman said. "Well, then. So it begins."

Persephone looked over in surprise. Was there unmistakable malice in her tone? And *what* begins?

Poof. The woman was gone. Persephone searched for a place the stranger could have quickly moved to, but there was none. Persephone tried again to rub the creeping cold from her arms. It should have been impossible for the woman to disappear, but the air was as thick as a wool blanket, and Persephone tasted power on her tongue. It was sweet, but slightly tart—like a crisp green apple.

Magic.

The woman. The island. Was it possible?

Persephone swallowed a hiccup of . . . hope. She shouldn't assume, she needed to be sure. Persephone scooped up her luggage, managing to set the small bag on top of her larger rolling suitcase and hefting the carry-on over her shoulder, and exited the boat.

Lightning lit the sky, and Persephone felt the hum rock into her bones like she'd stuck not just her finger, but her entire arm, into an electrical socket.

Magic.

The gentle light of the lanterns swayed along the dock, and in the distance Persephone finally spotted the passenger. She stood a good way up from Persephone on the beach, the stranger's hands cocked to her hips, her eyes stark and clear—and staring straight into Persephone's.

The air smelled strongly of salt, of a coming rain. It tasted like spiced wine, of mysteries batted away from the surface of the island. A sharp breeze swept by, swirling the ends of the other woman's coat.

"This autumnal equinox sets the ticking of the clock. Beware the tidings of Wile Isle," the passenger's voice impossibly whispered in her ear.

Persephone shuddered. Lightning flashed across the sky once more, skittering up from the earth where the stranger stood a hundred feet away. The other woman jumped back, her arms rose up as if in protection, and the lightning seemed to respond and shoot away from her.

The stranger lowered her arms and her eyes, now flecked with panic and ... something else, met Persephone's once more.

Persephone's breath caught. The stranger swept her coat behind her, turned, and marched up the shoreline. The night welcomed the stranger, wrapping itself around her. It was a long moment before Persephone let out a breath she didn't realize she'd been holding.

She wasn't sure what was going on, but Persephone couldn't wait to find Hyacinth.

She needed to ask her friend a hundred questions. She also knew she shouldn't get too far ahead of herself. The trouble with being on her own for so long was that Persephone had perfected the art of fantasizing. She was an expert at being in her head, skating just this side of reality. It was how she had survived her childhood. It made the traumatic bearable, but it also set her up for failure. She knew that. So Persephone forced herself to stay present. To not get ahead of herself. She would simply put one foot in front of the other.

She turned in the direction of town, and the moon's light shone brighter, illuming the way. Lanterns bordered the path leading from the dock, and the road curved as Persephone hurried along its side. To her left were thick bushes and to her right were mossy trees, the shades of green a quilt blanketing Persephone on either side of the narrow road. She gave room for any being that might come her way, but none did. The stroll turned into a climb, and once more her spine tingled. Persephone set down her luggage, held up her hands in wonder and turned in a slow circle.

She'd never been *anywhere* that felt like this.

Persephone looked over her shoulder; certain there was a town just over the path, but there was only the moon and the road and her shadow. To the right she saw two houses. One stood tall and was set off from the beach; the other looked as though it had been exhaled from the hill, half of it hidden. She studied the beach house and the small fire smoldering at the edge of it.

The smell of salt tickled her nose, chased by the sweet crisp ripening of the surrounding foliage. Her feet itched and an urge to turn, to dive into the greenery, pressed in against the sides of the path and crashed over her.

A second cobblestone path she'd overlooked stretched out to the right. Music. Laughter. The smell of roses out of bloom. She thought she saw a ripe apple tree. Between the pull of the moon and seduction of the woods, between magic and mayhem, Persephone was tempted to cut through the undergrowth. To let go, to just follow the narrow path and see where it took her. She stumbled after her own feet, taking two steps toward the inviting sound, compelled forward.

A bright light flashed down on her from up the other way, pausing her descent into the dark. A voice, soft and commanding, spoke. "Persephone May."

Persephone pivoted and looked into the shadows. Her pulse skittered and she peered up, seeking a voice to match the face.

A woman stepped out from behind her own curtain of darkness onto the path. Tall like an oak tree, and sturdy like a Renaissance sculpture, the woman cascaded forward, her long arms swaying as her hips swished closer toward Persephone. Her voice was older than her face, which couldn't be more than fifty. She took the last step to Persephone and as she did, goose bumps broke out along Persephone's arms.

"You are Persephone May."

"Yes," she said to the statement that should have been a question. "And you are?"

The woman twitched her nose. "I am Moira, keeper of Ever House." Moira nodded up toward the house tucked into the hill.

"Ah, of course!" Persephone said, and tried to brush the flyaway hairs from her face. "You're Hyacinth's sister. It's nice to meet you."

"Is it? Well then." Moira looked up at the moon. "Hyacinth invited you."

Her tone was flat, with a slight bite to it. Was she angry?

Moira's eyes met Persephone's then. Stared directly into them. Persephone blinked, prepared to look away, but Moira only tilted her head. Persephone took a deep breath. Counted down the seconds.

Nothing happened.

Persephone bit her lower lip as a rush of relief and wonder nearly knocked her off her feet. She had to force herself to keep from laughing out loud. Moira was *staring* at her. Meeting her eyes without so much as a hint of fear or craze.

"I've heard wonderful things about your island," Persephone said, struggling to keep a goofy smile from breaking out across her face. "It was so kind of Hyacinth to invite me. I'm so happy to be here."

Which was true. While Persephone was out of her element in navigating the particulars of a friendship, Hyacinth *was* her first friend. She was also, she suspected, if the power on the island was any indication, something more. Except Hyacinth had never struck Persephone as someone who didn't fit into her own world, unlike Persephone who didn't fit anywhere. And if the ability to hold eye contact was any indication—Moira was something more, too.

"My sister is many things," Moira said, turning and beckoning Persephone to follow. "I don't know that the first of them would be kind, but then a rose smells sweet to the bees and sorrowful to those leaving them for the dead."

Persephone studied her back in surprise. What an odd thing to say.

Moira turned to look back at her. "Why are you here?" She hooked a brow, and words loosened on Persephone's tongue.

"It seemed like the ideal time for a visit." Oh, this woman definitely had power. A thrill shivered up Persephone's spine. Moira was also clearly irritated at Persephone's presence, and that had her tampering her enthusiasm. "Hyacinth *did* ask me to come."

Now that Persephone was here, and after what happened with the stranger at the dock, she was eager to pose questions that Hyacinth, and perhaps Moira, could answer.

"My sister does a lot of things. She has grown fond of making decisions on her own, it appears."

Persephone bit the inside of her lip, for what could she say to that? The road curved, sharper this time, and the climb increased. They didn't speak as they embarked up the last hill, then up a steeper set of wide stones set deep into the earth. The house came into view and Persephone hesitated, but only for a moment.

Hyacinth *had* asked her to come, and this island was different from any place Persephone had ever been, as different as *she* was even. The island felt alive, and while it all seemed somewhat improbable, it was no more impossible than the other incredulous events of Persephone's life. Maybe this time, the impossible would finally work in her favor.

Persephone nodded to herself at her own resolution. Then she set her shoulders back and soaked up the view: the wide porch and hammock, the way potted plants were tucked along the final set of stairs, and faded rugs were thrown haphazardly across the planks. A stack of books rested on a cheery side table beside a rocking chair, and a mug of tea that smelled strongly of cinnamon was cooling next to a pair of jade reading glasses. Persephone sighed in relief. It was exactly as Hyacinth had described it.

A small white cat unfurled itself from beneath the rocker, and rushed out to greet the returning mistress and her guest. Its whole body shook with verve and joy, and Moira laughed. Persephone startled. Moira's was a laugh made deep in the belly, and it loosened the focus on her face. Moira's features watered, then softened as though someone had taken a severely colored cubism painting and transformed it into one of pastel watercolor. It was like seeing two sides of a coin at once.

"Hello, Opal," Moira said, addressing the cat. "I wasn't gone that long, now was I?" She picked up the tea, drank deeply, nodded. "See there, it's still warm, as I said it would be. I was back in plenty of time." She studied Persephone over the rim of her mug. "She worries, our Opal does, and the equinox is a special night for us all." Opal meowed loudly, as if in on the conversation. "Worry didn't use to be her nature, but seasons change and so do temperaments when the right pressure is released, or applied."

She cast a meaningful look at Persephone, who offered her best—albeit slightly confused—smile.

She wondered if Moira meant the equinox had something to do with her. When it came to it, Persephone had never bought into the seasons affecting anything. She understood the equinox was a day of equal hours of light and dark, but since Persephone always felt a decided lack of equal, of balance, she had wondered if the seasons got it wrong.

Persephone set down her luggage. Opal slinked to Persephone, her tail swishing as she came forward. The cat didn't pause to brush against her or dart away; instead she leapt straight into Persephone's arms.

"She's like a small lioness," Persephone said, after inhaling her musky scent to better study the cat's inquisitive face.

"Opal of the Night. It's who she is," Moira said, taking the glasses from the table. "There's something to the clean air and strong soil on this island. It calls to some of us. Hold these for me, would you?"

Cradling the cat like a porcelain baby in one arm, Persephone accepted the glasses with her other hand. They were warm to the touch. A comforting wave washed over her, and she tilted her chin up, certain she felt the sun's rays brush across her cheeks.

Moira made a sound that was part tut and murmur. "I see."

Persephone blinked in surprise, reminded that she was standing in the dark of night. What had that been about? She started to ask, but Moira cut her a look that had her words shriveling on her tongue.

"If you'll go on in through the door there, you'll find your room on the second floor, second door to the right," Moira told her. "Or you may find it to the left. Both rooms are open. Take your pick, but pick it well. The light seeks on one side and the dark whispers from the other."

It was a riddle, a magic riddle perhaps? "I'm sure I'll find my way," Persephone said. She felt like Moira was grading her for a test she didn't take, but she wouldn't let the other woman rattle her resolve.

From where Persephone stood on the porch, she felt a pulse, a breath, threading around her. Most of Persephone's life had been spent running, and for the first time in her thirty-two years, she felt as though she could stop. She wanted to savor the sensation.

Moira shrugged. "When Hyacinth offers, tell her you'll have the lavender and sage blend. Your unbalanced root chakra is distracting me." Then Moira dismissed her, sitting down in the rocker and hiding her face between the pages of a thick book with a navy cover.

She walked to the door, and felt Moira's eyes on her back as she went. Persephone looked over her shoulder at the last moment, and Moira ducked her chin. Right before she did, Persephone could have sworn the other woman was hiding a slight upturn of her lips.

Entering Ever House, Persephone decided, was like entering a portal back in time. As she crossed the threshold she was greeted by a rush of warm air, followed by the strong scent of freshly blooming jasmine. The room on the other side of the porch was wide, with high ceilings and light champagne-colored walls. Two oval marble tables beset a couch shaped like a crescent moon. More rugs were laid here, one across another. There was a large ticking antique clock the color of midnight on the wall with the phases of the moon painted in white around its face. A series of rectangle frames full of pictures of various flora and fauna adorned the farthest wall, and when she blinked, she was sure the images transformed into faces staring back at her.

As Persephone took a step to peer closer, Hyacinth burst through the white swinging doors on the opposite side of the room, carrying a tray with a teapot and wearing her signature grin.

"You're right on time," her friend said, dark eyes sparkling. "Don't you love when that happens? When the moments of past and future bow out to let in the present? It's so rare since they're always scrapping with each other like ruffian boys and girls looking to pull the first punch, or sample the best bite of pie, or just beat the other back for the thrill of getting on with it. But today, or rather now, or I suppose a moment ago, present wins."

As Hyacinth glided toward her, mouth running a mile a minute, Persephone felt the last dregs of worry drain away at the sight of her friend. There was warmth in the curve of Hyacinth's lips, a twinkle in her eyes, and laughter in her voice.

Hyacinth set the tray down on the circular ottoman tucked into the crescent couch, and pulled Persephone into a hug. After crushing her for five glorious seconds, no more no less, she pulled back to study her guest. "I'm thinking ginger. A nice ginger tea, and I'm not just saying that because of your hair."

"Lavender and sage blend," Persephone said, finding herself compelled to repeat Moira's instructions. "If you have it."

Hyacinth's head tilted, her eyes narrowing. She hummed a little in the back of her throat but gave a measured nod before she set to making the tea, mumbling about elderflower. The tea was loose leaf, and she built it like a jeweler stringing an emerald necklace. Inspecting the elements, sorting the order, and closing her eyes before she poured steaming water over the herbs.

"Blessed be, little cauldron," Hyacinth said, opening her eyes and holding it out. A smile tugged at her cheeks. "Go on then, it doesn't have any bite. All balance, all harmony."

Persephone paused to put down her bag. Opal, the tiny lioness at her feet, had yet to stretch a muscle. She, too, was watching Persephone.

"It's fantastic to see you again," Persephone said, with a little laugh, meaning it. She raised the teacup to her lips, still giddy with surprise that she finally found her first friend in Hyacinth. It felt right. Magical. The house, the island, Hyacinth, and even Moira—everything was familiar, clear but far apart. It was, Persephone decided, like seeing the ocean for the first time, after having only seen it in photographs and on film. Now that she had seen the view up close, she wanted to savor it. She wanted to make it last.

"I'm grateful you've come," said Hyacinth. "And on the night of the equinox, of all nights. It's a blessing, indeed."

"Thank you for having me," Persephone said, before pausing. "Though . . . I don't think your sister agrees."

Hyacinth averted her gaze. "Moira will. She doesn't like surprises, no matter how often I've tried to change her mind on the matter. But don't worry, you are a wonderful surprise and she will settle and be pleased as petunias you're here. I know I am."

Persephone sat down, unsure how to respond, wrapping her hands around her mug. Hyacinth reached over to fluff the pillow at Persephone's back, and Persephone laughed.

"I've missed you, too," Persephone said.

Hyacinth grinned, a flash of straight, gorgeous teeth. Her joy at seeing Persephone again was a tangible thing. It spread out into the room like perfume, tingeing the air. It wasn't a chore to feel happy around someone who smiled like you were a diamond they found when they were panning for gold.

Hyacinth leaned against the side of the sofa. "Did you get what you needed from your latest stint as a, what was it, coffee caretaker?"

Persephone frowned into her mug, thinking of the professor, of Larkin and Deandra, of all that did and could have gone wrong. "I'd say it ran its course."

"Oh, Persephone. You shouldn't be wasting your talents on pursuing dead ends."

She looked up, startled. "I guess I think of it as knocking on doors. At some point, I'll open the right one."

"Consider this an unlatched window," Hyacinth said, throwing open her arms before she sat down on the ottoman. "One I'm happy to give you a boost through." Hyacinth held eye contact with Persephone, her lips curving up. "Was your journey over-eventful?"

Persephone counted down like she had with Moira and waited. Nothing happened.

Persephone shook her head in wonder. "I'm sorry, what?"

"Your journey here. How was it?"

Could Hyacinth really not be affected by holding eye contact? Was it the island, or something else?

"Um," Persephone said, unable to hide her grin, trying to stay on track. Another five seconds passed, and Hyacinth only cocked her head.

"It's always different, coming here," Hyacinth said, tucking one of her curls behind her ear. "And I do mean that quite literally."

Persephone's lungs expanded as she took a deep breath. Hyacinth kept holding eye contact with her. It was the longest Persephone had locked eyes with another person, and absolutely *nothing* was happening.

It was almost too good to be true.

"I'm sorry, but what?" Persephone repeated, forcing herself to focus.

"Coming to Wile," Hyacinth said. "You can go north or south, but never the way shall twain again, once you've twained it one way. I last came in from the east, by helicopter. It was like riding on the tail of a very determined but distracted dragon."

The word *twain*, as Persephone knew it, meant two. Hyacinth could have a funny way of speaking. It was as though she was alluding to something—an inside joke Persephone wasn't quite in on. It was strange, and it was also a good distraction.

"I boated in with Captain Danvers and an . . . interesting woman," Persephone said, finally breaking eye contact, some of her joy dissolving as she recalled the stranger. She looked up, considered how to best ask Hyacinth if the island was magic.

Hyacinth shifted forward, her legs crossing at the ankles. "Clipped tones, gorgeous eyes, sophisticated clothes?"

"The woman? Yes." Persephone nodded, meeting Hyacinth's eyes again, marveling once more at the lack of change. "That's an acute summary. Do you know her?"

"It's a small island. I know everyone."

There was something to how Hyacinth said it. A layer of meaning behind it.

"It's a great place to call home," Hyacinth said, and the smile that bloomed across her face sent a shiver of envy through Persephone.

She tried to imagine what it would be like living on the island Hyacinth had described in her emails. In her heart of hearts, Persephone hoped it was like being cocooned on a floating Mayberry, as safe as a black-and-white sitcom with friends tucked into every corner. She took another drink of the tea. It was light and sweet. She drank again and her body grew heavy, like it was sewn into the soles of her shoes. She wanted to ask about magic, the woman from the boat, about Hyacinth and Moira, and how it could all be real. She wanted to ask her how you made a place a home.

Persephone yawned and her thoughts went fuzzy. She tried to remember why she'd ever been nervous about coming to Wile Isle.

"Asleep on your feet, are you?"

"I may be more tired than I realized," Persephone said, her shoulders relaxing. Suddenly, she was barely able to keep her eyes open.

"A good cuppa always reveals what you need, and I'd say you need proper rest." Hyacinth swiftly tucked her arm through Persephone's, picked up her larger bag, and led her up the long staircase situated on the left side of the room. Persephone didn't notice it until she was navigated toward it, and was grateful it wasn't nearly as steep as it looked.

There was a brush of welcome as Opal stole past them to lead the way up the stairs. When they came to the top, Hyacinth didn't bother to turn on the light. A sliver of moonlight lit the way. In the silver glow she guided Persephone down the long hall until, with an abrupt stop, she hummed again.

"I believe you're to be here." Hyacinth's arm swung out, though Persephone could only sense her movement. "Or you could go there."

It was like standing back on the cobblestone road again. There was a hard line, as though wrapped around Persephone's spine. It tugged her, hard, in each direction. She tried to take a breath, and the tug yanked again.

Closing her eyes, because she was already standing in the near dark so what could it matter, she felt something zap her in the back of her neck. The sense of *wrong* steered her away from the right.

"Left," she answered, her voice coming out breathless. "The room to the left, please."

Hyacinth squeezed her arm, and for a moment the grip was a hair too tight. Just as swift, she released her.

"As you will," said her friend.

Persephone acted on instinct and reached out, finding the handle immediately. When she opened the door, the light spilled out into the hallway.

Hyacinth smiled, and Persephone's vision fogged as she studied her. A strong and unfamiliar power pressed against her. The cat slipped past her into her room, and Persephone felt the effects of the tea try to take over. She raised her chin and *pushed* back. Her vision cleared. Hyacinth stood aglow, with the rest of the world behind her cast into darkness. Hyacinth's face bloomed unexpectedly into a wide grin.

"Well met," said Hyacinth, stepping back into the darkness before adding, "Cousin Persephone."

A green antique clock on a side table ticked off the seconds like a magician showing his cards.

One,

two,

three.

The word *cousin* pounded in Persephone's skull as the door clicked closed. She yanked the door back open, her eyes searching the darkness. Hyacinth was gone. In the hall, only the scent of cinnamon lingered.

Oh yes, Hyacinth was *definitely* something. Persephone raised a foot to step after her into the darkened hallway, and her legs jellied into sludge.

Suddenly sleep was closing in on her. The weight drove her to lock the door and stumble to the queen bed, which she fell into, pulling a worn quilt over her body. The bed exhaled under her, hugging her in a full embrace.

As she drifted under, Persephone could think of only one word.

Cousin.

HYACINTH EVER'S JOURNAL

Spring equinox, one year and a half ago

> *My bags are packed and my hopes are high.*
> *Higher than perhaps they should be. But I believe.*

I know that Moira would say it's a fool's optimism. That over the past ninety-eight years the prophecy hasn't proven to be more than the ramblings of a traumatized old woman. But come the morning light, the spell will lift and I will have six months to find her.

I've been scrolling for a long time, and tonight was the first time anything has been different. It was only a short exhale of a moment, but the obsidian I used dropped onto the map. Maybe it was that I chose to scry by the ocean or under the full moon, maybe it was the frankincense and lavender I anointed myself in—I can't be sure. But something tonight made it happen.

I didn't tell Moira.

It might be an omen, keeping this secret. But it isn't the first and it won't be the last.

I have to find her.

I think about the two sisters who caused this, how the divide between them split the world, and I know that isn't me and it isn't Moira. I am doing this for my sister. For myself. For us all.

The prophecy promised: a time walker of the Mayfair line will one day have the power to unmake the world. I've been scrying for a time walker all my life. I've been looking for the lost witch since Ariel told me about her ten years ago. Tonight I scryed for both and the obsidian listened.

It's her.

It has to be.

Three

Persephone woke to a face full of fur and the melodic sound of purring. Opal had curled across her neck. She shifted the feline and shook her head, the last dregs of sleep fading away. She'd been so tired the night before. Not at first, but after she'd drunk the tea. *The tea.* She ran a hand over her face. Had Hyacinth *drugged* her?

Surely not. And yet . . .

Persephone threw off the covers. She was quick to brush her teeth in the small but efficient bathroom with a claw tub and pedestal sink at the end of the hall as she prepared to confront her host.

She tried to mentally turn over what to say as she dressed in the smartest (and only) color she'd brought—gray—and left her auburn hair down. She decided to be straightforward, it was always her way, and went in search of Hyacinth.

As she approached the top of the landing a blissful scent wafted up to her: freshly baked scones and sausage frying in a pan. Persephone paused in her descent of the steep staircase as Moira's voice reached her.

"She doesn't know?"

Persephone leaned forward, her side pressing to the rail.

"No, not yet," Hyacinth said, her tone calmer than a yoga instructor's.

Moira's voice came out clipped with anger. "She doesn't know why you invited her and you couldn't be bothered to tell me you'd *found her*?"

Persephone's fingers gripped the banister.

"I wasn't certain it *was* her," Hyacinth said. "The only way to know for sure was for the island to allow her to come, and here she is."

Persephone thought she heard Moira growl. "You're reactionary, Hyacinth, and this time your perilous approach to danger could have cost us everything."

"It won't," Hyacinth said. "It's right she's here. We need her. Everything will work out now."

The air warmed ten degrees, heat rising to Persephone's cheeks. They had been looking for her? They needed her? She thought again of Hyacinth's remark. *Cousin.*

There was a lot to unpack from what the two women were saying, but one thing Persephone agreed with Hyacinth on was how right it was Persephone was here. She'd felt like she was where she was meant to be as soon as she'd stepped off the dock. But why did she feel this connection to a place she'd never heard of—and what did Hyacinth mean *the island* allowed her to come?

Persephone turned and walked back down the hall to the bath, where she splashed cold water on her face. She knew that eavesdropping—or lurking as one of her former foster mothers called it—rarely amounted to clear information.

She must demand Hyacinth tell her what was going on. It was time. Head high, Persephone walked back to the stairs and started down them.

"Morning," she said, seeing Hyacinth standing at the edge of the crescent couch, a deck of tarot cards in one hand, a blue lapis crystal the size of a small boulder in the other.

"Isn't it interesting how so many of our words have double meanings?" Hyacinth asked without looking up, setting the crystal down and moving the cards from one hand to the other as Persephone continued her descent and reached the first floor. "Morning. It's a statement, a greeting, and when the letters rearrange and you add in the u, it's a period of acknowledging great loss. When you think on it, morning isn't a time. It's a setting. I suppose it sounds better than 'Hello, it's nice to see you again in this different time period than when we last met,' but still. Double meanings. Funny little words."

Persephone studied Hyacinth. Sharp slashes of cheekbones, piercing eyes, golden skin. "I suppose," Persephone said, her fingers biting into her palms as she chose her next words. "The house smells like morning."

"Another way to use the word." Hyacinth waved a hand in the direction of the kitchen. "Moira's secrets are in her food. They're richly rewarding."

Persephone cleared her throat. "Were secrets also in the tea you served me last night?"

Hyacinth raised a single eyebrow, holding eye contact with Persephone. "Are you accusing me of something?"

"I'm asking."

"Ask then."

"Did you put something in my tea?"

"I put *tea* in your tea. Your chakras were out of alignment. The tea restored your vibrational harmony. It's medicinal, but not in the way you're implying."

"Oh." Persephone pressed a hand to her collarbone, trying to feel if she felt more aligned, uncertain she knew precisely where her chakras should be. "I overheard your conversation with Moira this morning."

"Did you now?" Hyacinth sat on the couch.

"You were looking for me?"

"I was."

Persephone's stomach flipped once at the thrill of being sought . . . and the accompanying thought that she was somehow being played a fool. "Why? Does it have something to do with why you called me cousin last night?"

Hyacinth's quiet smile didn't waver. "It's a good word, that."

"So what? It's just a friendly term of endearment?"

Hyacinth's smile stretched. "Of course it is."

"I don't believe you."

"Believe what you like. Only know I try very hard not to lie. Least of all to my kind."

"Your *kind*?"

Hyacinth didn't respond. She turned her attention away from Persephone to the banging of cabinets and the rattling of dishes being pulled down in the kitchen. Persephone took a slow breath.

Hyacinth clearly wanted to bait her, and as Persephone stood there waiting, being flagrantly ignored, possibly drugged, and tricked into believing they were friends so she would come to the island for who knows why, her temper sparked. Persephone grit her teeth and curled her hands into fists.

The lights in the room flickered twice, and with the precision of an exuberant child blowing out her birthday candles, every light in the ornate overhead chandelier whooshed out.

"Daughter of the Goddess!" Moira's shout from the kitchen came out as a curse as a dish clattered and broke. Persephone blinked, and Hyacinth let loose a wild laugh.

All of the lights in the house were dark.

"We *are* birds of a feather. Or flowers of a similar petal," Hyacinth reached over and gripped Persephone's still clutched hands. "Sit down, *cousin*."

Persephone studied the chandelier in shock. She hadn't meant to surge the electricity, her power had swelled inside her—much as it had since she'd stepped foot on the island, except now, it erupted.

"You can't control your magic at all, can you?" Hyacinth said, her eyes bright as she let go of Persephone. The room was awash in early morning sunshine, the natural light giving an extra glow to her skin. She shifted, reached behind the couch, and plucked a flower from nowhere.

A hyacinth.

Persephone's knees knocked together once, and she promptly dropped onto the sofa. She had blown half the fuses in Ever

House, and Hyacinth sat plucking flowers from the air as if it were all terrifically normal.

Moira pushed through the swinging doors. Her jade reading glasses bounced on top of her head, and her full mouth formed a judgmental scowl.

"*Everything* is not working out for the electrical," Moira said, shooting a glare at Hyacinth before brandishing a small plate at Persephone. "It's a full moon tonight. Eat this before you keel over or set something on fire."

Persephone glanced down, picked up the pastry from the plate, and sniffed. With Moira watching, hands fisted at her hips, Persephone took a bite. Like a tonic, the sugar and fruit of the blueberry scone knitted her resolve back together.

"It's a full moon nearly every night this month," Hyacinth said, reading the confusion on Persephone's face. "Wile makes its own rules."

"That's impossible," Persephone said.

"Nothing's impossible," Moira said. "Finish your scone."

Dazed, Persephone took another bite. "Blueberry?" she asked, her eyes on Moira's retreating back as the woman stomped to the kitchen.

"For protection," Hyacinth said.

"I don't understand," Persephone said, brushing her hair from her face.

Hyacinth scooted closer, reached over, and squeezed her shoulder ever so gently. "Anger is like kindling on a brush fire when it comes to sparking magic."

"You were being a jerk on purpose?"

"I was being a trigger."

Persephone rubbed the space between her eyebrows. She looked at Hyacinth. "What am I?"

"What do you think you are? You're a witch same as me."

Persephone dropped her hand. She held the word in her mouth, rolled it out on her tongue. "A witch."

Hyacinth's eyes twinkled.

Persephone considered the word, applied it to herself like it was a new pair of shoes she could step into, and found it fit. "You knew, didn't you? When we first met."

"About who you were, magically speaking?" Hyacinth shrugged. "I guessed. You wouldn't look me in the eyes. Witches' eyes hold power, and until we know how to store it we can accidentally let it seep out. It's easy to transfer power through eye contact. Yours set off sparks."

"You don't mean that literally, do you?" Persephone asked, conjuring an image of her eyes showering sparks like a comic book villain.

"Of course not. It's more like an electrical jolt. Here."

Hyacinth reached for her hand. She stared at her full-on, and something in her eyes shifted. It was as though a curtain pulled away from Hyacinth's eyes and a flame lit inside of Persephone in response. The blow of it had her attempt to drop her friend's hands. Hyacinth's eyes shifted again, she released her grip, and the flame died.

"But when others look at me, they . . ."

"Act insane?"

"Hurt themselves."

Hyacinth considered Persephone. "You think you're the reason they do that."

Persephone's brow furrowed. "How could I *not* be? It's my power seeping out, right?"

"Are you wishing these people harm when you look at them?"

"What? No, of course not." She rubbed her neck. "It just happens."

"There is dark in all of us. Witches and humans alike. What you draw forth may be *their* dark, but that doesn't mean *you're* dark."

"So how do I stop it?" Persephone asked, leaning back. "How did you learn to control it?"

"Training."

"Oh."

"Of which you've had none."

"Clearly," Persephone said.

"*Obviously*," Moira's muffled voice called from what sounded like under the house, before the lights flickered back on. A door swung open and shut before the older woman stomped back through the kitchen and out into the gathering room where Hyacinth and Persephone sat. "You're like a Roman candle on the Fourth of July in some small Yankee town."

"Which is where *we* come in," Hyacinth said, rolling her eyes at her sister.

"Because you need my help?" Persephone asked, thinking of their conversation she overheard.

"That's still debatable," Moira said, doing an impressive job of ignoring and scolding Hyacinth all at once.

"We can help you," Hyacinth said. "And we *do* need your help. This island isn't like other islands." She exchanged a blink-and-you-miss-it look with Moira. "It's cursed."

Persephone blinked. "Cursed."

"Yes."

"I . . . didn't think curses were real."

"Magic is real, but curses you doubt?" Moira asked.

Persephone shook her head. "I don't know. Curses just seem like something else."

"They're as real as magic," Hyacinth said. "And we can train you to control yours. Magic, I mean."

Moira snorted. "Again, debatable."

"You saw what she can do," Hyacinth snapped.

Moira lifted a shoulder. "I saw what her *temper* can do." She looked at Persephone. "*Can* you control your power?"

Persephone rubbed at her temple, trying to process everything they were throwing at her. She was as unaccustomed to speaking about magic and curses as she was making eye contact. "Sometimes."

Moira harrumphed. "Like I said."

"And we can help her with that, like *I* said." Hyacinth wrinkled her nose at her sister.

"But how can I help you break a curse?"

Moira muttered something under her breath, shot her sister

a look, and left the room. Hyacinth waited until her sister was ensconced in the kitchen, and offered a dimple of a smile.

"There is a spell. A very particular spell that invokes the power of three. Moira and I are two, with you, we are three."

"I don't understand."

"*Yet.* You will."

Persephone blew out a slow breath. Hyacinth smiled at her and hope, the biggest bubble of it she had ever felt, washed over Persephone. Persephone blinked and realized she was crying.

"Oh, Persephone," Hyacinth said, and reached forward. She wrapped her arms around her, and didn't let go for thirty-eight whole seconds.

"Sorry," Persephone said, savoring the feeling of being held, really held. "I didn't mean to do that." She sniffled and wiped her face as Hyacinth leaned back. "I think I may be in shock."

"You aren't in shock," Hyacinth said, as Moira walked back into the room holding a tea tray. She passed Persephone a thick mug of alabaster marble.

Hyacinth nodded at her. "You're found."

"Drink up," Moira said, before she turned and left again.

Persephone was struck with the realization the irritable woman was trying to take care of her by giving her the scones and the tea. All of a sudden, Persephone wanted to laugh, and cry harder.

"She's prickly on the outside and gooey on the inside," Hyacinth said. "Like a cactus."

Persephone hiccupped a laugh, drank the tea, and embraced the calm that settled over her. The heat of the mug warmed her hands, and the sparkling eyes on her friend's face thawed her down to her bones. Hyacinth was staring at Persephone like she saw her; she saw her and welcomed who she was. More, she *needed* her.

No one ever wanted Persephone, let alone needed her.

"I really don't understand," Persephone said, feeling like everything was about to change, hoping she could handle whatever was coming.

"I know. There's a lot to explain." Hyacinth held out a hand, and Persephone didn't hesitate. She slipped hers inside it, and followed Hyacinth to the kitchen. It was the first time Persephone had seen the heart of the house, and she couldn't stop staring. The long room was the perfect combination of modern rustic southern (white farm sink, counters and cabinets with perfectly matched robin's-egg blue appliances and copper fixtures) coupled with the insides of what could have come from Mary Poppins's carpetbag.

There was a large oak table with a peacock Tiffany lamp resting in the center, seven vintage Coca-Cola signs, and a collection of thirteen cuckoo clocks along one entire hall. The windows over the sink were wide and rectangular, bringing in a slew of natural light. An upright cream antique stove sat in the corner and appeared in working order, while over the small squat wooden island was a baker's rack filled with an assortment of cast-iron cooking wear. The room appeared well loved, and hinted at being a place where secrets and scents and impossible tastes sprang to life.

Moira leaned against the farm sink, a bright red kitchen towel tucked into the back of her pants, flour dusting across one cheek, and those same reading glasses perched atop her head like a beauty pageant's finest crown. Her face gave nothing away.

"We should take this conversation to where the walls can't hear," Hyacinth said.

Moira nodded. She untucked the towel from her waistband, brushing the flour from her face with it. "If she turns out to be the wrong Persephone, I'm casting her memory of the island and you from her mind before we send her back on her way."

Moira swept from the kitchen toward the hall full of clocks, leaving Persephone gaping after her.

"Like I said, a cactus," Hyacinth said in a tone that did little to reassure Persephone. "You are our third, Persephone. Of this I have no doubts."

Persephone swallowed, but followed after the sisters. She finally knew what she was, knew they had to be the same. A thrill shimmied its way up her spine, because for the first time in her life, Persephone May was going to get answers.

▸ ▸ ▸

MOIRA STOOD IN front of what Persephone mistook at first glance for an antique Bavarian timepiece. It featured a Craftsman-style house with a balcony, and a chronometer in the center for a face—but where the Bavarian tended to showcase dancing boys and girls with men brandishing pints of ale, this clock costarred only women, dancing with scrolls and hourglasses with the sand frozen halfway in time. It was a puzzle of a message Persephone felt certain she should be able to figure out if there were but one more piece to it.

Moira stepped up and whispered something into the ear of the tiny carved woman closest to the center of the timepiece. The wall groaned and began to slide back. It shifted four feet away and ground to a halt.

"After you," Moira said, her smile a promise or a challenge or both.

Doubt crept in. Persephone didn't really know these two women. She didn't know anyone other than herself . . .

And that was the problem.

She could stay here, in the hall, and nothing would change. Or she could go with Hyacinth and Moira and take a chance that something good would happen for once.

Persephone squared her shoulders and stepped into the darkened space. As she walked deeper down a narrow hallway, the light grew brighter and brighter until Persephone was standing in front of a well-lit arch. The arch was made of brilliant stained glass in a hundred shades of blue and white sea glass, and featured a thick copper handle on a door.

Hyacinth's face was half hidden in the dark, and from where Persephone stood, Hyacinth appeared more specter than person.

"To where it began," said Moira, whose own face was steeped in shadow much as it had been the first time Persephone saw her. "Our cliffs."

Hyacinth stepped next to Persephone and reached out. Her right hand closed around the handle and she flashed a grin, then Hyacinth gave the door a gentle tug and it opened.

The room before them was not a room at all. It was a doorway into the impossible.

Into another world.

Persephone gasped and stepped through the arch. The land beneath Persephone's feet was firm but yielding. The grass grew long in some places and short in others, its shade of green vibrant in the way all living things are when they reach the peak of their season.

Before Persephone lay a path perhaps ten feet wide. The edges of the path dropped off, the land sloughing and cascading down into the beckoning waters of the deep blue sea.

"These are your cliffs?" Persephone had never seen nature so raw and complete. She pressed a hand to her stomach at the sight of the crashing waves. "Are we on the island?"

"We are on *an* island," said Moira, the words spoken with reverence before a crisp breeze captured them. "The cliffs of Skye, in Scotland."

"How?"

"Magic," Moira said, in a tone that implied *duh*.

Persephone stepped forward, her gaze drawn to the meadow buttercup, the small, friendly yellow wildflowers growing in groups along the path like swaths of paint sprinkled across the ground. The clouds overhead were a deep neon pink bleeding into orange, rolling into purple, and shifting into a paler shade of gray and misty morning blue. Persephone had never felt such peace in a place.

She walked the rest of the path, studying how the flat surface of the cliff was rocky enough to be imperfect and dramatic enough to feel like a painting come to life. The view stole the last of her breath.

"This was once our island," Hyacinth said, coming to stand beside her. "This is a memory. It's the gift of the Arch to Anywhere. When you pass through the arch, if magic runs in your veins, it will take you where your heart desires."

"I don't think this was my heart's desire," Persephone said. She would never have known to dream up such a place.

"Your desire to follow us brought you here. Here is where our story begins." Hyacinth took a deep breath, and seemed to grow taller from breathing the sea air. She slipped a hand into the front pocket of her shirt, and pulled out three seeds. "Two hundred years ago there were three islands. Elusia, Olympia, and Wile. These three islands were sisters, having broken off from a larger peninsula."

Hyacinth held up a seed and waved a hand over it. Persephone watched as it grew into a pomegranate.

"My ancestors escaped to Wile in 1620," Hyacinth continued, "but they weren't the only refugees. Other covens of witches had already found their way here. In their journals, they noted it was like the islands had sprung up from the water just for them. The people of the three islands brokered peace with one another, and found that the longer they lived on the soil of the islands, the more powerful they became."

"How?" Persephone asked, studying how the pomegranate seemed to flush pink with life.

"Magic sprung up from the earth, and it went into their crops and became nourishment for their bodies and their minds and their souls," Hyacinth said. She waved a hand and the other two pomegranates grew ripe in front of Persephone's eyes.

"For one hundred years, our people flourished on the islands. Then, as time has a way of doing, life caught up to them." Persephone watched as Hyacinth's words shift into worlds, scene after scene unfolding before her eyes like a movie projected onto the sky.

"In 1720 dark magic spread on the islands of Olympia and Elusia as the witches' greed for power corrupted them, and the two lands began to waste from the inside out. Treacherous, selfish magic turned the heart of each person on Olympia and Elusia dark." Persephone watched as the darkness spread across the islands, witnessed the sky and lands grow black, the waves of the sea rise, and the land get sucked back into the ocean that had once borne it.

"By 1820 the two islands disappeared back into the sea. The people who lived and worked the land were lost."

The scene blinked out, and Hyacinth held up the fruit—two of the pomegranates lost their luster. Where before they had bloomed with life, now they decayed in death. Hyacinth waved a hand and the decayed fruit returned to the two seeds. She held up the other remaining pomegranate in her hand. "Only Wile Isle remained. Our small island. Then, one hundred years ago come Samhain, it was cursed."

"Right. Cursed." Persephone said, giving a shake of her head. It was a lot to take in. "How?"

And so Hyacinth began her strange tale.

THE TALE OF THE BLOOD MOON CROWN

Once upon a time Amara Mayfair had it all. She was young, gorgeous, magical, and clever. Her sister True never felt half as fair. Then one day the two teenage sisters found their mother's sacred grimoire, and decided to cast a real spell.

It was a simple spell, one used to make roses bloom in winter. Their island already grew flowers that shouldn't grow in times when they shouldn't bloom, so they decided to manipulate the spell and see if they could make a tree grow apples out of season.

Following what they had learned from their mother and aunts, they cast their circle by placing three gemstones, four seashells, and eight candles around them, clasping hands, and calling their intention. This was the first time they were practicing deep magic (they usually served as amplifiers in a circle or were confined to helping their grandmother make tisanes in the kitchen), and the rebellious freedom was seductive and thrilling.

Once their circle was set, they called to the corners of their land—the guardians of North, East, South, and West—and were delighted as the small flames they had struggled to keep lit bloomed with light.

The spell asked for proof of intent and promise of dedication. Amara offered blood in the pricking of her thumb. She pressed the droplets to the apple core she carried, and buried it deep into the earth. True confessed her truth to the circle: she wasn't as clever or powerful as her sister, and she was jealous. True whispered the words into the earth as she slid the dirt over the apple and sealed the spell with her tears.

The sisters' intent planted into the ground. Like seedlings, the spell sprouted and spread. From the earth, a tree grew overnight. It bloomed bright with apples the color of blood. Then the roots of the tree tethered to each sleeping girl, and magic flooded into a single sleeping sister: Amara.

When they awoke, both sisters were delighted to find their tree alive. Amara reached for an apple, and found it too hot to touch under the noonday sun. She wished it were cooler so she could pluck and eat it . . . and the apples shook on the vine. They shifted in color, as ice spread out across the surface and froze them solid. Ice apples, the shade of plums, now rested in place of the fresh juicy apples.

Amara's magic was potent, but True found hers was unchanged. She couldn't turn fruit on the vine, or stir the wind, or rush the tide.

As True's jealousy grew at the injustice, so did Amara's magic—which was too powerful to reside in only one person. Magic choked Amara in her sleep and ate her from the inside out. The next day she awoke to discover she was too sick to leave her bed. The sisters tried to get rid of the magic, to chop down the ice apple tree and send the new power back into the ground. But axes, spells, and wishes all ricocheted off the tree's needle-sharp bark.

True, desperate to help her sister, found another spell in the grimoire called the Bound-Thorn Stave. The Bound-Thorn Stave was a spell for taking magic. All witches knew stealing another's power was dark magic, and besides being dark, this spell hinted at something else—a prior bargain having once been made.

With Amara's magic, they discovered the Bound-Thorn Stave was the spell their ancestors had used one hundred years before, striking a bargain with Wile after their two sister islands, Elusia and Olympia, sunk into the sea. Those witches bound themselves to Wile, swearing to give their magic to the island and in return, the island would trade its magic freely.

"It's a curse," Amara said, her voice hoarse, the magic that filled her also draining her. "That's why the island gave me the magic and not you. Because when we cast our spell I gave it blood. Our blood is tied to our essence, and is tied to our magic. We're connected to Wile, that's what the vision showed. We are what it needs. We're addicted to its power and it to us."

"Is that why we don't leave?"

"People leave," Amara said. "I've traveled with the aunts and I can't wait to leave again. To find a place I truly belong. You are the one who doesn't leave, sister."

Unlike Amara, who was restless and never felt like she fit with the puzzle that was her family or the land they tended, True loved everything about the island. The way the garden could grow any fruit or vegetable she'd ever wanted. The way people seemed to love coming to visit, and how no one ever looked twice at how the witches spent more hours asleep in the day and awake at night.

True read over the Bound spell carefully while her sister slept. It was simple, really. The spell required bound rope, a blood promise, and the light of the moon. It would siphon the power of another, and grant it to the other person. If the sisters bound *themselves to each other, then maybe it would flow back and forth between them. True knew that the spell could have strings, magic often did, but if it could save her sister, she didn't care.*

"We can use the spell," she told Amara, "because we aren't making a deal with the island. We only want to share what we have, not take from anything or anyone else."

Amara tried to argue. There was a loophole somewhere, or a price—magic always claimed its price. But she grew sicker and sicker and she eventually gave in.

The spell took an extra hour and a lock of hair, but it worked. The two witches bound themselves to each other. True was able to siphon power from Amara (and in the process acquire the kind of power she'd only dared dream of), and Amara was able to grow strong enough to live her life again.

But dark magic is clever.

As the years passed, it bid its time. The ice apple tree didn't wither, and neither did the magic's connection to the sisters. For that was the loophole. What they shared wasn't only theirs to command.

When Amara and True were twenty-five, the deep dark magic seeped back into them. Amara's nails grew razor sharp overnight, True's eyes changed from green to copper, and when the sisters would snore in their sleep sparks would fly from their mouths. The island's visitor population was growing, and the dark was ready to come out and play.

"We have to do something," Amara said one night, feeling the dark as it tried to push its way into her will and convince her to turn an unruly neighbor child into a puppy. "We need a way to rid ourselves of this."

True only studied the moon and sighed. She did not agree.

So her sister scoured Wile and the family books on magic, and traveled off island to look for a cure. Meanwhile, True stayed on island, busy testing the boundaries of what her strong magic could do.

True met a man, charmed him to her, and then did the same with four more. Unlike her sister, True couldn't fathom leaving Wile Isle—especially when she realized anything she desired to learn about life off island she could simply discover by dipping into a traveler's memory and taking possession of their mind.

With heightened senses and abilities, True grew intoxicated by the power. What she discovered about the outside world only strengthened her dislike of it. This was the same world, after all, that killed their kind and made martyrs of women and witches alike.

Amara returned from her travels weary and worried. She noticed the change in her sister, and realized it wasn't only she who had been affected by the dark magic. But True seemed to flourish from it while Amara wilted.

"It's time to break the bond," Amara told True. "The bargains we've struck have cursed us."

But True didn't want to lose her power any more than she wanted to lose her sister.

"I won't do it," she said, vehement in her resolve. "Breaking our bond would kill you."

Amara tried to cut off the siphon to her sister, to destroy the spell, but it was no use. They were bound and the darkness was growing. So she came up with a new plan. "We only need a place to store the excess magic, the darker shades," she wrote in her journal one night. "We are amplifiers, but we aren't meant to hold or amplify this magic." Amara remembered her grandmother mentioning a hinterland—a lost land behind the veil of this one. It was a place only witches

of great power had access to, and Amara planned
to use it as a kind of vessel to hold the dark magic
running in her veins.

True, on the other hand, was busy with her own
plans. True saw how her power could empower not
only the other witches on the island but also the
visitors. She created the Menagerie of Magic, a night
to display her magic and its power to the people of
Wile. True believed with the dark, they might find
the light, and use the magic to teach every woman
how to tap into their inner witch. To throw off those
trying to oppress them.

So it came to be that one sister wanted to keep the
dark, and the other to drive it out.

"It's too much," Amara told True, which was not a
lie. She took to her bed after she poisoned herself with
bloodroot in her last effort to break the bond.

True felt the effects of her sister's ailment through
the bond. The weakness and pain. She did not feel
how, without her permission, Amara had woven a
spell connecting herself to the island beyond the veil.
Amara, who loved her sister fiercely and had never
felt like she belonged anywhere to begin with, made
a new bargain using her blood: she offered her life to
the hinterland in exchange for ridding Wile of the dark
magic the sisters had invited in.

The night of the menagerie arrived, and True
acted to save her sister. She knew she could do more
good with the dark. She could free her sister and
remake their world at the same time. True called
down the blood moon and siphoned her sister's magic
without her permission, pulling it all into herself. At
the same moment, Amara slipped into the menagerie
and wove her own spell, which would open a door
to the hinterland. She would save her sister and

*her island from the poison she could feel fighting to
get free.*

*In the end, the spells ricocheted and both witches
were cast beyond the veil—each bound to the other
and the promises they made. Amara and True were
trapped inside the hinterland, along with those True
had promised freedom and magic to—the visitors
in the menagerie and the witches on the island who
came for the show.*

*True had planned to share the powerful magic
with the witches, to siphon strong magic into each of
the visitors to the menagerie, to grant them all power,
and in that power, freedom. She had tethered herself
to the magic of the island and the souls she had
ushered into the menagerie, and Amara had failed
to break her bond with her sister—tethering herself,
and the hinterland, to them all.*

*Like a tree with its roots spreading out, each
connecting to another, every life on Wile Isle inside
the menagerie was now a bargain struck, and a debt
unpaid.*

▸ ▸ ▸

HYACINTH LEANED BACK onto a rock, her tale concluded. The world within the arch had grown silent as the witch spoke, and now distant seagulls crooned, waves crested and clapped back against the base of the cliffs, and thunder rumbled far off in the atmosphere like an afterthought to the rain Persephone tasted on her lips.

"How are you here, if all the witches were locked away in the hinterland?" Persephone asked, rubbing her arms to try and rid the chill that had settled in.

"All were, save two who skipped the menagerie at the last minute—our great-grandmother and her sister. They went off island to perform a gratitude spell to the Goddess in the ocean when the curse was cast," Moira said. "Eleanor Mayfair had a vision later that night. She foretold it would be one hundred years before the curse could be broken."

"Though the prophecy hasn't stopped us from trying," Hyacinth added. "There are a thousand ways to attempt to break a curse." She winced, and for a moment a deep sadness passed behind her eyes. "Failing to break a curse carries a cost, and unfortunately none of our attempts ever worked."

"And you think *I'm* going to be able to break it? Just like that?" Persephone asked.

"Not just like that, no," Hyacinth said. "But yes, we do think you are the one." Moira made a noise like a horse huffing at hay and Hyacinth reached for Persephone's hand. "I know it's you."

Before Hyacinth could continue, Persephone took back her hand. "How? What is this island to me? I mean, no offense, it's horrible and tragic what happened to them, but who are these people *to me?*"

"Who do you think?" Hyacinth asked, her tone gentle, eyes kind.

Persephone looked from Moira to Hyacinth, licked her lips, and asked the question that had been resting on the tip of her tongue. "Are you my family?"

Hyacinth tilted her head. "Yes."

Persephone let the answer wrapped itself around her. She studied Hyacinth, with her expressive eyes and quick smile. Her cousin. Her *family*.

The feeling of air slipping under her feet, of floating, tugged her up. This is what she had dreamed of her whole life. But . . .

She drew in a deep breath. "Where is my mother, my father? I . . . all I've ever wanted is to find my family. To find *them*."

Moira's and Hyacinth's eyes met for the briefest of seconds, and in it Persephone was certain an entire conversation passed.

She tried again, speaking past the lump growing in the back of her throat. "Why did they abandon me?"

"Your gran left Wile Isle sixty years ago," Moira said.

"And?"

"She never came back."

Persephone wrapped her arms around her waist. "Why not?"

Hyacinth offered an apologetic shake of her head. "We don't know. I've been scrying for years, and you only popped up on my map a little over a year ago."

"I don't understand. What does that mean?"

"It means . . ." Hyacinth hesitated, reached again and squeezed Persephone's arm. "I wasn't *only* scrying for you. I've been trying to track your grandmother Viola for most of my life. For any member of your family. Since you were the only one we could find . . . we believe you are the only living member of your line. I'm so sorry."

Persephone had to force herself to keep breathing. Her mother and grandmother. Viola. She had a name and yet . . . "They're *gone*? Just like that? I was so sure—" She looked around. She *knew* the island, had as soon as she'd stepped foot on it. Deep down, she'd been so close to certain that everything she'd wanted was waiting for her.

"We are truly sorry," Hyacinth said, pain for Persephone raw on her face.

Persephone couldn't swallow past the lump lodged in her throat. She felt like a child who had been given a handful of balloons—she had family!—only to have two immediately popped. Persephone may have never known her mother or her grandmother . . . but dear god how she had wanted to.

She closed her eyes for a moment, and the next thought rammed into her. "And my father?"

Moira brushed the question off with the wave of her own hand. "Only the Goddess knows. He was not of the island, and so he is not of us."

"What does *that* mean?"

"It means we can't track people not of our lineage," Hyacinth explained. "Your father was never on island, that we know of, so he's out of our reach."

Persephone tried to grasp that single straw of hope like it was a lifeline. He *could* still be out there.

She turned back to the view, tears pricking her eyes faster than she could blink them away. Persephone thought of the peace the view had afforded her moments ago and found her gaze drawn to the angry way the waves smashed against the base of the cliff on the northern shore. Peace could so quickly turn to violence in the blink of an eye. "How on earth can I help you break a curse? I can't control my magic. I don't understand it at all."

"This is the land of your ancestors," Hyacinth said, as she watched the tears stain Persephone's face.

Moira's low hum in the back of her throat had the hairs prickling down Persephone's spine. "Witches of Wile can do anything, Persephone."

Persephone thought of the stranger from the boat. "It's not just the two of you, is it? Witches on this island, I mean."

Moira's stare was cold, and Persephone rubbed her arms to try and block the frost. "No. There are also the Way sisters, Ellison and Ariel, who live in the yellow cottage on the beach."

"There was also our mother and aunt," Hyacinth said, "but they both . . . left." She cleared her throat. "Fifteen years ago was their last attempt and failure to defeat the curse. Once you leave Wile with the intention of staying gone, you can't return. It's part of the curse."

"That's awful," Persephone said. "But if you need help, why not ask the other sisters—"

"Unlike us," Hyacinth interrupted, "the Way sisters don't want to save the island. In fact, they want you off this island. *You* are their greatest threat."

Persephone's mouth dropped open. "How am *I* the threat?"

"Without you the curse cannot be broken."

"But why would they . . ."

"Because they fear freeing the trapped witches will be all of our undoing."

Persephone rubbed at her eyes. "I'm confused." She looked at Moira. Looking into her eyes was like looking into a curtain. "Undoing how?"

"No one knows Amara's or True's current state of mind, or what either has been planning for a hundred years," Hyacinth said. "What power they have amassed in the hinterland, or what exactly they plan on doing with it. The rules there aren't finite. The land is cut off from us completely, and that makes it a danger. Once it and they are freed . . . well, fear of the unknown can lead people down the darkest of roads."

"You don't share their fear?"

"We have faith in the Goddess," Moira said, not quite meeting Persephone's eyes.

"I still don't understand how *I* can help. You said it yourself; I don't know what I'm doing. I don't know how to use my magic, I never have."

"If you are the key, Persephone May," Moira said, "then you were fated to return."

"The prophecy?"

Moira nodded. "Eleanor Mayfair foretold that a time walker of the Mayfair line will one day have the power to unmake the world."

As the sky around them darkened, Hyacinth plucked a sprig of jasmine from a low-hanging vine. She tucked the jasmine into her dark curls, and considered Persephone. "It *is* you."

"I don't walk in time, whatever that means."

"You don't know what you can and can't do."

Persephone paused. "How much power do you think I have?"

"Enough."

"Is it really just you and the other witches? You're all alone here on this island? I mean, can't someone else help?"

"We are the only remaining members of the original witches here, besides the Ways," Hyacinth said. "But we were not the only people who were on island when the curse fell. An island such as Wile has always pulled in travelers, vacationers—those seeking the light. Just as it called to you, it has called to others. Their ancestors are here yet, but they have little in the way of magic."

"And they can leave," Moira added, her face turned away.

"Yes," Hyacinth said, her mouth turning down. "As I mentioned, that's part of the curse. We witches of Wile can only leave the island from the spring equinox to the eve of the autumnal equinox, and we must return before sunset. We are cursed to remain on island the other half of the year. Frozen in our own way. You shouldn't have been able to arrive on island on the equinox, but you are of our blood. You *are* who we've been seeking."

Persephone tried to digest all the information the witches had dumped in her lap. She tugged at the skin on her elbows. "I don't know what to say."

"It's a lot to process," Hyacinth said, her smile slow but reassuring. "I wish we had more time. Unfortunately, that's the thing we are shortest on. Eleanor saw the curse would be broken in one hundred years from when it was cast because it has to be. The magic won't hold beyond a hundred years; if we don't break it now, all of the witches will remain lost forever. We have until Samhain. Will you help us?"

Persephone looked up at the sky. She thought of all they had told her. The improbable and the impossible. She thought of her faceless mother and grandmother, and all the forgettable foster parents. She looked over at the witches, and they stared back.

"I want to know how to use my magic," she said at last. "I need to control it."

"So?" Hyacinth asked.

Persephone took a breath, because there was really only one thing to do. "So yes. I'll help you."

▸ ▸ ▸

PERSEPHONE WRAPPED THE afghan Hyacinth had handed her more tightly around herself. She was vibrating, a strange combination of adrenaline and overstimulation. She had family, but was still missing the gaping hole that was her parents. She wasn't made wrong, like she'd always feared, but was made a witch. Which was a lot to get her head around. She was relieved and heartbroken, and still buoyed by hope because Hyacinth sat on one side of her and Moira across from them.

It was clear she, Persephone, mattered to them. Moira might be a stern, brash person, but she was blending tea from five little sachets, and murmuring to herself about Persephone's color being peakish. Hyacinth was offering Persephone a magician's bag of smiles. Worried, kind, compassionate. She flashed them all over and over.

"Tea is good for the soul," Moira said. "Drink this up, save for two sips at the end."

Persephone accepted the second cup of tea this morning from Moira. "Save two sips?"

"She wants to read your leaves," Hyacinth said, pulling a blanket over her lap and wiggling her toes with the bright pink polish. "You have to save a little so your essence is good and locked in."

Persephone looked down into the cup, at the loose tea floating inside it. "Am I supposed to know what that means?"

"Your saliva," Moira said, building a second cup, not bothering to look up. "Saliva is sacred. It's your life force. Drink the tea, taste the tea, but don't drink it all. It's not pocket science."

Hyacinth let out a fierce giggle. "She means rocket science." She accepted her cup from her sister. "*Pocket* science."

"I mean what I say, little flower," Moira said, though her own lips twitched.

Persephone smiled into her cup, and drank. It tasted of roses and honey and something else, light and sweet.

"What kind of tea is this?" she asked.

Hyacinth peered over into Persephone's cup. "Mmm. Moira's hibiscus blend." She wiggled her brows and settled back into her seat.

Persephone focused on the taste even as she savored being cocooned in the house with the two extraordinary women. There was a sacred hush in the room. Everything was warmer, brighter, but not in an intense way. In the way that sunshine feels against your eyelids when you close them and lift your face up. Persephone wondered if this was what people meant when they talked about finding peace.

"I love this," Persephone said, then ducked her chin when she realized she'd spoken out loud.

"It is good tea," Moira said.

"That isn't what she means," Hyacinth said, tossing a throw pillow at her sister's feet. "Is it?"

Persephone smiled. "It *is* good tea, but I guess I meant being here. It's really something."

Hyacinth's grin flashed bright, and even Moira raised her cup—slightly—in the direction of Persephone.

"It's home," Moira said.

"I've never had one," Persephone said, her words light to escape the heaviness of her meaning. "You're lucky."

Moira considered her, and her mouth softened. "Perhaps we are."

"Did you never have anywhere that felt like home?" Hyacinth asked, before taking another sip of her own tea. "You mentioned traveling in almost every email you wrote. I assumed you had wanderlust."

"Quite the opposite," Persephone said. "I've always longed for a home. Like the ones I read in stories, but I was never Anne of Green Gables or even Pippi Longstocking," Persephone said, thinking of the orphans she had wanted to be, the ones who found true family, who were secure in knowing who they were. "My trajectory was a transient one."

"Until now," Hyacinth said, a knowing glint in her dark amber eyes.

Persephone's heart squeezed in her chest. Oh, how she wished that could be true.

"How much tea remains?" Moira asked, setting her cup aside and looking pointedly at Persephone's hand.

She realized she'd almost drunk every last drop. "Just a bit." She swished the remaining tea. "Two sips."

Moira nodded. "Then take the cup into your left hand and circle it clockwise three times."

Persephone did as Moira asked.

"Now place this saucer on top of the cup."

She accepted the saucer, and did as she was instructed.

"Flip the cup over onto the saucer to drain, and pass it to me when you are ready for your leaves to be read."

Persephone closed her eyes, flipped the cup over, and felt a tug at the center of her stomach. She squeezed her eyes together, and a row of books being trailed over by long, slender fingers flashed before her eyes. Persephone's breath caught.

Hyacinth leaned forward. "What just happened?"

Persephone opened her eyes, started to tell her, and the words dried up.

Moira raised a brow.

"I . . ." Persephone shook her head. "I don't know."

"Cup?" Moira asked.

Persephone gave a short laugh of confusion. Hyacinth leaned back, rubbed at her cheek.

"Did you . . . have a vision?" Hyacinth asked.

"I've never had one before," Persephone said, which was true. But it wasn't the whole truth. What she'd seen was lodged in her throat. The words refused to be spoken.

Hyacinth took a sip of tea, and gave Persephone her own shrug.

Moira removed the cup and set the saucer aside. She pulled her reading glasses down from her head and slipped them onto her nose.

Persephone, suddenly nervous, looked at Hyacinth. Her friend gave her one of those comforting grins, and Persephone smiled back.

Moira looked up at Persephone, studied her. "There are three symbols here," she said. "A plus sign, an X, and what could be a figure eight."

Hyacinth shifted beside her on the sofa.

"What do they mean?"

Moira looked back at her findings in the cup. "Interpretations vary, but I would say changes are coming. Obstacles, loss, success, too."

"That's a little vague," Persephone said, not wanting to insult Moira, but feeling a bit let down by the ambiguity of the reading.

"The figure eight is intriguing," Moira added. "To some it might look like a ring. Like a proposal. Is there someone in your life? A man or woman?"

Persephone blushed, unable to hold back the snort. "Not even a hint of a someone."

"Then perhaps he or she is coming."

Hyacinth peered down into her cup. "Is there a new she coming for me?"

"You've had enough ladies. One can only hope the next one is the right one."

"What is enough?" Hyacinth asked, blowing Moira a kiss and earning a laugh from Persephone.

Moira paused, looking into her own cup. She took a final sip, slipped her own saucer over the cup, and flipped it. For a moment Persephone wasn't sure Moira was going to look—the strangest expression slipped over her face. In the end Moira peered into the cup, and then re-covered it once more.

"The last man I was interested in," Persephone said, wondering what Moira had seen in her own cup, hating the touch of sadness she saw on the other woman's face, "walked into rush-hour traffic after we held eye contact for too long."

"Ouch," Hyacinth said, sympathy tugging one corner of her mouth up.

"Yes, it would have been quite painful for him, had his student not pulled him from the road."

"Men can be the greatest of fools," Moira said, staring at her upturned cup, a frown line creasing her furrowed brow.

"They can also be quite charming," Persephone said. "Especially the ones who carry themselves like they're ten feet tall. Who smile with their shoulders and have fingers that look as clever as their words sound."

Hyacinth quirked a brow. "Calling Mr. Darcy."

Persephone laughed. "Oh gods, am I that transparent?"

"I've always been more for Captain Wentworth over Mr. Darcy," Moira said, running her thumb and forefinger around the base of her ring finger. "A lover scorned who returns is a hopeful thing."

Hyacinth frowned at her sister, who glanced over and caught the look. Moira shook off her reverie and stood, collecting the tea saucers and cups. "I better check the bread before it bakes itself burnt."

They watched her go, before Persephone asked Hyacinth, "Who broke your sister's heart?"

Hyacinth merely shook her head. "No one that I know of." She ran a finger over her left eyebrow. "Moira's always had a string of suitors. Off islanders who find themselves drawn to her like a fish on a well-wormed line. But while Moira's never turned down a good romp, she always tosses the fish back in the water when she's done."

Persephone wrinkled her nose at the notion of men being fish and women being bait and fisherpeople. She also thought, perhaps, Hyacinth did not know everything about her sister's love life. At least, not if the pain in Moira's eyes were any indication.

"What about you?" Persephone asked Hyacinth. "No special lady? Truly?"

Hyacinth bit her lip for the briefest moment. "The truth?"

Persephone nodded.

"I've always thought she was waiting for me somewhere else. On a different island, in a different part of the world."

"Then let's hope you get to her soon," Persephone said.

Hyacinth raised an imaginary shot glass and then tossed it back, ending it with a bite at the air. Persephone laughed and Hyacinth grinned her cheeriest smile.

"Let's hope he doesn't wait too long either," Hyacinth said.

"Who?" Persephone asked.

"Whoever was waiting in the base of your cup." Hyacinth suppressed a yawn and stretched out onto the couch. "That's the thing about Moira, cousin. She always sees them coming."

▸ ▸ ▸

PERSEPHONE SLEPT DEEPLY that night, after a meal of the most delicious cheese plate, homemade bread, and fresh vegetables. Most of which were out of season and yet grown in Hyacinth's garden. Persephone didn't know if she could really help the sisters break their curse. She wasn't entirely sure she believed in curses, no matter what they said, but she did believe in their and her power. What Persephone knew, without a doubt, was that she had never been so relaxed in her life. After the morning's hard revelations, she had somehow spent an afternoon laughing, drinking tea, talking about love and, later, which celebrities had the best backsides (basically, none of the women would kick any of the Avengers out of bed, though Hyacinth and Persephone had to Google Marvel to show Moira what an Avenger was). It was the first time Persephone had felt so protected, and she knew it wasn't a feeling she would ever forget.

The following afternoon, Hyacinth asked Persephone if she was ready to show them what she could really do. Trepidatious, but eager to please, Persephone jumped at the opportunity.

To practice their magic, the three witches went back through the Arch. They stood in a clearing in a forest as thick as any jungle and as bright as any polished emerald. The air smelled of moss and ferns, of sage and thyme. Persephone walked barefoot, instinctively removing her shoes as she stepped through the door onto the lush green grass.

"Think of this first practice as an experiment," Hyacinth said.

"One that will prove if you are our third," Moira added, though not unkindly.

Persephone rolled out her shoulders, determined not to fail even though she had no idea how to control any of her power. "What do I have to do?"

Moira moved to stand before her. "Your element is personal to you. Elements are the fundamental building blocks of nature, but we are more than elemental magicians or spell casters or even witches. We are goddesses in training, keepers of the island. Protectors of her power and secrets. You will need to claim and call forth your element."

Persephone held Moira's gaze, and took a breath down deep into her belly.

"Are you ready?"

Persephone nodded.

"Then let us begin."

Hyacinth had given Persephone slips of paper an hour before they made their way back through the Arch into the new land. Each had an element written across it: fire, water, air, earth.

Moira held out her hands and called forth the first of the elements, fire. It sparked in Moira's palm. She waved her other hand over it, and the spark grew into an orange flame half a foot high before she blew it out.

Hyacinth did not call forth earth, from which she could make things grow, but air. Hyacinth blew up a tiny tornado that twisted the ends of her hair into a perfectly knotted updo.

When it was Persephone's turn, she thought of the two remaining elements: water and earth. Persephone reached for a connection, for the tug she'd discovered on Wile Isle, and found it lacking. There was no familiarity to water, no connection to earth.

Persephone once had a dream of a man with nimble hands and sharp eyes. In the dream, Persephone was the most powerful person in the world. In it, she no longer felt lost, but known. Cherished. As Persephone focused on her magic a second time, she pulled the feeling of the dream back to her: a secret desire, her heart's truest wish. To be known. To be loved.

Persephone thought she heard a whisper of her name, felt the brush of lips across the edge of her jaw and the lightest caress of a fingertip trailing down her arm before it brushed against the inside of her wrist. Persephone thought, *Please,* and cupped her hands.

A brilliant white light leapt to life in the center of Persephone's palms.

There was a quick inhale of breath to her left. A gasp to her right. Persephone kept her gaze focused on the warmth she cupped. She drew it to her, closer, going on instinct alone.

Persephone pressed her palms to her chest and the light grew twice its size before it cooled to a single ember.

She bent down, her feet grounded like any strong oak whose branches take root. Persephone waved a hand over the grass, sent the ember into it, and reached deep into the earth. Down went her thoughts, down alongside her steady heartbeat, down with her intentions.

Persephone suddenly knew the earth, knew and saw, and she

began to work. She called forth reddish brown flakes of soil, breathed them up and into the air. They shimmered like snow caught in a fresh gust of wind, then flew up and spread out over the heads of the three women.

The flakes hovered, trapped on pause. For the briefest moment even the forest did not dare to breathe. Then Hyacinth let loose a wild laugh and the flakes tumbled down, brushing across the witches' hair and shoulders, noses and cheeks, before spilling back into the land.

"Copper," Moira said, her tone giving nothing away. "You mined copper."

"Aether," Hyacinth said, with reverence. "Persephone, you carry within you *aether*."

"Aether?"

"The strongest of all elements," Moira said, tilting her chin, a rare smile finally gracing her lips. "The life force of the universe."

Persephone couldn't have stopped from grinning if she tried. In a voice filled with a strength she had never heard herself possess, she said, "Then blessed be."

The three witches called forth their magic, spreading it across the land. Persephone pulling out earth while Hyacinth blew it into the air and Moira set the sediments to flame. Barefoot, brazen, the three women laughed and danced and tried to outdo one another. They brought the moon low and the tide high. They placed new stars in the sky and doused old ones out. They did not come inside from the Arch until they were so spent, they nearly had to crawl to bed.

▶ ▶ ▶

FOR THE NEXT few days, when she wasn't working on her magic with the sisters, Persephone was immersed in books. She read all she could on her element, aether, also known as spirit.

From physics, Persephone learned aether was suggested as the channel for the spreading of electromagnetic and/or gravitational forces. And in Plato's *Timaeus*, he said, "there is the most translucent kind (of air) which is called by the name of aether," while Aristotle argued that it was fire that was often mistaken for aether.

From this argument, aether became known as the fifth element.

As Persephone understood it, aether was spirit or space. Or, as Moira further explained, "Aether is what exists in the space outside the celestial sphere. In the realm of the Goddess, think of aether as the substance through which light travels. It is also the air the Goddess breathes. It is the most powerful and elusive of elements."

Persephone also devoured books on herbs, on the history of magic and alchemy, on Scotland and Wile Isle, and even one book on the unmitigated benefits of channeling your cat. The last one Persephone was mostly certain Hyacinth had thrown in as a joke.

Persephone's days slipped into a comfortable rhythm. She woke early, before sunrise, and joined Moira on the long front porch. At first, Moira was quiet, used to savoring her alone time, but Persephone's quiet perseverance paid off. At sunrise each day they shared a pot of lemon balm, Saint-John's-wort, chamomile flowers, and green tea—all for setting Persephone's intention and channeling balance.

A week into her new routine on Wile Isle, Persephone sat down with one of her books, *The Art of Herbs*, and sipped from the cup Moira had set out for her.

Moira moved across the porch, arms and legs slow to shift from pose to pose as she moved through the thirteen postures in Tai Chi. It was like watching poetry in motion. Moira's eyes stayed closed, her face devoid of lines as she breathed and performed what Persephone had taken to calling her slow-motion dance.

Where Hyacinth was almost always moving, Moira was one of the stillest people Persephone had ever met. It was when she practiced her Tai Chi that Persephone felt she saw the truth behind the regal woman.

It was how Moira's hands seemed to shift on an internal clock. How her feet followed her palms, and her spine did not yield. Moira held her head like she didn't even need her neck, as though it was another accessory she simply made the best of. There was such performance to her movements, on and off the porch. You only had to be patient enough to watch to learn that Moira had perfected the art of restraint.

When she finished, Moira came to sit in the rocking chair to the right of Persephone, her navy book with its gold bookmark slipped between the pages.

"That was lovely," Persephone told Moira, wishing she were confident enough to perform any type of exercise in a flowing skirt.

Moira crossed her ankles, and picked up her cup of tea. She stirred it with a copper spoon, three times counterclockwise, and steam rose from its surface.

Moira's magic, Persephone was learning, was no small power.

"It takes a hundred days to grow a foundation," Moira said, looking at Persephone. "I plant a seed daily, and in the end, I harvest what I've grown."

"What are you growing?"

"I hope the ability to bend the curse."

Persephone leaned forward. "How does Tai Chi help?"

"It's about habit," Moira said. "You can create a good habit, and bring yourself success, or you can cultivate bad ones, and bring about failure." She looked out over the hill, to where the path led back down toward town and the ocean. "The problem is that it is much easier to create a bad habit than a good one."

"Do you worry you're doing it wrong? The movements?"

Moira turned back to Persephone. "It's not about right or wrong. It's the doing that is important. All I need is to breathe in and out, and let my arms follow the air like a tide follows the water."

"Was that what you were doing?" Persephone reached her own palm out to press against the breeze passing through the open porch. "It did look a bit like you were pulling a wave to you and sending it away."

Moira smiled at Persephone, and the quiet grin was almost as good as a hug. "That's exactly what I was doing."

Persephone tucked her arm back into her side, and restarted the sway of her rocking chair. "How did you learn? Is it something your mother taught you?"

Moira's cup rattled as she set it in the saucer. A tiny drop spilled over the edge onto the side. "No. My mother was not one for slow movements, she was interested in going fast. Always."

Like Hyacinth. Persephone wanted to ask a hundred questions. Where was their mother? What happened when she tried to break the curse? Why did she have to leave the island? Why did Hyacinth not speak of her at all? Why did talking about her cause the pretty flush in Moira's cheeks to drop away?

But Moira was holding herself so rigid, Persephone was afraid the wrong question would send her out of her seat and back into the house. She feared the relative ease and comfort they'd grown over the past days would scatter with the wrong words spoken.

Instead she asked, "So how *did* you learn the practice?"

The flush returned in the blink of an eye, spreading from Moira's cheeks to her chest. "A man I once knew taught me."

Ah. Persephone bit back a smile. "Was he a Tai Chi master?"

Moira's laugh filled the porch. "Most assuredly not. He liked to make up his own poses and rename them ridiculous things, like Stroking the Tree and Mooning the Moon."

Persephone snorted out a laugh. "What?"

"We were practically kids," Moira said, grinning. "He was a young chef. Came on for a season, and stayed for one more."

Persephone caught the wistful tone in Moira's voice. "He was special?"

Moira dropped her gaze. Studied her bare feet. "It was a long time ago." After a moment, Moira looked back at Persephone, and gave her a sad smile.

"Still," Persephone said, sighing a bit. "I envy you."

Moira laughed. "Don't waste your time with envy. Fill it with facts." She nodded to the book sitting on Persephone's lap, before picking up her own and returning to reading.

After tea, they had a light lunch before Hyacinth wandered in from the garden. Hyacinth ate a cucumber sandwich over the sink, quizzing Persephone on her morning *Art of Herbs* studies, while Moira swept up the dirt Hyacinth trekked in and threw it out through the side door.

As the afternoon wore on, they shifted to training, and entered through the Arch to one of the three "green" dimensions. These dimensions were a variation of cliffs and forests, the best places to meditate, according to Moira. Persephone learned these locations weren't real, but a magical memory that existed only through the Arch.

Some of the spells she learned during training came easier than others. Stirring the air and reading what Moira was feeling when the witch was open to it (which she was surprisingly more willing to do than Hyacinth, who kept her emotions more closed off than a forgotten forest) were spells Persephone took to casting naturally. Trying to perform the more demanding variations or consistently calling aether on demand wasn't as easy.

When it came to summoning her element, Persephone would stand in the spot where the earth warmed to her touch, thinking of the white light of aether. She would call and call, her brow perspiring and her hands shaking.

"That's enough," Moira finally said one day, after Persephone swayed from the effort. "You're draining yourself."

"Just a bit more," Hyacinth said, giving Persephone an encouraging smile.

"I said *no*," Moira said.

Persephone watched the two women stare at each other until Hyacinth looked away first.

"You're trying your best," Moira told Persephone. "That's more than enough for now."

Hyacinth studied Persephone and winced. "She's right. Besides, I think you're ready to put your newfound knowledge of herbs to use."

Persephone knew that regardless of how powerful she was, she wasn't making the kind of progress the women wanted or needed. Mary Miller, the foster mother who almost adopted Persephone, once told her that expectations were the road to resentment, and Persephone couldn't have agreed more. However, Mary Miller wasn't under a time crunch to break a curse.

They left the Arch for Hyacinth's garden, stopping in the

kitchen for a chocolate biscuit and tall glass of milk on Moira's orders.

Persephone loved the garden at Ever House. It was a garden with a mind of its own. It grew what the witches needed, and what it thought they should have. Hyacinth said it was a divine kind of magic.

Hyacinth sat in the garden, with two small pots by her feet, a tiny bag of soil in her lap, and a sultry indie singer crooning from the portable speakers she had set high up in the tree behind her.

"Why do I feel like this is not what a real horticulture class experience would have been like?"

Hyacinth flashed her teeth. "It would if you'd gone to school on island. Miss Sully was a stickler for incorporating fun into even the hardest lessons."

Persephone sat down and dug her toes into the soil, savoring the feel of the cool earth. Grounding was a way of life for the witches, and Persephone couldn't imagine going back to wearing shoes after she left. She banished the darkening thoughts trying to creep in at the idea of leaving Wile Isle, and reached over to scoop a handful of soil from Hyacinth's open bag.

"What was it like going to high school? My impression of it is a strange compilation of John Hughes movies meets *Mean Girls* meets *Clueless*."

Hyacinth blinked twice. "That sounds . . . savagely fashionable."

"You didn't have an outfit-focused, self-organizing closet then? One you magically tricked out?"

"If only I'd thought of such a thing," Hyacinth said with a laugh.

Persephone tossed a sprinkling of dirt at her, and followed Hyacinth's movements and filled the small pot with the rest of the soil.

"School was pretty average. Boring mostly. I grew up with the people who attended and there weren't a lot of surprises. The hardest thing was not using magic on someone if they annoyed me. Hormones were the most formidable frenemy I had." Hyacinth reached into the pocket of her loose flannel and pulled out a packet of seeds. She passed the packet to Persephone. "What about you?"

"I didn't attend an in-person school," Persephone said. "It was hard at times, easy at others. Lonely, mostly."

She didn't mean to say the last part out loud and flushed at the admission. It was embarrassing to admit that you never fit in, never had the kind of friends you coveted from make-believe movies.

"I think high school can be lonely for anyone, in person or not," Hyacinth said. "But it totally sucks you didn't get to go if that's what you wanted."

Persephone brushed her bangs back from her face. "Thanks. On the plus side, no one ever tried to shaving cream my locker."

"I don't even want to know why you think that's a thing," Hyacinth said, suppressing a grin. "But if you want, I can freeze your bra later tonight."

Persephone grinned, and gave her head a solid shake. "Hard pass."

Hyacinth pulled a second packet of seeds from her pocket and shook it at Persephone. "Well, then. As the incomparable Miss Sully would have said, 'It's time to begin today's lesson, class.' Which means, let's make some mothertrucking magic."

The lesson of the day was growing an herb from the kernel of a seed.

"These are rosemary seeds," Persephone said, giving the seeds a closer look.

"Correct. A plus to my best student! Now can you tell me what they are used for?"

"Sautéing chicken?"

"Ha ha."

"Okay, fine." Persephone studied the seed, and the words she had read earlier that morning sprang into her mind. "Rosemary is a clever herb, and it can be used to aid in memorization, for purification, in a wreath for handfasting, as an aid in fertility—those two seem to go together, don't they? For protection, to repel bugs, and in place of frankincense."

"Very good," Hyacinth said, clapping her hands together. "How do we grow the seeds?"

"Water and sun?" Persephone asked, mostly teasing.

"And a bit of this and a bit of that," Hyacinth said, and waved Persephone on. "Demonstration time, dear student."

"I'm starting to think I might have been one of those students who skipped a lot of class," Persephone said, rolling her eyes, but she did as Hyacinth asked. Holding a seed between her middle finger and thumb, she used the pointer finger of her free hand to dip into the soil and create a little pouch. Then Persephone licked the seed, dropped it into the hole, blew dirt ever-so-gently across it in a covering, and closed her eyes.

She saw the seed nestled in its bed, saw the way it should look in the stages of growth and the end result as a full-fledged sprig of rosemary.

"Grow," Persephone whispered.

The air shifted. A breeze caught the edge of her bangs, the tips of her ponytail, and blew them back. Hyacinth let out a little sound of delight, and that deep vibration of the island pulsed once between Persephone's hands.

When she opened her eyes, a beautiful four-inch rosemary plant waited, small but sturdy, in her pot.

Persephone gave a squeal as she brushed her fingertips across the soft spikes of the plant.

"You have earned a gold star and a smiley face," Hyacinth said, clapping.

Persephone beamed at her, and then gaped, as Hyacinth waved a hand over her own small pot and her own sprig sprung up.

"In the garden," Hyacinth said, "we learn how to give life."

Persephone gave a happy sigh. "What you do is incredible."

Hyacinth set the pot aside and leaned back onto her hands. "I'm good at this, here. The plants, the garden, it comes natural."

"It's amazing."

Hyacinth shrugged, not quite meeting Persephone's eyes. "It is what it is, I suppose. How has it been for you? Do you remember the first time you used your power?"

Persephone ran another finger over the rosemary plant. "Hmm. When I was three a bee stung me and I stung it back. Is that what you mean?"

"Emotional sparks can trigger magic," Hyacinth said, with a nod. "Magic is energy, and energy charges."

"It's stronger here." Persephone looked off, along the herbs growing in the neat six-by-eight square planters. She swore she could hear the flowers waking up. "It's like being plugged into the island."

"Because you're meant to be here," Hyacinth said. "I knew it the moment I saw you. It's in the blood."

Persephone sighed, an ache right beneath her rib cage opening up. "I wish I knew more. About my blood, about my parents."

"I do, too," Hyacinth said. "The Goddess knows I tried to find out. There's just . . . nothing there."

"But we *are* cousins."

"Third cousins, twice removed," Hyacinth said, with a smile. She turned to the clove tree behind her and, using not a shear but her fingers, sealed off a break in the stem of the clove plant before passing it to Persephone. Persephone ran the sprig under her nose without breaking eye contact. She still wasn't used to the sensation, and it was one she savored.

"We share great-great-grandparents. Three times down, and so we are third cousins removed by two generations."

"Two generations of witches?" Persephone asked, because some moments it all felt too big, too extraordinary, to be true.

"Yes. Our great-great-grandmothers were cunning folk like their parents before them. And their parents' parents are the original settlers of Wile Isle."

Persephone nodded and stretched.

"How are you doing?" Hyacinth asked. "I know it's a lot to take in."

"It is." Persephone felt the pang of loss every time she thought of her mother and grandmother. Of how she had spent her whole life tending the secret, fervent dream that one day the family she so desperately wanted would be hers. "But I'm glad to be here with you and Moira."

"If you don't mind putting a pin in this lesson, I think I'll walk a bit," Persephone continued, the ache of loss rubbing raw.

"Of course," Hyacinth said, studying Persephone's face.

Persephone gave a forced smile, before standing, dusting off, and crossing to the road. "Oh," Hyacinth called, before Persephone had traveled too far, "don't follow the wind."

Persephone looked toward the path. "I don't know what that means," Persephone called back, on a sigh. She wished there wasn't still so much unknown to her.

"Yes, you do, Persephone," Hyacinth replied, her voice sounding like it was circling Persephone's feet. "You're waking up. Keep your eyes open and *don't follow the wind.*"

Persephone wrapped her sweater more tightly around herself and gave a nod. Breathing in the salty air, she closed her eyes and tried to find her balance.

I am a witch, Persephone told herself. *I have magic. I just grew a freaking plant from a seed.*

Persephone walked until the garden and home were out of sight. Turning back, she studied the house on the hill, which appeared to shoulder part of the small mountain. She really was grateful to Hyacinth and Moira. She hoped she could be who they needed her to become. They thought she was powerful, special.

She hoped she wouldn't let them down.

Giving in to instinct, she dropped down to press her palms to the road. Persephone asked the earth which way to go, closed her eyes, and felt the decisive *tug*. It was the same as the one she'd felt the first night in Ever House, while deciding which room would be hers.

Persephone followed the tug to a bend in the road. A strong gale blew up from the east and nearly knocked her over. She stumbled a step forward and the earth beneath her gave a violent shudder.

Don't follow the wind.

Persephone's feet froze, and she looked left to right at a split in the road she was certain had *not* been there a moment ago. She peered into the distance, and studied the inviting yellow house standing like a proud flamingo on the beach. An invisible arm wrapped around Persephone's middle and yanked, once. *Toward* the house. She felt the urge rise, and within a blink it was gone. Another tug rose up, like hands slipping into hers, and pulled Persephone in the opposite direction.

How do you know which way the wind is blowing you on an island that pulls a body both ways?

She took a step forward and the space in front of her went white around the edges. The air itself wavered.

Looking over her shoulder, Persephone saw a third path she'd missed the night before. It was covered by wispy hanging branches of two oak trees. Crossing to it, Persephone peered beneath the branches, and pushed them aside. A small sign posted to the left of the larger oak read: WELCOME TO WILE ISLE (EST. 1620).

The wooden sign announcing Wile Isle looked old at first glance, but on a second look Persephone realized the carving was fresh. Hyacinth and Moira said they didn't go into town often, and Persephone's heart sped up at the thought of getting to look around on her own, to see if there was a library or town hall with records, something Hyacinth may have overlooked that might help Persephone glean new insight into who her grandmother had been. She reached out and ran her fingers along the grooves of the words imprinted on the sign.

The sound of laughter and the straining notes of music caught in her hair as the wind blew the strands back from her face. Through the canopy of trees Persephone crept, tasting the sea on her tongue, savoring the scent of sap.

She followed the music. Her boots beat a gentle rhythm on the road as anticipation sped her feet forward. She emerged on the other side of the crop of trees, and stepped into . . . a fairy tale. There was no better description for the picture before her.

The road was flagstone; gray and white stone buildings along the border, slight and cheerful. The grass was a bright green, brilliant in a way Persephone hadn't expected to find on an island. The roofs of the little cottages were slate, the paint along the trim new. Laughter tinkled out from the open window of the shop nearest to Persephone, and she crossed to it. The door stuck on the first try, but after a second heave it gave and Persephone tumbled across the threshold.

Inside, the shop looked nothing like the outside. It was a bakery of sorts, and smelled of sweet biscuits, raspberry jam, and fresh buttermilk cookies. It was the patrons, though, who gave Persephone pause. They were dressed in period costumes made up of bustles, hoops, and petticoats, tux and tails, and the world's tiniest hats atop ribbons of curls.

"Your dress is wonderful," Persephone said to the woman nearest to her.

"Oh!" The woman looked down, and brushed invisible crumbs from her bodice. "The finery is for the festival. We're preparing for it, you know." The stranger tilted her head. "You aren't from the island. You must be a guest."

The last town Persephone had lived in over the Christmas holiday had a similar dress-up holiday festival, but they were months from Christmas and seeing so many people in costume in one small shop at once was startling.

"I'm staying at Ever House," Persephone said, studying the timepiece pinned to the woman's lapel. The hour was wrong, but the piece itself looked authentic and reminded her of the clocks in Moira's kitchen.

"Ah." The woman offered another smile. "The center of things. Are you coming to the festival then?"

"Festival?"

"It's really more of a show than a festival, but I guarantee you it's the only show worth seeing in any town or port." The woman waved her arm like a queen addressing an imaginary audience. "A spectacle of wonder for the senses to behold. The most marvelous magnificent show." The stranger hopped up, gave a twirl, and ran over to the window.

Watching her reminded Persephone of Audrey Hepburn in *My Fair Lady*. In fact, the way everyone in the shop moved felt like it was out of a film. The costumes, the pauses . . .

The pauses.

In time. In space.

Persephone looked around more carefully. She hadn't put it together at first, but the people weren't all talking or moving at the same time. Some paused, others swept into action as though awakened from a dream.

Persephone looked over to the counter. A woman with auburn hair and pale skin ran the workspace. She exited through a door on the side of the room after looking up and seeing Persephone. Time slowed, and Persephone watched as the rest of the patrons in the room shifted from in motion to in repose. Persephone took a breath, exhaled, and saw the air had turned to mist.

Something was very, very wrong.

The mist *moved*. It formed the shape of a person, and took one step, then another, and another, heading straight for Persephone. The blood in Persephone's veins turned to ice, and she ran for the door, yanked it open, and tumbled outside.

Persephone exhaled a stream of cold air. She looked for the path back to Ever House, but it was gone. Panic set in and her heels rapped against the cobblestones as she hurried away from the bakery. Two streets over she saw an individual cottage. It was beset by two black iron streetlights, like something from a gothic novel. Beside the wide front window was a handmade sign with carved elegant script. It advertised: LIBRARY FOR THE LOST.

She crossed to the library with its funny name, and looked over her shoulder.

The mist was gone.

Persephone let out a slow, careful exhalation.

She waited, counted down the seconds, until a full minute had passed.

No one, mist made or otherwise, was following her. No one was there at all.

The sense of danger faded. Had her imagination run wild from an overuse of magic this afternoon in the garden? Whatever it was, real or not real, there was nothing there now.

Persephone took a second, deeper breath, and peered into the library through a dusty window. She spied a polished wooden table tucked between two cream wingback chairs. Along the wall behind it were floor-to-ceiling bookshelves adorned with row after row of books. A new sense, this one of longing and belonging, washed over Persephone, and she decided danger or no, she might as well escape inside.

Persephone raised a hand to reach for the door when it swung open.

The young man on the other side of the door wore navy suspenders, a cream button-up shirt, and dark green pants. His long hair was tied back with a leather cord, and his cheekbones looked like they could slice through glass. Persephone's heart gave a hard knock in her chest. She thought he looked impossibly dangerous for a librarian, until he startled when he saw her. Then he looked as irritated as any interrupted intellectual.

"You're a surprise," he said.

"Excuse me?"

He flashed half a smile and Persephone's breath caught. His smile looked lived in, worn around the edges. The sleeping dragon in her belly woke, its wings unfurling and giving a hard flap.

"That sounded rude, didn't it? I'm not expecting anyone." He studied Persephone, and his smile dimmed. "Who are you?"

"Persephone," she said, before glancing over her shoulder again.

The man's eyes narrowed a fraction before he looked beyond her. A hard wind pushed down the path, nearly knocking Persephone off balance. She blamed his square jawline shadowed with stubble, and the delicious imperfection of his crooked front tooth for how her knees went weak.

He sighed, a long and irritated sound. "The temperature is dropping. You aren't meant to be here. You should be on your way."

The wind gusted again and he stepped inside the door. Persephone huffed at his rudeness, but stepped in after him, eager to escape its chill. He turned to look at her, an expression of incredulity on his face, and she quickly averted her eyes.

"Is the library not open?" Persephone asked.

"No."

"Why not?"

"Because it's not that kind of library."

She looked around the room full of books. All her life libraries had been safe havens. "What kind is it?"

He waved in the direction of the sign. "A library for lost people, lost things."

What an odd thing to say. He glanced back, and Persephone tried hard not to stare at how his shirt strained across his chest. "I'm lost."

"You're not lost," he made a half motion she couldn't interpret as a shrug or shake. "You're in the wrong place."

He slipped further into the room. Beyond him the shop was warm and smelled of ink and paper. Antique oil lamps with large glass domes were tucked into corners, the light pushing into the room like a beacon of welcome. The dark hardwood beneath their feet was blanketed with a deep burgundy rug, and a path was worn in the way of usual foot traffic. The library was large, with stacks going back as far as she could see.

It looked like any number of libraries Persephone had visited before. Then a vibration ran up her legs, clamoring onto her shoulders. Persephone leaned into the sensation. Into the call of magic.

The library may look ordinary, but it was not. She stepped further inside. The walls in front of her were adorned with books, and in the center of the room was a small castle made of leather-bound journals. Persephone crossed to it immediately, drawn to how enchanting it was.

"How many books did it take to make this?" she asked, squatting down to study it.

"I didn't count." He moved to a chair behind her, the arms of it creaking as he sighed and sank into the deep-cushioned seat.

The right wall of the book castle was missing three books, and her fingers brushed where the spines should be. Persephone studied the curious way he'd left a door off the castle. No way in and no way out.

The librarian cleared his throat, and she turned, careful to focus above his eyes. He was studying Persephone like a deer might eye a hunter. The feeling from when she was a child, a *giggle*, worked its way up her spine. Persephone tucked her hair behind her ear, wishing he wasn't affecting her so much. He closed his eyes, and Persephone grew warm.

"Is this a . . . magical library?"

"It's a library for the lost," he repeated.

Power thrummed in the room, making her head swim. "The magical lost," she decided, and turned back to the books in front of her. She smiled to herself. "I wrote a book once. A long time ago. You wouldn't have heard of it."

"*The Upside of Down Magicks.*" His eyes snapped open and roamed over her face. One of his hands gripped the edge of his seat. "Persephone May."

She startled, knocking over four books leaned together to form a turret. "No one's heard of my book or me."

"Consider me no one," he said, the gravel in his voice causing her to suppress a shiver. He leaned back into his chair. "I know most tomes that have anything to do with magic."

"Because . . . ?"

He didn't bother to hide his frown as he conceded what she already knew. "The library is a warehouse of magic."

"Like I said," she muttered.

He stood up and walked to the long reading desk in the center of the room. Persephone stared after him. Magic was all around her, and this man *knew*.

He was also very nearly gorgeous, and limping. His right leg shuffled, the foot dragging a little along the floor. He slid onto a worn stool, and watched her for a moment, before turning to a large book, roughly the size of an Oxford dictionary, with the image of a moon sliver wrapped around a large tree across its front.

"Hey," Persephone said, her gaze transfixed on the cover. "I know this."

"You've seen something like it before?"

She shook her head. "No. I . . . I don't know."

"It calls to you?"

"Yes, maybe." Persephone tried to look away, but ended up leaning closer to study it.

He stared at her. She could feel the heat of his eyes, smell the minty air of his breath.

"Have we met before?" Persephone asked, unable to shake the sense of *knowing*.

"Not quite," he said, with a small smile that transformed his face from handsome to stunning. He ran a finger along the spine of the book, looked down at his hand. "Some people believe when you see something and it draws you in, you have already seen or learned it before." His voice dropped dangerously low. "It's a re-membering. You remember what you've already known, as though in this life you are catching up with pieces of your past life."

His hand closed over the book as she leaned forward, ready to take it from him. A flash of anger flared to life in the pit of her stomach. His brows lifted like question marks and Persephone fought the deep desire to stare at him. To study his eyes, so later she could remember *him*. With effort, she looked back to the book.

She thought of Devon and the forgettable faces from her past, of Thom and Larkin. She thought of how she should definitely *not* make eye contact with this man, magical library or no. She felt him watching her, his gaze drawing heat as it traveled across her face. The sleeping dragon of desire in her belly flapped its wings relentlessly, like a horde of butterflies warning her to be careful even as she made up her mind. Magic was here, couldn't that make the difference?

Persephone lifted her face. She stared back at the librarian.

The hazel in his eyes shifted to amber. Tawny eyes, full of strength and something else, something Persephone could not name.

Persephone and the librarian locked eyes in a war of gazes for five long breaths. Her hands clenched. His breath caught. She waited, terrified of watching the change come over him.

He lifted one thick, sloping brow, and inclined his head. Then, he smirked.

For a moment, she wanted to shove him. To throw him down and, she didn't know . . . steal the book, slap him, kiss him hard. Maybe all three.

Then his cheeks flushed. Persephone looked down and saw her raised hand. *Reaching* for him. She backed up. He blinked at her, staring with such focus her knees knocked.

Persephone tried to think of something normal to say. To play off her reaction. Because *he* wasn't reacting. He was standing there, staring at her, as calm as the winter moon. No words came, and instead of saying anything at all, she turned and left.

He was entirely unaffected *by her*. The idea of it left her so off balance, she had to reach out a hand to the stone wall outside of the library and hold on.

Outside the streets were deserted. Persephone shook her head, trying to gather her wits. Desire coursed through her and she grit her teeth. He hadn't been affected, and yet, oh gods—how she wished he *had*. Not in the way where looking into her eyes sent him to the edge of insanity, but she wanted him to . . . want her. The normal way. The way one person craved another. The idea of it thrilled her.

A throat cleared and Persephone swiveled on her heels to face it. The man stood in the library's doorway. His head was tilted, his eyes keen like a wolf's. Persephone swallowed, had to force herself to meet them.

"Where did everyone go?" she asked, clearing her throat, needing to keep him from seeing too much of her.

"Go?"

Her hand waved toward the flagstones, and Persephone peered down the path. "The people dress-rehearsing for the festival."

"What festival would this be?" he asked, but there was something in his voice, steel and curiosity.

"For . . . the show?" What did the woman in the bakery say? "The most marvelous magnificent show?"

His hand gripped tighter on the door frame, and she stared at it. His hand. How could she find those fingers so familiar?

"Persephone," he said, and her head whipped back to him. "There hasn't been a festival or a show of any kind on Wile Isle for one hundred years."

Persephone blinked, the sun bursting from behind the clouds, blinding her. She looked away, able to clearly see the shops lining the road. For a moment, they shimmered and Persephone saw thatched roofs, turrets puffing smoke, fresh paint gleaming in the sun.

A second later, and the same row of stores were worn to near decay. The slate of the roofs chipping from age, the shutters hanging sideways if they were there at all. The buildings seemed to shrug at their own decay, their paint worn away, the remains a ghostly imprint of what once was.

"I don't understand," Persephone said.

The man's jaw was tight, his expression bleak. "You're in the wrong world," he said, as the clouds shifted to engulf the sun. "You need to go."

Wind kicked up, pushing Persephone forward, then trying to tug her back.

The clouds in the sky changed from somber gray to the purple of a healing bruise. A low whistle cut through the wind, the air scented with rain. Static slipped its way up Persephone's arms, clung to her skin.

Lightning cracked across the sky.

In bolts of three.

Persephone gaped at the horizon, and what appeared to be worlds intertwined within other worlds. It was like looking at the edge of a globe to realize two other globes were trapped inside.

"You shouldn't be here," the man said, his voice shifting into something dangerous. "*Go.*"

He shut the door before Persephone could demand his name, an explanation, anything. Everything.

The wind drew closer, brushing against her skirt, tugging at her shirt, scraping at her hair. Persephone's shadow grew long on

the stones beneath her, and she felt that unruly tug, this time in her chest—this time as a warning.

Adrenaline took root at the base of Persephone's spine. She took three steps forward as the shops changed again. The air crackled with electricity and the hair along her arms lifted. Persephone tasted metal on her tongue.

Across the street a door to a shop the color of burnt wood opened, and a woman stepped out. The woman was dressed in a dark gray three-piece suit, cupping a hidden object in one hand. Her face was in shadow, or made of them. Persephone could not see the stranger's eyes, but could feel them watching. The warning was back, and a sick sort of excitement pooled in Persephone's belly as the shadow woman took a step forward.

She moved like she was born of nightmares, an improperly assembled marionette. Her free hand plucked imaginary strings in the air.

Then, as if they were living in a slow-motion filter, the woman smiled. Her awful delight worked its way inside Persephone's mind, and a scream exploded from the back of Persephone's throat.

HYACINTH EVER'S JOURNAL

SUMMER SOLSTICE, TEN YEARS BEFORE

I never used to think magic could be dangerous.
It was always clever and charming, seductive but welcoming. But dangerous? No way.
Now . . . I'm not so sure.
My cousin Ariel's magic is changing.
The other day I made her a doll from corn husk and ivy, sewn together with elder bark and clovers. I only had to think what I wanted to grow and it appeared. Moira says anything will grow on the island if you have the right seeds and words, but I've found if I wish hard enough, I don't need anything else to make the earth respond. That's how I got the

caraway to weave into Ariel's doll. I closed my eyes, asked, and when I opened them the little plant was sprouting at my feet.

It's funny, but I didn't have an idea for the doll other than to make it. It turned out to be blond with eyes like an owl's, large and knowing. I didn't plan to make a girl, but the doll knew what she needed to be, I suppose, the way most things in magic know. The caraway, I hope, will bring Ariel love.

Once I finished pinning the marjoram flower in the doll's hair, I handed it to Ariel. She took it without looking up, her nose still in a book.

"For the Goddess' sake," I said. "Ariel."

Turning her face to the sun, because she moves like a sunflower, she eyed the doll I'd placed in her hand. Her smile took its time as she studied it. Finally, once even the blades of grass had grown bored from watching her, she said, "Well hello, little beasty. Who are you?"

She stroked her fingers over the doll's hair, leaned down to smell it. I watched as her fingertips hovered over its cheeks, and Ariel brushed the doll's face with the sweetest caress. It was as though she had forgotten I was there. I started to brag on how it only took me half an afternoon to create it, when she plucked at the clover closest to where the doll's ears should be.

Ariel leaned closer and whispered words I couldn't hear. A moment later, green light flickered behind the doll's eyes.

I watched the eyes blink and then turn in the face to look up at Ariel. She grinned down at it, and I sank back onto my heels. The doll was alive. My breath was a little startled in my laugh, and Ariel swiveled to look at me. She smiled, and tucked the doll under her arm, hiding it from me.

"Thanks, Hye," she said. "She's what I've always wanted."

Then Ariel went back to reading, and I went back to studying the grass and thinking that no matter what I wished to grow from the island's powerful earth, I would never have the kind of power my cousin does—and while I'm pretty sure that's a good thing, I also can't help but wish otherwise.

FOUR

T HE GROUND RUMBLED BENEATH Persephone's feet; she
tried to keep them planted but was forced to her knees. Her
vision darkened at the edges as the being in front of her wavered.
Persephone blinked, trying to see more clearly, and the person,
the thing made of shadows and refracted light, dove at her.

Persephone didn't have time to think. The scent of coconuts
and rain slammed into the back of her throat, cutting off the
scream. She tasted honey, blood, salt of the sea. A melody, coupled with garbled words and the notes of a song with roots as
deep as time's oldest tree, pulsed into her mind.

Persephone's fingers dug at the cobblestones. She arched her
spine, threw back her head, tried to shake herself free.

What was happening was wrong. It was an invasion.

Something—or someone—wanted all the way in.

Persephone fought. She would not give in to the pain scraping
its way down her spine, or clawing at her throat. She was finally
so close to everything—to finding her way, to having something
more than the life she'd barely been living, that she refused to let
the thing in.

She refused to allow it to take her.

Persephone felt for the tug at her midsection, and she yanked it *deeper*. She pulled power into her palms like Moira had taught her, and the magic answered. Radiant currents of energy flooded her system.

Persephone thought of the tomes she'd pored over at Ever House, of the spells she'd learned and seen performed. She raised her hands to her lips and through trembling fingers she found the words waiting.

> "*I am my own,*
> *more than ash and bone.*
> *As I will to know,*
> *your will* will *let me go.*"

Persephone tugged each line of magic tight to her and spelled it into a chant, turning the words over and over times three. She wrapped the words and magic around her head and heart.

A low mournful cry begged from inside Persephone's mind. Earnest and demanding, a strange call bore into Persephone's thoughts and echoed twice before the pressure inside her skull relented, and her vision cleared.

Persephone stayed crouched on the ground, clutching her palms to her chest. When she could take a breath without a moan, she slowly rolled herself up to standing.

Testing, Persephone spread her fingers in front of her face, and looked between them like a child sneaking a peek between the crack of a door and its frame. She should be scared, she thought. Whatever *that* just was, it should have her weeping in terror, stumbling for safety.

Instead Persephone felt strong.

The magic she had pulled into her flared once more, and she threw her head back. Persephone inhaled the crisp air and let the power simmer down low into the marrow of her bones. She had known terror before. After all, she grew up with fear—the fear of not belonging, of never fitting in, never being loved or enough. That fear had once been her constant companion.

Not anymore.

The difference was her cousins. It was the island.

Here, she was not alone.

Persephone looked to the library, expecting to find the strange man peering back at her, expecting answers. The man was no longer there. The library was gone.

She looked around, noting the changes in the street. The shops were similar, but not the same.

Persephone thought of the librarian. She set aside how he had made her feel, how much she liked looking into his eyes — the desire and comfort, and *craving* it caused — and focused on what he'd said before he disappeared.

He'd said she was in the wrong world. Persephone studied the exterior of the expansive stone building, and it shimmered before disappearing completely.

In its wake was the cobblestone road, bordered by lanterns. Persephone turned in a circle, and lightning crossed the horizon. She ran a hand over her eyes, and looked again. She turned back to face where the street had faded, and standing on this road, with a frown marring her face, stood the passenger from the ferry.

The first thing Persephone recognized was that the stranger was the exact same height and shape of the shadow being. Then thunder rumbled in the distance, and Persephone had a second realization. The stranger was not alone. Another woman stood beside her, and they both wore twin expressions of rage and disbelief.

Lightning struck again, this time at the feet of the passenger. The woman's eyes widened, and she *growled*. Going on instinct, Persephone threw up an arm as a shield.

The lightning storm scattered around the women. It was like someone was standing overhead, dropping bolts down on the two strangers like a child skittering rocks into a pond.

The passenger muttered a curse, raised her hand into the air, and clutched her hand into a fist.

Persephone gasped for air and doubled over. She peeked at the women through the pain. They appeared to be in their mid-thirties, and magic sparked off them like an electrical storm. Ariel and Ellison Way. They had to be. They were powerful, more powerful than she had guessed, than Hyacinth and Moira had alluded.

"*Give. It. Back,*" the shorter of the Way sisters said.

"What?" Persephone coughed twice, hard, and felt the magic inside her lift up and out. It was like the previous attack, only focused in a different direction. On instinct, Persephone reached her hand up and grabbed at the air. "I don't know what you're talking about."

The passenger's other hand came up and fisted and Persephone cried out in pain.

"Liar."

Persephone tried to breathe, tried to tap back into the vein.

"You dare?" the passenger said, her eyes narrowing.

"I beat you before, I can beat you again," said Persephone, a deep pool of rage roiling beneath her skin. Screw these witches. Persephone *was* stronger. She couldn't let them win. She wouldn't fail Hyacinth and Moira. She gnashed her teeth and wrapped the invisible line tighter around her.

The tall woman stepped forward, and the passenger's arm shot out to stop her. The passenger's face had gone from livid to uncertain.

The passenger sniffed the air and said something low and in a language Persephone did not understand, and the tall woman's expression lost its edge as the three women stood facing one another.

"You are not of the way," said the passenger. "You are something else." She looked up into the trees, before gazing at the spot on the ground where Persephone had fought off her attack. The passenger studied it like it was a riddle.

A seed of doubt sprang up in Persephone. "Wasn't that you?" Persephone asked, thinking of the shadow monster, of the first attack, certain it must have been from them.

The witches only stared, eyes narrowed, brows creased.

A shudder worked its way through Persephone, and she

wrapped her arms around her waist, trying to physically hold herself together.

Persephone got her answer when the woman looked at her and flashed a grim line of lip and teeth. "You are not of the way, but you are *in* the way." The passenger closed her eyes, took a breath, and raised her hands, palms face up. "Return now."

The gentle words scattered like leaves on the wind. Persephone felt them trickle up her legs and clamor onto her thighs. They undid the magic Persephone had wrapped around herself in one fell swoop.

The power she had pulled washed away and Persephone shuddered violently. The spell's undoing stole Persephone's breath and took her strength. She fought to keep herself upright.

"Come for my power again, witch, and I will end you in the most creative ways," the witch from the ferry said. She turned on her heel and walked with her head high, back down the cobblestone path.

The other woman, the tall one, shook her head. "Ariel always has to make a show of it." She studied Persephone, sighed, and lifted her own hands. "But really, you should know better."

Ellison Way snapped her fingers and everything, in and out of Persephone's line of vision, went black.

▸ ▸ ▸

PERSEPHONE WOKE ON the white crescent couch in Hyacinth and Moira's sitting room. Hyacinth sat at her feet, Opal at her head, and as her vision snapped into focus, Persephone saw a line of purple crystals varying in size resting along her right arm. "What—?"

"Amethysts," Hyacinth told Persephone. "You're depleted." Hyacinth held up a sachet of herbs, and tied it shut with red thread. Standing, she placed it in Persephone's palm. "I didn't think you'd need so much protection right away. I was wrong and I'm sorry."

"Protection?" Persephone asked, the rising aroma waking her faster than a cup of coffee ever could. The memory of facing the witches washed over her. "What did they *do* to me?"

"Drained you. I knew they wouldn't respond well to your being on island, but neither Moira nor I anticipated they would attack you like that."

Persephone studied the sachet in her palm.

"That will help," Hyacinth said, giving her hand a gentle, reassuring squeeze. "It's a bit of rosemary, angelica, and sage, three cloves, and a pinch of salt. While it's on you it wards off negativity."

"Does it work?"

"It does if you believe."

Persephone struggled to roll over, knocking the stones from her arm. "And these?"

"The Way sisters bled you of your energy, and the crystals aid in a faster process of calling it back." Hyacinth reached behind her to the long table, and brought a cup of tea forward. "Cinnamon for healing, among other things. Drink, and then we'll talk."

Persephone accepted the cup and drank deeply. As she did, the sachet warmed in her other hand and a feeling of peace rooted deep in her. Persephone's shoulders inched down from her ears. Whatever magic Hyacinth was doing, it was working.

Persephone finished the cup, pocketed the sachet, and swung her legs forward. Resting her head against the back of the couch she took a slow breath, and found the pain around her middle had abated.

"How did I get back to your house?" Persephone asked, her thoughts going to the library and the man there.

"Moira felt you fall," Hyacinth said. "She sent me and I brought you back." She brushed a loose lock of hair behind Persephone's shoulder. "You've really grown on her. I haven't seen her so worried since . . . well, it's been a long time."

"I'm growing on her like a boil," Persephone said, with a quiet smile.

"More like a freckle." Hyacinth said, flashing her trademark grin before her mouth pulled down and she looked to the side. Her expression reminded Persephone of someone biting off a secret.

Persephone thought of one she carried, and opened her mouth

to tell Hyacinth of the man and the library, and the words stuck to the roof of her mouth.

Magic.

She closed her eyes for a moment, seeing the man's hazel ones, and bit back a growl at whatever spell he'd worked to quiet her tongue.

"Those Way witches . . ." Persephone said, instead.

"They certainly give the term a bad name, don't they?"

"Without a doubt." Persephone ran a hand across her lips, tasting the fear from before, trying to recall precisely *what* happened. "I think, before they attacked me, that there was someone or something else there. It was . . . made of shadows?"

Hyacinth offered a subtle lift of the brow. "It could have been either Ariel or Ellison. Magic distorts our perception when we're under attack."

Persephone heaved out a sigh. "They really hate me."

Hyacinth ran her palm along her jaw. "They don't love you."

"But they don't know me."

"They know what you could be." Hyacinth sighed. "It isn't fair, Persephone." She looked her over. "Are you up for going outside, or do you need more time to rest?"

"I'm okay," Persephone said, stretching her legs and finding all her aches had eased.

Hyacinth nodded and helped Persephone up, and they went out onto the expansive porch, down the steep steps, and onto the pretty cobblestone path.

Persephone drew a breath down deep into her belly, relishing how the clean sea air seemed to reenergize and lift her spirits. "It's hard to imagine anything bad ever happens here," she said, looking at the rolling hills and deep foliage that merged together almost as though they were in a race for the sea waiting at the base of the island.

"Bad things happen everywhere, don't they?" Hyacinth said, her voice drawing Persephone's gaze. She nodded toward the mountain on the other side of them, and they followed the road up rather than down.

"I suppose," Persephone agreed after a beat. "I mean, bad things certainly happened everywhere I went before, but I assumed those times were from my own doing. You know, with the creepy eye magic."

Hyacinth looked over. "You haven't had it easy, have you?"

Persephone shrugged. "Who has?"

"You don't complain."

Persephone gave a short laugh. "What good is complaining?" She rolled out her shoulders, tested her neck muscles by tilting her head from side to side. "I've never wanted to be the victim, I've only ever wanted to be . . ."

"The hero?" Hyacinth supplied.

"I was going to say a survivor," Persephone said, wrapping her arms around her waist. "I read a self-help book at the last group home that said we should aim to thrive instead of only survive, so I guess that's what I've wanted, really." She shrugged to hide the feeling of being too exposed.

"To thrive," Hyacinth said, and her arm came up and around Persephone's shoulder. The side hug was gentle but reassuring. It lasted twelve seconds.

Persephone turned around to face her friend. "What about you?"

"I'm no hero," Hyacinth said, her mouth curving into a crooked smile.

"You know what I mean. What do you want?"

"To break the curse," Hyacinth reached over to pluck a leaf from a flowering bush. "To help you. To be free. To break the curse."

The path looped and they took it to the right, deeper into the forest where thick moss was draped over curvy forked oaks like decorative scarves wrapped around voluptuous women.

"If you are working with me," Hyacinth said after a long beat, "you are working against Ariel. She once wanted to break the curse, but time has a way of changing minds. After our mothers tried to break the curse and were banished, it changed Ariel."

Persephone studied the trees in the distance. She could empathize with that loss, to a degree, but perhaps it was harder to lose what you've had than what you've only dreamed of.

"Did you ever scry for your mom? Like you looked for me?"

Hyacinth nodded. "I thought I found her once, on the winter solstice." Hyacinth rubbed at her collarbone in a way that made Persephone think she wasn't aware she was doing it. "She doesn't want to be found. I couldn't hold the connection, it was like it was everywhere at once. Like maybe she didn't want to be traced."

"Oh," Persephone said, her heart breaking at the pain on her friend's face.

"She has her reasons, I suppose. When you leave without the island's magic, it can corrupt you if you aren't strong enough. She knew she could never return, so maybe she did what she needed to survive."

Persephone didn't think there was a cost she wouldn't pay to be reunited with her family. For Hyacinth's mother to cast her daughter off so easily . . . it was unimaginable to her.

Hyacinth brushed her hair from her face. "Ariel couldn't forgive the curse for forcing our mothers to leave, so she decided everything about the curse was evil. Including breaking it. She and Ellison now believe that to break the curse will free the darkness. They think to break the curse will destroy us *and* the island." She shook her head. "Ari's wrong, though. Saving the lost witches, our family, is what will save us."

Persephone considered the pinch of her cousin's lips, the determined set of her jaw. "Maybe it will even save your mothers."

Hyacinth didn't respond right away, only raised a hand and pulled a current of wind toward them so it sent her chocolate curls fluttering in the wind. After another weighted moment, she spoke. "Maybe."

Persephone didn't want to cause Hyacinth more pain and linger on the subject of her mother, so she rolled out her neck, freeing a few of the knots. "They wanted to hurt me, Ariel and Ellison. To stop me."

"Perhaps."

"I was able to control my magic," she said, thinking back to the powerlessness she felt facing the other witches. "But *I* didn't know how to stop *them*."

Hyacinth rubbed her forehead. "They are strong, and we haven't faced them in a long time. They are stronger now than before. I shouldn't have underestimated them." Hyacinth took a slow breath, released it. "Do you want to continue? Talking about magic and practicing your craft is one thing, but facing the Ways . . . that is another."

Persephone turned her face up to the sky. She meant what she had said to Hyacinth, she didn't want to be a victim to her life. She finally had family, family who made her feel seen and supported, and she didn't want to let them—or herself—down.

"I'm not afraid of the Ways," Persephone decided. "Though I'd sure like to not get my ass kicked if we face them again."

Hyacinth finally flashed her dazzling grin. "Then after you've had a bit more time to recover, I say we up our training and go for serious defense spells."

With that, Hyacinth and Persephone returned to Ever House. Hyacinth drew her a bath of rosehips and salt from the deep of the sea before she went out to her garden to work. When the last of Persephone's muscles no longer carried a lingering twinge from the fight, she dressed and went downstairs.

Moira stood in the kitchen, dancing to the Indigo Girls, preparing a lunch of roast duck and buttered potatoes. On the table sat a thick coconut cake that should have been illegal.

"It smells like whatever tempted the fates into giving up their souls," Persephone said, her mouth watering.

"Ha," Moira said, and gave her hips a wiggle. "As if the fates would ever give up *their* souls. They'd trade one of ours first." She turned around and waved a pitcher of tea in Persephone's direction. "How are you feeling?"

"Better." She considered the flour on Moira's face, the batter on her apron, and the mismatched slippers on her feet. In moments like this, it was easy to forget the power of this particular witch. "Hyacinth said you felt me fall?"

"I did." Moira reached for Persephone's hand. She placed her palm across hers, and a jolt ran into Persephone's toes. "We are connected."

Persephone smiled at the idea. Then, thinking it over, she asked, "Is there a reason Hyacinth didn't feel me fall?

Moira set the pitcher beside the cake. "Her magic isn't quite so strong as yours, it's a bit of a different wavelength so to speak."

Persephone nodded, looked out the window over the kitchen sink to where she could see Hyacinth in the garden, bent over a bed of hibiscus.

"She knows, doesn't she? It's why she works so hard."

Moira came to stand beside her. "Don't those who feel a lack always work twice as hard for what they want?"

Persephone thought of her mother and grandmother, and tugged at a pilled thread at the edge of her shirt. "Can I help with anything?" she asked, turning to Moira.

"That depends, how are you at setting a table?"

Persephone wiggled her brows. "I am a veritable badass when it comes to donning silverware and plates."

Moira's eyes twinkled before she nodded in the direction of the cloth napkins.

They made quick work of it, and as Persephone laid plate over plate and fork beside knife, she couldn't help but think of how many generations had gathered in the kitchen of Ever House. It made her heart squeeze to know her grandmother likely had stood where she stood.

It made her sad to recall what Hyacinth had said of her own mother, and how she would never stand here again.

"Do you miss your mom?" she asked Moira, the question popping out.

The fork Moira was holding clattered to the plate. She looked over at Persephone, her gaze sharp. Moira set the rest of her forks down, methodical in her motions, before she pulled out a chair and sat.

"How do you feel about thunderstorms?"

"You're asking me about the weather?"

"I am."

Persephone looked out the window, to where the sun cascaded gorgeous rays of gold across the grass, considering. "I love thunderstorms when they don't bring tornadoes or hurricanes."

"I hate them," Moira said, her voice level. "They are loud, bright, and aggressive. But they water the earth, they change the land, and change is necessary as well as inevitable." She ran a hand through her hair. "My mother was like a thunderstorm."

"Oh," Persephone said. She opened her mouth to ask Moira more, as footsteps sounded on the porch.

Moira reached for the spoons. She went about nestling them beside the plates, while Persephone held the wooden ring for a cloth napkin, her eyes on Moira, and the slight, barely there, tremble that ran down her cousin's arm, into her fingertips.

▸ ▸ ▸

THE WOMEN ATE, savoring each bite, and talking about nothing and everything. When they finished, Persephone helped Moira wash and dry the dishes after Hyacinth cleared the table. Ever House had a dishwasher, but Moira believed it was for special occasions. "Busy hands help clear minds," she told Persephone.

Once the dishes were dry, Moira and Persephone went out to the porch for a restorative meditation session. An hour and a half later, Hyacinth led Persephone through the Arch, and out onto a meadow bordered with wildflowers and apple trees.

"Welcome to Alternate Wile," Hyacinth said, waving an arm at the world around them. "This is what we imagine the other islands could have looked like had they not sunk into the ocean."

The air was cleaner on this land, the grass more lush than on Wile Isle. It was a type of oasis, Persephone realized, unmarred by a single imperfection. She immediately decided she preferred the real thing to the illusion. Persephone held out a hand to see if she could catch the breeze, and shuddered. Her whole body shook from the effort like leaves clinging to a thin branch during a windstorm.

"Your energy is blocked," Hyacinth said, as Persephone shook out her hands, trying to rid herself of the cold that flooded in when she tried to channel her power. "It happens when we let our minds believe what they should not. When we forget we have the power to manifest our world. To clear it, we need to release the imprint of negative energy left behind by the Way sisters."

Persephone's teeth chattered. "How do I do that?"

"By untangling the thread."

"What kind of thread?" Persephone asked, envisioning herself as one giant scarf and if Hyacinth tugged the wrong end she'd fall apart.

"The root thread, of course. It ties you to this new belief you're forming that *they* are stronger than you. You need to pluck out the feeling of fear from your encounter with them, and cast it aside."

"How do you pluck out a feeling?" Persephone asked. After all, emotions weren't feathers on a chicken.

Hyacinth dimpled a grin at her. "You rewind and review the emotion of the memory. It's like EMDR for witches."

Persephone had no idea what EMDR was. "Does it hurt?"

Hyacinth shook her head. "No, it's actually pretty peaceful. You close your eyes, root into the earth, and tug out the root. It can be a bit complex, the first attempt. I can assist you in the journey, though it's a pretty intimate spell to work that way. I'll be inside your memory, which can be unsettling."

Persephone scratched at her elbow. The idea of someone inside her memories left her itchy all over. And yet.

"I think I'd like you to help me," she said, summoning her courage. For all of her life, Persephone had been on her own, and she'd made a mess of things more often than not. She did not want to screw this up.

Hyacinth gave her an encouraging smile. "You can think of me as a road map to guide you, so you don't accidentally rewind the wrong memory."

Persephone raised her brows. "You mean so I don't accidentally replay one of the endless nights of Larkin and Deandra arguing over the merits of organic whole fat creamer versus natural almond milk while Larkin rubs up against Deandra's apron like she's a cat and Deandra dumps coffee grounds in his latte?"

Hyacinth let out a low laugh. "Yes, well, nobody needs *that* argument on repeat." She reached into her pocket and pulled out a small leather pouch. Waving Persephone closer, she opened the pouch and tilted it to its side. A group of lavender nestles tumbled out into her palm. "These are from our garden. One of the reasons we tend it so carefully is to help influence its growth. I sing lullabies to the roses, read poetry to the sunflowers, and tell stories to the lavender. This lavender knows memory, understands the importance of it. It will hold tight to yours, and—when you're ready—it will blow the intensity of the too strong memory away."

Persephone cupped her hand and accepted the nestles. Their sweet fragrance perfumed her fingertips, and a bit of the fear she'd been carrying since facing the Way sisters dissipated as she inhaled the calming scent.

"Take my hand," Hyacinth instructed, and Persephone grasped it with her free one.

"Close your eyes and inhale deeply. Focus on the scent of lavender. Breathe it in as your heels press into the earth, as the wind brushes against your cheeks. Think of a memory as a page in the book of time. It's one page in a billion, and lucky for you it's bookmarked with your thumbprint. Only you can recall it."

Persephone took a deep breath in, held it, and pressed her feet more firmly down into the ground. The wind tickled her neck as it shifted a few loose strands of her hair. She thought of the moment she'd looked into Ariel's eyes and the scene went from feeling soft and pliable in her mind to hard, tangible, real. Her knees shook, her feet wobbled, and the wind grew cold against her skin.

She bit back a ragged breath as adrenaline spiked in the pit of her stomach, and Hyacinth squeezed her hand.

"It's not real," Persephone said, her voice high and a little breathless.

"No," Hyacinth said, her voice quiet but strong. "It's not real. It's done and gone. It can't hurt you."

Persephone let the memory play out in her mind, telling herself it was over, it had no power. As she did, her breath evened out and the tremor in her knees subsided. She let the memory wind its way up and down throughout her mind, finding it was like rereading a scene in a story. The more she reviewed it, telling herself it couldn't hurt her, the easier it was to see details she'd missed the first or second time around.

How Ariel's face had flashed with confusion before it shifted into anger, how Ellison's fingernails were painted a cyan blue Persephone had never seen before, and how the two sisters had looked so different and yet like they very much were a pair. How the cobblestone path had glittered and the clouds shifted from black to gray to white while the three of them had stood facing off. The more she saw, the less she feared, the less power she allowed the memory to have over her.

Finally, Persephone's legs grew heavy in contentment. She held the memory close, and cupped the hand holding the lavender nestles. She opened her palm and let the nestles go, relieving herself of the fear she'd wrung out, but keeping the memory intact.

Persephone turned her face to the sun, and shifted her chin in the direction of Hyacinth. She could feel her cousin there, just beyond her mental border.

Persephone tried to open her eyes, but the sound of Hyacinth's panting, struggled breath, froze her in place.

She searched beyond her memories to the present moment. A light green mist shrouded the door in her mind to where Hyacinth was.

Something was wrong. She could feel the anguish lurking. Persephone reached out and pushed through the boundary. It wasn't difficult, the barricade may as well have been made of cotton candy for how pliable it was to move through.

Hyacinth's hand went rigid in Persephone's, and Persephone gasped at the bone-chilling cold that rocked through her. Persephone cupped her hand again, and tugged. Hyacinth's memory revealed itself.

Hyacinth was younger than today, her hair shorter, her skirt longer, her hands moving a mile a minute. She stood in the center of town, whispering into the ear of a girl with thick black eyebrows. The girl's cheeks were flushed, and her eyes bright. She kept looking off to the side, and then back to Hyacinth again. The girl nodded once, twice, and Hyacinth stepped back with a wink.

Then the girl turned as though called, and Hyacinth quickly walked away, hiding behind the market. Ariel came striding into town, her hair pageboy short, her face round and vibrant. She grinned at the girl, her whole face lighting up before she looked over and saw Hyacinth. Her expression twisted into irritation and then something closer to rage.

"No!"

Hyacinth twisted her hand from Persephone's in a furious tug, and Persephone stumbled a step back.

Her eyes flew open and she stared at her cousin, who was breathing hard and shaking.

"What?" Persephone asked, as Hyacinth looked at her curled hand.

The memory. Persephone had been holding Hyacinth's memory. Oh no.

"I'm sorry," Persephone said, "I thought you were under some sort of attack. You were frozen, and I was only trying to help—"

Hyacinth wrapped her arms around her waist, her face pale and determined. "What did you see?"

Persephone swallowed. "You and a girl. It looked like you were a bit younger than now, but it didn't seem . . ." She was going to say *special,* but then realized the right adjective should have been *scary.* It was the purpose of the lavender, and the spell. To pull a memory and release it.

Why would Hyacinth want to be rid of that memory?

Hyacinth ran a hand over her face for a moment, patting her lips. "It was nothing. But you can't do that, Persephone." She shook her head. "I didn't think you'd be able to cross into my memories. I should have realized."

"I'm truly sorry, I didn't mean to violate your privacy. I was worried, and thought to help."

Hyacinth stared out into the pristine world beyond. The wind moved around them, but Persephone couldn't feel it. The blades of grass sat unchanged, untouched by their feet or the weather. The world wasn't real, but their magic was. Her cousin gave a shudder, before dragging her gaze back to Persephone.

Hyacinth nodded, and failed at a smile. "I understand. In the moment, it just—surprised me. You have a habit of doing that."

Hyacinth went to the edge of the meadow, and a small stream appeared. She pulled what Persephone thought of as a singing bowl from the stream and sprinkled a handful of seeds from her pocket into it. Then Hyacinth closed her eyes, ran a hand over the brim, and said, "Awaken."

Nothing happened.

Hyacinth's mouth pulled into an irritated slash. "Awaken," she said again, her tone firm.

There was a simmer of smoke, but nothing more.

Persephone watched as her friend and cousin took three deep breaths. Hyacinth bit her lip and raised her hand, and this time the word rolled out of her on a near yell. "Awaken!"

The bowl filled with smoke, and Hyacinth's smile lit across her face. "One last step and the ritual is complete."

Persephone gave a quick nod, still searching Hyacinth's face for the fear her cousin had directed at her when she'd accidentally seen her memory. Not finding a trace of it, Persephone stepped closer.

"See the path, and repeat after me," Hyacinth said, giving Persephone the smallest of smiles.

> *"Return to the source of your power,*
> *for under darkness I will not cower.*
> *As I will it, I set you free,*
> *As I will it, so mote it be."*

Persephone spoke the words, and the remaining tension in Persephone's neck and elbows, the weight in her joints, released from her body. Persephone summoned her own smile, and looked over only to see envy flash across Hyacinth's face. It was gone almost as quick as it came, and Persephone's brow furrowed.

"I wish it were that easy for me," Hyacinth said with a shrug, seeing Persephone's expression. "Even with the words as a guide I have trouble with that spell. But we all have our gifts."

For the rest of the hour, Hyacinth focused on teaching Persephone protection spells relying on Persephone's element, aether. Here, Persephone struggled. She could go through the motions of calling space, but could not truly summon her element again—no matter how hard she tried. Persephone did master how to release nervous energy by sowing it into the earth, and how to wrap a cloak of confusion around her enemies by glamouring the air that surrounded them.

They did not speak again of the memory spell or what Persephone had seen in Hyacinth's mind.

That night, with a few new defense spells to show for her efforts along with a mammoth headache and a mountain of frustration, Persephone stood on the other side of the Arch to Anywhere, her eyes firmly on the cuckoo clock and its frozen hourglasses. She thought of the man in the library, how it had felt to be seen by him and to see him. The *thrill* of it. She thought of how each time she tried to tell Hyacinth or Moira about him and what he'd said, or the strange villagers preparing for the festival, the words lodged in her throat.

There were many magics on Wile, and so few Persephone understood. The clock in front of her ticked louder. There was something about the device that bothered Persephone. The way the grains of sand worked through the slender part of the glass. They didn't move in seconds, Persephone realized. Time inside the hourglasses slowed and sped up on its own accord.

That night Persephone dreamed of the three islands, the Way witches, and a curse that kept her frozen in time. In the dream, Persephone couldn't breathe, couldn't move, could only watch in horror as the family she never knew was killed by a mob of faceless witches.

The next morning, Persephone woke in a sweat. Her scalp

itched, her chest felt tight. She took a deep breath, then another. The room was shrinking, or the air was losing its oxygen, because her lungs and vision were constricting.

Persephone thought of her struggle with aether in the training session and Hyacinth's disappointment.

How could she help her cousins when she couldn't help herself?

Persephone was disoriented, terrified in her state of panic. She stumbled downstairs, seeking Hyacinth or Moira, but the downstairs was empty. She tried to access the Arch in case they had gone through it, but the door wouldn't open. She turned and hurried out the back door of the kitchen and down the side steps leading to the road. She searched the garden, porch, and the side of the house.

Her skin vibrated, a hum of adrenaline skittering inside her veins. Persephone was, once again, all alone.

The need to run, to sprint, to flee—a feeling she'd worked hard during her teenage years to overcome—overtook her. Persephone stopped thinking about the panic firing inside her, and she gave in to the raw reaction of fight or flight.

Persephone was not a runner. She preferred to take her time, to walk with measured steps and study the world around her. Because she'd had to move often, and failed for so long at connecting with other people, Persephone had developed a strong need to connect with her surroundings. Since she'd stepped foot on the island, Wile Isle had felt like home in a way nowhere else ever had. Which is why it was so terrifying that Persephone had awakened that morning and felt so unsafe.

With panic clinging to her shoulders, Persephone ran down the hill, toward town. She ran with the wind in her eyes, the breeze stealing breath she couldn't catch, and tears she didn't try to hold back leaking down her face. Persephone ran until the air rippled around her, the path under her feet shimmered, and she thought she would pass out. She ran until the worn cobblestones resumed a polished gleam, the aged trees along the path shrunk down to infancy, and the beach along the island's edge transformed from a short walk to an endless one.

Persephone's feet slowed.

Her choked pant was lost in the heady breeze . . . a breeze that was nothing like the one Persephone experienced when she stepped out of Ever House forty minutes earlier. Overhead the sun was shining. Persephone removed her heavy sweater, finding the temperature had warmed at least thirty degrees.

Persephone turned in a circle, trying to make sense of what she saw. The island had changed again.

She thought of the librarian, and her heart sped up. "You're in the wrong world," he'd said.

Persephone gave her head a shake as she looked around. She turned and walked up the path that looked like it had only just been laid. She pushed through thick undergrowth, and found herself in front of a large building—the very one she had witnessed disappear a day earlier.

The Library for the Lost.

Persephone's breath caught. She turned to look past the heavy wooden door when it swung open and a gruff voice drifted out from inside. "You don't know when to quit, do you?"

Persephone jumped, and the sweater she'd loosely tied to her waist dropped to the ground. Cursing, she bent over and picked it up. When she straightened the librarian was standing in the doorway like a sexy, bad-mannered jack-in-the-box.

Persephone pushed the hair from her face and flicked him a glance. "*Who* are you, and *why* are you so rude?"

"She's angry," the librarian said, leaning into the frame with his folded arms across his broad chest. Persephone couldn't help staring at the tattoo on his exposed forearm, a symbol so crudely drawn it looked as though he had done it himself after a heavy round of drinking. Her fingers itched to touch it. "You can call me Dorian, though I'd rather you didn't call me at all, and *I'm* not the one who is trespassing."

"I'm not trespassing," Persephone said, although since she wasn't sure *where* she was, and she couldn't be certain her magic hadn't in fact gone faulty . . . she might be hallucinating the whole experience. She looked over at him, and deeply hoped she wasn't. "At least I don't think I am."

Persephone shook out the sweater and accidentally tossed it to the ground again, this time a few feet from where Dorian stood. He didn't make a move to pick it up, only stood there, staring at her with those wolf eyes, unblinking.

"Rude," she repeated, her pulse speeding up. She forced a steady hand to tuck her hair her over her shoulder.

"Rude?" he asked, with a determined lift of his chin.

"What else would you call not assisting someone in distress?"

"If the person in distress is a walker like you, I'd say it's good old common sense."

Then he stepped back into the library and shut the door. Persephone glared at it, considered smacking it or turning on her heel and marching off. She decided if this *was* her hallucination, if she had indeed tipped over the point of sanity into the realm of magical madness, she might as well go all in.

Persephone scooped up the sweater and tied it into a knot around her waist, then marched forward and shoved at the door. It opened with ease. Persephone charged in, looked around the room for Dorian. She found him in front of a large fireplace she'd overlooked before. He was crouched in front of the open stone mouth, feeding large hunks of wood into it.

His whole body sighed as Persephone stepped closer to him.

"You seem to have a firm opinion of me, considering you don't even know me," Persephone said. It shouldn't bother her, but there was something about how he made her feel, that desire, coupled with how much she put him out. It wasn't her magic driving his irritation. Eye contact didn't faze him. No, this was something else, and that was a very peculiar puzzle indeed.

"I know your kind well enough." He prodded at the fire before shifting his weight and sitting all the way down. Crossing one arm over his bent knee, he looked up at her. Dorian met her eyes, and stared. Five, four, three, two, one. Persephone counted down. Again, and again. He raised both brows. "You're thinking hard, aren't you?"

"You're staring at me."

"You're staring back."

She blinked. He blinked. Persephone narrowed her gaze. He smiled.

"You're a witch," she said, crossing her arms over her chest, trying to hold down her excitement at the discovery.

"Not even a little," Dorian said, his tone indicating she had implied he had crawled out of the sewer and licked her boot.

She dropped her arms to her side. "How come I can't tell anyone about you if you're not a witch? That's serious power to prevent me from speaking your existence."

"It's none of your business speaking about me, and I'm not a witch." He took a step back from her, the clench of his jaw telling her he was more affected than he wanted to let on. She thrilled at the realization. "I'm a librarian, of sorts. Your blood's the one humming with the ancients." He shifted further away from her.

Persephone leaned forward. "Am I making you uncomfortable?"

"You keep showing up like a bad penny, so yeah. I'd say that's a word for it."

"But you're still staring at me."

"Are we in a contest? Because if so, I'll have you know I mean to win. I'm frightfully good at winning." He quirked up a corner of his full lips. "Except when I lose, but even then I do so spectacularly."

Persephone's eyes drifted to his slightly crooked, chipped tooth and a blush crept up her chest. She dropped her gaze to the fire.

"Looks like I'm the one making you uncomfortable now," he said.

Persephone gave her head a small shake and crossed to the bookshelf nearest to her. It was filled with old journals, row after row of them. He might not be a witch, but he was something. He could see her, and the *way* he looked at her sent need licking along her spine.

"Why can't I speak about you?"

"You can't speak about the library. I'm in it."

She considered that, and him. "You called me a walker. Why?"

"You're here uninvited, so a *walker* you are, Persephone May."

Persephone reached out for a thick-paged journal in front of her, her hand brushing air. She tried again but grasped at nothing. Persephone stared at the shelf in disbelief. The books were *there*, on the shelf, inches away. "The library is magic," she said, narrowing her eyes. She reached again, but it was like trying to grab a puff of smoke. "Wait." She looked at him. *Walker.*

Time walker. The prophecy. "How do you *know* I'm a . . . walker?"

He raised his brow in response. "People don't just come here, Persephone. Not even witches."

"I am a witch and I'm here."

Dorian stood and strolled across the room, his limp less pronounced than it had been earlier. He turned and as he did, the room turned with him. Persephone's head spun, but only for a moment. A hallway appeared to the left, and Dorian started down it. Persephone hurried after him, and crossed through an open door, then another, and another, and another. Dorian ambled ahead of her, and something in how he leaned forward made her think he was laughing at her.

Persephone picked up the pace, and still he stayed the same distance ahead. He went through one more door and turned down a hall with floor-to-ceiling books of various shapes, sizes, and preservation. One tome was so thin, Persephone thought if she were able to touch it, its spine would collapse in on itself.

The hallway was a heady mixture of pine and sea, the scents nothing like a library and everything like a forest at the edge of an ocean. Dorian turned once more, and they entered a room with high ceilings. It looked to be three times bigger than the exterior of the library.

She blinked at the long navy sofa, the only piece of furniture in the entire room. It rested on top of a threadbare oriental rug that may have once been turquoise but had faded to a dull, inviting blue. Beside it was a thin telescope pointed at the far wall. The wall featured a painted mural of a jungle set in a much more exotic landscape. She couldn't be sure, but as she stepped closer, Persephone thought one of the banana trees in the painting swayed.

She peered nearer, and a small creature scurried from limb to limb. Startled, Persephone fell back, directly into Dorian.

FIVE

D ORIAN'S CHEST WAS LIKE a delicious pine-scented wall.
Persephone fell into it and his hands clamped down under
her elbows, catching her. For a moment, Persephone leaned into
the feel of him, before he spun her around to face him.

They stood inches apart. She was so close she could see the
honey and amber mixed with the deeper shade of green in his eyes.

"You say you're a witch, but you walk through worlds," he
said, his hands warm against her forearms.

She suppressed a shiver. "I didn't mean to."

"That, Persephone May, doesn't change what you're doing."
His palms remained on her arms, and when he finally removed
them, Persephone was tempted to put her hand over the spot to
try and keep the warmth trapped there.

"I haven't been in this room in a very long time," he said,
looking around.

"So why bring me here?"

"I didn't." His brows lifted.

"What are you talking about?"

Dorian ran a hand over his hair, tugging at where it was knotted at the nape of his neck. "You brought us here. The magic in

you, it's how you're moving through the library. You are the first walker in a hundred years."

Persephone shook her head and looked around the room, still not understanding.

"Have you never experienced anything like this before?" he asked. "You shouldn't be here, and yet you are. Have you never walked through a world before?"

Persephone met his eyes.

"How about this? Have you ever felt time move around you, control events within it?"

Persephone had a flash of Larkin, of telling him to *release*.

"Yes," she said, understanding clicking over.

Dorian gave her a slow, complicated smile. "Magic's a bit like this library. It has its own rules."

"Which are?"

"None of your business."

"Gee, way to be a jerk."

"It's the truth, walker."

Dorian's lips thinned, and Persephone's temper flared. Who cared that the man made her toes curl when he looked into her eyes, he was an ass. "Fine. If you'll just show me the door, I'll be happy to go."

He waved a hand around the room. "I didn't bring us here. You did. I'm sure you can take yourself anywhere else."

Persephone raised a brow. "Would it leave you trapped here? For all eternity, perhaps?"

He snorted at the hope in her voice. "You'd like that, wouldn't you?"

"I can't say I wouldn't mind it."

He glared at her, and the urge to hit him coursed through her so strongly Persephone had to grip her hands together.

"You'll break your bones if you squeeze any harder," Dorian said, flicking his eyes to her hands and back to her face. "So much power, so barely contained. Why are you here, walker, and what is it you really want?"

"Right now? I would like to get the hell out of this place."

Something flashed in his eyes. A spark of interest that burnt bright before he doused it out. "What made you choose this door? To come here of all places?"

Persephone looked back to the hall they'd entered from. "I . . . followed you through the opened doors and we ended up here."

He considered, and turned and walked to the telescope pointed at the mural that wasn't a mural. He peered deep into it, to the jungle.

A moment later he looked up and back to her. "Care to have a look?" There was an edge to his voice, a challenge.

Persephone rolled back her shoulders. She stepped over and grabbed the handle, pulled the scope down an inch and looked.

A shadow moved from behind the banana trees.

Persephone took a step back. She looked at Dorian and he cocked his head. She looked at the mural, and nothing had changed.

Persephone reached out again, and looked once more into the telescope. The shadow crept in, like a fog riding on a sunrise as it came closer into view. The blood in Persephone's hands chilled, ice moving into her arteries.

This time she took three steps back before knocking into a side table.

Dorian turned as slowly as a yawn. "You don't know what or where that is, do you?"

"It's bad." Persephone stepped again, around the little table. "I know enough to know that."

He didn't speak, but waved a hand and the mural of a wall that was or wasn't a window into another land shifted into a labyrinth of shelves leading from the floor up into the ceiling. Only the telescope remained behind.

"What was it?" she asked. "That . . . thing?"

"That is not for me to say." He held up a hand. "Before you protest, I don't have permission to tell you. I *can* say you shouldn't be able to see it, but you can." He paused, appeared to struggle with his words. "Only walkers can access beyond the veil."

Persephone gulped. She wanted to ask him about the prophecy, to ask more about the veil, but in the next moment the ground shook. Persephone reached over to steady herself and shelves shifted forward into the room. A new wall rotated up into the library and before them stood a never-ending wall of manuscripts, journals, books, and maps.

"I didn't do that," she said. "Did I?"

"No. The library has a mind of its own," Dorian replied, crossing his arms.

Persephone squinted and saw that across the room, *those* shelves were full of various items and objects of all shapes, lengths, and sizes. A collection her fingers itched to touch.

"Be our guest," he said, watching her, speaking once again as though he were issuing a challenge. "If you can."

Persephone studied the books, bit down on her irritation with the attractive, bad-mannered librarian, and pulled her intention to her center.

I need a way, she thought. *To find my family, to get answers.*

Nothing happened.

She took a breath. *As I will, so mote it be.*

An unseen whisper brushed against Persephone's cheek.

A low rumbling knocked its way along the endless shelves.

Dorian's brows arched.

Persephone took a step closer to the wall, took another breath, and reached.

Her fingers pressed against the wooden edge. Persephone slid them up toward the closest journal and they brushed through it as though it wasn't there.

Persephone bit back a frustrated groan, and returned to the wooden portion of the shelf. The vibration pulsed beneath her fingers and she trailed them along the edge. The tremor grew, building until Persephone's whole hand was shaking, the vibrato climbing up her arm. She had to grip into the threshold to keep her focus.

Sweat beaded along her brow and dripped down her back. Persephone took another steadying breath, and her vision grayed at the edges.

Persephone's fingers crawled along the shelf until she stood in front of a photograph. She reached out, hesitated, and hovered her fingers over it.

"Hmm. There's a surprise," Dorian said, his low voice carrying in the great echoing room. "Know if you pick it up, you agree to the library's terms."

"I don't suppose you'll tell me what those terms are," Persephone said, trying to keep her voice light and finding it as breathless as the rest of her. Using her magic to penetrate the boundary took all of her effort.

"I don't suppose I will."

Persephone gave a quick nod, imagined sticking her tongue out at him, and dropped her hand onto the image. She scooped the photo up, and her legs gave out like a newborn colt taking its tremulous first step.

Persephone stumbled back, raw, aching, and drenched with sweat. She felt as if she had spent six days cramming for the exam of her life without bothering to sleep or eat. Her hands shook as the image on the picture began to shift into focus.

She flipped it over and read the words on the back.

May you ever find your way.

Persephone turned it over and stared. "It's a photograph," she said, brushing a finger across the face captured there. "Of a woman . . . who looks like me."

Dorian moved closer to her, far enough away not to be touching, near enough to offer some form of comfort. And it *was* comforting to have someone there, even if that someone was the surly librarian who made her palms sweat.

Persephone stared at the photo for so long her eyes watered and her mouth grew dry. This picture was the first real evidence that Persephone belonged to someone. Someone who had the same nose as she did, the same eyes.

Dorian leaned over her shoulder, his piney scent intoxicating. "I've never seen *that* particular image before."

She studied him. "Do you know who it is? Who I am?"

His tawny eyes searched hers. "I can't tell you who you aren't," he said, tapping the edge of the photo. "Or who you come from. The library may have answers, but I do not."

Persephone had to force her gaze from the fullness of his lower lip. "You and this library are a right pain in the ass."

"Says the pot to the kettle."

Persephone glared at him for a moment, before turning her gaze back to the picture.

Dorian let out a loud, infuriating sigh. "The library holds all manner of magic, of answers and truths. It is a keeper of time and memories. I don't know who this is, but if I'm guessing, I'd say from the era and the fact that you have bits of her face in yours, it's your grandmother."

"Yes." She sighed. "Viola. I wish I knew more about her."

Dorian made a noncommittal noise.

"Can you ask the library and tell me?"

"That's not how this works."

"You're not a very helpful librarian." She rolled out her neck. "So how does it work?"

"You can ask, and the library will help or it won't."

Persephone ran a finger across her brow, pressing at the headache trying to form. "How do I know that you aren't lying about everything you have already told me?"

"You don't."

Persephone looked over and he shrugged.

"And I'm supposed to trust you?"

"You aren't supposed to *do* anything. You keep showing up and getting your way, though, so I suspect that's what you'll keep trying to do."

Her eyes narrowed. "Were you born this big of an ass or is that a secret, too?"

He bit off part of a laugh, and she swallowed. Dorian was stunning when he smiled.

"You said this is the Library for the Lost," Persephone said after a rather long silence and staring game neither of them won. "My family is lost."

He blinked, a slow and methodical movement. "That is not quite the right question to ask."

Persephone straightened and stretched. "What is? Never mind. I know what you'll say." She attempted to mimic his deeper voice. "I cannot tell you the right questions to ask." Persephone took a breath, searched the room, and returned her gaze to his. "Are all the items in here like this? Are they all magic or under a spell?"

"Yes." He nudged her with his shoulder. "Keep going."

She held very still, fighting the shiver that rose up at brush of his arm. "The . . . library won't let me tell my cousins about you or it?"

He gave a slow nod.

Persephone tapped her finger along the photo's edge. "Is . . . is the library the most powerful place in existence?"

He cocked his head, and Persephone knew she was close to something. "It is one of them. It holds all magic that has been imagined. Some real, some fictional."

"Fictional?"

"The library has a sense of humor. If something has been written as magic, be it in a story or in reality, it can exist here."

"And it's *not* the most powerful place in existence?" Persephone asked, thinking of all the magical novels and non-fiction books on power she'd read in her life.

Dorian thought for a moment, and cocked his head. "It's no Menagerie of Magic, but it's powerful in a different way." His eyes cut to hers.

"The Menagerie of Magic?" Persephone said. "You know of it?"

Dorian closed his eyes for a moment, tried to work his lips, but only ended up shaking his head. When he blinked his eyes open there was something like concern, or pain, there. "I can't say anything further."

Hmm. Maybe even the librarian could be bound by silence on certain subjects. "You *do* know of it, so you must know of Amara and True Mayfair," Persephone said.

He hesitated, nodded. "Lost witches."

"Lost, like the library?"

His lips curved infinitesimally but he did not speak.

Persephone sighed. "I'm so tired of all the things I don't know. You clearly have answers, but can't tell me."

"Does it help that I wish I could?"

She smiled, her heart giving a painful thump at the way his eyes roamed over her face. Craving unfurled in her belly, a strong tug of wanting. "A little."

"The library has answers. It gave you that one." He nodded at the photograph in her hand.

"I don't know anything about her, or what happened to her or my mother."

"You will."

"What makes you so sure of that?"

"Just a hunch."

He smiled then, a flash of crooked teeth, and Persephone's bones hummed in response. She brushed at her bangs and looked away. "I should go. I've got some walking to do, and magic to sort."

She could feel him staring at her, feel the blush flood into her cheeks. Dorian stood slowly, and started for the door. His limp growing more pronounced with every step. He waited for her to unwind herself from the floor, and when Persephone crossed to him, he held out his arm. "I'd rather go the short way than the long," he said. "So I'll need you to let me lead."

"Fine by me, Dorian. Lead on." Persephone tucked her arm through his, trying her best not to get lost in the heady scent of him. Within a few short steps, they walked through the doorway, and out into the main room. Persephone blinked, her head reeling for one long second as the floor rolled beneath her feet. She blinked again and the discombobulation righted itself out of her. "How in the world—?"

Dorian shifted beside her. "Things don't always follow the natural order here," he said, his touch gentle as he unspooled his arm from hers.

"Here?" His meaning sunk in. "Because this is another world?"

He hesitated. "Because this is not your island."

Persephone searched his eyes, the cinnamon color brighter in the firelight than it had been before.

"Is it unsafe to be here?"

"It is if you arrive uninvited." He smiled, and this time it reached his eyes. She wanted to run her finger along its seams.

"Which as you keep pointing out, I am."

"Yes. Though it's been . . . interesting, finding you."

"I think you mean I found you," Persephone said, and ducked her chin as she moved to the front door.

Dorian was proving to be the most confusing man. She didn't like how drawn she was to him, how distracted she was becoming by the irrational, growing urge to taste the scar just under his chin. He was impossible to read, and she was struck by the thought that, for once, *she* wasn't the most dangerous person in the equation.

When she looked back, a look of indecision crossed his face. "Wait a moment, please," he said, and went to the fireplace.

Persephone clasped and unclasped her hands as she waited, watching Dorian's backside and scolding herself for giving in to the distraction. Dorian reached into a compartment beside the fireplace, but when he stepped back there was nothing but stone in front of him.

He walked back to her. In his hand he carried an hourglass locket. He passed it to Persephone. "Walkers can lose track of time."

Dorian's cheeks were faintly flushed, and Persephone realized his own actions had embarrassed him.

Persephone had never been given a present by a man, let alone a necklace. The gift touched her more than she dared admit. She accepted it, murmuring thanks, trying to ignore the furious knock of her heart in her chest.

On the bottom of the hourglass was the inscription: *Walker Mayfair. May you ever find your way.*

"Like the inscription on the photo," Persephone said, looking up at him, her gaze sharp. "What does it mean?"

He shrugged one shoulder. "I do not know. I catalogued it some years ago. I think, perhaps, it was waiting on you."

"Because of the picture or because I . . . walk through worlds?"

"Both, and because I think you are looking for a way." He pushed the door open and stepped back. "Now you have your direction. The rest, I'm afraid, is up to you."

Persephone pulled her sweater from her waist and slipped her arms inside it. "What if I need to return here, invitation or not?"

Dorian's smile was quick and it punched a small hole in her heart. "I suppose you will find a different way to do that, too."

Persephone stepped through the door frame, feeling like when he said *suppose* he really meant *hope*, and when she turned to thank him and simply get one last look, the building was fading. Persephone stayed where she was, watching the light shimmer, and the hues of amber and jade weave together.

Persephone did not see the shadow slinking from the windows.

She never noticed it disappear into the cracks by her feet.

Persephone did not sense it as it slipped across her own shadow and held on tight.

▸ ▸ ▸

THE HOURGLASS SAT heavy in Persephone's pocket. She stood on the cobblestone road, squinting in the distance like she could make the library reappear by sheer will. And maybe Persephone could. She did not yet know, magically, what all she could and could not do.

Why not try to bring it back? Persephone stared ahead, seeing the building once more in her mind. The fabric of air, of earth, of worlds, rippled around her.

A rush of euphoria spiked into Persephone's bloodstream. She thought of the library. She thought of Dorian's smile.

Persephone lifted her hands . . . and . . . nothing.

A cold wash of frustration followed as the vision faded. Persephone tried again, but she could not pull the world back.

A little breathless, and severely agitated, Persephone tugged the hourglass from her pocket and studied it. It was exquisite, and one hell of a first gift to be given. Persephone closed her eyes for a moment, bringing Dorian's face back into her mind. That he could meet her gaze, and how it felt when he did, flooded her with an ocean's worth of emotions.

Persephone loved staring into her cousins' eyes, it was comforting and reassuring. Staring into Dorian's however . . . she hadn't realized how charged a room could become, how seeing someone and having them see you could lead to such *need*. It was its own kind of magic, perhaps. One that made her heart gallop in her chest, her mouth water, and her toes curl. It was foolish, but Persephone knew she wouldn't stop replaying every millisecond of her run-in with the librarian anytime soon.

The timepiece grew heavier in her hand on the island than it had been in the library. Persephone tucked it into her bra, the safest place to keep anything on her person, and checked the time on her phone. She blinked, read the numbers again, and blinked once more. Five minutes had passed since Persephone had left Hyacinth and Moira's house that morning.

Five minutes and what felt like a day. Persephone shook her head at the wonder of it, and rolled out her neck. The intense wear of using magic no longer wore at her fringes. The bone-deep tired she'd carried dissipated as she stood under the cool noonday sun. It must be the island, Persephone thought, that replenished her so fast.

Persephone needed to know the truth of that connection. It was time to return to Ever House and try and find a way to tell Hyacinth and Moira about the library and Dorian, show them the photograph, tell them about being a walker. They were closer now, surely, to breaking the curse.

She turned to walk back, and her feet froze on the stones. Persephone tried to move, but the tug around the center of her spine jerked her in the opposite direction.

Toward Way House.

Oh no. No, no, no.

She tried to yank her feet up, unspool herself from her stuck position. Nothing happened. Persephone growled in frustration, twisted her body left and right, she even tried to throw herself forward. It was all to no avail.

Persephone stood there, eyes closed, irritated, and worked to clear her mind.

Dorian's face drifted in, and she heard him telling her: *there was a way* to her answers.

Persephone let out a groan. What if he had meant *a Way*, as in a person?

She wanted to break the curse, needed to help Hyacinth and Moira, wanted to save her family. What if this was what she needed to do next?

Persephone took a breath, held it, and felt the tug grow stronger. Her bones hummed with the knowledge—the island wanted her to go see the two witches.

She looked down at her feet and sighed. "Fine. If this is what's needed, I'll do it. But if you want me to go talk to them, then *you* can keep them from trying to kill me."

The island released Persephone, and she stumbled a step forward. She rolled her eyes. Wile Isle had a will almost as strong as hers—clearly she was on a magical island with control issues.

The journey to the beach was picturesque even as heavy, low resting clouds swept the sun away in the sky. Seagulls perched at the edge of the wharf, standing on wooden posts and hopping along sand dunes. The cream-colored sand was pockmarked from the lapping of the ocean's waves, and Persephone's bare feet dipped into the ground as she heel-toed her way across the earth. The briny scent of the sea wrapped itself around her, and Persephone pulled it closer. She tucked the fresh air into her muscles, wove the calm into her bones, pulled in magic, and fortified her will.

Persephone did not see the darkness reflected against the water as it inked its way along her shadow.

▸ ▸ ▸

THE TWO WITCHES who claimed the beach, and therefore the ocean brushing against it, had built their house on stilts. It was a pale yellow vision with more windows than walls. A lengthy porch wrapped around the home's west side, perfect for watching sunsets and admiring fishermen who attempted to come to shore.

Ellison and Ariel Way loved to admire fishermen. Fishermen, fisherwomen, fisherpeople in general. Any body of beauty was a welcomed sight to their eyes.

Unless the body was connected to Persephone May.

Ellison walked outside and stood on the porch, watching Persephone approach. Ellison loved her porch that wrapped like a crescent moon halfway around the house. She loved the smell of the salt in the air that being by the beach afforded. Loved the way the sky would shift from ripe carrot into rosy red as the sun set and reflected off the water like a hundred shimmering lights trapped beneath the surface. Mostly, she loved sitting on the porch and daydreaming about the places she had yet to go. Unlike her sister, Ellison dreamed of travel and seeing sunsets around the world.

What she didn't dream of was leaving her sister behind, still nursing a broken heart and untrusting of said world. Ellison decided she couldn't begrudge Ariel entirely for untrusting people, as she watched the witch from the mainland approach her porch, because people—especially witches—could be tricky.

And yet Ellison didn't call for Ari as she watched Persephone approach. Unlike her sister, she wasn't quite as certain Persephone posed real danger. There were too many threads to this particular web, and too many spiders hiding in plain sight. Ellison only needed to find the right thread and tug.

The window in the attic opened and Ellison sighed.

"Really, Elsie?" Ari called down. "You look like a welcome party. Want me to bring out a poisoned fruitcake or a nice basket of barbed wire to entice her closer to our door?"

"Better than one of your maniacal beasties," Ellison said, quiet enough to be a whisper, loud enough her sister could hear.

The truth was there were very few secrets between the two sisters, and irritation was never one of them. Part of the curse of being one of only two sets of witches on island was the gift of having a sister as a best friend. While Ellison missed her mother, and even at times Moira and Hyacinth, she never found herself lonely with Ari around.

"They're *mechanical*, not maniacal. You want maniacal, look to the girl with auburn hair mucking about in our freshly swept sand."

Ari was certain the ocean was hers. Everything that hugged the water along Wile Isle belonged to the Ways. That was what Ariel believed and what she expected her sister to believe.

Ellison believed they were cursed, and she was tired of it.

As a child, she never cared that they spent their winter months watching the waves and studying the stars, but when she turned twenty, an itch started between Ellison's shoulder blades. Like all itches, this one was desire. Specifically, the desire to come and go from Wile Isle as Ellison pleased, for months or even years at a time. Over the past decade the itch grew, and it now covered most of her body.

"She's coming regardless," Ellison said, scratching behind her ear. Ari harrumphed as the window slid shut.

Her sister clomped down the stairs inside, navigating all four floors like a deranged fairy waking from a delightful nightmare. Ari was the size of a sprite, with the temper of an avenging angel. Her copper skin shined as she stepped out onto the porch, the striking sprinkle of freckles danced across the bridge of her nose. Ellison's own skin was the color of cream, her eyes as stormy as the seas, and her hair as golden as the hiding sun. They were more than sisters, they were Irish twins, but that didn't prevent them from looking like they belonged to separate families. Ellison looked like a Norwegian priestess and Ariel a Native American warrior princess. It was a reminder that some small part of who they were was because of who their fathers had been, even if they could not recall the men their mother had spent a season or two enchanting.

"Two sides of one coin reflected in two souls," Ellison's mother had said of the near twins when they were children, and this much, at least, was true.

True twins ran in their family. It was their lineage, and it was said that since power couldn't be evenly shared, having twins was a harbinger of darkness. For these two, though, sisterhood meant being as close as twins without having shared the same zygote. They were in no greater danger of twinning than the next pair of magical siblings, and their close nature rarely reared its ugly side except when they were arguing over how involved in town they should be during the on season.

Ariel did not like tourists. Ellison knew they were crucial to supporting their livelihood, and the connections they made—especially during the dark months, when the island closed to outsiders and magically disappeared from maps and navigation tools—made the rest of the year run smoother.

Some people called Wile Isle the Salem of the South, but Ellison liked to joke it was closer to the True Bermuda Triangle. From the autumn equinox to spring equinox, the way in was shut. Like Willy Wonka's Chocolate Factory, during those months nobody ever came in, and nobody ever went out. They couldn't. Thanks to Amara and True Mayfair.

Like Hades and his Persephone, their spell had splintered the island's welcome in two. Half the year it pulled in people and half the year it refused them. They weren't frozen like their lost ancestors, but they might as well be during the winter months. Ellison knew the islands had once been a thriving land, where all year-round festivals ran, people celebrated, and neighbors were family. Now, well, now life was split in two seasons: on and off. And they were knee-deep in the off season.

During the off season there was little to do. Little money to be made on island, and less entertainment to be found. Ellison ran an anonymous (but well-paid through sponsorship) blog called *Witch, Please* to help make ends meet. She wrote tongue-in-cheek articles on witchcraft and wizardry for money, and sold "blessed" necklaces of dried flowers pressed in glass pendants attached to silver chains for entertainment.

For her part, Ariel made mechanical automatons and sold them online through her popular Etsy store during winter, and at a booth in town during the summer months when she could be bothered to show up. While Ellison didn't use her magic to infuse her work—she did rather the opposite, certain no one in their right mind should invest in her posts on "Ten Supremely Adorable Things Every Witch Needs in her Life" and "Crystal-infused Salves to Rev Up Your Lover's Sex Drive"—Ari delighted in bespelling her creatures. If a person didn't believe in possessed dolls before they ordered one, that would soon change when they got them home.

"They're automatons, Elsie," Ari said when her sister complained about the risk of exposure from her little joke. "They are doing what they were named to do, and acting on their own will. It's not my fault no one ever reads the fine print of etymology."

The Ways' magic was a strong magic. Ellison knew that was part of what initially divided them from the Evers. While Moira and Hyacinth were direct descendants of True, Ariel and Ellison came from Amara's line, as did their mother. The magic between the two lines wasn't the same, even though they were all descendants. That's why when their mother and aunt foolishly tried to splinter the curse the magic went unbearably wrong, and did what it did. Strong magic was its own curse, and Ellison believed it was also what caused Hyacinth and Ariel to fight over that girl and cement the divide between the families. Though after what happened with their mothers, perhaps the unbreakable divide was only a matter of time.

Ellison worried about the magic Ariel used. Aether was tricky. Ari was pulling it from space, and it wasn't the kind of magic where you could see where it started and ended.

At least Ari had stopped making the cuckoo clocks; those had been *too* lifelike and honest. These, well, dolls she supposed you'd call them, Ariel advertised as "purchase at your own risk." That warning seemed to be to the delight of her customers, but still. A warning was a warning.

It was the Goddesses' great sense of humor that had people taking Ellison's ridiculous works as real and Ari's as false.

All in all, even with the curse, they had a good life. A settled and quiet enough life. And all of that, Ellison knew, was about to change as the redheaded witch from the mainland walked up to the base of their steps.

Ellison, never one to run from a confrontation, started down the stairs to meet her. Her steps faltered when she registered the billowing black cloak, as thick as smoke, trailing after Persephone.

"What in the Goddess?" Ellison murmured, studying the way the shadow bled and blended.

Persephone waved, a half smile on her face. "Sorry to intrude," she called, "and please don't blast me again, but I really need to speak with you."

"Stay where you are," Ellison said, her eyes flicking from the shadow that was not a shadow to Persephone. The side door clanged open, and within seconds Ariel stood at her sister's side, a small bag clutched in her hand.

Magic rippled in the air. The tide rose in the ocean. Darkness drew near.

▸ ▸ ▸

PERSEPHONE WAS PRETTY certain the two Way witches were unhinged. Maybe it was their natural state—the way the island soothed and revived her, maybe it soured them. Resting witch face, that's what she called the look they exchanged. Persephone decided she was crazy to come here. Perhaps she'd always been crazy and she was finally claiming her birthright.

Persephone ran a hand over her hair, finding small tangles knotting it. The hourglass was warm where it was tucked against her heart. Persephone sighed, doubting she'd get much help but hoping she could make sense of the fragments of information floating in her head. If the island sent her here, Persephone had to try.

"I'm not about to come closer," Persephone called. "I learned my lesson after the stunt you pulled this morning."

"Stunt?" Ariel's voice rose an octave. "I can show you a stunt, you demonic little tart."

Ellison put a hand over her sister's. "If you bade our warning true, you wouldn't be here at all."

"If it could be helped, I *wouldn't* be here, but here I am."
Persephone slipped her hands in her pockets, needing something
to do with her restless fingers. Persephone tugged at the fabric
inside her pants, growing more edgy the longer she had to hold
still. "I'm looking for information. I think, perhaps, you may be
the ones who can help me." Persephone saw the bottom of the
necklace in her mind's eye, drew herself up in courage, and said,
"Walker Mayfair?"

There was a long beat before either of the sisters spoke.

"I need a tonic," Ariel said, before swiveling on her heels and
going inside.

Ellison stood as she was, watching the winds run through the
freed strands of Persephone's hair like underwater seaweed being
tossed by the current. Ellison's eyes were as calm as still waters,
as dark as any oncoming storm.

"Walker Mayfair?" Ellison repeated.

"Yes," Persephone gave a short nod, wishing they would make
this whole process a little easier. Hyacinth and Moira could see
her for who she was, but these witches disliked her because of her
power, even though they, too, carried magic. Nothing added up.

Persephone shook off a tingle climbing its way up her calves.
"I found something with the . . . name on it?"

Behind Persephone the shadow that was not a shadow swept
against her feet. Persephone yanked her hands from her pockets and scratched at her lower back. Ellison tracked both movements, keeping her head tilted to one side.

"Walker Mayfair isn't a person," Ellison said.

Persephone tilted her head, and reached up for her collarbone. She rubbed at the growing itch there. "You know what
it is?"

"The prophecy," Ariel said, stepping out onto the porch holding a tumbler of clear liquid and passing a small sachet to her
sister. "The prophecy of the rise of the true dark witch."

Thinking of the prophecy Hyacinth had told her about, that
a *time walker* of the Mayfair line will one day have the power to

unmake the world, Persephone shook her head. Her magic, the Evers' magic, wasn't dark.

Was it?

"That doesn't make sense."

"Nothing about you being here does," Ariel said, and she showed her teeth in a grin that had Persephone's stomach turning.

Persephone took a step back and the shadow wrapped itself around her ankles.

It was like stepping into a web of cling wrap. One minute Persephone was irritated, bordering on nervous about the sharp-eyed witch holding the amber liquid, and the next she couldn't move. Persephone tried to breathe, tried to shout, tried to run, but she was rooted to the earth, frozen in her spot.

Ellison whispered something as determination settled across her features. For Persephone, fear turned into panic, bloomed into terror at the studied expression both witches wore. Persephone tried to thrash beneath the dark air that tugged at her arms and legs. Persephone was losing control, could feel something dark inside her trying to work its way out, to take over.

Ariel clasped one hand with her sister and raised the sachet up to the sky.

She called a single word out into the air, "*Release.*"

The sand beneath Persephone shifted, rumbling under her feet. There was a tight pull in Persephone's midsection, and the ropes binding her loosened. She lurched forward, bending at the waist. The darkness ebbed for one blessed, glorious second, before it rushed back in faster, stronger, deeper.

"*Return,*" she heard Ariel say, and a cold fear replaced the panic Persephone had been fighting.

Ariel drew her arm back, and catapulted the sachet toward Persephone. As it neared, Persephone closed her eyes, and briefly wondered how she'd ended up here, with misfiring magic and angry witches who were going to kill her.

Lightning crashed across the sky and splintered into the sand. Persephone's eyes shot open and the sachet ricocheted back and landed in the water. The sea bubbled around it like a cauldron rejecting the ingredients.

The water turned a seething red before it foamed white and settled.

Golden light blinded Persephone, and the darkness that had been holding her released. Persephone staggered back, her arms coming up, ready to fight.

"*Stop!*" Coming from nowhere and everywhere, Moira's voice cut through the air—clear, focused, and vibrating with so much anger Persephone had to grit her teeth against the sound.

Lightning cracked again, splintering boards, imploding the lower steps leading up to Way House.

Moira's voice boomed out.

> "*I call to the East,*
> *South, West, and North,*
> *my intentions manifest this mighty force.*"

Wind whipped forward against the two witches standing on the porch, pushing them back onto their own ground.

Hyacinth came around the other side of the house, striding through the storm like it wasn't bringing torrential winds down with the angry wrath of the Goddess. Hyacinth crossed to Persephone, wrapped her arm around her, and a pressed a sachet into her pocket. A blanketing sense of calm descended over Persephone.

"The time for you to fight is not yet born," Hyacinth said.

Persephone slipped an arm around Hyacinth's waist, and leaned heavily on her friend.

Moira emerged from the mist, and stood like a proud general facing a firing squad. Moira did not back down, not even as Ariel fought her way forward, sending sparks of green down onto the beach.

Moira crossed to her sister and took her hand. She spared the briefest glance at Persephone before she raised her chin up another notch and spoke. Moira's voice boomed into the distance even as lighting split the sky and the winds wrapped around the house and beach like a desperate tornado seeking a way in.

> *"I call to the Guardians of the Island*
> *Today is not the day*
> *Protect what has gone astray*
> *Return the power to us now*
> *Release the bond and break the bow*
> *Three unto three*
> *As we will, so mote it be."*

Light flashed so bright Persephone let out a small scream. Hyacinth's grip on her tightened, and in the next instance the wind died down to a cool breeze.

Ellison and Ariel were gone from the porch; a deep crack splintered their staircase dividing what was one into two.

Hyacinth let out a low, gleeful chuckle, flashing a delighted grin before Moira cleared her throat. Hyacinth looked over, saw the state of Persephone, and blanched.

"Apologies, cousin. It's been some time since we've faced the Ways, and I hate to admit how much I'd been spoiling to see that fight. Let's get you home."

Moira's face was drawn and pale, but she wrapped an arm around the other side of Persephone, and with the support of the two witches, Persephone walked away from the yellow house. The water beside them crept further inland, trying to reach their feet as they went, the current urgent in its message.

Persephone paid it no mind. Persephone was looking back, up into the attic, into the dark and furious eyes of Ellison Way.

HYACINTH EVER'S JOURNAL

Two weeks after the summer solstice, ten years ago

> *Ariel believes all magic is magic. She said this*
> *to me while we were at the beach, watching the*
> *first July arrivals from off island boat in. She's been*

building a cuckoo clock for the Arch, one that could hold sands of time if we were brave enough to collect them. I told her that kind of magic isn't regular.

"Sure it is. It's magic for memories, dreams, and moments." Then she laughed. "You can fill it with whatever you want, since you spend all your time there."

I spend so much time beyond the Arch because I'm practicing. Her magic isn't my magic. I don't know how she makes the impossible possible. I've told Moira that Ariel might be the witch to break the curse, but Moira only shook her head.

"She can pull space to her, but she can't walk through it. It's manipulation, not mastery."

Moira's big on mastery. Boring on it. She spends all day working on her recipes and practicing Tai Chi, while I sit in the garden watching things grow.

So we sat on the beach, Ariel ignoring my latest rant on the hinterland and the curse and how I wish we could break it, and we watched the waves nip at the edge of the shore. If we did break the curse, we'd have more magic, and more company to keep all year-round. If we broke it, maybe our mothers could return and the island would finally be a home.

"Who is that?" Ariel asked, finally looking up.

A girl had stepped off the boat. She had light hair, full lips, and walked like she was on a runway. Swish, swish went her hips.

"Tourist?" I said, watching her continue down the dock, and onto the path.

"It's the girl," Ariel said, breathing the word in a way I'd never heard before. She pulled the corn husk doll from her bag, and passed it over.

I looked down, and startled in surprise. The little doll I'd made Ariel, with its dandelion curls, looked remarkably like the girl stepping off the boat.

"Ari," I said, my stomach flipping once. "Did you do something to this doll?"

She smiled at me, and pulled her bag over her neck. "You can keep her. I have the real thing now."

Then Ariel danced over the sand and onto the path, her shoulders squared, her eyes flashing.

I was left holding the doll, forgotten on the beach, once more all alone.

SIX

ONCE PERSEPHONE AND THE Evers were off the beach and back on the cobblestone path, Hyacinth and Moira gently released her. Persephone found she could stand on her own, and did so, brushing the hair from her face and turning to them in gratitude.

"Thank you for showing up when you did." Persephone gave her head a shake. "I don't understand what happened."

"Back at the house," Hyacinth said, giving Persephone's hand a gentle squeeze before casting a glance over her shoulder. "We'll talk where it's safe."

Moira led the way home, her pale face growing gray as they walked up the hill. Power crackled off her, filling the air with a sharp tang of bitterness and the bite of static electricity. Persephone wanted to ask her if she was okay, but the way Moira moved with such focus reminded Persephone of when she practiced Tai Chi, and had her biting her tongue.

The walk was long, and the salt in the air stung Persephone's eyes. Her body grew heavy, and the weight of her heels dug deep into the cobblestones. Persephone's elbows ached with each swing of her arms, and her neck felt as though it had been yanked to one side and stretched too far. She tried to hold her pulsing head with one hand, but the effort was too much.

"She needs grounding," Moira said, wiping sweat from her brow.

"She needs better access to her powers," Hyacinth said.

"The island," Persephone murmured. "I thought it would restore me."

"It will," Moira said, shooting Hyacinth a look. "But you need more than a healthy breath of fresh air. That was powerful magic you fought off. Grounding is the thing."

"It's not safe here," Hyacinth said, holding one hand out to assist Persephone, her eyes studying the hill they had yet to climb. "Just a little farther, we're almost to our protection barrier." Hyacinth wrapped an arm tightly around Persephone's waist. "Lean in, cousin."

Persephone did so, and though each step was measured and tedious, she could bear the burden better from the support. It struck Persephone that she had never had the chance to lean on anyone before coming to Wile Isle. Persephone had missed out on occasions to allow herself such frailty, and finding it now she discovered she did not enjoy the experience in the slightest.

When they finally reached the house, Persephone was perspiring and breathless. Hyacinth left her to sit on the stoop, saying she would be right back. Moira moved her feet and dug her toes deep into the earth, shaking off energy like a dog shakes off water, as she studied the horizon.

Hyacinth returned with two cups of tea, gave one to each of the women and told Persephone to "down it in one good swallow." She did, watching Moira do the same. Persephone sputtered after, while Moira didn't bat a lash. Whatever tonic was in the tea was hidden by the strong taste of whiskey.

"We should head for the Arch," Hyacinth said. "We could work on binding your powers to all of us, so we can make sure this doesn't happen again."

"I don't think I have the energy for spell work," Persephone said, not sure that she liked the idea of a binding of any kind.

"We need to restore your strength." Moira crossed to her, studied Persephone. "Perhaps we need the blessing tree."

Hyacinth helped Moira assist Persephone up before she went back inside to consult her books, while Moira led Persephone to a mossy tree that looked more gnarled than an arthritic man's knuckles.

"*That* is the blessing tree?"

"Of a kind. You've heard the term *tree hugger* before?" Moira asked, arching her brows. "Now you'll get to enact it."

"Oh goody, just what I've always wanted," Persephone said on a sigh.

Moira bit back a laugh, and helped Persephone find the base of the tree, moving the hanging limbs aside. Persephone straddled the roots with care, feeling only mostly ridiculous, and wrapped her arms around the moss. It was a bit like Persephone imagined hugging a shaggy dog would feel, only with more musk to clog her senses.

Her toes dug into the soft earth, and Persephone gave in to the urge, and closed her eyes.

"The trees are older than we, stronger than we, and they remember their strength easier than we ever could," Moira said, her voice wrapping itself around Persephone. "We are of the earth. We are born from it and to it we return. Allow your spirit and body to bridge the gap. Imagine your feet sinking into outlets of energy. Now, plug in. From the top of your head down to the base of your spine, see a line of strength. Imagine white healing energy, salty and born of the land, to fill your body. Invite it inward to recharge your soul."

Persephone imagined a white light. She saw the crown of her head lit with it, and the light entering through a door she kept hidden beneath her hair. The warm light flooded Persephone's system, pushing along her spine, pulsing into her feet. As it did so, a golden light filled her from her toes up to her teeth. Energy from the earth and from the air poured in until all Persephone heard was her beating heart and the echo of her exhalation.

Persephone did not know how long she stood hugging the ancient tree. She held on until it no longer felt silly, until it felt like someone was hugging her back. When it was time to let go, a whisper of a wound Persephone carried deep in her core had grown silent.

▸ ▸ ▸

BACK INSIDE EVER House, Persephone sat on one end of the moon-shaped couch. Hyacinth claimed the other end as Moira fed the crackling fire, and Opal the cat warmed a pillow on the floor. It smelled of cinder and ash, of cinnamon tea, and roasting apples cooking on the stove in a heady red wine concoction Moira had not yet perfected.

"What happened?" Persephone asked. "On the beach, what did they do to me?"

Hyacinth gave her head a short shake, and held up a hand. "Not yet."

Moira went into the kitchen and returned with a basket. In it were herbs, candles, a jar of salt, and three strands of cord. "There is still a presence, a darkness following you. Do you feel it?"

Persephone thought back to the feeling of unrest standing on the beach, of not being able to move, of the shadow creature. She gave Moira a nod.

"Casting a circle will shut out any disruptive influences to keep us safe," Moira said, pulling four thick candles from the basket and setting them at different corners of the area where Persephone and Hyacinth were gathered. "This is a type of psychic protection."

"I'm not sure I follow," Persephone said, watching.

"Magical energy is energy in its natural habit," Hyacinth explained. "Energy has a bad habit of bouncing around and scampering off into the universe. For some, like Moira, who are naturally gifted in their power, it's easy to call it back. For those like me who aren't born with the same talents, magic energy is a balance we constantly work to control. Today we're using the circle to gather up more energy and hold on to it longer."

"Does the circle itself make the magic stronger?" Persephone asked, sniffing the air as Moira pulled herbs from their sachets.

"A vast oversimplification, but yes," Moira said. "It will keep the magic in, and any disturbances out."

"The rosemary, angelica, sage, cloves, and salt build protection from prying ears and eyes," Hyacinth added, on a yawn.

"And those bits of cord?"

"You hold them," Moira said with a hint of a smile, passing one to Persephone.

Moira finished laying out her herbs. She walked the circle three times, calling on the guardians of each direction as she went. Hyacinth didn't speak, but held her palms up, as though in offering.

When the circle was sealed, Moira took a seat in the stiff-backed chair, a serene smile crossing her face. Persephone understood the smile, for as the circle was completed, the air had changed.

They sat in comfortable silence for a stretch of time before Moira spoke.

"That was dark magic you felt on the beach. A powerful spell of control. I didn't think the Way witches dealt in such magic, but you must pose more of a threat to them than we surmised."

"What did they throw at me?"

"A binding sachet," Moira said. "To control you or hold you, I can't be sure which."

The boundary inside the circle gave off heat, and tingles ran along the side of Persephone's right foot and leg that were closest to the line. She tried to respond to Moira, but couldn't. Being inside the circle was like being in a frozen glass globe, trying to see through to the world beyond it—for Persephone, everything was out of focus.

"All is well now," Hyacinth said.

Hyacinth's words were blurry, settling into Persephone's skin like a child's first attempts at cursive writing. It took Persephone a moment to decipher their meaning. She inhaled a steadying breath, and put both feet solidly on the ground. It helped.

"You're safe," Hyacinth added.

The truth of her cousin's words floated down over Persephone.

Safe. One moment Persephone was stuck, the next she was exhaling a long release. A euphoric kind of shield enveloped Persephone and she sighed back into the pillows.

Persephone tilted her head. "The Way witches said something about the rise of the true witch when I spoke to them. Who did they mean?"

Hyacinth shifted in her seat.

"Who do you think they were referring to?" Moira asked.

"The way they said it, it sounded like me." Persephone rolled out her neck, savoring the motion. "But I'm barely a basic witch." Persephone smiled at her own joke.

"You're stronger than you know," Hyacinth said.

Persephone rubbed at the crown of her head. "I feel like it's an uphill battle. The training, the curse, all of it."

"You have innate magic in you. When the time comes, you will be able to do what you need to do," Moira said.

"And what the Ways said?"

Moira hesitated for the briefest of moments. "The thing about prophecies is they are open to interpretation, and the Ways read it one way, and as a warning."

"What do they believe?"

"That the true witch will bring about the end of the Mayfair line," Hyacinth said.

"Who are the Mayfairs?"

"The Way sisters," Hyacinth said.

Persephone cocked her head in confusion, and Hyacinth nodded. "They changed their last name a few generations back when they tried to reinvent themselves. It didn't work." Hyacinth smiled. "They're still awful."

Moira tutted out a breath. "Really, Hyacinth." She turned to Persephone. "The Ways didn't use to be so . . . volatile. A lot has happened over the past decade, and like water shifts foundation, change alters a person. The prophecy foretells that a time walker of the Mayfair line will one day have the power to unmake the world. Whether or not she ends the line *is* a matter of interpretation."

"*I'm* a Mayfair?" Persephone asked.

"Yes," Hyacinth said. "Your grandmother changed her last name when she left. Likely trying to do what she could to cut the tethers to the island. Each generation who tried to break the curse has failed, and rather spectacularly. Your grandmother did what she thought was best by leaving, like my mother and aunt."

Moira flexed her fingers at the mention of her mother and aunt. When neither she nor Hyacinth said anything more, Persephone went to reach for the photograph, to try again to tell the witches about what she'd found, about the library, and Dorian. Persephone opened her mouth and the words on the tip of her tongue spoiled. She couldn't utter a vowel. Damn the befuddling librarian and his library's rules of magic.

"Shouldn't we try to convince the other witches?" Persephone asked instead. "To help us instead of fighting us? I . . . I think that's what the island wants."

"We've tried to look into the curse with their help before," Hyacinth said. "That won't be happening again."

Persephone scrunched her nose. "They've helped before?"

"Yes, and trust me when I say there is no way Ariel's going to assist us in anything other than perhaps trying to drown me."

Persephone's eyes widened, and Hyacinth shrugged.

"My sister is right," Moira said. "Not about the drowning, perhaps, but there is no way either Way sister will help us today." Moira said, gazing toward the crackling fire, "Fear holds power of a different sort, and they are scared of what you represent. They have twice made attempts on your life. The third time I worry you may not fare so lucky."

Persephone tried not to picture a third time. "What changed? If they were once willing to help?"

Moira set her piece of cord in her lap. She tilted her head, her gaze drifting to the twin band of rings Persephone wore on her thumb.

"Did you know bad things don't come in threes?"

Persephone cocked her head, gave it a slight shake.

"They arrive in twos. A sunrise leads to a sunset, light must have dark, yin needs its yang. Success is balanced by failure."

Moira rubbed at her eyebrow, before dropping her hand into her lap. "In our family, twos can get into the most magical of trouble, and our aunt and mother proved this a decade ago.

"Every generation has tried to break the curse since it was cast. It never goes well. A curse is a haunted kind of magic. When you attempt to interrupt it, it disrupts. Our mother and aunt knew they weren't going to be able to break it. They were only two, after all, not three, and they had seen how previous failed attempts blinded my great-aunt and turned my grandmother's hair white. My mother and her sister thought to be more clever than the curse. To bend instead of break." Moira looked out the window, to where the mountain rose. Persephone's heart squeezed at the pain on her cousin's face.

"It didn't go well?" she asked, her voice soft.

"No, it did not."

Hyacinth cleared her throat. "As Moira always says, there is a cost to magic. Theirs was to be cast off of the island for try-ing to alter that which refused to budge. They left . . . without a word, as soon as their spell backfired." Hyacinth looked to the fire. "We have not seen them since."

"Do the sisters blame you?"

"Not for that," Hyacinth said, while Moira said nothing. "They blame us for what came after." Hyacinth ran a hand through her curls. "Ariel and I were once great friends. After our mothers were forced to leave, we tried to find a loophole to get them back. We knew when a witch left the island they were cut off from the coven. We just didn't realize it could happen to us, to our parents. We also knew better than to cast, lest we be cast off, too, so we looked instead—to see if there was a way to fix it." Hyacinth bit her lip. "We found something we didn't expect."

"What did you find?"

"A girl." Hyacinth swallowed and gave her head a shake. "A girl . . . who came between Ariel and me." A look of discomfort moved across her cousin's face. "She wasn't who we thought she was, though, and in the end, she showed us that the hinterland is like any tap—over time it can corrode and cracks can appear."

"Cracks?"

Hyacinth nodded. "When they do, a leak occurs."

"Like a magic leak?"

"Yes."

"So you what, made contact with the hinterland through the girl? Was she a medium?"

"No, the hinterland made contact with us," Hyacinth said, looking Persephone in the eyes, the agony behind them clear. "A powerful witch found a way to crack through the world. I believed she was trying to ask for help, but the Ways took it as an attack."

"I don't understand," Persephone said. "Who was the girl?"

"She . . ." Hyacinth opened her mouth, and a crash came from outside. Wind nipped against the windows, an incoming storm pressing against the house.

"It doesn't matter," Hyacinth said, standing. She swallowed twice, her usual joy dimming into embers of nothing. "Not anymore. Not the girl, not Ariel, none of it. The only way out now is to go forward." She tossed the cord she still gripped aside. "We can't go back."

Hyacinth broke the circle then, as she brushed the line clear with her foot.

"Moira," Persephone said, after Hyacinth scurried outside, the back screen door clanging shut behind her. "What happened? Who was the girl?"

Moira gave her head a small shake. "An interloper. One who broke Ariel's heart and Hyacinth's." She paused, lifted her chin and stared hard at Persephone. It was a look Persephone had grown to understand over the past few weeks. Moira was deciding something.

"I'm going to trust you with a truth," she said. "One that Hyacinth does not know. Something the Ways do not know."

Persephone's heart gave a thump against her chest at the sharp crack in Moira's voice. She had grown closer to the serene woman who seemed made of steel. There were visible chinks in Moira's armor now, and it caused a tremble in Persephone's stomach. "Of course," she said. "I will be glad to bear your trust."

Moira nodded. "I do not know who the girl was, but I know that death brought her. Hyacinth's and my mother left not because of the curse, but because I told her to, because it was unsafe for her to remain on island." She took a slow breath. "Persephone, my aunt never left the island. She did not survive the attempt to bend the curse."

As the words and their meaning rooted in Persephone, Moira squeezed her eyes shut tight. "My mother told me of what happened, of her sister dying, made me promise not to tell." She opened her eyes. "I agreed to but only if she left. My mother carried darkness with her when she returned. I could see it, feel it. It wasn't safe for us, for Hyacinth, for her to remain."

Persephone swallowed, and Moira placed a hand to her heart. "There is a leak from the hinterland, and hungry, malevolent magic is spilling onto the island. The curse is deep and dark, and will have its way until the crack is wide enough for us to slip through. We must break the curse, and it cannot be broken without the power of three. We cannot fail, Persephone. We have already lost so much, and the cost for failing again will be immeasurable."

▸ ▸ ▸

AFTER UNBURDENING HER soul, Moira returned to the kitchen, more shaken than Persephone had ever seen her. Persephone sat staring at the fire. She watched the flames crackle, the wood smolder, and ash grow in the hearth.

She tried to make sense of what she'd been told. Moira had lied to Hyacinth, had lied to her other cousins. Their mother, her aunt, was dead.

Persephone wondered if at this point, all loss felt the same to Moira. Whether a parent was cast from the island or died, they were cut off from you for the rest of your living days. Perhaps being a witch also meant accepting death with the kind of ease Persephone herself did not possess.

Persephone thought of the painful cost of bearing a secret. She thought of Dorian and the library, and how she knew what it was to hold her own secrets on the island.

Finally, Persephone thought of the fear on Moira's face and

urgency in her voice when she said the cost for not breaking the curse would be steep.

Moira had spoken of bad things coming in twos, not threes, and Persephone couldn't help but wonder what kind of price could come with success.

When the sun began to shift from the sky, Persephone went in search of her other cousin. She found Hyacinth in the garden, talking to the flowers and herbs.

"Hyacinth?" Persephone asked, watching Hyacinth tend an overgrown summer rosebush somehow blooming in the start of winter. At her name, Hyacinth's ears climbed to her shoulders. It was clear she expected Persephone to press her on the girl, and Ariel, on everything that had transpired before.

Persephone didn't want to add to the heartache Hyacinth appeared to carry, and she didn't want to let something of what Moira had shared show on her face, so she asked the other question on her mind. "Have the Way sisters been looking for me all this time, too?"

Hyacinth glanced up at the question, relief clear in her eyes. "No, definitely not. Ariel would rather hide in her house and pretend the rest of the world doesn't exist . . . until it shows up on her doorstep."

"I guess I delivered myself then," Persephone said, earning a slip of a smile from Hyacinth. "But you found me. You sought me out."

"I—" Hyacinth's hand slipped, and the rose she'd been trying to revive faltered and drooped in death. "Drat." Hyacinth let out a low curse and placed the rose in a large flowerpot full of her failed attempts.

Magic took great concentration for Hyacinth. She seemed to work twice as hard for half the results, and Persephone was learning that not being as gifted as her sister was an area of great pain for her cousin.

When Hyacinth held up her hand, her thumb was pricked with a single drop of blood. "*Rosa spinosissima*," she said, naming the rose. She shrugged a shoulder. "Everything takes its cost."

Hyacinth went in to cleanse the wound, leaving Persephone to wonder if she meant the cost of taking the rose from its natural state or of finding Persephone.

Persephone reached a hand into her pocket. Hyacinth had gifted her a small moss green stone with splashes of pink the previous day. It was the sixth crystal she'd given Persephone, in hopes that one of them would be Persephone's grounding stone. So far the rocks were simply added weights when they were in her pockets or palms, and nothing more. Still, Persephone took the unakite jasper from her pocket, cupped it, and thought, *Rise*.

"You're too focused on it," Hyacinth said, when she returned to the garden and witnessed Persephone struggling to make the stone in her hand levitate.

The truth was, for whatever reason, when Persephone tried to pull her aether to her, nothing happened. The nothing was *frustrating*.

Persephone focused again, stared hard at the rock, and willed it to leave the laws of gravity behind. It didn't even twitch.

"Try to see it with your mind."

Persephone closed her eyes, saw her aether, saw the rock . . . and gasped as Dorian's quirk of a smile flashed before her.

The stone sat unmoved.

She growled, irritation at the man and the gemstone flaring, and threw the stone as hard as she could. She hit a furrow-browed gnome tucked beside the Saint-John's-wort, taking out one of his eyes completely and leaving a gaping hole in the little man's porcelain head.

Persephone's hand flew to her mouth in horror as she looked at Hyacinth, who broke into a gale of laughter.

"Whoops."

"Whoops indeed," Hyacinth said, her laugh morphing into a giggle.

Persephone grinned back, glad her temper was good for something. If she could bring the color back to her cousin's cheeks, she'd throw a hundred stupid stones.

Hyacinth went over to better inspect the hole. "You're lucky the broken bits fell out into the grass and not into Saint John's bushel. Otherwise, the fairy folk might consider it a trespass and come for you in your sleep."

"Ha ha," Persephone said. She considered Hyacinth's raised brow. "You're joking about the fairies, right?"

Hyacinth's only response was to scoop up the porcelain and pocket it before turning back to the house. "I'm gathering our shoes. I need a break, and so do the wee keepers of the garden." Hyacinth looked at the one-eyed gnome. "I imagine it's hard to be on the lookout when you don't have a way to look out."

Hyacinth was in and out of the house in a matter of minutes. When she returned, she was bearing shoes, sweaters, sunglasses for the gnome, and Persephone's small bag.

"Where are we going?" Persephone asked, wrapping the burgundy sweater around her shoulders.

"Where else is there to go on island this time of year?" Hyacinth asked, put the shades on the little gnome's face. "To town."

"Really?" Persephone knew how little Hyacinth enjoyed going into town. Neither sister liked to be away from the house for long.

"Yes, really. I need to see the postmistress, and I can't delay the trip any longer."

Persephone rubbed her hands together. "Fabulous."

They walked out of the yard onto the path. All around them wildflowers grew, bringing a wild kind of charm to the view.

"It's incredible here," Persephone said, sighing at the sense of peace being on the island brought to her—even amid the chaos of trying to break a curse.

Hyacinth gave a halfhearted murmur of agreement.

Persephone studied the side of her cousin's face, and a thought struck her. "Hyacinth? Do you . . . ever wish you lived somewhere else?"

A quiet smile curved her lips. "All the time." Persephone's eyes widened at the vehemence in the words, and Hyacinth waved a hand. "I love the island. But I grew up here. There have been so many days where I wake up wishing I could fold into the busyness of a big city for the winter, somewhere you forget yourself like New York City, or Paris, where there are cafés and strangers on every street corner. Where no one knows my name, and the world doesn't care what I do or don't do."

"That makes sense," Persephone said, tugging the edge of her sleeve. "I hadn't thought of it quite that way."

Persephone knew the sisters said they couldn't leave during the winter months. That her arrival was a gift, because the island didn't allow anyone to come to it during what the sisters called the "off" season. As she thought on the implications, she found it both romantic and horrifying—to be so isolated for half the year.

"Magic often has a cost," Moira had said, when explaining it. Persephone was beginning to understand there were many angles to cost on Wile Isle.

Still. Having seen so much of the world herself, even while struggling to make ends meet, Persephone realized she was lucky—she had never felt locked away. "It must be frustrating."

Hyacinth shrugged. "It is what it is. Thankfully our business does well enough all year-round that I can travel more when the spring equinox comes. Everyone's business does, really. Luck—or curse—of the island. Our postmistress stays the busiest, with the grocer following. Laurel and Holly do better than the rest of us, well, and Our Delights."

"Our Delights?"

"The bakery and luncheonette in town."

Persephone nodded. "That must be where I stumbled into the other day. It smelled heavenly."

"Did it?" Hyacinth asked, raising a single brow in a motion Persephone herself had tried and failed to achieve a hundred times before.

"Yes, though it was a little off-putting. The magic inside seemed wonky."

"Oh?"

"Yes. Time moved sluggishly, and the costumes the people wore threw me a little. Does the bakery not ever interfere with Moira's business?" Persephone asked. Moira ran her own online bakery of a sort, called the Secret Ingredient.

"No," Hyacinth said, with a quirk of her lip. "Our goods vary enough from the bakery in town. They don't offer lavender-infused serenity bites or chocolate biscuits for the brokenhearted. We do a high turnover in the holiday season, particularly from word of mouth that on-season guests provide, and I've learned my fair share of online marketing from a girl I hired off island. The internet is rather its own alchemy."

"It's certainly something," Persephone said, stepping widely over a crack in the cobblestone path.

Hyacinth reached out and ran her fingers over the white little fence that bordered the right side of this part of their walk into town. "Still. Business isn't life," Hyacinth said. "It's a passing of time. The more time passes, the worse off we are, and the more aware we are of who and what we're missing on Wile."

"Do you miss her? Ariel? I'm sorry," Persephone said, kicking herself for bringing it up after seeing Hyacinth's smile fall. "It's really none of my business."

"It's okay," Hyacinth said after a moment. "The truth is there are family feuds and then there are witch family feuds. You've stepped into a history of knots."

"Have you never tried to work it out?"

"Some wounds require more than a bandage. Maybe one day Ariel will be ready," Hyacinth said. They turned a corner and ducked through the brush to step from the cobblestone walkway into the village. "The truth is that she has every right to her feelings. All I can do is forget the dark and focus on the light."

The light seemed to spread out as the village stood before them, and it had transformed again. Dusk was settling in, the twinkly lights previously strung through the trees sparkled down at Persephone. Persephone lifted a hand to brush against the lowest limb of a moss-wrapped tree, and the light blinked bright in her palm.

"It's a bit like Goblin Market, isn't it?" Hyacinth asked. "That's what Moira and I decided when we were girls."

Persephone grinned at the idea of the two sisters running through the village, spouting Rossetti's epic poem, searching for forbidden fruit. "No wonder you're worried about the gnome."

Hyacinth let out a ringing laugh, and Persephone grinned before she studied the scene before her.

The dusky sky offered a more forgiving view of the town than during daylight. The fading shutters and chipped slate tiles appeared worn with charm instead of wear, and while half the shops were closed, Persephone smiled to see there was a handful open with their friendly chimneys smoking. Hyacinth led her to the post office, where she pulled slips from her bag for the mail. Persephone spent twenty minutes getting a short history lesson on spirits of the drinkable kind from Laurel the postmistress, whose hair was a vibrant shade of pale blue and whose eyes were as green as the laurel tree Persephone hoped she was named after.

She was also the girl from Hyacinth's memory. From the look Hyacinth shot Persephone as she greeted Laurel, Persephone knew she wasn't the only one putting those pieces together. Persephone tried her best to smile at Hyacinth, in hopes she understood Persephone wasn't looking back but forward.

"Most people haven't a clue our island makes its own small batch rum and vodka," Laurel told Persephone, showing her where the distillery was marked on the pretty map framed on the wall of the office. "The vanilla vodka is worth its weight in rubies but the coconut rum is only to be drunk under a full moon when you're of a mind to make a fool of yourself." Laurel wiggled her hips, Hyacinth laughed, and Persephone felt the tension in her shoulders loosen at Hyacinth's ease. She joined in, thankful to feel the balance between them restored.

From the post office, their progress was a slow, gentle turn about the cobblestones. Hyacinth paused here and there to bid good evening to the few faces wandering the village after dark.

"The visitors who stayed," Persephone said. "What kept them? Didn't they sense the change in the village after what happened and everyone disappeared?"

Hyacinth shook her head.

"How?"

"Our remaining ancestors had enough magic to bind their memories, and perhaps plant the seeds to keep them from leaving. You

can't have a thriving village without the people to help it grow."
Hyacinth ran a hand over a browning vine and Persephone watched
as new growth rippled and unfurled, changing its color to a lively
green. "It could also be the magic that drew them to the Menagerie
of Magic rooted in the soil."

"What kind of magic do you think drew them?"

"Our gran used to say True planned 'to give back life to those
afraid to live' by showing them glimpses of miracles and magic —
promises of what they could become. It was rumored she lay with
a man who snuck into the menagerie before it was finished. He
stole her idea, and a piece of her heart, and took both back to
the mainland. Soon thereafter he announced his first circus. True
had thought to bring the magic of life to the masses, to show that
power was nothing to fear but a way to help heal the world. The
man who betrayed her decided to twist her idea into a perverse
freak show."

Persephone couldn't help the flare of pity for True. Having
never been in love herself, Persephone had read countless books
on love. In heartbreaking stories, the heroine was betrayed and
left broken by the wrong man. She imagined love could poison a
person in a thousand insidious ways.

"Do you think her broken heart changed her dream to something sinister?"

Hyacinth glanced over to Persephone. "No. There is a reason
the women in our line mate but do not marry. We have learned
the lessons of foolish hearts. True may never have forgiven her
man for perverting her vision, but she didn't stop from planning
the Menagerie of Magic. When it finally opened to the public, it
brought in a successful showing of two hundred open-minded
people who were gifted shades of magic and a night of wonder."

Persephone watched a young woman on a pale yellow bicycle
with a white wicker basket ride past.

"No one is certain of the precise mechanics for *how* the exact curse was cast, that was lost along with the witches. We only
know what came after."

"Lost witches. All of them frozen in time."

"That's the easiest way to put it," Hyacinth said. "They are locked away."

Another villager strolled past, pausing to bid them good evening. Then Hyacinth resumed her explanation.

"Aside from our ancestors and a few visiting families, the island lost all its inhabitants when the curse fell. The non-magical people who stayed here today carry a whisper of sight, and some make the most of it. Off land, Wile Isle is known for being something special, and it is the people of the island who feed that story when tourists come. They make and sell their tisanes or speak in their affected fortune-teller ways, and profess they can read the stars—for a price. The truth is they, too, are cursed. Only . . . they don't know it." Hyacinth tilted her head back so the new rays of the moon slanted across the planes of her face. Hyacinth filled her lungs with the crisp air and blew an even exhale. "Still. The island holds its beauty. Even now."

"Yes, that it does," Persephone said, turning over the idea of the Menagerie of Magic, the curse, and how to break something when you don't know precisely how it was formed. Persephone studied a row of shop houses with their large windows and bright, if not faded, shutters.

"You mentioned seeing costumes last week," Hyacinth said, glancing at Persephone. "What kind of costumes were the townspeople wearing?"

"Ah, Victorian nobility, I think."

Hyacinth paused, and pointed at the thatched roof cottage standing before them. "In this bakery?" Hyacinth proceeded ahead, pushing open the navy blue door and walking inside. Persephone blinked at the shop, and the sign hanging beneath the awning: OUR DELIGHTS.

This was *not* the same bakery.

Persephone took an unsteady breath. What had Dorian said? *You're in the wrong world.* What if it wasn't only the library in the wrong world, what if the bakery was, too?

Persephone turned around, looking for the right bakery, and

did not see it anywhere. Fighting a flash of panic, she followed Hyacinth inside.

Our Delights was a lovely and welcoming shop. It boasted seven cheery white tables with mismatched pastel-colored chairs, cream walls, beautiful Gaelic decor, and a tearable paper scroll on the wall with an inspiring "quote of the week" reminding Persephone that "Those who say it cannot be done should not interrupt those doing it." It smelled of freshly baked pastries and pancakes, spices, and chocolate. The counter was filled with a variety of succulent treats, each more decadent than the one before.

And Persephone had never stepped a foot inside the shop a day in her life.

"This is not the bakery I was in earlier," Persephone said, her voice a faint whisper.

"No," Hyacinth said, surveying the quiet scene before them. "I rather thought not."

Persephone sat down hard onto the nearest chair, and rubbed at her eyebrow. She'd seen the other bakery before she saw Dorian and the library. Before the first attack from the Way witches and the dark force they controlled. A chill worked its way down her neck and Persephone let loose a shudder, trying to mentally retrace her steps.

"Tell me about the other bakery," Hyacinth said, her tone so light it nearly brushed past Persephone.

Persephone studied the room, and an urge to run out of the bakery and back to the library washed over her. She gripped the edge of the chair and watched two middle-aged women with kind eyes and busy hands bustle at their stations, going from the kitchen back to the kneading station with its large marble slab as they worked what appeared to be caramel across its heavy surface.

"It was darker," Persephone said. "The colors were less cream and amber and more . . ."

"Forest green and midnight blue?"

Persephone gave a short nod. "Yes."

"Hmm."

"You know it?"

"Of it."

Hyacinth said nothing more, and the pieces knit together for Persephone. Persephone should have realized it sooner, after Dorian explained about the library. She should have put it together—it had been so obvious and she'd been obtuse.

Persephone truly *was* a walker.

"I was in a different world."

"Or one hidden within another one," Hyacinth said. She turned her eyes to Persephone, and there was something calculating in them. A knowing, and a hiding.

It was disorienting, being able to see so clearly into someone else. For the first time Persephone wondered if being unable to maintain eye contact hadn't been a blessing in disguise. Persephone had been certain the windows to the soul would bring a deeper connection, would help her find her place in other people's hearts and lives. It had seemed to be working, in Moira and Hyacinth she experienced peace at being seen.

When she met Hyacinth's eyes this time, Persephone did not feel understood or settled. The balance she'd held moments before wavered. Hyacinth tried to school her features, but it was no use. Persephone's powers hadn't manifested in all the ways the other witches expected, but as she studied her friend, Persephone knew one of her gifts was to see through—the veil of space, the realms of place, and the subterfuge of someone hiding something they very much did not want the other person to know.

Persephone leaned back in her chair, trying to figure out *what* Hyacinth could be hiding. Was it more of the same—the witches speaking in near riddles because they lived their life in shadows and were so heavily cloaked in secrets they forgot they wore them? Or was this something else?

Hyacinth, for her part, offered a temporary deflection by getting up to order a fresh pot of mint tea and cherry blossom cheesecake for them both. Hyacinth said it was the best on the island and yet Hyacinth barely did more than move her slice around on the plate.

Hyacinth took a delicate sip of her tea. "Can you tell me more about where you were?"

Persephone ran the teeth of her fork over the slice of cake, drawing three roads down its center. Something about the three roads stood out in the back of Persephone's mind, but when she tried to see it clearly, her vision blurred and the cheesecake was just a cheesecake.

Persephone thought of the current running underneath Hyacinth's easy tone. Everything on the island had a current. The people, the water, the ground. She imagined the cheesecake and the three lines formed their own currents. Persephone saw the island of Wile, the Library for the Lost, and the other bakery. Each three separate places, each three individual worlds.

Persephone looked up. "The colors stand out, and the smell of freshly baked goods." She looked around the bakery. "It smelled much like this one, but there were people in costumes—or so I thought."

Hyacinth considered her cousin, and rapped her knuckles on the table, a decision made. "You walked into the bakery that was. It's in the hinterland now, a mirror image I imagine of what existed on Wile Isle before the curse. You are a world walker, Persephone. When you walked through space you crossed beyond the veil into the hinterland."

Persephone released a breath, relieved Hyacinth answered her honestly, even if she wasn't telling her anything she hadn't figured out.

"But how? I don't know how to control 'walking' any more than I understand how to call and control aether."

"I don't know." Hyacinth took another sip of her tea, her eyes focused on her cup. "Success is about steps, and many of those steps are getting something wrong . . . or almost right. Failing is finding your way to success, and you're going to get a handle on your magic soon."

"But will it be soon enough? We're at the end of September, only a month remains."

Hyacinth picked up her fork. "If the Goddess wills it." She took a bite, and Persephone finally gave in and followed suit.

"Yes." Hyacinth nodded firmly. "What will be will be."

▸ ▸ ▸

FOR THE NEXT week Persephone worked twice as hard to grow control over her magic. September shifted into October and her level of skill ebbed and flowed. Magic was simply not what Persephone had thought it would be. It was practice and sweat, blood and tears, and giving far more of yourself over than you could expect in return. She'd imagined controlling her magic would become easy as breathing, but then Persephone supposed breathing was a complicated business—one just forgot to recognize all the mechanics to something they had perfected in utero.

As her days grew longer with study, Persephone found her skills seemed to be going in reverse. She could hold light for moments, and bring flame to fire, but she also set two bushes ablaze and shorted all the fuses in the house four times when her magic overpowered her.

Beyond the Arch, she practiced memory spells with Moira and continued learning defensive ones with Hyacinth. They tried only once to blend their individual power into three, and ended knocking Hyacinth unconscious for five excruciatingly long minutes.

Moira pulled spell after spell from her grimoire. She showed Persephone how to freeze rain from the sky and then explode each droplet of rain—trying to break a barrier of frozen magic. When Persephone tried, each droplet turned to snow and sludged to the earth. Hyacinth grew a tangled bramble of tree roots and Moira dug out a flame, while Persephone tried to douse the flame with water pulled from a river beneath their feet. Instead the flame grew as tall as a giraffe and threatened to engulf Persephone. Moira singed the hair off both her arms wrestling it away from her.

Each spell backfired. Nothing they tried seemed to lead them closer to breaking the curse, or Persephone gaining pure understanding of her gifts. She decided it was like looking into the mud for a flower. You knew something could grow there, but it was impossible to see through it to a viable root.

Persephone bled for her craft. She dug deep into the roots of the earth, pulled in the air, and pushed fire across water. None of it was enough.

"We aren't there," Hyacinth said one afternoon, a current of worry running through her voice.

"I know," Persephone said, wiping sweat from her brow with the back of her arm. Her hem was caked in mud and her cheeks were the color of a ripe tomato from effort. "I'm doing my best."

"Of course you are," Hyacinth said, biting her lip.

"We have time," Moira said.

"Very little of it," Hyacinth said. "It's a few short weeks to Samhain." She tapped her fingertips along her jaw. "Why don't you try to walk? If you can cross the spatial boundary you went to before when you saw the bakery, maybe it will reveal something we are missing."

Persephone nodded. It was worth a shot. She closed her eyes, held up her hands, and pushed.

Nothing.

She squeezed her eyes tighter, blew out a breath, and said, "Bakery bakery bakery bakery bakery," under her breath.

The world did not change.

Frustrated, but refusing to give up, Persephone kept at it. For the rest of that afternoon, and the next, and the next, she spent hour upon hour attempting to leave the island and walk into worlds she barely knew. Her success became a near obsession for her and Hyacinth. Persephone tried her best, but the truth was it was *difficult* to walk through worlds.

When Persephone had walked previously, it was because she was scared or angry. Hyacinth and Moira were firm in the belief that magic was best achieved with a clear head. Following their line of thought, Persephone eventually managed, with a little luck and a lot of perspiration, to slip through the veil of *a* world.

She imagined a new place inside the arch. She wanted to see the real cliffs of Scotland, to feel the spray of the sea on her cheeks and the salt of the brine on her tongue. The air shimmered around her, and Persephone stepped out into a space void of anything.

She opened her eyes and saw the rolling hills that built into cliffs. She reached out a single hand and the vision wavered. Persephone blinked and she had returned.

Out of breath, Persephone turned to Hyacinth.

Hyacinth scratched her nose. "That was like watching a light flicker on and off. One minute you were here, the next . . ." She ran a hand through her dark curls. "I can't see where you go. I don't like that," Hyacinth said, her forehead furrowed in worry.

Persephone had only tried once to return to the hinterland, and the library, with Hyacinth watching. When she had attempted it, there was the tug in her midsection, leading her anywhere other than to those locations.

"I went to the cliffs of Scotland. It was beautiful, but there wasn't anything out of the ordinary waiting."

Hyacinth frowned. "Try again. Maybe we overlooked something."

For the rest of the day, Persephone returned to Scotland. Each time she returned, Hyacinth was standing a little closer, her eyes a little darker, her mouth more compressed.

When she wasn't practicing magic, Persephone was persistent in her search for information on her family. Her cousins kept diligent records on everything, from which plants they harvested during which season, to the allergies of returning tourists who regularly placed orders for Moira's baked goods, to when the earth's soil produced the best crop of lavandin—a type of lavender that should only grow in Provence, but flourished in their garden. If only they had more on Persephone's family. In all the books she read, Persephone could not find a single line on her grandmother mentioned.

In the evenings, Moira taught Persephone lessons in the fine art of flour. "Life isn't all magic," Moira told her. "It's about heart, too. About building a life even around the extraordinary. When we bake, we live in the present moment."

Persephone learned how to sift all-purpose flour with the gentle shake of her wrist and strain it through cheesecloth. She took joy in measuring butter and sugar, and adding freshly ground berries and peeled apples to craft perfectly sponged cakes. She became a master of fashioning cream cheese icing from scratch and whipping up scones with her head half in the clouds. And Persephone listened, as Moira would whisper poetry (the witch truly had a heart for Christina Rossetti) with flair and flourish while she worked.

As Persephone's knowledge of the island and her connection to her cousins grew, her sense of magic stalled. Whatever power Persephone *was* able to tap into began to sputter as her thoughts inevitably drifted to the mother and grandmother who weren't on island with her.

Persephone also felt a debt mounting in her heart. Her payment to the Ever sisters for their kindness and acceptance was meant to be her power—"As three we are stronger than Ellison and Ariel Way can ever pretend to be," Hyacinth told Persephone time and again—but their power was only fortified if Persephone's was tamed.

Persephone's guilt grew the more Hyacinth's concern blossomed. Her friend and cousin had taken to spending the hours she wasn't coaching Persephone in the garden, studying her books, talking to the trees, and searching for answers. Time was running out, and the more agitated Hyacinth became the calmer Moira got.

Persephone also couldn't stop thinking of Dorian and the library, but each time Persephone tried to speak of either to one of her cousins, the words curled up and turned to ash on her tongue.

The annoying truth was that Persephone thought about him— the angles of his face, the crooked tooth, and the smile that never quite reached his eyes—more than she cared to admit. When Persephone dreamed, she saw him crouched by the fire, the endless stacks of the library moving all around him.

Then, on the thirteenth day of the second month of being on the island, Persephone woke to a searing pain in her chest. She sat up, and the pain spread like fire slathered across her skin. Persephone reached for her shirt and her hand clasped the hourglass tucked beneath the fabric. She gasped and jerked her fingers away, a burn searing the tips.

Thinking fast, Persephone yanked off her shirt and swung around onto her knees and hands so the hourglass dangled in the air below her neck. It pulsed a bright, brilliant green three times before the color faded to a rosy gold. She didn't trust touching the metal, so she leaned forward and worked her fingers around to the clasp at the base of her neck. Undone, the locket dropped to the bed. Persephone sucked on her singed fingertips. After a few moments the pain was dull enough for her to gingerly press a pinky to the hourglass timepiece. It was no longer hot, but ice-cold to the touch. She pressed the two injured fingers to it and cool comfort spread through them before the aching burn left entirely. Persephone studied the tips in wonder—the red had faded to pink, the injury gone. She scooped up the necklace and found it was heavier in her hands than before.

As she tugged her shirt back on, the bottom of the hourglass swung open. Miraculously, a note on thick parchment weighted like a stone tumbled from it into her palm before the hourglass swung closed on its own. None of the grain of sands inside the timepiece had moved.

The note read:

> *A walker is meant to travel alone.*
> *She is not meant to burn out.*
> *Your scent lingers on the books.*

Persephone's heart fluttered at the last sentence. She reread it until the words faded into the page and dissolved into a single rose quartz she cradled in her palm.

Dorian.

Persephone stood, tucked the hourglass and the rose quartz into her pocket—she didn't trust either yet against her skin—and walked into the hall, still wearing her flannel pajamas. The urge to see him, one she'd barely kept banked, spread faster than a wildfire.

Persephone tiptoed down the stairs, brushed past the crescent couch and a dozing Opal, and quiet as a dormouse unlatched the front door and slipped outside.

The shadows watched, and waited.

Persephone stepped into the garden, and moved to the cobble-stone path. Her feet picked up the pace as she went from a quiet stride into a soft run to an all-out sprint. Persephone pulled the images of the library into her mind. As the images appeared, she saw the sign to the library and the wooden door, and wove and unwove time, or rather space, like braiding and unbraiding golden threads around her. The process was nothing like before, when she was forcing—or reacting—to her power. She knew what she wanted, and this kind of wanting made all the difference.

Past and present swirled as though made of strands of light divided by silver and gold that formed a path under her feet. The colors enveloped her as she walked farther. Moments passed, the air warmed. She reached a hand forward and whispered his name. *Dorian.*

Persephone stepped out of the swirling colors and up to the front door of the Library for the Lost.

Persephone knocked once, and the door quickly swung open. Dorian stood in the archway, breathing heavy as though he'd been the one sprinting instead of her. His hair was wet, and his eyes burned with a focused intensity. Persephone held out a hand. There, cupped in her palm, a flame of light, of spirit finally summoned, danced.

Persephone asked, "May I come in?"

▸ ▸ ▸

ARIEL WAY HAD woken early. She often slept, like a cat, in long, luxurious snatches of time. Her naps usually left her clear-eyed and focused, but for the past few weeks she had slept fitfully.

Her sister was barely sleeping at all.

When Ellison did sleep, she spoke from within the confines of a dream, rhapsodizing of coming storms and a doorway she needed to keep locked. Ariel watched her sister lose weight even as she denied there was a problem at all.

Such was the way of the Way women.

Before her mother had gone off with their aunt to foolishly try and bend the rules around the curse, she'd stopped sleeping.

It happened a month after her mother had an affair with a sandy-haired fisherman with a toothy smile and bright eyes. A man who her mother—her bold, rash, and independent *mother*—begged to stay on the island. Ariel had overheard their conversation after coming home later than usual one night. She'd spent the evening making out with Laurel, who had recently broken up with her college boyfriend, and was—Ariel was fairly certain—stringing her along. She was distracted, her crush on Laurel being no small thing, and didn't realize anyone was on the porch. When she heard her mom *plead* with the man to stay, Ariel nearly fell into the water.

He was the first man her mother had gotten lust drunk over, and in the end his leaving is what Ariel was certain led her mother to do it. Try to fracture the curse. She didn't believe her mother thought she and her aunt would succeed. No, she believed her mother *wanted* to fail, to get thrown off island, tossed into the sea like a siren so she could be on her way to tracking that man down.

That she left without a word told Ariel everything.

Now Ellison wasn't sleeping and that damn curse was threatening to fuck everything up yet again.

Ariel sat in the attic on her favorite tree trunk of a stool, turning her attention to the little automaton who knelt before her. He was a delightful beastie, with his golden eyes and green pants and suspenders. Something about the breadth of his shoulders reminded her of someone. Perhaps a leading man she had once seen in a black-and-white movie.

The mechanical man she created had been ordered by one of her favorite couples who came on island each May. As Ariel worked the final wires together, she added the little jacket she'd sewn the week before and set the little man before the great oval window. "Time to wake up, my friend."

She turned the switch in the back, at the base of his neck, and waited for his whirring and burring to commence. He creaked and groaned, and there was an unexpected flash of green light. Ariel leaned forward, squinting at where the light went in.

"Shit," Ariel said, leaning back. She had purposefully kept her magic at bay while working on him, trying to keep the pocus out.

It was difficult not to use her power, but she had long ago learned magic, like her heart, like love itself, was not to be blindly trusted.

Ariel glanced at the mechanical lady she'd been working on for a young woman who had commissioned it for her mother's birthday. In the new light, she realized the lady, like the mechanical man, also looked familiar. *Too* familiar.

It was the dark eyes and curly hair, the combination of Italian and Spanish ancestry gorgeously showcased by sharp cheekbones and a full mouth. She'd been so absorbed in her work she hadn't realized she had created a miniature Hyacinth from memory without even trying.

Growling out a frustrated curse, Ariel set the female automaton aside. She'd figure out what to do with her later. For now, she focused on the whirring man, and how his eyes lit as he creaked his head to one side and blinked his slow methodical blink at her.

"Ah, there we are," Ariel said.

He opened and shut his mouth, turned his head from left to right and lifted his chin up and down. Satisfied with his range of motion, Ariel reached out to turn him off when his mouth opened again and a word tumbled out in a voice as real as any curse could be.

He said simply, "Persephone."

Ariel's scalp tingled and she looked across the room. The female automaton's eyes opened and her lips curved into a twisted, mechanical smile.

▸ ▸ ▸

"PERSEPHONE." DORIAN STARED at her, blinking rapidly. "You shouldn't be here."

"I got your note."

He reached a hand out, hesitated, and dropped it.

"What?" Persephone asked, wanting to step to him, afraid if she did he might disappear. Which was almost as ridiculous as her being able to cross time and space to stand outside his doorway.

"Come in," he said, and stepped out of the frame.

Inside the library two navy wingback chairs sat in front of the wide-mouthed fireplace. A small table was pressed between them. Dorian waved a hand, and two cups appeared. Persephone crossed to the closest chair and studied the cup. The scent of cocoa and cinnamon rose up to greet her.

"Library magic?"

"One of the few perks." He stood at his chair, and she realized he was waiting.

Persephone sat, and he followed suit, lifting his cup to his lips on an almost smile. He drank deep, and the smile shifted up to his eyes. The corners creased, and Persephone studied his face. It was a combination of sharp angles and deep slashes—the cheekbones, nose, eyebrows, and then there were those wolf eyes. Dorian would never be cast as the hero of any story. Persephone liked that about him.

She sank back into the seat, and took a sip from the mug. "Oh," she said, delighted. She drank again. "Hot chocolate."

"Spiced chocolate," he corrected. "It's one of my favorites."

"I've worked in coffee shops," Persephone said, thinking about how that life was worlds away from where she was now. "The air would sometimes smell like this tastes. Do you like coffee?"

"I prefer sweet to savory."

She nodded into her mug, and watched him drum his fingers across the top of the chair. Was he nervous?

"I don't . . ." His fingers now ran along his jawline, drawing her gaze. "I haven't shared a drink with someone in some time."

Persephone looked over to the fire, at how the tips of the flames wavered blue. She thought about the endless cups of coffee and tea she had steeped and served. Not once had she sat down to have a cup with anyone. Not even Deandra or Larkin.

"Me either," she said. "It wouldn't have been in a library either. I'd be terrified to bring water inside, let alone something that could spill and stain. Most librarians are . . ." She trailed off, a laugh gurgling in the back of her throat.

"Are what?"

"Terrifying," she said, the laugh bubbling over and out.

Dorian raised a brow, and the laugh turned into a cough.
"I don't know if I should be flattered or flummoxed," he said,
and scratched his chin. "I think I'm offended."

Persephone let out a breath she hadn't realized she was holding. "You're scary enough," she said.

"And yet."

"And yet?"

"Here you sit," he said, his dark eyes piercing as they met hers.

Persephone lifted the cup and drank, trying very hard not to
react. There was so much of Dorian, it was like he was surrounding her in the room, rather than sitting across from her.

His gaze dropped to her hands and she cleared her throat.
"Why did you send me the note?"

"I shouldn't have sent it," Dorian said, leaning forward. "But
I needed to warn you."

She set the cup down with a clatter. "Warn me?"

He nodded. "You aren't safe on the island."

Persephone frowned. "Not safe how?"

Dorian stood up, crossed to the fireplace, and then walked
back to her. "There's too much in the way." He gave his head a
small shake. "I can't see it all, but I see enough."

"Enough of what?"

"Dark magic. Something's coming."

Indecision hung thick in the air. It clouded Persephone's senses
and sent her heart thumping. She climbed to her feet. She took a
step forward, and for an impossible moment, Persephone thought
he would reach for her.

Dorian kept his hands at his side, but stepped closer. He
smelled of ink and rain, of pages drying with story and a crackling fire roaring to life. Persephone met his eyes and he smiled—
the finest, truest smile she'd ever seen. She held his gaze for the
longest seconds of her life before his smile faded and he stepped
away.

"There are shadows clinging to your edges, trying to break
free. I can't see enough to know what they mean, and until I

do, you have to stop testing time and space. You have to take care."

"Shadows?" Persephone lifted a hand and tugged at the chain of her hourglass necklace. "Like the one the Way witches sent after me?"

"The Ways?" Dorian shook his head. "It's not their fate trying to undo yours. No, this is something else. The curse and something . . . hidden from me."

"How do I fight what I can't see?" Persephone asked, her irritation growing with each word. She wanted clarity, needed to understand.

"I'm looking," Dorian said, and this time he did not hesitate. He reached out, and brushed a hand along the edges of her hair, cupping the strands. She wanted to lean in, press her nose to his palm, breathe him in. "If I can find out," he said, "I will call for you."

A crash sounded from somewhere deep in the library, and Dorian stepped back. A gust of wind rose up from inside the room and pushed its way toward the far wall. Books dropped to the floor and scattered, their pages bucking, spines cracking.

Persephone backed away from it, stepping to the door.

"Dorian."

"It's fine. You need to go." He stared deep into her eyes. "You have to go."

She swallowed hard around the sudden sense of loss, and crossed through the door.

"*Don't* follow the wind," Dorian shouted over the rising noise. He gave Persephone one last look, and pushed the door closed behind her.

Persephone tried to call for him, but time sped up and dissolved around her. She stumbled back and found herself standing in the center of town, on the cobblestone path.

She looked up to find she was facing a grim-looking Ellison Way.

▸ ▸ ▸

ELLISON HAD BEEN pacing the beach when she'd seen the flash in the attic. It was the same green she'd seen in her vision, the one where the island was drowning. For weeks she had been having nightmares of the island sinking into the ocean whenever she fell asleep, and now understood what the nightmare meant. She had been wrong to dismiss the red-haired witch.

Persephone May was the faceless witch she'd been dreaming of, the one who brought them to their knees and sent them down deep into the slumbering waters of the Atlantic.

As soon as Ellison saw the flash of green, she knew. The blasted curse was a ticking clock of a time bomb, and everything had shifted once the witch set foot on Wile Isle. First it was the little lightning storms stalking Ariel and Ellison during their afternoon walks on the beach after Persephone arrived. Then it was the dead fish washing up on their shore. And last night droves of fireflies with green lights for tails had chased Ellison inside from her evening tea on the porch. Ellison had even taken to wearing an enchanted face mask when checking their magical perimeter to keep the overgrown gnats from darting into her mouth.

Yes, Ellison had been a fool, and she had been wrong. Something must be done, and Ellison decided she was the one to do the doing. As a witch, she knew what was to be would be. The only thing to do was cower . . . or meet it face on. For all her faults, and she felt she had many, Ellison never cowered.

Not when jellyfish swarmed the shore and she had to convince them to return to the depths, not when drunken louts wandered too close to her house during the summer months and needed to be charmed back off the island, not even when the Goddess showed her the vision of her mother's death ten years before and the only thing Ellison could do was bear witness and protect her sister from the devastating truth.

No, Ellison was not the sort to shrink from the fates. Throwing on her warmest cloak, and bespelling her sister in the attic to keep her safe, Ellison left the house, and her post as guardian over the ocean and the beach, and headed into town.

The Way sisters did not often leave home if they could help it. Town, during the on season, found its way to them. Once, a decade before, they had gone regularly. They had, in fact, sat for tea in Our Delights with the Ever sisters, visited with the postmistress, and attended every in-season festival. Once upon a time, when Ellison thought of the Evers, she thought *family*. That was back when Ariel Way looked at Hyacinth Ever and saw a kindred spirit.

"She's a wild, and occasionally reckless, witch like myself," Ariel had once told Ellison. "Hyacinth loves her family and who she is. She isn't pretending about anything."

Ariel had seen a friend who understood her. Back then Ellison had agreed. After all, she had foreseen that Hyacinth would introduce Ariel to the woman who would hold the key to Ari's heart.

The problem was Ellison couldn't see *everything*. Just as she never saw Persephone coming, she never saw Hyacinth stealing Ariel's girlfriend for herself, or using Ari's ex as a means to hurt Ariel. She didn't see that the girl wasn't who she said she was, or that she would solidify a divide between the Ways and the Evers. That time, Ellison saw everything far too late.

Ellison's feet moved softly over the cobblestone path as she walked into town. She rolled her shoulders back and lifted her nose to the sky. The world outside the beach smelled of blooming roses and a sweetly salted brine. It was a mix of Way and Ever, of curse and life. It was, Ellison knew, the smell of home.

The oaks bordering the path were thick with moss and mist. The morning was rolling back, bringing the warmth of the sun out even as cool air chilled down into her marrow. Ellison could see the dark, the shadows that arrived the moment Persephone stepped off the boat and onto the beach. Part of Ellison wanted to blame her sister for tempting fate, for traveling with the boat master to the dock to test the boundaries and try and leave the island during the winter months. Ari had been itching to try for years, determined the curse was finally weakening as time ran out.

Ellison knew she missed their mother, missed a woman she believed had abandoned them over the curse. Ariel also missed the combined passion she and Hyacinth had for trying to bring home their mothers. She missed her bosom friend. A part of Ari may have even wanted to find a way to break the damned curse on her own, to show Hyacinth, to show their mother, she didn't need either of them.

Ariel had mistaken the lack of activity on the island, the lack of wards being unbroken and time moving without incident, as a promise of safety. It had been a lure, and it had cost them. For when Ariel left the island for less than an hour, Persephone had arrived.

Ever since the delivering of that particular woman to the shore, things had gone from annoying to worse for the Way sisters.

Ellison stepped through the hanging foliage and past the WELCOME TO WILE ISLE sign. She waved a hand over the trailing roses, pulling a bit of moisture from the pricking leaves onto the tips of her fingers as she passed. The water called to Ellison, knew her as only like can know like. She tried to see into the bead on her fingertip, to find the vision clearly nestled there, but the Goddess was quiet.

It was early enough that shopkeepers were just setting their kettles to boil, shaking the linens out, and readying their stores for the day. It was late enough for mischief to be born.

She paused and watched a pretty man with hair the color of copper navigate the walkway. Her fingers itched to toss back the long bangs that fell across the bridge of his nose and hid his eyes. She wondered if they were as gray as the sky before a storm, or as blue as the horizon after. She imagined how they'd widen if she walked over and pushed him down into the nearby bench and climbed atop him. How quickly those eyes could fill with lust. How easy it might be to show him how to please her.

Ellison longed for connection, she longed to share her bed and her heart, and she was rather desperate to do so anywhere but here.

Forcing her gaze away from the man's devastatingly sharp jawline and broad shoulders, and her thoughts away from the trouble a tumble could bring her longing heart, Ellison saw the maelstrom as it swirled in the center of town. One minute the air was empty, the next it was an upturn of a tempest, cutting through space and bringing a flash of green amid a contrast of bright aether light. She knew it for who it was, rather than what it meant.

"Fool of a witch," Ellison said, picking up her stride and crossing to stand before it as it slowed to a stop.

Looking disheveled and very nearly heartbroken, Persephone May came to solidity and looked up at Ellison.

Persephone's mouth opened and closed as she stared in surprise. Ellison quirked a brow, and worked through the words she'd mentally recited thirteen times on the way into town in an effort to get them just right. Before Ellison could mutter so much as a vowel, the sky split apart.

Lightning shot up from Ellison's feet and Ellison raised her hands, blocking the surge. It bounced off her protection spell and sparks skittered across the sky.

Green light sparked down from clouds, and Persephone stumbled back.

Ellison tried to call out, but her voice was frozen in her throat. She looked down at the glow coming from her fingers. Space. Time. The fibers of her being were being pulled from her like a thread tugged at just the right angle to unravel a sweater.

Persephone was *siphoning* her power.

Ellison growled out in anger. She looked across the way and saw that the man with the copper hair was frozen in form. Space was being manipulated, and freezing the world outside their grain of sand. Ellison held up her hands higher. The lightning crashed across the sky once more. She gazed over at Persephone, and past her to the shadows hovering at the edge of the stone path. Ellison pulled her power back into her and tried to bind it to her being.

Thunder rumbled, and another shot of green light sparked down from the sky. Ellison looked at Persephone's face. Time seemed to speed up as she took in the quivering lower lip, how Persephone held up her trembling right hand.

Then Persephone May flung out her arm, and shot pure white light straight into Ellison's heart.

HYACINTH EVER'S JOURNAL

Autumn solstice, ten years ago

Change is coming.

I know it because the wind is unable to find its course. It comes in from all directions at all hours.

I've been having strange dreams about a woman and a sea of people. In the dream, I'm underwater, too—just beneath the surface, but I'm still breathing. When I wake up, I feel so sad.

The truth is I feel sad all the time.

I'm going to see if Moira will come with me to Wile's Great Mountain tonight. Try and find where the wind is getting caught. There's something off with the wards Gran set there, the ones that only sound when something crosses from another world into this one—it's the only explanation I have for it.

Ariel isn't speaking to me, or I'd ask her.

I miss my friend.

Change is coming. I fear it's already here, and I wish I could say I didn't feel so lost.

seven

PERSEPHONE WATCHED IN HORROR as Ellison Way staggered back and crumpled to the ground. One second Ellison was standing in front of Persephone, with an imposing set of her shoulders and a glint in her eye. The next, like rocks tumbling down a steep cliff, Ellison collapsed to the earth.

Persephone hadn't meant to do it. She didn't know why the witch had charged her and attacked her like she had. She didn't understand why the Ways hated her so. But Persephone had simply wanted her to stop. She acted in defense. Her hand had gone up and all she could think in that moment was: *No more.*

Now Persephone's hands flew up to cover her mouth in horror. As the storm around them receded, Persephone stumbled forward, and quickly bent over the fallen witch, searching for a pulse. A door opened behind Persephone and Laurel rushed out.

"Elsie?" Laurel called, seeing Ellison lying on the ground as limp as any unpuppeted marionette. Laurel's face lost its color as she stared down, and she, too, dropped to her knees to search for signs of life.

"She just collapsed," Persephone said, which was a kind of

truth. Her voice shook and her hands trembled as she clasped them to her chest.

"We need her sister," Laurel said, not bothering to look up. "Ariel Way. The number's in the office on the inside wall behind the desk." A wind blew in from the east and Laurel looked up. "Never mind, she knows." She turned now to Persephone, who wore nothing but flannel pajamas and a worried frown. "Go," Laurel said. "You're staying with the Evers, so it's best if you're not here when Ari arrives. Theirs is a line you won't want to cross."

"But—"

"*Go*," Laurel repeated, more sharply this time. Then softening her tone, added, "Please."

Persephone nodded and stood. She turned and increased her speed as she walked out of the center of town down the side walkway behind the shops, and onto the cobblestone path. Persephone didn't feel her feet, could barely register the racing of her heart. She heard nothing and saw no one as she gave in to the fear and horror of her own thoughts.

Persephone had attacked, possibly killed, Ellison Way. She'd never killed anything bigger than a spider, and even then had profusely apologized for her actions. True, Ellison was likely about to attack her first—and not for the first time—but Persephone had crossed a line.

Persephone's magic had not failed her this time, but she'd used it for harm. What did Moira start every morning meditation with? *And harm none.* Persephone had broken the first rule.

As she staggered up the road, she didn't feel the blood rushing to her head, or the sweat pooling down her spine. She didn't blink away the tears or register them as they fell.

Persephone never realized she was following the wind, until it blew her over.

One minute she was upright, the next she was on her face. Persephone tried to stand but the darkness wrapped itself around her.

Persephone fought. She rolled to her side, and through the shadows, saw the town beyond them. She realized she was no longer in the present world.

The island was as it had been before, picture-perfect, newly built and adorned. This time, however, Persephone saw the spire of what could only be a carnival or circus tent. A white awning rippled in the wind, and the sounds of laughter and music flowed out and around Persephone like a snow globe encasing a lonely snowwoman.

A voice whispered in her head. A soft sigh that grew louder and louder until it nearly split her apart.

The way. The way.

The world spun faster and faster. Cracks splintered down Persephone's spine, inside her arms, along her sides.

Persephone screamed.

The very seams where the universe had sewn her together were coming apart. Persephone tried to quiet her mind, to call on the training Moira had instructed her in day after day to help prevent any mental attack, but the voice was nestled too deep.

The way, Persephone.

Persephone was losing her battle against the darkness pressing in on her. Her strength was fading faster than a tide turning a current. Persephone knew she didn't have long, and as she drifted to oblivion, she closed her eyes and saw Dorian's concerned face shining in the darkness. Her heart lurched at the loss of a chance to finally, maybe, discover someone else in a way that made her heart race.

A keening deep within Persephone sparked at the thought. At the realization of all she did not know, and never would if she gave in to the dark.

Persephone dug her nails into her palms and saw the white light she'd sent into Ellison Way. It was aether, space, in its truest essence.

It was a door to open all the blocks barricading Persephone into herself. The choice was hers. She could break down the walls within herself and see what she was truly made of, or she could crawl into herself and die.

Persephone reached deep into the depths of her soul, of her heartbreak, of her long-standing and impossible dream of wanting to be more, to be known, to be found.

And Persephone May opened her eyes.

She saw, clearly, who she was and who she might become. Two selves reflected in one mirror, splintered in half, waiting to be reknit. Persephone knew who she wanted to be.

She reached deep and screamed for all she was worth. Pushing, fighting, forcing it back, the darkness pooled around her. It sloughed off in ripples and waves, rolling back into the cracks in the earth.

For a long time, Persephone did not move.

When she could, she rolled over and pressed her face and fingers into the grass at the edge of the path. Slowly, with the last of her focus, she dragged her strength from the land.

When she could open her eyes without crying out in pain, Persephone reached out with her mind and called one name.

▸ ▸ ▸

DORIAN WAS IN the middle of scouring the stacks for a very specific book when he felt the earth shake beneath his feet. He stumbled away from the shelves and watched as they warped and curved. The Library for the Lost changed its shape, reworking the geometrically angled room into a large cylinder. Magic ripped through the air, cracked down the hall and burst toward the stacks. The book Dorian had been seeking flew off the shelf. The book wrote and rewrote itself, pages tumbling out and shredding into nothing as new words and fresh ink and parchment fluttered in.

In all his years, so very *many* years, as the guardian of the library, Dorian had never seen such a sight. The library was thrown to its regular fits, particularly when he challenged its wishes, but this was something else.

The rest of the books shifted and straightened. New rows appeared, others deleted, and a chandelier made of prisms and balls of white flowing light encased in water descended from the ceiling in the center of the room. Dorian knew what those glowing orbs were before the word solidified in his mind.

Aether.

How?

The walls of the building shook as rooms were rewritten.

Shadows moved against the walls, slinking in as far as the edge of the stacks. They reached out, trying to grasp a way in but were propelled back by the light.

"It's not your time, friends," Dorian said, his voice solemn as he watched them wait and retreat. "But time is certainly trying to speed up."

Dorian waited out the last of the aftershocks, and when the room was as silent as a prayer, he took a calm step forward. The book he'd been seeking fluttered its cover once, like a lady shaking out her skirt. Dorian reached for his stepladder, and counted the new steps in its wake. Seven more had appeared. He climbed up until he was eye to spine with the book in question.

"Ah," he said, giving a small bow to the book with the ash tree and crescent moon on the cover. The Mayfair grimoire. "It's as I thought."

He stepped back down the ladder and crossed to the door. Dorian's hand was on the knob when he heard his name cried out, heard the wound in her voice, as she tried to rip him through time and space.

Dorian leaned in. He tried like hell to hold on. He didn't stand a chance.

Dorian crumpled to his knees as pain overtook him.

It was as though a knife slashed into his side and yanked down and up, down and up. Each time it completed its journey, the seams of his soul were reknit. Dorian was being torn apart, knitted back together, and torn apart. The layers of his soul shredded as Persephone tried and failed to yank him from the library.

He didn't know how long it lasted, how long magic fought an impossible war to move an immovable object through time. In the space of seconds or hours or days or years, Dorian bled apart and was reknit again.

That was the problem with curses. They cannot unmake themselves, no matter how hard a walker might try.

When it finally stopped, and Dorian was whole once more, he wiped the sweat from his brow, and let a single tear slide down his cheek.

He said her name once, and only once.

Oh, Persephone.

▸ ▸ ▸

THE BOAT PULLED up to the dock. A girl opened a red umbrella before she stepped off the skiff. The captain of the vessel had never been to Wile Isle before, and he liked the look of the island as much as he'd trusted the smile on that wicked girl's face the moment she'd placed her money in his hand.

The girl, for she was just young enough to still be in girl-hood, looked like an impressionist painting come to life. Delicate lines, soft colors, lovely features—all except the eyes. There was something banked in them, embers of an alien nature that had the boat captain looking over his shoulder every hundred yards or so after he left her on the island to make sure she hadn't somehow materialized out of the water and back into the boat.

As she stood on the dock, Deandra Bishop studied the island and turned her gaze to the little yellow house some ways down along the beach. Seagulls and crabs skittered along the dunes and sand. She turned to step closer, and found a magical barrier had been erected making the way impassable.

Clever witches.

She lifted a single thick brow, cocked her head, and turned back to the cobblestones. Then, umbrella held high enough to keep the mist and rain from doing more than dusting across her shoes, she swiveled her hips and sashayed up the path toward the large house built into the hill.

Deandra was alone, which was disappointing, for there was no one to hear her song.

> *"Swish swish*
> *A siren's wish*
> *Come come*
> *She beckons me on."*

Deandra smiled her sharpest smile, the one that bore the uncanny resemblance to a pair of pinking shears. She had known magic was building, knew it was only time before someone did something foolish—like try to break apart the worlds locked within Wile Isle before they understood what they even were. Deandra had bided her time and hidden herself well after what happened last time, and as the water gave way to carrying all things along its channels, she heard the spell when it struck.

Then she hitched her ride on the closest boat and crossed the barrier.

It was the first time in one hundred years the barrier had dropped enough to permit someone like her to cross.

Now Deandra walked up the long hill to Ever House. It was time for the final piece to return home to the board.

It was time for the games to begin.

▶ ▶ ▶

PERSEPHONE ROLLED HERSELF into a seated position, a lump lodged in the back of her throat. She had given all of her power over in calling for Dorian, and *nothing* happened.

Nothing.

She tried not to hyperventilate as she scrubbed her hands across her face. She may have just *killed* another witch, and yet she couldn't reach the librarian even when she put all her magic behind it. And this was where her thoughts went. What the hell was *wrong* with her?

Trying to dampen the panic exploding in her chest, Persephone closed her eyes and whispered all the beautiful things Moira had taught her to make. Buttermilk scones and coconut cakes. Crustless cherry pies and chocolate cupcakes with cream frosting so bright it glittered. Cinnamon and sugar, nutmeg and extracts—the kind that taste bitter and sweet and hold whole worlds in their flavors.

The start of a sob escaped through her lips and she bit it off. What would Moira say when she found out Persephone had killed her cousin? Moira and Hyacinth may not like the Ways, but like had little to do with love when it came to family. Of that, Persephone was now almost certain.

Tears ran down her cheeks and she dashed them aside. That

Persephone had been a part of something so joyful these past weeks was no small wonder.

It was a wonder, but it was not real. Persephone flashed on Ellison crumpled on the ground, the life seeping out of her, and the sob burst free. That was real. That was the destruction Persephone's magic craved.

Because Persephone was broken. She had been born broken and if she stayed on the island, she would break everything and everyone around her. The ground shook, her head spun, and she saw an image of Moira and Hyacinth dead at her feet. She saw them in stark contrast: the paleness of their faces, the deadness in their eyes.

It was a foretelling of what was to come. A vision of a sort, one she could not ignore. Persephone knew this would be their fate if she stayed.

She pulled herself upright as the vision faded. With waning strength, she managed to limp the rest of the walk to the dock. She smelled jasmine as she crossed through a side path and entered the cobblestones by the water. She knew the smell, had an instant recognition of the colorful notes, but couldn't recall how or where.

She crossed to the dinghy moored to the narrow dock. The wind came hard across Persephone, trying to push her forward, tug her back. As she held on, she wondered if it would send her spiraling into the ocean's depths.

Persephone persisted in pushing forward, and climbed into the small craft. She reached out one shaking hand to the meager motor attached to the back of the faded white vessel, and reverently hoped starting a boat would be similar to igniting a lawnmower.

She cranked the motor over and over until her arm was heavy with effort. Finally, on her last attempt, the engine gave a craggy roar to life.

Persephone let out a shaky sigh of relief as she lifted her face to the horizon. Her pajamas were half soaked through, her hair plastered to her face, and she had a variety of shallow cuts and lacerations along her arms and legs from where she had fought back the darkness.

Persephone had come to the island with a dream in her pocket, and she was leaving with all her hopes crumbled by her feet. But if she did not go, Persephone saw what she would bring. She would not let the same fate befall her cousins as what she had done to Ellison.

The sound of a heartbeat thrummed to life, and Persephone looked down at her chest. The hourglass flared, a bright white light trying to get out. Sorrow rose in her chest, but Persephone pushed it aside.

She couldn't think of Dorian now. She would fail Hyacinth and Moira if she stayed. For that, Persephone decided, was what she must have been born to do.

Daughter of a faceless woman. Granddaughter to a ghost. Descendent of the cursed.

Persephone set her shoulders, grit her teeth together, and untethered the final rope of the boat from the shore. The dinghy gave a violent jerk, sprang forward, and shot into a wave. It gave another start, tried to propel itself again, and the engine sputtered.

"No, no, no," Persephone said, crawling forward to try to will the boat on. "Don't stop, we have to *go*."

The boat shot out again, and as it did the wind wrapped around Persephone, clamping itself to her wrists and ankles, wrapping around her waist like chains. The tug was back, and this time it was in control. The little dinghy jolted and broke free. The invisible force yanked Persephone from the boat as it careened into the waves heading out to sea and piloted itself nowhere.

Persephone was tossed back onto the beach, where she fell hard onto the soft sand. She turned her head to the sky, another sob wrenching free. Persephone watched the escaped boat until it was a mere speck in the distance. Until it, too, was a memory.

For Persephone may have decided she was of no use in breaking the curse or saving the island, but the island would decide if and when it allowed her to go free.

EIGHT

PERSEPHONE KNELT ON THE beach, her knees sinking deeper into the sand, the water lapping closer but never brushing against her skin. The wind stirred around her, the skies blue and serene. She did not move, letting the minutes rush past, leaving her behind.

The winds changed again. Persephone blinked and the skies were the color of mud, the sand beneath her swirls of beige and amber. She studied the grains, dotted with rain, and pulled her gaze up. Her clothing, like her hair, like the sky itself, was soaked through.

Persephone felt muted, hollow.

She blinked again and puddles of water had pooled around her. The sun had moved behind the clouds, refreshing the sky from an aggressive navy to a somber blue. The air, which only moments before smelled full of rain, was clean and crisp.

None of it mattered.

Persephone thought of Ellison Way, and looked up the beach. She could not fully see the yellow house, but should go to it. Turn herself over to Ariel. Maybe the other woman would kill her. Maybe Ariel would only arrest her or have her thrown in their dungeon. Perhaps that would be enough to keep everyone safe.

What other unimagined horrors, Persephone wondered, could await her on this side of the dark? She looked down into the puddle closest to her and the water shimmered. Persephone leaned in, and it glazed like ice freezing over.

She tilted her head, studying it, then crawled onto her hands to stare directly above it. The reflective surface showed her own face, the brows severe and forehead furrowed. Persephone's mouth was drawn tighter than a fresh hemline, and there was a vacancy to her eyes that made her think of a blank-faced store mannequin.

She tried to pinch color in her cheeks but left two pink slashes that looked more like mistakes. "Mistakes are all I make," Persephone told her reflection. "You're a fool, Persephone May. You knew better than to think you were special."

She wished for the hundredth time she could be someone else, someone better.

Persephone blinked again and saw a different face. This one sure and strong, dark brows and a wide forehead. Eyes that saw too much, a mouth that held a crooked tooth behind full lips with a smile that could rival the sun.

Dorian.

Persephone didn't question the drive to reach for the puddle. The island wanted her to stay, but she wanted to go.

Persephone no longer felt the cold or loneliness that was worse and more familiar than the frigid rain. She put one hand into the water, and watched the waves ripple and part. The scene solidified, the colors inside the Library for the Lost blended and merged. Persephone took a hopeful breath, and dove in.

▸ ▸ ▸

ELLISON WAY WAS suspended in time. She knew this because she could see the magical layers of the island. If the earth was made of a crust, outer core, and inner core, Wile Isle was made of shell, time, and aether. Ellison was somewhere between the three. Not the hinterland, but some other place—where you go when you have no other place to go.

From the moment Persephone had hit her with white light and Ellison had fallen into time, she'd felt a tug sending her to the middle layer. A door had flashed through her mind. Wooden, thick, and malleable. It looked a little like an entrance to a library.

For no time and all time, Ellison had been studying it, trying to make up her mind if she should open it.

Something about the door bothered her. It reminded Ellison of a vision she'd once had . . . before. An important vision, which was part of why she had ended up in this predicament. The problem was that the longer she floated, debating, the less she knew. The edges of knowledge were fraying apart, and Ellison was forgetting.

There was someone she needed to get to. Someone she did not want to leave. But where were they? Maybe they were through that door. Ellison put out one hand, and tasted static building in the air as it bubbled like carbonation on the tip of her tongue.

Names are powerful seals. When called with certainty and trust and truth, they are bindings.

Ellison.

Ellison knew that voice.

Ellison Lenora Wayfair.

She turned from the door.

Damn it, Elsie.

Ellison shook her head, trying to clear the cobwebs.

Please, Elsie.

Ellison lifted her chin and studied the door. The number eight flashed before her, and a crackle of unease climbed up her spine. She took a step back.

Elsie! Now!

Ariel.

Ellison turned her mind away from the door, and the number. Ellison took one step, another, giving a last glance over her shoulder to the shimmering layer of aether bound in the island's outer core.

Then Ellison took a breath and opened her eyes.

▸ ▸ ▸

PERSEPHONE FELL THROUGH the ceiling of the library and landed with a hard *thump* on the multiple rugs overlayered across the wooden floor. She wheezed out a cough, which rattled down into her lungs and rumbled against her rib cage. Everything in her ached and moaned.

"Persephone?" The shock in Dorian's voice had her looking up.

"Help?" Persephone managed, before dropping her face into her arm.

He crossed to her, his large hands gentle as they propped her up. He ran fingers over her skull, down her side and over arms. Checked her legs for broken bones and brushed his calloused thumbs across her cheeks. "How are you here?"

"You like to ask me that, don't you?" Persephone asked, as he assisted her, a giddiness bubbled up beneath the pain as she studied his face.

She couldn't believe she'd managed to reach him, and she tried to find the humor in the situation, considering she looked like a drowned rat and felt far worse. "Everyone likes to ask me questions I have no answers to, and give me answers that never quite satisfy my questions. It's rather annoying."

"You don't understand," Dorian said, shifting back onto his heels. "No one can travel into the library unless it's through the front door."

"Your library has too many rules," Persephone asked. She pressed a palm to the side of her dizzy head. She wished she had a giant aspirin and human-sized bottle of Coca-Cola. "What will the punishment be? I have no change for an overdue fee." She gestured to the pajamas and its lack of money.

"You're speaking gibberish," he said, guiding her to her feet, and walking her to a small plush sofa in the center of the now circular library. "And no one should be able to travel here like you just did." Dorian sniffed the air. "That's serious magic."

"I'm remarkable like that," Persephone said, trying and failing for a winsome smile. Her heart cracked as she thought of Ellison, of Moira and Hyacinth. "It was a fluke, Dorian. I don't think my magic brings anything but devastation."

He stared at her, waiting, hovering, making her palms sweat. Persephone looked over her shoulder and registered the new space. "What room is this?"

"It's the main room, or the outer level of the library," he said. "You're not the only new magic or rule being broken. The library rewrote itself a few hours ago."

"Like a story?"

Dorian winced as he sat next to her, and she realized his limp had grown more pronounced. Persephone wasn't the only one in pain.

"Did you hurt yourself?"

Dorian barked out a small laugh, still looking as dazed as she felt. "Funny you should ask it that way. I don't think it was me who did the hurting."

At her puzzled look, he waved a hand and a fire roared to life in the large stone fireplace opposite them. Then he pulled a blanket from a small ottoman next to the sofa and laid it around her shoulders. "I can't charm your clothing, as they and you don't come from the library. You're out of your time here. The best we can do is give heat the opportunity to do the work for us." He leaned back and ran a hand over his hair, pausing as he touched his ear with another wince. "The library isn't a story, or not in a way anyone could write it. It's a being. One you tried to steal from and then broke into. You're a puzzle of a library thief, Persephone May."

"I'm not a thief," Persephone said, and shivered at how he used her full name, the way the syllables rolled off his tongue. "What kind of a being?"

Dorian opened his mouth, appeared to be trying to speak, but only shook his head. "I've said too much. I guard the secrets, but they aren't mine to keep."

"Do those secrets have anything to do with me?"

"Did you or did you not try to break the worlds apart today?"

Persephone looked at him sharply. "What? No. I can't break a world." Dorian arched a brow and Persephone thought of the blood draining from Ellison's face as her body dropped like a puppet with its strings cut. "That . . . can't be right."

"Tell me?" Dorian asked, peering at her like he was trying to read her mind through her eyes. Maybe he could, maybe he could read the very wishes printed on her soul.

He leaned in, and Persephone smelled the pine and musk of him. The fear in her relaxed, and she felt the steady beat of his heart when she shifted closer in response. The warmth of his skin brushed against hers and sent her own heart fluttering. Persephone thought it was dangerous, in a way she didn't fully understand yet, being so close to this man.

Taking a calming breath, she turned her attention to the crackle of kindling and flame in the fireplace. She studied the way the hearth spilled shadows across the floor even with the lights on in the room.

Persephone cleared her throat. "I haven't been able to make my magic work proper. I've struggled to access and control my aether . . . until today. This morning I faced off against Ellison Way after I left you." Her hands shook, and Dorian took them in his. "When I stepped back through the veil, she was there. I saw something in her eyes, and she started to speak, and I . . . reacted. I didn't think, or not overly, I just didn't want to be attacked again. I only meant to stop her, but I did something else."

Dorian squeezed her hands, his touch gentle but sure. It helped as much as it distracted. "What did you do?"

Persephone grimaced. "I shot something at her . . . aether, or the essence of it? I'm still learning. Ellison fell, and then I tried to find a pulse . . ." Her voice trailed off, the words chased away by the ghosts of regret. "But I . . . I think she was gone."

▸ ▸ ▸

DORIAN WATCHED WHAT little color Persephone had won back from the fire leach from her face and lips. He made a decision. It was time for action, and if he was honest with himself, he'd already made the choice to act the moment he had opened the door and saw Persephone standing there. It had really only been a matter of time.

"She's not dead," he said, bending, not quite breaking, a law of the library.

Persephone lifted her chin from where she had tucked it into her chest. "What?" She turned her body so she was facing him square on. "How can you know that?"

Dorian waved an arm around the room. "The books aren't mourning her. I haven't seen her. If she was dead, I would know."

"What do you mean?"

"I mean lost things come here, Persephone. *All* lost things connected to the islands." As the implication of what he was saying settled on her shoulders, he continued. "That wasn't what I was referring to, though. What you did, you tried to cross the borders without being lost. I thought perhaps you were trying a new angle against the curse, attempting to fracture the worlds, but you weren't?"

Persephone turned her face from his, averting her eyes as a blush climbed up her neck and cheeks. "I was trying to reach *into* this world," she said, her voice whisper soft.

"You—oh." He blinked, trying to clear the shock. "You were trying to pull *me* to you?"

He had heard her say his name, but he didn't realize her call had been *for* him. Dorian's soul did not belong to him, and therefore *no one* could call it through space.

Now he understood the price he paid when someone tried.

Persephone squirmed. "After I left Ellison—which wasn't my choice, the postmistress ordered me to leave—I lost my way."

"You followed the wind?" he asked, still trying to understand how she could have risked everything to pull him from his station.

"Not intentionally." She brushed her drying bangs from her brow. "Something came for me." She remembered the hold, the fight, and the voice in her mind. "It was like before, when I faced the Way witches on the beach. *Oh.* Ariel must have sent it." Persephone tugged at her hair. "Of course she did. I tried to kill her sister." She looked at Dorian, feeling utterly stupid for not comprehending it before. "Whatever the thing was, it almost won. I thought I was going to die, and then—"

Persephone glanced at him, a small smile on her lips. The

embarrassed quirk of her lips was so honest it sent his own heart thumping a painful staccato against his rib cage. "Then I thought of you. It gave me solace, to think of you." She gnawed on her lip, turning her eyes down. "I managed to get away." She reached for the timepiece beneath the collar of her nightclothes. "I called out for you after but I didn't intend to steal anything." She released the locket. "Or anyone."

Dorian thought of a child in the night, waking from a terrible dream and clutching a teddy bear. He thought of what her actions cost, how his soul had been splintered from his body and re-sewn into him again and again, until time no longer existed for him. She lifted her lashes, and he swallowed the truth. He couldn't tell her what she'd done, at least not yet when there was so much she didn't understand.

"You tried to pull me from the Library for the Lost, but I cannot move through worlds. Time moves with me, but only as the natural order wills it."

"There is nothing natural about the order of this place, or the island."

"Not as you understand it." Dorian reached for her hand, turned it over, and tucked it into his. It was a small gesture, but this was the first time Dorian had reached for someone to steady him, rather than the other way around. "I need to gather a few things," he said. "See if I can find you something dry to wear. I'll be back in a few minutes. Stay close to the fire, and don't try to touch anything until I return."

Persephone gave him a sad upturn of one corner of her mouth but nodded her agreement.

Dorian rose on shaky legs, and limped from the inner library to the outer hall. He turned down the corridor, noting how it had changed yet again. He wound through a small labyrinth, and found himself, after an odd number of right turns, on the other side of his quarters.

His room did not hold a bed or a chair, but two well-placed hammocks and the softest rug he'd ever walked across. He was quick to grab a spare change of clothing from his wardrobe, one of only five outfits he owned. He returned to the outer sanctum and found Persephone curled up on the sofa, sound asleep.

She was beautiful. She looked like something he would have dreamed up, if he still allowed himself to believe in dreams. Setting the clothing beside her feet, he walked to the front door of the library and looked up at the hanging chandelier. The small orbs of her element, of aether, glimmered and shined.

Dorian closed his eyes and let his mind wander.

It came over him as it always did. A steady thrum of energy. It was the cacophony of a thousand hearts beating as one. A thousand souls locked in this place he kept watch over.

He listened to the soothing rhythm they took when they moved together. He saw the number eight repeated over and over along the grooves of the library, built into the walls and ceiling, across the floor, down into the fibers of the joist and foundation. He made the symbol with his hands. Two circles, brought together. Like the two islands that once interconnected with Wile Isle.

He turned to face the sofa, and saw the sleeping eight. Infinity. It was Persephone's symbol. Yin and yang, good and evil. There were always two sides, and what she didn't yet understand was that the duality would be how she would break the Curse of Nightmares if she was to succeed. In order to take, she would also have to give.

The library whispered in his mind. Words from many varied tongues, rolling together into a knowing he welcomed. Dorian cared for the woman slumbering on his couch. He was afraid his care could grow into more.

But it was no matter.

He was guardian for the Library for the Lost, and Persephone had broken through the wards. The library was willed by the Goddess, it was tethered to the three islands, and housed their magical energy.

As the library was the point place for all magic that flowed to and from the islands, Dorian had no choice but to listen and do as he was tasked. If he did not, the library was not shy about what it would do in return.

The cost of failing the library wasn't death, not for Dorian. The cost of failure was to exist for all eternity and *wish* you were dead.

The library whispered again, and Dorian nodded. Yes, he would do as it asked. He would hold the library's test for the mystifying creature slumbering on the sofa—whether he wanted to or not.

Dorian opened his eyes and crossed back to Persephone. The library was pleased he'd agreed, and as he stepped the sharp pain in his hip ebbed. He reached her and, with ease, squatted down in front of her.

Persephone's lips were two perfect rose petals, and he was tempted to press his thumb against them, to try and memorize the way they sculpted against his skin.

He would do as the library asked, true. He would also do everything in his power to help Persephone.

Dorian watched her sleep for another long moment before he pressed his palm to her shoulder and gently shook her awake.

"If a good must exist," he said as her eyes fluttered open to meet his. "Then a complete evil must exist as well. Your Wile Isle is the gray, but we are in the black. I owe a debt, one that must be paid. You do not owe my debt, but maybe I can help lessen the load of yours." Dorian took a breath. "It is time to tell you the story of the Library for the Lost, and then you can decide what you wish to risk for this being of a place, should it decide to help you."

NINE

WHEN PERSEPHONE AWOKE, THERE were candles suspended above them. Persephone did not know how he did it, but Dorian had lit the entire main room of the library in floating, glistening light. He stared at her with such urgency as he told her he would tell her the story of the library, and yet his eyes crinkled at the edges as her own lit in wonder.

"It's like something out of Hogwarts," she said, focusing on the library rather than his distracting face.

"Harry Potter," Dorian said, with a small nod. "His story is on these shelves."

Persephone smiled in response. She stretched, stood, and agreed to hear Dorian's story before she slid behind a recessed stack to change into the clothes he had brought her.

She felt an overwhelming urge to lift the clothing to her face and inhale the scent of him. It was so overwhelming, she had to bite the inside of her cheek to steady her focus.

"I secretly kind of hated those books," she called to him, before tugging the shirt over her head in one swift motion. She slipped on the strange pajama-like pants and turned to study the rows before her. Line after line of books without titles visible to her.

Something about how the light shimmered over the aged spines made her wonder if they weren't simply hidden from her sight. "I was jealous of how Harry, Ron, and Hermione found family in each other, though I very much admired how they didn't give up on the light even when darkness seemed like it would prevail." She rolled up the long sleeves of the billowy shirt, cuffed up the pants, and sighed. The candles illuminated the stacks of books that encircled the room. The stacks seemed to go on and on, endlessly.

Persephone walked out from the alcove. "How did you do all this, if you aren't magical?"

"I never said I wasn't magical, only that I wasn't a witch." He ran a hand over the books, and sparks flew up from them. "All magic exists in the library from the worlds of Three Daughters— Elusia, Olympia, and Wile. The islands aren't like other islands, and what they harnessed and harness has different limits. That includes being able to pull from magic written in stories. I ask the library for favors. Some she grants, others she does not."

Persephone ran her fingers through the tangles of her hair. "I think the island may be pissed at me."

Dorian raised a brow.

"I tried to leave."

He shifted his weight and slowly tipped his chin down to look at her in a way that had her shivering. "You tried to leave."

It wasn't a question. Dorian said it with an edge of amusement . . . and anger.

"I can't do what anyone needs me to do." She clasped her hands together, squeezed them so tight the skin whitened, then dropped them to her sides. "I had a vision. If I break the curse, I will kill my cousins."

Dorian didn't move a muscle. "What happens if you don't break it?"

"I'm sorry?"

"Visions are like prophecies, Persephone. Two sides, differing angles. They're also only one piece of a picture, a scene in a chapter if you will."

She gave her head a slow shake. "I don't know. I've never had this type of a vision before."

He ran a hand across his stubbled cheek. "You can't know anything for certain from a vision."

Persephone sighed. "You said the library grants favors. You called her a she?"

Dorian looked over his shoulder. "Our library is a mistress of deception when it suits her, but for the most part she is forthright and honest."

"You think the library is a being. And female."

He looked back at her. "It's not a thought, Persephone. It's reality."

Persephone pressed her toes into the rug. If she had learned anything these past many weeks on Wile Isle, it was that there were many realities when it came to the world of magic.

Not all of them were wise.

"Does she have a name?"

Something flickered across his face. "There aren't enough words to name her."

"Good or bad ones?"

The corner of Dorian's mouth twitched, but he only shook his head.

"You don't call her something in your mind?"

"I call her Library for the Lost. I'm literal that way."

Persephone's lips betrayed her by curving. "And you said the library might help me?"

He nodded. "She has the power to do so, if she deems it, but you'll have to prove your intent is true."

"Does the library know about visions?"

Dorian winced. It was so quick, the pinch of skin around his eyes and mouth, that Persephone wasn't entirely certain she hadn't imagined it.

"She knows many things."

Persephone sighed, and ran a hand threw the tangled ends of her hair. "And the library wants to give me a test?"

"Something like that."

She crossed her arms. "I hate to point it out, but that sounds pretty stereotypical of a library."

He gave a low chuckle that made her stomach flip in the most delicious way. "Bet you wish you'd studied."

Persephone gave her head a shake, and rubbed her hands against her crossed arms, letting her fingertips linger on the worn fabric of the oversized shirt Dorian had lent her. It was once linen or something equally stiff and abrasive, but time and the contours of his body had worn it velvety soft. She wondered what his smile would feel like if she held it in her hands.

Persephone realized she was staring at him, possibly revealing too much of the longing on her face, and quickly jumped to the next question. "So the story of the library?"

"I'm waiting for you to get the nervous energy out of your limbs." Now he did give her a rare slash of an almost smile. "You keep tugging on the shirt and tapping your feet on the rug. I thought perhaps it best to make certain you wouldn't dance out of here once I start."

Persephone dropped her hands, which had in fact been fidgeting against the fabric of the opposite sleeves. "Funny." She leveled her gaze. "I'm here, listening, as still as tepid water."

Dorian's eyebrows were dark slashes against the copper tone of his face, his eyes an indeterminate shade. Persephone wished she had years to spend studying the way the green and gray and brown flecked together. He reached out one hand to the closest shelf, and said, "Water is precisely where our tale begins."

Dorian lugged a book over that was the size of a small table. He opened it and Persephone blinked in surprise. It was like looking into the pool of water she'd seen during the storm. She reached forward to touch it and found the surface, which held the image of a roaring sea in motion, as solid and cold as a sheet of glass.

"What is this?"

"This is the story of what was. It's the *Shanachie* and it may show you what has come to pass. Not quite a vision, but more of as a visual history, so to speak."

"What do you mean *may* show me?"

Dorian didn't look over. "I mean, just as you don't show all sides of your person to everyone you meet the minute you meet them, a story doesn't show all truths to each reader who reads it. You'll find what is most prevalent to your course here."

"I feel like you're having an existential argument with me over a magical tome."

"I'm not arguing at all, I'm explaining. You're trying to reject my explanation."

Dorian's voice had dropped an octave. It went deeper when he was irritated, and learning that thrilled Persephone. She wanted to needle him further, but then he looked over at her, and she caught the slight dimple in his cheek from where he was suppressing a smile. Her heart thunked loudly in her chest, and she forgot entirely what she had planned next to say.

"How about I make you a deal," he said, when she did nothing more but stare. "If I believe you haven't been shown something important, I will tell you the parts of the story you are missing."

Persephone held out a hand. "Deal."

▸ ▸ ▸

DORIAN TOOK HER hand, but did not release it. Persephone savored the way her palm tingled against his.

He cleared his throat. "This tale begins like all great tales. Once, many moons ago, the world was a simpler and more complex place."

As Dorian spoke, the first page of the *Shanachie*—if you could call it a page—rippled and shifted. Persephone went from staring at the images, to standing inside of the story. There was no shift in the fabric of worlds, no notice of going from here to there. One minute Persephone sat on the sofa, the next she stood inside a new storied world.

Persephone caught her breath and looked down, and found her hand was still connected to Dorian's. Dorian stood beside her, but he was a younger and rougher version of the man she'd been sitting beside only moments before. He squeezed her hand and let go.

Dorian stepped further into the story. Persephone decided it was like watching a video game from the inside, as if a player was called in and came on screen to take his turn. Persephone was still off screen, and yet very much inside the action.

The sea surrounding them was dark and grim. White foam tossed over deep angry water as the surface churned over and over. Dorian manned the large vessel they had boarded, a black flag flying at the mast. The upper deck of the boat smelled of fish and salt water, and Persephone plugged her nose until she lost her footing. The boat rose and fell, fighting and losing the battle against steel-armed waves. Dorian was nonplussed, focused solely on fighting for control of the current.

"Of course he's a pirate," Persephone said to herself, eyeing the tattoos running along his forearms. It was the first time she'd seen Dorian without sleeves to his wrists, and she marveled at the strength in the cords of muscle as well as the extensive ink. A compass tattoo was nestled against his chest where his shirt was undone, and he looked as dangerous as the water as he called out orders to the men who rushed past.

Suddenly a swell of a wave collapsed over the side of the boat, brushing men, casks, and ropes into the sea. Dorian didn't pause.

"Avast ye," he yelled, taking to the main sails. "Pull!"

The crew responded, all men on deck, scurrying in his wake, pulling and pushing, tugging and freeing ropes and pulleys as Dorian commanded. He called orders as he navigated the waters, taking control of the wheel. His men were left to fight the depths as the boat sailed on.

Dorian was ruthless in his approach, and it both chilled and excited her. Persephone started to cross to him, when she heard the steady *thump thump, thump thump*, from beneath the floorboards. Persephone had to remind herself that she was here to see what had happened. This, presumably, was the ship showing her the way. Listening intently, she turned and walked in the direction of the stairs, away from a struggling but arrogantly determined Dorian. Down she went into the belly of the boat, seeking the steady *thump thump*.

Persephone navigated the final step only to stumble her way down a narrow and shaky corridor. In the last quarters, at the very end of the hall, a red door waited. She hesitated, but opened it, the rough seas throwing her forward as it swung wide.

Cursing as she tumbled headfirst inside, Persephone fell onto the cluttered planked floor. The door swung shut behind her and the rocking of the boat ceased.

There was a hush in the room, and Persephone swallowed as she took stock of the objects before her. Piled along the floor, and covered by tattered oilcloths, was a sea of bric-a-brac. In the center of the assorted items, like a lighthouse beacon, a light blinked on.

Thump thump, thump thump.

Persephone dusted herself off and stood. She was careful to navigate the edges of the room, but even so her arm caught on a cloth as the boat rocked side to side, and she unraveled a section. As the dusty covering fell away, her mouth ran dry.

Gemstones of smooth and rough surfaces, large and small sizes lay before her. Behind them were musical instruments, books of various sizes, potions in a crate, masks that had her backing up a step, and a collection of weapons, chalices, and what looked to be decorative swords drawing her nearer.

Her palms itched with power. "It's a magical treasure trove," Persephone said, spying a waterlogged crate in one corner. Beyond it, she estimated there were ten casks or so more. There were tridents and knives so aged and worn they looked like they'd been stolen from a mermaid's palace. Persephone tiptoed through the array of jewels, barely able to resist the urge to scoop them up and place them in her shirt.

Maybe she could. Perhaps that meant they were free to take.

"And perhaps they can keep you here."

Persephone stopped moving, and looked around. "Dorian?"

There was no reply.

Persephone took a light step forward, waited, but no one spoke. Instead sound rushed back into the room, the boat rocked again, and she braced her feet.

"I'm losing it," she said to herself, taking another step forward, careful not to fall over. "Talking to myself and imagining the objects talking back."

"Who said anything about an object, lost girl?"

Persephone banged her shin into the chest to her right and spun around. "Okay, that's it. Come out, Dorian."

Persephone heard a soft laugh, and turned again. The laugh wasn't Dorian's. It was female.

The light in the center of the room pulsed red and she narrowed her eyes at it. Stepping high and fast, Persephone cut across the room to where the light was still hidden beneath the remaining sheet.

"I don't have time for this." Persephone wasn't going to let an inanimate object, no matter how magical, mock her. She reached down, plucked the sheet up and threw it back.

Persephone's hand flew to her neck, as she stared in shock. Beneath the blanket, blazing as red as any pulsing heart, was the hourglass she wore. It was draped over a golden telescope.

"How?" Persephone stepped forward to grab it, and the light around her neck blazed from green to gold.

"Wrong question, Persephone."

Persephone stared down at the light shining from her chest. Golden white, brilliant and true. She looked back at the telescope. She had seen it before, looked through it. In the Library for the Lost.

What did it mean?

Persephone was careful to retrace her steps back to the front of the galley, where she peered down into the case of stones. There, nestled back in the corner, was a rose quartz. She pulled out the stone she'd tucked into the pocket of the pants Dorian lent her out. Persephone held it up. Twin stones, like the twin lockets.

Persephone gave her head a shake. She was staring at a portion of the belongings she had seen on the shelves at the Library for the Lost. Why was the library showing her this, what did it mean?

She turned and hurried back up the corridor and stairs as the boat lurched forward again. Persephone stumbled up the last of the stairs, and took one step out before her feet were swept from beneath her. It took her precious seconds to realize the boat was going down, and by the time she'd put it all together, Persephone was overboard.

▸ ▸ ▸

PERSEPHONE SHOOK OFF the spray of chilled water and realized she was on the shore of a beach. It could be Wile Isle—long dock, white sands, storybook trees—aside from the mist blanketing it. Thick as smoke, vaguely gray in color with a hint of yellow, *this* mist was a menace.

Dorian, sopping wet and half drowned, lay beside Persephone. Persephone looked around for the boat as she crawled to check his pulse. She knew this wasn't real, he'd said as much, but her stomach lurched at the sight of his face so pale. Before Persephone could reach him, he rolled onto his side and coughed up a gallon of water. Then Dorian staggered up to his feet, not seeing Persephone beside him, looking only ahead to something in the fog.

"Mr. Moskito," a soft female voice called out from somewhere beyond the gray. "You have made it to Three Daughters, but you seem to have lost your ship."

"It's swimming in the depths of Davy Jones's locker, Mayfair," Dorian rasped, pushing his hair from his face, wringing out the edge of his shirt. "You didn't tell me these waters were of a mind of their own. The storm took everything down."

"The kijker?"

He shook his head. "I don't know what that is?"

"The looking portal. Made of gold."

"It's all gone," he growled out.

"And yet *you* managed to escape the fate of our treasures."

He shifted his weight, wrinkled his brow even as a sneer pursed his lips. "You blame me for keeping my life?"

"I blame you for not living up to your promise."

The woman stepped out. She was short, barely coming to Dorian's shoulders in height, with hair the color of the new moon and posture as perfect as any company ballerina.

"A promise is not a bargain, Mayfair," Dorian said. "I'm a private ship captain, and I privately captained my ship to my *near demise* bringing you treasures that the renegade Watchman in your homeland agreed don't belong to you. I lost fifteen men before we set sail off the coast of Orkney. This voyage has cost me everything, and you've a mind to argue against me saving myself?"

Lady Mayfair did not move so much as an eyelash.

"What do you want me to do?" he said, his tone exasperated.

"Do?" Now Lady Mayfair smiled, and it was as sharp as a barracuda's. "Why, Mr. Moskito, there is nothing for *you* to do. You have failed, and in your failure, you have cost us more than you can know. It is now in the hands of the Goddess, who controls the natural order. Yours is a debt you will have to settle with her."

The woman turned and walked back into the fog. Dorian took a step to follow, and the ground shook. The waves from low tide surged forward, the water choppy and swirling. Like an octopus rising and releasing its tentacles, tendrils of water cascaded toward an unsuspecting Dorian. Persephone cried out, but it was no use. Persephone wasn't really there.

The water reached like a claw for his legs, swirling around and pulling him down. Dorian tried to kick free, and the water responded by rising to his shoulders. It wrapped around his head, and tugged him off the shore and deep, down, into the inky black sea.

Persephone tried to follow after him, but she was frozen in place. Glued to the sand, paused in time.

The debt must be paid in full.

Persephone heard the voice from the boat. She saw the words it spoke written along the sand, scrawled by an invisible hand.

What you give comes back to you three times three.

Persephone watched the words wash away as new ones were written.

Until we are all freed, none shall be.

The laugh started low, a giggle of a child. It morphed into a throaty chuckle that spawned into a cackle. Persephone covered her ears as the voice went from one to two to twenty to a hundred. The voices rose and rose, laughing Persephone out of her mind.

▸ ▸ ▸

WHEN PERSEPHONE COULD next draw a breath, she inhaled pine. Dorian's hand was once again gripped in hers. They sat side by side on the couch in the Library for the Lost as though no time had passed.

Persephone rasped in a second, deeper breath, squeezing his hand hard. "What *the hell* was that?"

Dorian's face was whiter than freshly fallen snow. His lips trembled as he struggled to find his breath. Persephone reached over and smacked him hard on the back. He coughed a handful of water onto the floor, and Persephone rubbed his shoulder until he was able to properly breathe.

The water stank of the sea. "That was *real*?"

Dorian released her hand and wiped his mouth. "As real as it could be." He gave her a pained look. "Magic always takes its price."

"And you paid for both of us." Persephone shook her head. "You idiot. You could have just told me that you were a pirate, and not a very good one, who sunk magical items belonging to the islands. That's what happened, isn't it? And the island took your . . ."

Dorian waited for her mind to catch up to her brain. "Life," Persephone finished. "You were drowned. You're dead."

The very air Persephone had been breathing caught in her lungs. It cycled up and down as she held it in, trying to make sense of the senseless.

"You're dead and some of the items housed in the library are from your boat." Persephone rubbed hard at her brow. "Items that sank, including the telescope you had me look through? If I've got that right?"

"I failed on delivering in a bargain I made."

"With my ancestors? I'm assuming that's who that scary woman was."

He made noise. "Scary is one word for Marela Mayfair. I was hired to deliver magical items buried in Scotland. The Goddess needed them to place her roots, and the telescope was a gift to Marela from her lover. The Mayfairs could not bring their bounty over when they fled. I didn't realize there was life magic in them."

"Life magic?"

"It's how the Goddess stays connected to the souls she ferrets."

"I don't understand."

"When the witches were cast out of Scotland, they had to take the core of magic with them. The way to tether magic and spread it. The Goddess stores her magic in various ways. I lost the ones she needed."

"Couldn't she just pull the objects you lost from the sea?"

He smiled. "I asked the same question. The answer was no." He hesitated. "Maybe she never wanted to."

Persephone didn't know what to say to that. If there was a grand design to all things, or if magic like life was accidental—she did not know.

"It wasn't your fault. I saw it, the storm prevented you from making it to the island."

"That was no storm." Dorian sighed. "It was a curse."

"A curse?"

"I . . . wasn't going to deliver the items," Dorian said, with a shrug. "The magic knew, that damn storm was retribution from the Goddess. This is a Library for the Lost. As I was lost to the sea, so was my bounty. The Goddess created her library to house lost or forgotten magical items, so here they came."

"So you're what? Cursed to be their keeper?"

Dorian lifted a shoulder, let it drop. "You could say that."

She leveled him a look. "Worst librarian job ever."

Persephone stood. She had to move, had to walk. The first man she really cared for was a *dead man*. In a library. A library lost in, what, time? Space?

She stopped pacing, turned around. "You said the library is a person."

"A being."

"I heard someone on the boat." Persephone reached up and tugged at her hourglass necklace. She thought of the laughing voices. "Or many someones? I don't know."

Dorian winced, shifted his arms overhead as he stretched. "The library is legion."

"It's not biblical," Persephone said, practically spitting the words at him, tempted to stamp a foot his direction. "How are you so calm? You just told me you're a dead captive in a magical library lost in space."

"I've been all of those things for some time."

Persephone resumed her pacing, waving a hand at his blasé attitude. "What keeps you here in the library? The Goddess?" She squinted up at the ceiling. "Is that why I couldn't draw you out?"

"You do love to ask your questions."

The look she cut him had him crossing his legs.

"I can't give you all the answers you seek." Dorian sighed, his color returning to his cheeks as he shifted his chin onto his palm. "I'm here until my debt is paid, but I wouldn't say I'm a *prisoner*. I was given a choice, and I chose this."

"When did you make that call? Before or after the ocean swallowed you whole like the whale swallowed Pinocchio?"

"You're comparing me to a puppet?"

"Should I have gone with Jonah?"

"*I'm* not biblical," Dorian said with a shake of his head. "I'm no hero. I made my choice after the sea reclaimed me." He stood up and limped to the closest stack, ran a hand along the sea of spines.

She studied his leg with the limp, and looked over to the fireplace. "Dorian?"

He didn't answer right away.

She cleared her throat. "I don't know about you, but I could use a cup of your spiced chocolate. Is that possible?"

He looked over his shoulder, surprise crossing his face. "Yes," he nodded. "I think so."

Dorian waved a hand, and two mugs appeared on the table closest to him. He picked them up and brought them over. His limp was even more pronounced.

He stood waiting, and Persephone blew out a small sigh before she sat. Only then did he hand her a cup and sit as well.

They drank in silence for a few minutes, absorbing the heat of the cocoa and the kick of the caffeine. Persephone tucked a leg under her and turned to him. "Do you miss it? Your old life?"

Dorian stretched his legs out in front of him. "I miss . . . certain aspects of that life, yes."

"The ocean?" When he looked over, she smiled. "You looked fierce facing it, but also like, I don't know, thrilled at the fight? Even though the ship was going down."

"I didn't know we would go down," he said. "A relationship with the sea is unpredictable at best, that's part of the draw. She's a great seductress."

"The ocean is female, too, like the library?"

"For me she is," he said.

"Why did you do it? Steal all of those things. Was your job also seductive?"

"No. My job was a means to an end." He gave a small shake of his head. "The end it brought was not the one I intended."

"So why then?"

"Steal?"

She nodded.

"I wasn't born noble, so I made my own way. I was good at making a plan, organizing the way to get what was needed, and doing so without being noticed."

"You have to be bright to be a thief," Persephone said, unable to resist the urge to lean into him.

Dorian exhaled at the brush of her shoulder. "And terribly stupid. Tempting the Goddess was a fool's errand and I played the fool."

She nudged him with her elbow. "Is this all really so bad?"

"There is still so much you don't see. So much you can't."

"What am I missing?"

"For starters? The library," Dorian said, rapping a knuckle against the shelf, "is not made of time."

"So how am I here?" Persephone studied the stacks beside

her, ran her fingers through where the books appeared and disappeared. "Magic?" Persephone studied the back of her hand. "I can walk through worlds, so I can enter into this one?"

"Yes."

"And *what* exactly is this world?"

Dorian cleared his throat. "It is a world for the lost."

Persephone's shoulders drooped. "The real reason I can be here is because *I* am lost."

"Are you?" He slid a hand over hers. "You haven't asked the most important question yet."

"How dead am I?"

"Not as dead as me."

"Funny."

He removed his hand. "I believe you are here because the library allows you."

"*She* wants me to be here?"

"I wonder why."

Persephone studied him, and Dorian gave a small wave at the room.

"You think the library is trying to help me?"

Dorian treated her to a rare half smile.

"Why?"

"Perhaps you're the right witch at the right time."

"I don't have a use for magical items from your sunken boat, Dorian."

He waved an arm and the corridor off the east end of the room reappeared. "The library is endless. It makes and remakes itself as it sees fit, and it stores a countless collection. Some items I know and catalogue, others are hidden even from me."

Persephone studied the way his eyes traced the lines of her face, like he was trying to nudge her on. She thought of how she would like to free him, how she wished she could protect her cousins, free them all.

Free them. From the curse. *Oh*.

"Dorian, is there something specific here I need to break the curse?"

He quirked a brow, shifted his hands in front of him like he was balancing scales.

"Terrific." More vagueness for answers. "How do I find it?"

Dorian studied the floating candles, burning in a lazy manner. He snapped his fingers and the flames flared high and bright. The room glowed so fiercely Persephone wanted to shade her eyes. Dorian grinned and the candlelight doused itself out.

"As you step out onto the way," he said, his voice soft, "the way appears. Only you can access what you need."

Persephone huffed, preparing to respond, and there was a *tug* in her core. She didn't question it. Persephone reached out, and said a single word.

Meum.

Mine.

The light returned, and Persephone found herself in an unfamiliar room with a tall podium in the center. The podium was cut in the shape of a crescent moon. On it sat an aging leatherbound book with an ash tree and moon on its cover. Its pages were worn, and the color of sand. Four metal latches, rusting at the hinges, crisscrossed over its cover.

Persephone moved to it, and peered down at the inscription of a single word scrawled across the tome.

MAYFAIR

The air tasted of honey and copper, of cinnamon and nutmeg. Persephone held a hand over the book and the soft light of spirit awakened. It glowed as a soft white orb spread out into the room, illuminating the yellow of the pages.

Suddenly the book changed. The spine rotted away. On a gasp, Persephone reached out, trying to catch the pages, and they crumbled to ash.

The form shifted once more. In the place of the book sat a binder full of mismatched sheets. A stack of documents, all depicting words in various languages. Persephone's breath caught in her chest as she tried to find a word she understood.

Then, like liquid flowing down a drain, the words swirled and the pages morphed into a newly bound book with a cover of forest green and sheets as crisp as the first leaves to fall in autumn.

"How?" she asked, and her voice trailed off into an echo.

The book rose, hovered in the air.

Pages fluttered, turning rapidly one to the next. The sound amplified into the room, and Persephone covered her ears.

When the last page settled, the book shuddered. Persephone had only a moment to react before it dropped into her hands.

The weight was substantial. She shifted and the book adjusted so that it felt no heavier than a paperback.

Persephone took a deep breath, ran a shaky finger over the front cover. She tapped one finger over the refurbished iron latches . . . and they glowed green. Persephone held on tighter, and the clasp unclasped.

Someone clapped from behind her, and Persephone spun around, holding the book tightly to her chest.

"Transfiguration," Dorian said. "You are constantly full of surprises."

"Transfi-what?"

"You convinced the book to show you its true self."

"But . . ." All she did was approach it. "I don't understand."

"The reward is yours."

"Reward?"

"The grimoire in your hands."

"Grimoire?" Persephone looked down, gripped the book tighter. "It's mine." That was what she had asked for, what was hers. The library had answered the request.

"Your family grimoire." Dorian studied the book in her hands. "The collection of Mayfair history and spells, of all things lost, relating to who you are, where you come from, and where you may yet have to go."

"Mayfair."

He nodded. "Yes," he said with a smile, as she ran a hand over the spine of the book. "You are no longer unclaimed."

Persephone startled, looked at him. "I am claimed."

"Aye," Dorian looked around. "And you've conjured another room." He studied her. "The library wants to help, even if you did try to take me from it." Dorian bit back a smile as he walked toward the door. "If you'd like to stay here, I think you'll most likely find your way out, but if you prefer to come with me, I find the main room has the best lighting for reading."

Persephone shifted the book in her arms. Her heart was a steady thrum in her chest even as her palms itched to crack open the book and devour the contents. She was *claimed*. Could it be true, was it too much to hope that the answers about her family, all the things she wanted to know and never could, were finally here after all these years—or, was this another trick of magic?

She took a steady breath and one last look about the room, and followed after Dorian, who once again surprised her by taking her arm.

Dorian led Persephone down a complicated series of hallways. It was a lot of left turns, a complex opening and closing of doors. While he might think the library had shown her favor, Persephone wasn't at all sure she could find her way out of anywhere. She heaved a sigh of relief when they entered the main chamber of the library.

A new square oak table with a series of reading lamps outfitted with stained glass lampshades waited for them.

"I'd say that's the place," Dorian said, nodding at the table. He squeezed her arm once, and she sighed at the loss of heat from him when he let her go. He took his seat on the spare leather sofa, throwing a leg across the center and resting an arm along the edge.

"You aren't planning to read over my shoulder?" she asked, smiling a little at how hard he was trying to appear uninterested.

"That wouldn't be proper."

Persephone set the book down, keeping a palm on its cover. "You haven't read this already? You *are* the guardian."

"It doesn't quite work that way," Dorian said, turning over a palm and pulling a book from thin air. "I am only allowed what the library wants me to read, or allows me to read. It's rather a lot of fiction about sailing and mermaids, if I'm honest with you."

She watched as he turned the book face out. Persephone's lips twitched as she read the title. "*How to Dance Like a Rake?*"

"The lady is not without her sense of humor."

Persephone sat at the table, the book calling her forward. "Are you certain your library *is* a lady?"

"Of course," Dorian said, opening his book and turning the liner notes to find the first page. "A lady always keeps her secrets."

Persephone couldn't disagree . . . but she thought back to earlier when the library was speaking to her—if that is what it was doing inside Dorian's *Shanachie*. Something about the laugh, it had been too full—too complete to be just one voice.

What if the library was more than a single lady?

It was, she decided, a puzzle for another time. Persephone had a book to read, and she placed both hands over the grimoire and watched as the cover opened on its own accord.

Persephone rolled out her shoulders, and she began to read.

Ten

THE WITCHING HOUR

THE BOOK OF MAYFAIR started with a simple opening:

> *Only those with blood of my blood may know me*
> *Only those with eyes of my eyes may see me*
> *Only those with hearts purer than mine may read me*
> *Know this, child,*
> *There is a right path*
> *There is a wrong path*
> *Then there is the forest beyond them both*
> *The answers lie here.*

This was the only page she could read. Try as she might, Persephone couldn't turn the rest.

She pried, pushed, and whispered incantations over the edges, but the pages wouldn't budge.

Persephone tried spells and might, begging and bolstering. Just when she was prepared to throw the book at the wall, Persephone ran her fingers over the words, and something pricked her palm. She pulled her hand back, and a perfect crimson tear of blood dripped onto the page.

The opening lines faded, and the pages fluttered as if passed over by a breeze. When she tried again, this time they turned.

The book of Mayfair was full of spells.

Simple kitchen spells, spells to enchant, spells to open locked doors, and others to quell a worried mind. Spells to protect, to aid, to sway, and make an unwanted object disappear. The more pages she turned, the more spells appeared, and . . .

Spells weren't all the book contained.

There were journal pages, recordings of births and deaths, family recipes and lists, measurements and admonishments. Little love notes and poems, angry dictations and harsh curses.

There were letters from one member of the Mayfair family to another.

"There's so much," Persephone said, pausing hours *in,* after her eyes had begun to tear from reading and her neck muscles protested from the strain.

"May I?" Dorian asked, his voice a whisper's caress.

Persephone realized he hadn't spoken a single word the entire time she'd been reading. Dorian had shown her grace and kindness by leaving her the space to be.

"Please," she said, touched by his restraint. She waved him over.

Dorian stepped close, and peered over her shoulder. He asked her to turn pages and flip ahead or back. After a few exceedingly long minutes, he stepped back.

"What are you looking for, in particular?" he said, his voice a low rumble. "These are the lost pages of your ancestors. Everything written that was lost found its way here."

"And the things written that aren't lost?" Persephone asked, turning a page.

Dorian didn't respond.

She turned to look at him. "I was joking." She studied the furrow in his brow. "But your face isn't laughing." Persephone leaned back. "If there is a Library for the Lost, does that mean there is a Library for the Found?"

Dorian's lips compressed into a tight line. He looked like he was trying to say something, but couldn't get the words out.

"You can't tell me, can you?"

She waited for him to answer, knowing confirmation of any kind would be its own answer.

He smoothed out his expression. "*Logic* would certainly intimate that one may exist." Dorian offered a tight smile. "What is it you're looking for? If you're specific, the book may better be able to handle your request."

Persephone put the knowledge of the other library in her back pocket, and focused on the grimoire before her. She wanted to know everything, but everything took longer than a day, and she didn't think even she had that much time to give—regardless of how the library manipulated the ticking of the clock.

She didn't know the right question to ask—it was all too big, too daunting. "I . . . I'd like to know about my mother and grandmother, for the book to show me how to save the island, how I can help my family."

Dorian studied the book, glanced back at Persephone.

"Well then," he said. "What are you waiting for?"

Persephone shifted back in her chair. Good question. "I just ask it?"

"Won't know if you don't try."

She cleared her throat and a command, not a question, rolled off her tongue. "*Show me.*" Persephone watched the color and shape of the words she exhaled glisten like bubbles blown into the air. They fell like tears onto the pages, absorbed in an instant.

The book didn't shift pages forward or back, instead it shuffled like a typewriter trying to reset its keys. Soon pages were spit out of the book, up into the air, and dropped back into the seam, reknitting along the spine.

Persephone stared at the unfamiliar handwriting as a chill trickled down her back.

> *Dearest Persephone,*
>   *If you are reading this, I am gone and you are*
> *truly lost to us. My darling girl, were there any other*
> *way, we would walk it. To say you are loved is a*

severe understatement, and yet love is often brave but not always enough. Forgive your grandmother and me, leaving the island was the only way she knew to protect you. Giving you up was the only way I could continue to keep you safe.

Prophecies are a tricky thing, and my mother saw you coming. She saw what you would have to face and give up, and could not bear it. When the vision passed to me on the day you were born, I understood.

Love is giving up the whole world for the people you love. I gave up mine for you, and I would do it again in a heartbeat. The only way to keep you safe was to give you a fresh start. I may not have been beside you, but I have always been with you.

All my love—

Your mother,
Artemis May

A breeze stirred the page, and Persephone did not feel it. She did not move. She could not.

Tears leaked soundlessly from her eyes.

Artemis May. *Her mother.*

Persephone had been loved. The words were right there. Loved . . . but abandoned. She reread it once, twice, and tried to hear her mother's voice. To give way to a new inner narrator, but it was no use. She couldn't hear her mother's voice because she had never known it in the first place. Even with this new knowledge, Persephone felt as alone as ever, and that broke her heart.

Dorian shifted beside her, and she turned to him.

"It's a letter to me. From my mother." Her voice sounded strange to her own ears, and she cleared her throat, trying to suck back up the tears she couldn't prevent from escaping. Persephone did not understand how to heal this ache, the pain clinging to it.

"She is lost then," he said, his words soft but their meaning hard. "I am sorry, Persephone."

She nodded, picked up her grimoire, and walked across the

circular room to a small reading chair on the other side. The lighting was poor and the chair was lumpy. Dorian brought her a handkerchief that looked as old as the library. She let the tears come and watched as they soaked the book, but never made it wet.

She thought of the words her mother had written. *Love is giving up the whole world for the people you love.* She didn't know that she agreed. If you really loved someone, you found a way to stay.

When her tears had quelled enough for her to catch her breath, Persephone held a hand over the book. She thought of Moira and Hyacinth in her vision, dead beneath her feet, and shuddered.

She closed her eyes and asked: *How do I break the curse and keep them safe?*

The book quivered in her hands, and moments later the ground beneath the library shook. Dorian let out a lengthy string of words that promised he was a sailor yet, before the lights flickered and went out.

The library was silent.

Persephone gasped as the book began to glow. Pages fluttered back and forth, rustling and shuddering. Persephone heard her heart thump loudly and pressed a palm to her chest, only to realize the sound did not belong to her.

The book's heart was racing.

It shuddered again, and spit out an envelope. Persephone caught it in one hand. The paper was yellowed from age, the edges worn.

Addressed to no one, Persephone used her pinky nail to slice it open.

A handful of rose petals tumbled out, browned from time. They were followed by a few spare pages, ripped from a journal. Here was a letter the writer had known would never be sent.

> *September 20, 1958*
> *Beatrice,*
>   *This morning I left the island for the first and final time. I am sorry to go like a thief in the night, to leave you without answers.*

*The curse is not yours to break, and it is not
mine. It will be not be our daughters' but those who
come from them. I have foreseen it, and I won't let
it happen. I won't let it claim her as it claimed the
others, I see her strength*

[Persephone held the page up, trying to find the
rest of the sentence. It was as though it had been
scrubbed away, only faded markings left in the wake
of what once were words. She read on.]

*Amara and True wanted power. Now magic is
failing, the island revolts as the witch tries to cross the
boundary and bring back that which must remain
lost. It is from her I must hide the truth.*
*Beware the worlds, ward your hearth and home,
and ward yourself. Know I am with you always, and
I am sorry.*

All my love,
Viola

Viola. Her *grandmother*. She ran a finger across the name, pressing hard into the page.

Then, flipping back and forth, Persephone tried to determine
what the smudged letters could say. The pebble of unease in her
stomach had grown into a boulder of worry.

"Dorian," she said, turning to face him. "Who was Beatrice?"

He lowered his book, and stood. Dorian crossed to the shelves
and ran his hand along the spines of the books closest to him.
"Your great-aunt Beatrice. You would know Beatrice Mayfair
as Beatrice Way. She, too, changed her name. The aunts in your
family are fond of doing that."

"Oh." Persephone sat on the ground, her legs giving out. "Of
course. I keep forgetting, or perhaps choosing to forget, that Ariel
and Ellison are my family, too." She gave her head a shake. "I
don't understand the letter, or *what* my grandmother wouldn't
let happen."

Dorian, who was preternaturally still to begin with, did not blink. The only show of his emotion was how fast his chest rose and fell as he watched her.

Persephone gripped the grimoire, trying to process so much new information. "I wish I understood." She looked at him, and his eyebrow twitched.

"Dorian?" she asked, as he ran a hand over his hip.

"Hmm?"

"Do you know what she meant?"

He closed his eyes, reached up, and rubbed at the space between his brows. "I cannot say enough," he said, his words so low she barely heard them. "I can only say what is available to me." He opened and closed his mouth, looked like he was trying to say something. After a moment he threw his hands in the air like he was surrendering. Persephone thought that would be that, when his eyes widened.

He raised a brow, tilted his head, and dropped one of his hands.

A very attractive smirk crept over his wide mouth. Dorian made the remaining hand into the motion of a gun, and pointed it. Straight at her.

She looked at him, and how he trained the finger gun at her. Did he mean . . . ? She pointed to herself and raised her brows.

Dorian lips parted but no sound came out. He held the finger gun up to his mouth. The universal librarian sign for *shh*, with an edge.

Persephone's thoughts spun. Was she the thing to be protected? If so, it made a certain kind of sense why her grandmother left the island. But protected from what? The curse?

"I don't understand," she whispered, staring at the letter before her. "I thought this would tell me who I am, and now I feel more lost than before."

Dorian hesitated. He ran a hand over his face, winced, and then gave himself a nod. Dorian reached into his pocket and pulled out a pen. He brought it to her, and nodded for her to pocket it.

"You are who you have always been," he said.

She tried to smile and failed. "I know who *you* are." She looked down. "What is this for?"

"Emergencies," he said.

She slipped the pen in her pocket. She wasn't sure what emergencies a pen could fix, but if he meant for her to have it, she would gladly take it. Because Persephone might not understand the layers of her story, but she knew without a doubt, somehow in the past few weeks she had grown to trust this man.

She went to reach for him, but stalled. Her fingers fisted.

"How do I help you, Dorian?"

"You cannot," he said, failing to keep the surprise from his face. "Or rather, you help me by helping yourself."

Persephone looked around the room, heard the murmur of the voice from before urging her on. She looked back at him. Dorian believed in her. This library of extraordinary things believed in her. Her cousins, Moira and Hyacinth, believed in her. She did not understand what her grandmother's letter meant, or how to change the vision she'd had, but Persephone finally understood.

If she wanted to break the curse and save her family, it was time for her to believe in herself.

"I have to go back to my cousins," she said, and then she did the one thing she'd never dreamt she would be brave enough to do.

Persephone reached out, drew Dorian's face down to hers and brushed her lips against his.

Once.

Twice.

She let out a soft sigh, and Dorian's hand came to her waist. His grip tightened as he pulled her closer. In the brilliant candlelight of a place that existed neither here nor there, Persephone learned a new definition to the word *hungry*.

Dorian's mouth was not gentle, his touch not light, nor sweet. His was the call of a drowning man, breathing her in like she was air, like she was life. Persephone answered, her mouth claiming his as his lips sought, savored, devoured. He deepened the kiss again and again. Testing. Tasting. It was the shifting of weight, the brushing of fabric against her stomach, a moan rolling from her mouth into his, and his answer growing taut against her thigh.

Dorian backed her into the edge of the sofa, and she shifted onto the arm. Persephone wrapped her arms around his neck, fisted her hands in his hair, and slid her leg up and around him.

A bell chimed, long and low, from far off.

"*More,*" Dorian demanded, and so Persephone gave. She clung to, writhed against him, and nearly went over the edge.

The light shifted, the bell chimed again, and Dorian began to fade.

"*No,*" Persephone growled, reaching, trying to hold him to her.

The last thing Persephone saw before he and the library were lost to space and time, was the desire and promise in his eyes.

HYACINTH EVER'S JOURNAL

Ten years ago, July 15th

Her name is Stevie and she's a Sagittarius. Her blond hair is always worn down, even when the summer sun is so hot my sweat sweats. Ariel can't stop looking at her. She does everything but crawl in her lap.

At the diner Stevie gets up to go to the bathroom and Ariel stands to let her pass, making sure her fingers graze her shoulder. When they sit side by side on the lawn for the outdoor showing of Some Like It Hot, Ari's knee inches over until it presses against Stevie's. She's first to refill her soda and has read Emily Dickinson to her aloud, but it was when Ariel made her the clover crown that I stopped glaring and started seething.

My best friend is gone. A pod person has replaced the girl who counted the stars with me and laughed at my jokes until our sides hurt. This new Ariel only has time for Stevie.

And Stevie? Stevie is a moron.

"What are you doing with that spoon?" Stevie asked me, when she came out into the garden the other morning. She's staying at Ever House, and I've yet to work out the best way to get rid of her.

"It's a spade," I said, rolling my eyes because she couldn't see them. "And I'm digging. Planting in the soil."

"Oh." She sat beside me and watched. Not moving an inch when I scooted over to reach for the new bulbs, just breathing down my neck and staring like a drunken owl.

"What are you trying to grow?" she asked. "A beanstalk?"

"Yeah, that's not a thing."

"How else did Jack escape?"

I snorted. "You mean the children's story 'Jack and the Beanstalk'? That's bullshit."

"All stories have an element of truth," she said, leaning closer so I could smell her jasmine perfume.

I thought about it. "Then the element to that particular story is Jack got into magic he knew nothing about and it screwed him over."

"I thought it was that he wanted to escape," she said, biting on her lower lip.

The truth of that hit too close to home, and I squinted at my bulbs. They were not beanstalks. They couldn't take me where I wanted to go.

"Do you plan to travel?" she asked. "Or are you staying on island like Ariel?"

The shake I gave my head was so fierce it rattled my teeth. "I'll leave one day," I told her. "And I will go everywhere and see everything."

She laughed like I said something extraordinary, and bumped me with her shoulder. Then she asked me what the "tiny fork" was, and I had to explain the trowel.

And this is who Ariel has chosen over me. A girl with hair the color of straw, and the IQ of a carrot.

It's enough to drive a being to hate.

ELEVEN

THE KNOCK ON THE door came at precisely one thirteen in the afternoon. It was an ominous time in Moira's estimation, as she had never liked the number thirteen. Other witches might swear by the numerical significance as a great foretelling, but for Moira, thirteen was the age when she relinquished her virginity to a tourist with fast lips and hips who took far more than he gave. It was the number of times Moira had tried and failed to fall in love before she met the one who got away, and the number of years separating her sister from her. Having practically raised Hyacinth, and loving her in a way Moira imagined a mother loved a daughter, Moira thought this should cancel out some of the negative association she had with the power number. But the truth was Hyacinth kept *at least* thirteen secrets from Moira and none of them were good.

Moira supposed, as she thought on it, she actually associated the number thirteen most with her sister. Which might have been why when the knock fell, she knew it wasn't for her.

Still, Moira opened the door.

The woman on the other side wore the body of a girl and the

eyes of a witch. She did not smile at Moira, or adorn a pretense at all. Instead the woman peered past her inside the house.

"I'd ask to be invited in, but you'll find I don't need any invitation."

Then the stranger swept past a gaping Moira into the main room.

Moira herself had spelled the house, warding it with herbs collected on a full moon and whispered over at midnight, during the peak of her power. She'd done this three times, salting the perimeter and carefully pressing promises upon the grains. No one should be able to pass who was not of Ever blood. It was the simplest and most common spell in the book.

"Who are you?" Moira asked the stranger.

The woman crossed to the sofa and sat sniffing the air. "Jasmine," the stranger said. "The house still smells of jasmine. Get your sister, Moira Mae Ever, tell her the truth has come home."

Moira did not want to leave the woman-child she had never before seen standing in her living room, but once the command was issued she found herself compelled to walk up the stairs to the second floor and to Hyacinth's rooms. She found her sister inside, settled on her window seat, growing hyacinths from the palm of her hand. It was a trick Hyacinth had used when she was eight and didn't want to face her punishment for feeding posies to the girl who pulled her hair.

"What have you done?" Moira growled, standing in the doorway, arms pinched across her chest. "Someone, who I do not know but clearly has been here before, has walked into our home and demanded your presence."

Hyacinth blew the flowers into the air. They drifted down to the hardwood beneath her feet, the petals falling free. Hyacinth stood and reached for the hand mirror on the window seat. Moira watched the tremble take over her sister's hands. The mirror shook as she tried to hold it.

"I have done what needed to be done," she said, not meeting her sister's eyes. "The curse will be broken."

"Of course it will," Moira said, her words sharp. "We have Mayfair blood on our side, we have our Persephone. Your plan *will* work." She studied the stubbornness settling across her sister's face. "This person is *not* the plan."

Hyacinth gave her head a hard shake. "For six weeks we have trained our Mayfair witch. She can barely control her magic. You know it, I know it. Aether is the hardest of elements to control, and hers is refusing to merge with her." Hyacinth hesitated, sighed. "Plus, she's about to switch sides."

"What? What on Wile Isle do you mean, switch sides?"

"The Ways."

Moira rubbed at her forehead. "That's impossible. She would never go to them, especially not after all they've done to harm her, harm us. Hyacinth, Persephone is family. She loves us."

"It's happening." Hyacinth swallowed, but lifted her gaze to her sister's. "I knew it would, but I tried to stop the tide. I failed. We're out of time, sister."

Hyacinth moved past Moira into the hallway, glided down the stairs, and marched into the living room. She stopped a foot from the stranger. Took her measure. Then, with a deliberate coldness that made Moira's skin crawl, Hyacinth bowed her head and pasted a smile on her lips.

"May the Goddess bless you," Hyacinth said.

"And keep you well," the stranger replied.

Then Hyacinth handed the mirror over, and the woman held it up to her face. Moira could see the image reflected there.

"It's . . . it's not possible," Moira said, her words clouded with shock.

"I am many things," the stranger replied. "Possible is only one of them. Come, daughters, the clock is ticking down and we have spells to cast and worlds to save."

▸ ▸ ▸

Too soon Persephone was back on the cobblestone path. Her arms empty of Dorian, of the grimoire. Her mind overflowing. As Persephone walked, static crackled in the air around her, clinging to her hair, causing the ends to rise up. Her powers, long dormant and buried, were waking.

Aether coursed through her veins, her senses heightened. Persephone paused to take a deep breath, coughing out as she tasted the salt of the seawater and the buttery flavor of the tuna fish swimming offshore.

The tug returned, a strong yank to her midsection. Persephone turned against it, in the direction of Ever House and her cousins, only to find her feet refused to budge.

"Oh, *come on*," Persephone said, grinding the words out. "I don't have time for this."

"*Wrong way.*"

A shiver rankled up her spine at the sound of the voice. Then the voice shifted, one growing into two, and two into twenty. First the voices were a whisper against her mind, and Persephone fought it. She pressed her hands to her head, and tried to shake them away.

They grew louder.

Persephone tried to drown them out by humming. She sang the alphabet as loud as she could, but the voices would not be denied. Thinking to just ignore them, she attempted to walk away, but the island refused to let her pass. She couldn't budge a toe forward.

She let out a frustrated groan and looked up at the sky. "*Fine, I give up.*"

The voices quieted.

Persephone looked around, then down at her hands. "Who are you?"

"*We are with you always, we are the Many.*"

Persephone closed her eyes. "You're from the library."

"*We are from everywhere.*"

"*Are* you the library?"

"*No. We are the Many.*"

Persephone ran a hand over her face. Talking spirits. From the library. Terrific. Her element was technically called spirit, so Persephone supposed it could make a certain kind of sense that she would hear them, except . . . why now?

She opened her eyes. "Why are you here?"

"*We are the Many. We would never hurt you, daughter of Artemis, granddaughter to Viola. We are with you always.*"

Persephone had dealt with a lot this day, but this was too much. She turned and tried to return to the library and demand Dorian help her. Nothing happened. The tug yanked against her core. The island wanted her to follow through in another direction. It would not be denied.

She stomped her feet, knowing what little good the temper tantrum would do. If magic had shown Persephone anything, it was that to fight this would come with a price and there was a good chance she would fail.

"You win," Persephone said to the island, and to the spirits she could hear but not see. "Show me the right way to go, then."

Persephone followed the wind. It carried her to the beach, onto the sand, and unsurprisingly, to Way House.

"Of course," Persephone said. "I'm doing this now, am I? Showing up, again, all alone after what I did to Ellison. This is brilliant."

"*The locket. You are not alone.*"

"No, I'm not. I have an hourglass and a host of vague voices in my head from a mythical land no one else can travel to unless they're dead. I'm so glad to have such good company."

Persephone reached beneath the oversized shirt and felt at the hourglass talisman. She pulled it free. The locket had grown. With great care, Persephone opened the false bottom and a small ruby tumbled out.

"A stone," Persephone said, her tone wry. "I suppose I throw this at Ariel when she tries to kill me for attacking her sister."

Her power thrummed steadily through her, a combination of energy, adrenaline, and determination, and she sighed again but kept walking. Persephone walked around to the back of the house, and took the narrow stairs. She did not do so as an effort to sneak up on the women, but to show she was meeting them as family might, as equals. It was the last bit of hope she had.

By the time she reached the top of the stairs, Ariel Way stood waiting.

▸ ▸ ▸

ARIEL HAD FOUND her sister in an immovable state hours earlier, and her own rage had threatened to consume her. But as soon
as she called for Ellison, had reached out and shaken her, Ellison
coughed herself back to life. Ellison was frozen, not dead, and it
was the first time Ariel had ever seen the particular spell performed.
Calling the Veil was not a simple casting—only an extremely powerful witch could pull such magic off. Ariel had only heard of one
other being able to achieve its results. Amara Mayfair. It was Calling the Veil that had frozen the witches away in the hinterland.
Ariel should know; she and Hyacinth had both tried and failed.

When Ariel and Hyacinth attempted to perform the spell,
Stevie got caught in the cross fire. She was frozen for one day. In
the Arch. Where she had followed Ariel and Hyacinth without
their knowing. When they were finally able to undo the magic,
Stevie was altered.

She was also infatuated with Hyacinth, and Hyacinth did not
turn her away.

To say Ariel disliked the particular spell was a *severe* understatement. If it were a bug, she'd pull its wings and head from its
body and grind the leftover for good measure.

Now Persephone stood in front of Ariel, one of Hyacinth's
minions, with power rolling off her in waves so strong Ariel had
to force herself steady.

"Why are you here?" Ariel asked.

Persephone didn't speak; she only held her palm up, offering
the ruby sitting in her hand.

Ariel's eyes were as quick as lightning, looking from Persephone's face to her hand and back again.

Persephone tossed the stone into the air, and Ariel caught it
with ease. A green light flashed out between the two witches.

"I believe this must belong to you," Persephone said.

▸ ▸ ▸

SHE HADN'T ACTUALLY planned to throw the stone at the
witch, but it had grown hot in her hand at the sight of Ariel. So
Persephone followed her gut instinct and offered it.

Ariel whispered a word Persephone could not hear. The light faded and she studied Persephone with curiosity.

"Why would you bring me this?"

Truth or lie. Hyacinth had said witches could not lie to one another, but Persephone had learned that to be untrue. Persephone thought perhaps witches *should* not lie to one another, that to do so would be a mark of disrespect. She could only keep to her instincts for the choice she made next.

"It came to me within the past hour, and I thought it would be a good start in asking for a truce."

Ariel snorted. "What sort of fool are you, or do you take me for one?"

Persephone arched a brow in response. "You're my family."

"And yet you came to Wile and instead of seeking us, you sought the Evers."

"I wasn't aware of who you were when I arrived." Persephone clasped her hands together, hoping she looked more confident than she felt. "Up until two months ago, I didn't know who my family was, let alone that there was a curse or a feud. Hyacinth sought me out. I came to help, and once here all I have done is try to help break the curse."

A throat cleared as a shadow moved into sight. Persephone's gaze lifted to meet the steel blue eyes of Ellison Way.

"She knows nothing, Ariel. I told you."

"I'm sorry—" Persephone was cut off mid-sentence.

"There will be time enough for apologies," Ellison said with a no-nonsense wave of her hand. "Come inside, for the day grows short and the shadows linger. There is much you don't know Persephone May, and I fear much we all must learn before the Goddess is done with each of us."

Ellison plucked the stone from her sister's hand and went inside.

Ariel leaned in, her eyes on the locket hidden beneath Persephone's shirt. "Don't think I don't see you," she said, before she stepped around Persephone and walked inside.

Persephone checked her chest, and shook her head. They hadn't attacked, had instead invited her in. Maybe there was cause for hope yet.

She studied the silhouettes of the two sisters just inside the door. Warriors, both of them, queens in their own right. She wondered what that would make her, thought of Hyacinth and Moira, and hoped they would forgive her for crossing this line. Then, taking a deep breath, Persephone took one step, then another, opened the door, and walked inside.

▸ ▸ ▸

IF HYACINTH AND Moira's house was an example of cleanliness and order—even with a fair amount of magical clutter—this house was its polar opposite. It reminded Persephone of the expression "coloring outside of the lines," because everything was just this side of haphazard. A rug with a corner turned in, a bright purple wall with the brushstrokes sloppily pushing into the white edges of the connecting wall.

The sink she passed in the shotgun kitchen was full of dishes, and the counter smudged with crumbs. The living area was a sea of color. Purple sofa, bright jade sitting chairs, navy blue footstools. A wood-burning stove stood in the center of the room, on it a small black bowl sat with pink smoke fuming from its open mouth. In the corner was a large triangle bookshelf, with assorted tools stacked upon it, and a huge chunk of black obsidian sitting on the top shelf. Above it was a woven tapestry depicting the Theban alphabet. The ceiling was a maze of wooden beams, cut into intricate shapes that reminded Persephone of lace. The floors were a dark hardwood, and not one wall in the entire downstairs matched another.

Somehow though, it worked. The lingering smell of sage and hearth fire, the candles burning in almost every corner—the touches felt homey, inviting. There was a pillow on the sofa with cross-stitching that read: *Witch, Please*, and a sign over the hearth that announced: *I am never frightened, not even in the darkest forest, for I know that I am the darkest thing there.*

There was humor and heart here, and it struck Persephone that both were harder to come by in Ever House. For all its charms, Ever House felt like it had a mission. This house was simply a home.

"Sit," Ariel said, standing before the small pot wafting the faintly pink smoke. "You're making the house nervous."

"Does the house . . . feel things?" Persephone asked, sitting down on the jade chair and immediately falling back into a deep cushion. She struggled to sit upright while Ariel rolled her eyes.

"Yes, it's extremely sensitive to lethargy and assholery." Ariel crossed her legs. "No. I meant it as a figure of speech. The *ironic* figure."

Ellison sat in the opposite chair, her back as straight as her long blond hair. She shifted a little and Ariel tracked the movement. "I'm fine," Ellison told her sister. "Stop fretting."

"I am sorry," Persephone said, biting off the apology when Ariel growled out a sound.

"Did you mean to do it?" Ellison asked, picking up a mug from the table, and taking a small sip. "The binding spell?"

"A *binding* spell?" Persephone shook her head. Dorian had accused her of trying to split the worlds apart, not bind someone.

She thought back, and recalled what came after the attack on Ellison. When Persephone had tried to leave the island after she was unable to call Dorian to her. Was *that* what he meant by splitting the world apart?

The two witches were waiting, and Persephone tried to focus. "No, I just wanted you to stop. I thought you were . . ."

"Trying to kill you?"

Persephone shrugged a shoulder and Dorian's shirt slipped. She tugged it in place and Ellison set the cup down.

"That's an eighteenth-century man's work shirt, it looks authentic."

"Ellison is a history buff as well as a writer," Ariel said. "The writing runs in our family."

There was a long silence, the kind that dares, and Persephone wished she had her own cup of something to sip on. From the kitchen a cup clattered and Ariel turned toward the sound.

"Tea or coffee?" Ariel asked.

"What?"

"Your aura," Ellison said. "The house can't help but read you."

"Oh," Persephone blinked. "So it's not completely ironic then."

Ellison bit back a smile, while Ariel issued another low snarl.

"Tea, please," Persephone said.

"Chamomile, I'd wager," Ellison said, looking her over. "Caffeine will only increase your adrenaline and right now I'd say you're running at about ninety percent."

"It's . . ." Persephone brushed her hair behind her ear. "Been an interesting day."

Ariel walked into the kitchen and returned a few minutes later with a small silver teacup full of freshly steeped chamomile.

"It's not poisoned, is it?"

"I wouldn't need to trick you to end you," Ariel said, with a devilish smile.

Persephone barely refrained from rolling her eyes, but drank. Ellison was right; the herbs blunted the edges of Persephone's adrenaline even as they sharpened her senses.

"Why do witches always know what someone else needs in their tea?" Persephone asked, thinking of Moira and Hyacinth.

"We were trained," Ariel said. "Our mothers by their grandmothers, and us by them. It's part of our heritage—reading other witches, charming our homes to protect us and occasionally help us."

"You've known who I am since we met on the boat," Persephone said. "Haven't you?"

Ariel nodded while Ellison reached down for a floorboard, shifting it back to reveal a hidden compartment. From it, she pulled out a photo album. "You look like your gran."

Persephone's hand flew to her mouth as she took in the photo album. A hundred questions danced up to the tip of her tongue, and she took another sip of the tea to quiet them. Persephone might not yet be able to read every witch, but Ellison's expression was one Persephone could read with ease—it implored silence.

"When she left," Ellison said, "the images in the photos leapt into flames. Burnt themselves out from the pages or frames. The island tends to try and erase what is no longer here. Your grandmother turned her back on it and us, even if she had her reasons to leave. So what used to be an indulgent collection of photos, particularly considering the era, was reduced to one simple photograph."

"Our grandmother," Ariel said from where she paced in front of the fireplace like an impatient cat, "said your grandmother was doing her best to protect us, but she took something she should not have."

"What?"

"Your mother and you."

Just as Dorian thought.

If Persephone had had any question of her lineage, of her family truly being who her cousins and the library promised her they were, the picture would have been enough to squelch any remaining concern. The women in the photo were in their twenties, younger than the witches in the room today. One looked a good deal like Ellison, with long blond hair and overarching eyebrows. The woman happened to also have Ariel's determined eyes. The other woman had the shape of Persephone's face, her dark eyes and lashes. It was similar to the photo from the library, but in that picture Persephone's grandmother had been looking away, her face devoid of emotion. Here she was a prettier version of Persephone, the photo capturing her mid-laugh, her grandmother's eyes sparkling like they knew all the secrets in the world and were only too happy to keep them. The ladies were pressed close together, their arms entwined. It was easy to identify them as sisters, easier yet to see they were the best of friends.

"I've been seeking information about my family my whole life," Persephone said, and wondered what her grandmother would think if their situations were reversed and she was looking at a photo of her granddaughter. "You could have shown me this before, you know."

"You came to the island to seek Ever House," Ariel said. "I

asked if you knew where you were going that day on the boat when you arrived, and do you recall what you told me?"

Persephone thought back. To the first time she smelled the shore, saw the large oaks and the swaying lanterns along the dock. To the woman whose beauty had intimidated her, and whose rude reaction left a strong impression.

"I said that I was here to see a friend."

"A friend." Ariel spat the word out. "You chose the Evers and their path over ours, and then you attacked us." Ariel leveled Persephone a look that made her toes curl.

"I never attacked you."

"No," Ellison sighs, reaching over to squeeze her sister's hand. "That would be Hyacinth. Ari, you know where the blame lies."

The tiny witch only crossed to the window and stared out it.

"*Hyacinth*?" Persephone asked. They thought Hyacinth *attacked* them? "You're mistaken. She couldn't have, and wouldn't have done that."

"She has done worse," Ariel said, crossing her arms over her chest.

"Is this . . . ?" Persephone tucked her hair behind her ear. "Is this about the girl who came between you?"

"Stevie is just a small section of the footnote in why Hyacinth is evil," Ariel said, her cheeks flushing and her jaw clenching tight.

Persephone stared at Ariel, and had a sudden flashback to the memory she pulled from Hyacinth. Of Ariel and the postmistress, and how Laurel had looked at Ariel with an expression of fascination and something deeper.

Ariel stalked from window to window like a panther seeking its prey, and Persephone sighed.

"I'm sorry," Persephone said, because she knew well that at the root of strong anger rested hurt or fear, and that only Ariel could shift those emotions away.

"You don't need to be sorry," Ariel said, cutting her another look. "You should, however, be careful. Unless you're a moron. You may prove to be a moron."

"*Ari,*" Ellison said, admonishing her sister. She flashed an apologetic look at Persephone and pulled her long locks back into a ponytail. "What do you know of the curse of Wile Isle and the land beyond the veil?"

"The curse?" Persephone shifted in her seat, not thrilled with Ariel's low opinion of her being given so freely. "Quite a lot, seeing as how I'm here to break it." She cleared her throat. "Amara and True Mayfair caused it. Hyacinth and Moira filled me in on everything, and explained why Hyacinth went looking for me. That I am the key, prophesied to break the curse." She glared in Ariel's direction. "They also explained how you didn't want the curse broken."

Ariel stopped and turned. Persephone bared her teeth, and Ariel's lips quirked into a surprisingly charming smile before she sighed. She crossed to the other side of the room and blew into the wick of a long black candle, bringing the flame to life. "Obsidian base," she said, tapping the candle. "It will keep the negativity from the room, help block those nosy witches from trying to listen in, should they realize you're here."

"I can't imagine they would, or that Hyacinth would ever attack you," Persephone said, feeling like years had passed in one day instead of minutes.

"Then you *would* be a fool," said Ariel.

"And *you* would be a broken record."

Ellison bit off a laugh and Ariel rolled her eyes.

"They are craftier than you can imagine," Ellison said. "We trusted them once, and carry the scars for it."

Ellison didn't offer more, and seeing the sadness veil over her face, Persephone rubbed a hand across her eyes.

"You're being haunted, which I think you know," Ariel said, as though she were discussing the weather. "But we'll get to that in a moment."

"Wait, what?"

"Prophecies are usually self-fulfilling," Ariel said, waving a hand as she talked over Persephone. "You believe it to be so, you will work to make it so. In this case, I'm not against you working toward breaking the curse, if you really mean to break it and not further complicate things. *That's* what we are against."

"I'm sorry, did you say *haunted*?"

"Yes."

"But—"

Oh. Right.

The Many.

Ariel pursed her lips and Ellison gave Persephone a sympathetic nod.

Before Persephone could say another word the air in the room thickened. The pink vapor in the cauldron that sat by the fireplace grew from a gentle, soothing waft into a wall of thick smoke.

"The alarm," Ariel said before she muttered a curse, jumped up, and ran from the room. She was a smear of dark eyes and hair against the pink smoke. Persephone coughed, waved a hand in front of her face, but it was no use—she couldn't clear the air.

"There is wickedness on the island," Ellison said, her voice quiet but close. "That warning alarm was set before we were born. Something that should have remained lost has returned." Ellison began to murmur softly, a gentle incantation that swelled into the room:

> *"Goddess above me,*
> *goddess below me,*
> *goddess all around me.*
> *Cleanse the air and protect us well,*
> *as I will so mote it be."*

The smoke receded. Persephone watched Ellison's hands as they wove through the air, like they were plucking back each plume and returning it from whence it came.

"You're manipulating space," Persephone said, her eyes still watering.

"Yes," Ellison nodded. "That's one of my gifts."

Persephone gaped at her. "Your element is aether?"

"Of course."

"I can walk through worlds, manipulate space as well."

From the attic came a great crash. Persephone jumped, and looked over to find Ellison's hands, which seconds earlier had moved as if possessed by a dervish, hovered in the air.

"You're a walker?" Ellison asked, her brows drawn up.

"Yes, that's what . . ." Persephone paused, thought of Dorian. "My friend called it, yes."

"Moira and Hyacinth know this?"

Persephone nodded.

"Ah."

The next moment, Ariel returned downstairs. "I've reset the wards," Ariel said. In her arms she carried an object covered in a blanket. Ariel's face was so serene Persephone almost missed the fierceness banked in her eyes. Persephone was still not accustomed to holding eye contact, and the gleam in Ariel's had her back stiffening.

"You walk in worlds?" Ariel asked, her tone as sweet as freshly spun cotton candy.

"Yes."

"You walk in worlds, my sister weaves space at her will, and I can reach *into* certain spaces."

Ariel pulled back the sheet with a flourish, revealing the miniature man. Persephone's eyes grew as round as two full moons.

"*Oh.* Where did you get him?" Persephone asked, forgetting herself, forgetting her desire to stay still and centered, and crossing to snatch the mechanical man from Ariel's hands. He was two feet of metal, wires, and bore an unmistakable likeness to Dorian.

Persephone did not see the look that passed between the two sisters.

"He looks so much like him," Persephone said, a sense of longing rising from deep within her.

"Who?" Ellison asked, her voice as soft as a rose's petal.

"Dorian," Persephone said, the words loosened from her tongue and the green eyes of the mechanical man whirred to life.

The voices chorused out of Persephone.

"*We are the Many. We are here to guide. What way? We may.*"

The room spun once, twice. Ariel threw the sheet over the creature. Persephone put a hand out, and Ellison caught it, just before Persephone fainted face-first onto the couch.

> ▸ ▸ ▸

THE SOUND OF rain brought Persephone's eyes fluttering. She opened them to find the two witches seated with her on the sofa. Persephone lay with her head against Ellison's lap, her feet in Ariel's. Ellison had one palm on the crown of Persephone's head, and the other tucked into her sister's hand, while Ariel's free hand firmly cradled the heel of Persephone's foot.

"As I said earlier," Ariel murmured, giving her foot a gentle squeeze. "You are haunted."

"And the miniature Dorian?" Persephone asked, an illogical urge to protect it rising in her as she searched for it.

"He's a mechanical beastie, not a person," Ariel said. "I can manipulate space by creating a type of mental door between worlds. The doll spoke your name to me once. I needed to test and see if the doll is tethered to you. It is, but it's not what's haunting you." She nodded to the doll resting on a chair, and Persephone's shoulders relaxed. "The doll was the trigger for those that are."

"We are the Many," Ellison said, tapping Persephone's temple. "You spoke to us, and that is what you said, but you were not the one in charge of the words you spoke. *Many* indeed."

Persephone tried to tuck her feet in and sit up, but Ariel's strong hands held her in place.

"We can't break connection yet," Ariel said, her tone not quite apologetic. "We need to know if they're trying to hurt you."

"They aren't," Persephone said, unable to stop the possessive tone creeping into her voice.

"You've been lonely," Ellison said, running her palm in a soft caress over Persephone's hair. "Of course. You're protective of them, like you're protective of Moira and Hyacinth."

"Moira and Hyacinth are my family."

"They're relatively horrible people who share a few lines of coding in your DNA," Ariel said, before tapping Persephone's ankle. "We cannot find the exact source of the haunting, but it's got to be connected to Hyacinth."

"That's insane," Persephone said.

"Each time we have met, we have been attacked," Ariel said, counting off on her fingers. "Lightning, green energy, storms, and natural disasters."

"I . . ."

"Disagree?"

Persephone shook her head.

"I know only one witch with the type of power used to manipulate the natural world like that, and you've been staying with her."

"Hyacinth wouldn't want me harmed. I don't believe that." Persephone bit the inside of her cheek. "And she's not that powerful, you know. I've watched her struggle with her magic."

"Maybe Moira is assisting her."

"But why?"

"Best guess is she's using you."

"I need to get to Ever House," Persephone said, shaking the witches off.

"That's a good idea," Ellison said, releasing her, and surprising Persephone.

"You *want* to go there?"

"Our home has been rattling the windows. If we do not go to the Ever witches, they will come to us." Ellison closed her eyes, and said an incantation that sounded like a spoken lullaby.

Ariel stood up and Persephone followed suit. She tested her balance, found she was steady and the Many were silent.

"We don't know what we will face at Ever House." She turned to Persephone. "How adept are you with your new powers?"

"I've . . ." Persephone's head spun at the worry in Ariel's voice and the dread in her eyes. Could what the Way witches said be true about Hyacinth?

Or were *they* playing her?

She reached for the connection to the island, and found it secure. She was meant to be here, with the Ways. But did that mean she was safe with them? She took a steadying breath. "I've been working with Moira and Hyacinth for six weeks. I know how to protect myself."

Ariel flashed her teeth. "Do you, cousin?"

In the next moment, a bright spear of green exploded from Ariel, slamming Persephone against the wall. The air worked alongside Ariel, lifting Persephone and pinning her to the ceiling. The pretty lace design dug into Persephone's spine.

"Stop me," Ariel said, her voice bored. "If you can."

Persephone tried to lift her hands and force aether within them, but couldn't move. She worked her shoulders back and forth. Struggling only made it worse. Invisible binds tightened against her skin. Persephone couldn't move her hands, couldn't open her mouth to call a spell. All she could do was stare.

A seductive whisper slid through her mind. *We are the Many. We support you.*

Persephone blinked, and the room splintered into sections.

Light refracted as though through a prism. Persephone could see shadows breathing and moving along the floor. She could locate the shift in the room where one reality would lead to the next. Persephone could, if she chose, she realized, walk out of this time into another.

Persephone closed her eyes and focused on her breathing, on finding the next breath and the next moment as Moira had taught her.

Persephone couldn't move, but she could outlast Ariel.

She smiled down at her cousin, and the room's heat warmed. Ariel's arms trembled, shook. They grew heavy, her breathing ragged on the exhale.

The voices of the Many whispered against Persephone's mind.

Persephone turned inward, to a vision of a rolling sea and green cliffs. Of a land with white flowers and sunlight that made the dew sparkle. She found the answer waiting there.

Persephone opened her mouth and said, "Más é do thoil é."

Please. If it is your will.

The power seeped from Ariel and traveled along the prismed path up to where Persephone floated. Like petals of an iris opening after the rain, the power unfurled. She absorbed every single drop. Then, as Ariel crumpled to the floor, Persephone turned it around and threw it back to her.

Instead of breaking Ariel, she refilled the drained well of her cousin's reserve. As Persephone returned the magic, she released herself from her pinned prison against the ceiling and glided to the floor. Persephone's feet brushed the hardwood as they settled, her hair wafted back from her shoulders. Her cheeks flushed and her lips curved.

"Sweet Goddess," Ellison said, from where she stood in the corner. "I've never seen anyone siphon that much power at once."

Ariel, who was pulling herself together with jerky, agitated motions, rolled out her shoulders and dusted off her skirt. Ariel's skin had an extra shine to it. Her dark eyes and hair seemed a shade deeper, and the freckles across her own nose stood out like stars in a country night's sky.

"You drained me," Ariel said, two irritated lines bracketing between her brows. "Then you gave me *more* back?"

"It seemed the polite thing to do," Persephone said, biting back on a laugh fueled by power.

"I'm glad you find this funny," Ariel said, her eyes bright. "I wonder if you'll be laughing when you pay the price for that magic, for no theft of power is ever obtained without cost."

A ribbon of static skidded through the room. Persephone rubbed at a chill on her arms. Ariel's smile was smug, and Persephone felt a jolt of power tug at her middle.

"I've already paid," Persephone said, thinking of the losses she'd suffered so far.

"You only think you have," Ariel said, shaking her head. "Let's hope the Goddess doesn't test your good fortune."

With that she turned and marched out of the house, leaving Ellison and Persephone behind.

TWELVE

Ellison waited a moment before turning to Persephone. "Ariel loves a dramatic exit."

"As if all of this hasn't been dramatic enough," Persephone said, earning a nod in agreement from Ellison.

They went outside and met Ariel by the side of the house. "It will be faster to travel to Ever House on wheels," she said, of the wind-protected golf cart she stood beside. "I'd suggest broomsticks, but I can't guarantee I won't knock you off yours."

"Ha ha," Persephone said, while mentally preparing to block the witch should she try.

Ariel eyed the mechanical man on Persephone's hip. Persephone couldn't leave him behind, he even smelled like Dorian somehow, of pine and books.

"He's not a baby, cousin," Ariel said, her brow furrowing.

"Neither are you and yet you keep trying to prove me wrong," Persephone snapped.

Ariel surprised Persephone by offering a real grin before climbing into the driver's seat. "Snippy witches and their mechanical men ride in the back," Ariel said, before starting the cart and spinning it in a U-turn. "Whoever your Dorian is, I hope you've better luck than I when it comes to matters of the heart."

Persephone and Ellison climbed in. As they continued up the road, the grass around them deepened its shade from shamrock to olive to hunter green.

If it weren't for the way the shadows grew as they traveled up the path, Persephone would have found the ride almost idyllic.

"What are the smudges along the ground?" she asked. The wind swept up, swatting at them from both sides, causing the cart to sway. Persephone tightened her grip on the side of the white pleather seat. "And how can you choose not to follow the wind when it's stalking you?"

"That isn't the wind," Ellison said, one hand forcing her long blond tresses in place as they tried to whip free. "That is shady magic. Shadow magic. It clung to you when we first met, but now that you're free of it, it's revealing itself. It's an old magic and can't mean anything good."

There was a scent of grease in the air, oil and thyme, and something earthier, more pungent. Ever House appeared over the hill, and a dark presence edged along the ground.

"It's neither born of the light or the dark, but something in between." Ellison said, and reached back and took Persephone's hand. She dropped the ruby in it and offered a smile Mona Lisa would envy. "Our family stone, to give you strength."

"Stones," Persephone said, holding the mechanical man tighter, "are just what I always wanted."

When they crested the hill, power pulsed over them. Ariel stopped the cart, reached out, and pushed at the invisible field. "Fucking Hyacinth. She can't help but make everything harder." Ariel pulled off the road and got out. "The cart won't go beyond this point. We're meant to go on foot so they can watch us arrive. Like they're generals and we're plebeians in a war against the crown."

Ariel stalked forward. Ellison serenely followed, and Persephone peered into the growing mist surrounding the house, desperately hoping this was all a misunderstanding. She tried to carry the doll through the mist, and was pressed back. She set the mechanical version of Dorian in the cart, patting his cheek once before she left him behind.

Persephone thought of the letter her grandmother had written to her sister, of how she said it was up to them to break the curse, and how the curse would not be broken while they remained divided. Her grandmother had meant by evil, but Persephone thought maybe there was more to it. They were dividing each other, and wasn't that a powerful sort of wickedness?

When they reached the lawn to Ever House, the mist cleared.

Moira sat on the porch, tea in one hand, a book in the other. She offered Persephone a quiet look of reproach. "You trust too easily, little one."

"And you've been reading the same passage for ten years, Moira," Ellison cut in. "We're all who we are . . ." She lifted a hand and snapped an invisible thread. A shriek came from inside the house. "Well, most of us."

Moira set the book down and held out a hand. "Come, Persephone. You're on the wrong side of this divide. I don't know what spells they've been weaving to trick you to their side, but we are your family. Haven't we proven that?"

The hurt in her voice gave Persephone a pang. "I didn't choose them over you," Persephone said, taking a step forward. "I went to them for answers, but that was never apart from you or Hyacinth." She held up her hands as though they were white flags. "I was wrong before, they weren't trying to hurt me."

The screen door slammed as Hyacinth stalked outside, rubbing the back of her head. Hyacinth glared daggers at Ellison, but refused to even glance to the space where Ariel stood.

"They lie," she said to Moira. She turned to Persephone. "You can't trust them, Persephone. We *are* your family. Everything I've done is to show and prove that to you."

Persephone stared at her cousin in frustration. "They think you're behind the attacks. Did you attack them? Did you attack me?"

Moira gaped at her sister, while Hyacinth shook her head. "It's not what you think—I was *protecting* you."

"Hyacinth," Moira said, groaning. She stared at her sister like she'd sprouted a second head. "You didn't."

"Of course I did," Hyacinth snapped. "I am trying to save the island and protect Persephone. *They* couldn't be bothered to help us, and I knew they'd screw everything up if I didn't keep them away from her."

The air around them shimmered and black oil bubbled up from the side garden. Persephone gaped as the little gnome was turned onto his side and rolled down into the muck.

"Control yourself," Ariel said, her voice thick.

"That's not me," Hyacinth said, her eyes following the oil as it slicked through the garden.

"Sure it's not," Ariel said, her eyes steady on the front door. "Our barrier was broken—the one our grandmother set fifty years ago to alert us to returning evil. How did you do it, and how many creative ways do I get to kick your ass before you send whatever you called back?"

"Did you hear something?" Hyacinth asked Moira, cocking a hand on her hip. "It sounded vaguely like buzzing from an infected beehive. I hate when good creatures go bad, but I think I might need to put this one out of its misery."

"Try me," Ariel said, stepping forward. She bared her teeth and Ellison put an arm out, holding her back.

Persephone watched, her brows knitting together. Ellison saw her, and asked, "Don't you feel it?" She left her sister and walked to the edge of the steps. For ten long seconds Ellison stared up into the trees.

Hyacinth glared at the witch. "Don't even think about—"

Ariel flipped Hyacinth off. She ignored the outraged look on Hyacinth's face and the wary one on Moira's. "Do it," she told her sister.

Ellison raised her palms to the sky, and let her fingers dance. It looked to Persephone as though Ellison was playing imaginary notes on a piano across the air.

The house groaned and the mist pressed back in. A line of sweat broke out along Ellison's brow. Ariel raised her own hands, sending waves of energy toward where her sister stood. A crack reverberated through the air, settling into the ground and splintering it along the edge of the path.

Persephone gasped in wonder, the aether in her humming to life beneath her veins.

Space was being rewoven. A barren tree broke out in blooms, the sun shifted its position in the sky over the home, and the grass beneath their feet bent forward against an unseen wind. The natural order of Ever House was out of sync and Ellison was revealing what should be and what was hidden.

"That's enough," Hyacinth said, her teeth gnashed together.

"Is it?" Ariel asked, even as her arms trembled in support of her sister.

Ellison turned her face to Moira's. The witch had yet to voice an objection, and Persephone realized whatever was hidden inside, Moira did not want it there.

That was what made her do it. The need to protect Moira, to help. Persephone lifted her own palm and a shot of aether streamed out. It floated down like a sea of shooting stars, raining onto Ellison.

"You *can* control your magic," Hyacinth said, a victorious look passing over her face.

"Unlike some people," Ariel said to Hyacinth, her brow furrowed in concentration, a line of sweat trickling down her cheek.

The ground shook once more and the door to Ever House flew open. A shadow jerked into sight, before it was dragged onto the porch.

Persephone waited, but no one followed. A lone shadow stood, wringing its hands and tapping from foot to foot.

"That's *enough*," Hyacinth said, her eyes on Persephone's face.

"You brought a shadow creature into this world?" Ariel asked, her voice full of outrage as she stared at Hyacinth. "After what happened with Stevie last time, you still tried to trick the Goddess. *That's* what's been following Persephone?"

Hyacinth shook her head, but a sharp pain pinged in Persephone's chest. She was lying. It was all wrong, the shadow and Hyacinth's anger. Moira's face was grave, and Persephone rocked back onto her heels, rooting herself in the earth.

Ellison dipped her hands and Moira gave the slightest nod. Persephone raised her own, pouring power into her cousin. Ellison tugged down, like she was towing the stars from the sky, and a crooked form of a being fought its way out onto the porch. The limbs were agitated, the body moving out of sync with itself. When the light hit the face, Persephone swallowed a gasp and dropped her arm.

"I haven't been following anyone," the voice of the being said as it lulled from side to side. "I am protecting. You think Hyacinth could magic such forces of nature on her own? Hyacinth needed a siphon, and I am more powerful than you could ever hope to be. You should know that, Ariel Way."

"Oh dear Goddess," Persephone said, one hand flying to her throat. "Deandra?"

Deandra Bishop stood on the porch, refusing to look up. Her head was bent and cocked to the side, her arms rigid against her angled torso. The shadow cowered, separated from the girl.

"Hello, *Persephone*," Deandra said, her voice a broken whisper. "Do you know?"

"Know?" Persephone asked, her stomach flipping over as she watched the woman move.

Deandra turned her head back and forth, up and down, like a bobblehead nodding on a rotation. It was like watching the earth try to spin off its axis, and Persephone swallowed bile.

"What the hell you are," Deandra said, her mouth tilting up at one side.

Persephone's knees shook.

"That's not whoever you think it is," Ariel said, her face going pale.

"Oh, Ari, you're still just as dull as always." Deandra put her hands to both sides of her head and held it steady. "If you could keep those guard dogs from attacking, maybe I'll give you a kiss for old times' sake."

Ariel swayed where she stood and Ellison rushed to her side.

Deandra showed her teeth, and the poem Larkin had written one month ago rose up inside Persephone. The voice of the Many urged her in a fevered whisper, "*Swish, swish, a siren's wish.*"

Deandra gave a slow blink, one eye and then the other. Her lips tried to stretch into a smile, but the corners turned down.

Hyacinth watched, the first glimmer of concern flickering to life in her eyes.

Persephone pressed her fingernails into her palms to keep the panic and terror at bay. She had to do something. She crossed to the base of the stairs.

"Look at me, Deandra Bishop." Persephone cleared the tremor from her voice. "By your name, I call you to *look at me.*"

Deandra only rolled her head from side to side. "You're getting in my *way*, Persephone." She tilted her head forward at an angle, looked Persephone from top to bottom. "Hyacinth thinks you're the key. You shouldn't have gone to the Ways. They won't help you. They *can't* help you. You're not like them. You know what you are, you're *just like me.*"

"I am nothing like whatever you are," Persephone said, a wave of revulsion rising through her at the evil glee on the woman's face.

"Let's play a game," Deandra taunted. "Will you catch me or let me fall?"

The air cackled with static once more, and Deandra's form took flight. She rocketed up into the air, higher and higher until she was a dot in the sky. Then, with an unnatural speed, Deandra's body torpedoed back down to earth.

Persephone did not think. She saw the flying form of the woman who had stood beside her at the coffee counter with a bad attitude and a quick mind, and held her hands up as though in surrender. Power shot from her to the body as it tumbled from the sky.

Deandra's body didn't summersault, nor did it bounce.

It floated to the ground and hit with enough force to make Hyacinth wince, but not enough to seriously hurt Deandra. Then she rolled to her side and grinned up at Persephone.

"I see you," Deandra said.

Persephone took a step back. Shook her head as if to clear what she was seeing, and then stepped forward to peer closer.

Deandra's eyes were *wrong*.

Shadows along her face reflected in places where the nose was not, shading beneath cheekbones that didn't exist. The face was trying to map out its own lines in the light, but it couldn't because the face the body wore did not belong there.

Persephone could see the soul inside the body. How it was iniquitous. How it most definitely *did not* belong to Deandra Bishop.

"Who are you?" Persephone asked, her power crackling along her spine.

"Oh, she's figured it out," Deandra said, looking back to Hyacinth. "She's quicker than you."

Hyacinth gave a strangled cry. To Persephone, the woman gave a half bow from where she crouched against the earth.

"You thought you were the sad lost girl, didn't you? Scared to look anyone in the eye, to make true contact. Never really seeing what's there, never really seeing who isn't." Deandra laughed, and her voice dipped and changed. "Everything's been in front of your face, and you've been too stupid to know it." Her laugh was a blade, and it sliced at Persephone. "The eyes are the windows to the soul, and you were granted a gift to see the truth. *You looked away.*"

The witch wearing Deandra's face slowly rolled herself up into a standing position. Her body remained twisted, the arms not quite working in accordance with the shoulders or the hands.

Persephone couldn't take her eyes off her.

Deandra stepped to the gently shaking form of Persephone and ran a finger down her cheek. "I'll taste you all by the time I'm through."

The darkness that rolled off Deandra swirled around Persephone, cocooning the two of them together inside it. Ariel

rushed forward, but a tidal wave of power threw her back. Ellison and Moira aimed their magic at the maelstrom enveloping
Penelope and Deandra, and it ricocheted. The three witches were
thrown beyond the boundaries of the yard for their efforts. Only
Hyacinth stood unaffected, watching, frozen to her spot on the
porch.

Inside the storm the witch's eyes changed back into her own.

"Amara Mayfair," Persephone breathed the name, as recognition hit. Who else could the witch be?

The witch raised a brow. "You think you're clever but your
blood is tainted." She inhaled, craning forward. "The library has
granted you favor, and in return you've stolen from it. They're
whispering behind the walls, telling you what to do. You let
them out, but it won't matter. You can't set them free. You can't
free anyone." Her cruel mouth curved. "Didn't you wonder
what happened to your grandmother and mother? How the two
women who sacrificed everything for you stayed away? I've been
killing the people who loved you since before you were born."

Her face shifted like molding clay, reforming itself into the face
of a woman who looked too much like Persephone not to be her
mother, until it showed her the face of the woman from the photograph. Persephone's grandmother.

Persephone let out a low moan of pain.

"My magic is a clever kind of magic," the witch said. "My
body may be one place, but I long ago figured out how to extend
my reach outside of it. I am more powerful than you could ever
dream."

How to extend her . . . of course. It was simple and awful.
This witch, blood of her blood, was physically trapped in the
hinterland—but that didn't mean her mind wasn't able to travel.

As Deandra grinned, Persephone thought of how unaffected
Deandra had been in the coffee shop. She had been the only person unaltered by her spell. There was so much of magic Persephone didn't understand, but it was easy to see the witch before
her had been possessing people, including those in her life, for
years.

"It was you, all this time?" Persephone said, remembering the pain of so many failed adoptions, and the people in her life who seemed to want her and then not—as if by magic.

"You will never be a match for me." The witch's face shifted again to that of Deandra, and Persephone struck.

She opened the door to thirty-two years of rage and loss and said a single word.

"*Fuasgail.*"

Release.

Deandra let out a scream that split the day into night. It rattled down into Persephone's bones, cracked the earth beneath them.

The island shuddered as Persephone pulled all the light, all the aether, from the witch. Deandra's bones snapped, her heart squeezed, the smile crumpled from her face. She rasped out three final words. "You. Will. Lose."

The shadows receded, the maelstrom closed in on itself, and the eyes of Deandra Bishop blinked twice.

The witch was gone.

In her place, Persephone's co-worker stared up at her in open horror, before her heart gave a final beat and the true Deandra Bishop crumpled to the earth.

"*No,*" Persephone said, comprehension ebbing in. "No, no, nonononono." The word became a chant, a prayer, as the wards went down. Persephone tried to scoop the broken girl up. "Deandra, please." Persephone pulled her into her lap, cradled her close to her. "I'm sorry. I'm so sorry, wake up, wake up, *wake up.*"

She'd meant to cast out the witch, but Persephone had never considered the waiting soul. She patted the sides of Deandra's face, ran her hands over her hair, and tried to force life back into the person who never should have been there at all.

Persephone turned to the solemn faces of her sister witches who knelt against the earth along the perimeter. "Help me, *please.* You have to help me."

Ellison's eyes held compassion and pain, but she only shook her head. Ariel dipped her chin to her chest in prayer, while Moira's eyes filled with tears.

No one saw Hyacinth leave.

No one saw the threads of space open and part.

No one was able to bring the dead girl back to life.

▸ ▸ ▸

FOR THE FIRST time in ten years, Moira Ever helped a Way witch. She aided Ariel and Ellison as they dragged Persephone away after she collapsed over the girl's body. Helped force a tonic down Persephone's throat to subdue her enough for what must come next. Loaded them up in the cart, and sent them on their way.

Moira had not wanted to send Persephone away, but she had not seen another option. Moira had seen broken witches before. She was broken herself in many ways. But Moira had never been the one to do the breaking.

Moira knew it was her fault, hers and her sister's. They were responsible for bringing Persephone here.

Moira didn't know how Hyacinth had connected with the Mayfair witch, how Amara had worked the possession or for how long. There was so much beyond the veil she couldn't know. Moira didn't understand why Hyacinth had betrayed them. Moira had taken her sister at her word when she told her she scryed and the Goddess had finally listened, providing the location of Persephone May after so many years of searching. Moira assumed it was the mark of the one hundred year anniversary coming, that it was fortuitous. She assumed the bridge to the hinterland would open and so the key to unlock it would find its way back.

It was the Goddess' will. Fate, Moira had believed, was a fair-weather friend.

Fate was no friend at all.

Moira had grown to love Persephone like a sister, to appreciate the witch for her magic and wit, her kind heart and keen mind.

A mind that was surely cracked after this day.

Ariel and Ellison had agreed on taking Persephone back to Way House, and Moira had wrapped Persephone in her own blanket spelled with comfort and peace. They'd left Moira with Deandra's body, tasking her with preparing it for the burial. They all would send her to sea together when the witching hour was upon them. Pray to the Goddess that the girl would find peace in the afterlife.

As Moira worked, she listened for her sister to return. She did not know where she went, she only knew Hyacinth was responsible for this tragedy.

There had to be a reason.

Why bring over Amara Mayfair through a clumsy possession, why risk everything and lose their only way to break the curse? It was counterintuitive. It was baffling.

Once Moira had properly anointed the body, and prayed over her, she went upstairs. It was at the landing where she felt it. A void in the house, and a longing running through it as though the house was mourning something or someone, too. When she reached the hallway, blood chilled in her veins. The door opposite the room Persephone had stayed in was ajar. It was a room Moira did not like to enter, one that was too close to the beating heart of the mountain, to the secrets buried along the bridge hidden there.

Moira's scalp tingled as all her senses told her she would find her sister inside. Clasping a hand over the amethyst she wore around her neck, Moira opened the door.

Her legs gave out first as Moira collapsed at the sight.

It would not be a single funeral they held this night. For Hyacinth, her face as gray as the clouds before a storm, lay as cold as the deep of the ocean, dead on the bed.

Thirteen

T HERE WERE, DORIAN KNEW, prices even the dead could pay. Every light in the library had flicked to life an hour before, and he sat in the main room waiting. It was the first time since he'd come to be the guardian some two hundred years before that the library had reacted so strongly. He wasn't sure if it was a harbinger of good or bad, and he was growing more and more concerned about Persephone as the minutes ticked by. It wouldn't do to show it. He wasn't sure how that would be used against him, but after the kiss he knew he had essentially hand-picked the dagger and placed it in the library's hand. Should she need it, he knew the library would not hesitate to strike.

He hoped the library would not be able to move against Persephone. Dorian thought about how she had tapped into the life force of the library and used it to her advantage. She was tethered to it, but she wasn't completely under its spell—even if she didn't know what she wielded or how.

Dorian knew the curse Persephone needed to break would require more than one part. Like any well-oiled machine, there would be multiple bolts and screws to piece together. He just didn't know precisely what she'd need. He struggled with how to gain that knowledge.

He blinked and thought he saw Persephone's face peering intently down at his, blinked again and she was gone. It was the fourth time that hour he'd glimpsed her. He wasn't sure if it was his memory taunting him or the library—though he'd never been prone to visions or hallucinations before.

A long lazy knock sounded on the front door, and Dorian turned to face it.

There was a reason the library was called Library for the Lost, and it wasn't only to do with lost magical objects. He walked to the door, his body taut with tension. He tried to blow the edges out, turn his nerves to his advantage as his sails used to turn the wind to theirs. Instead the hair along his neck curled at attention.

Dorian opened the door and scowled.

"Hello, guardian," the woman said, her voice worn to a whisper. "Dead again so soon?"

The library's most prized possessions, the ones he couldn't show Persephone, were souls of witches who showed up on his doorstep when they departed the outer world for the inner.

The dead didn't haunt this library, they came home to it. The dead witches of the three islands were housed in the library, and oh were there many, each one kept where the Goddess wanted them.

Persephone, however, was not the first witch to show up when she should not, when she was not meant to die and arrive. That distinct honor went to the irritating witch on the other side of the door.

"Aren't you going to invite me in?"

"You aren't a vampire, Hyacinth Lenore Ever. If you were, I'd bottle sunlight and free it upon your head."

She sniffed, but walked past him to enter the library. "You are ridiculous."

"And you are unwanted. Why have you returned?"

Dorian didn't have to ask how—he knew now the witch had learned how to spell herself between life and death. For a few precious moments or minutes, Hyacinth could hover on the precipice long enough to cross the bridge here. She was the first of her kind to do it, and the first time she'd fooled him well into thinking she was something she wasn't.

Hyacinth leaned against the small wooden table and it shifted up a few inches to better suit her height. The damn library was most helpful when he didn't want it to be.

"I made a mistake," she said.

"No kidding."

"I . . ." Hyacinth swallowed. She closed her eyes. "I can't stop her. I can't stop any of it."

"It's hard to stop an avalanche, worse to watch it, I'd wager, especially when one causes it," he said, studying how she gripped her hands together, how the internal war within her waged.

Hyacinth kept her eyes squeezed shut. She reminded Dorian of a child playing hide-and-seek, forgetting to hide, thinking if you can't see the person seeking, then they can't see you.

"No one was doing anything to stop the curse. I couldn't let my ancestors die," she said. "My cousins were just letting fate fuck us. After what happened with Stevie . . . I did what I could. Did what I had to do."

"You mean what you thought you had to do."

She swallowed.

"You made your choice."

She nodded.

"It sounds like you have another to make."

"Yes." Hyacinth sighed and the books around them sighed with her. "I can't stop her." Her eyes opened. "There's only one thing to do."

Dorian waited.

Hyacinth studied the books lining the shelves, taking her time, thinking. Her eyes widened on the tallest shelf closest to them. Dorian watched Hyacinth nod to herself, and as she did, her spine straightened. She lost the frown pulling her lips down, her shoulders rolled down her back.

Hyacinth had made her choice.

"I need your help, Librarian."

"I helped you before," he said, turning to study the shelves as the spines of the closest books practically preened at the attention. "I won't do it again."

"You did," she said, her voice pleasant. "Thanks for that."

"I did not help you on purpose."

Months ago, Hyacinth had shown up as all wraiths do, lost and dead, confused and needy. She'd played him. No one had ever discovered the library before that wasn't meant to find it. But Hyacinth Ever with her beautiful eyes and cruel mouth had deceived him. She'd come like the rest, asking for knowledge before she settled into her place with the lost souls the Library for the Lost guarded. Only she hadn't meant to stay.

The dead did not always go easy. Because of that, they came looking for answers before they were ready to rest. Hyacinth's arrival wasn't unusual. Everything was as it had ever been, so Dorian didn't think twice to give her what she needed—the location of something lost. The library certainly hadn't stopped him.

"No, I suppose you didn't," Hyacinth said. "But if you hadn't told me the location of the lost Mayfair witch, Persephone would never have come, the island would stay cursed, and you wouldn't get the chance to have your heart broken."

He shot a look over his shoulder and she smiled.

"There's a book missing." She pointed. "A very specific grimoire that was on this shelf the last time I was in this room. The room reverts to the traveler, doesn't it? So that means this book is gone."

Dorian didn't say a word.

"I've seen her do it, you know. Travel. I should have known she'd come here." Hyacinth picked up a vase the color of eggplant and rolled it back and forth in her hands.

Dorian said nothing, and Hyacinth turned the vase upside down. She moved it in a feverish pace he couldn't follow, spinning the vase around and around, twisting and turning it so the color shifted into shades of midnight. "The thing is, I don't really need you to do anything this time. Rather, I need you to *not* do something." Hyacinth stilled the vase, and the smile she offered sent a shiver of fear walking down his spine. "This time, all you have to do is duck."

The vase flew from her hands, and Dorian foolishly headed her advice. He ducked.

He'd misjudged her, and the power she'd retained inside the walls of the library. Nothing was supposed to harm him here, but as the vase smashed against the side of his face and the herbs rained down onto him, he saw the hole in his logic.

Anything could happen inside the Library for the Lost—so long as the library willed it.

The world faded to black, and the last thing Dorian glimpsed in his mind, before he went under, was Persephone's hazel eyes, banked in sorrow, gazing down at him with tears freely cascading down the glorious angles of her face.

▸ ▸ ▸

PERSEPHONE SAT IN the jade chair in the living room of Way House, holding the mechanical man that wore Dorian's face. She hadn't turned him on, but every fifteen minutes for the last hour she could have sworn he was *looking* at her.

It was oddly comforting, because there was something in his eyes that even felt like Dorian. She wanted to go to him, to escape into the library. She wanted him to tell her it was all a mistake. Hyacinth hadn't betrayed her. Everything would be okay.

But she had and nothing was. Persephone was on the island to break a curse. But Persephone's curse was to be broken by those she loved, and there was nothing anyone could say to change it.

After Ariel and Ellison had reset the perimeter tests—adding new wards to the island to alert them if the evil from beyond the veil managed to penetrate the island again—they'd closed ranks on her. Persephone told them she doubted the dark witch would be able to regain the strength to return so soon, but it didn't deter them from settling themselves north and south of her as though they were a fortress.

Deandra Bishop was dead. She had died at Persephone's hand. An innocent girl was gone, and Persephone carried the mark of her loss.

Persephone wore it like you wear a car crash. It was visible in every step she took, every breath she tried to take. The death slashed deep into her soul, a rip down the center of her being.

There were so many questions. How long had Amara been Deandra? Why had she killed her mother and grandmother, why did she want to destroy Persephone?

And what about Hyacinth? How could she have thought she was protecting Persephone by teaming up with Amara? How did she contact Amara in the first place? Nothing made sense. Everything had shattered.

The betrayals and loss numbed the left side of Persephone's face. She didn't think she could blink if she tried. Persephone knew she was crying because the backs of her hands were wet, but she didn't bother to try and wipe the tears away.

Persephone could shed an ocean of tears and it would not matter. Her pain wouldn't change the tide, couldn't cause a ripple in the swell of heartbreak. The numbness was a sigh of relief. It was acceptance, the promise of a blank slate.

The curse could swallow them whole, if it meant Persephone wouldn't have to feel again.

"Moira needs us," Ellison said, sliding something into her pocket before standing and walking to the window.

"Telepathy?" Persephone asked, still studying the mechanical man's face.

"Of course not," Ariel said, speaking for the first time. "She can send a text on a cell phone."

Something was wrong with the ornery witch. Ariel was gray, as though the color had been drained from her. But Persephone couldn't help her. She couldn't even help herself.

"I'll go," Ariel said, talking to her sister, who had busied herself on the side ottoman in front of the large window. "You're better equipped for"—she waved a hand—"guiding her emotional devastation."

"You mean because you don't want to acknowledge your own emotions," Ellison said, her hands moving quickly as she performed an elegant knit and purl with a soft white yarn that looked like it had been conjured from a cloud's dream.

"People catch feelings like travelers intercept the common cold," Ariel said. "I've immunized myself to the bone." Ariel shivered and nearly lost her footing as she grabbed a light sweater off a hook. Ellison didn't call her on the lie, and Ariel took a deep breath before she grabbed a basket of herbs from beside the door and slipped outside.

"Her heart never healed," Ellison said, watching her go. "Too much time and not enough has passed, and suddenly we're back in each of their pockets like we're children again."

"You cannot fight the dark when you're battling a divide," Persephone said in a voice barely her own.

Ellison turned back. She lit a fire with a wave of her hand, and studied her cousin. "You're giving up."

Persephone did not respond.

"Hyacinth was a wicked fool, but all is not lost," Ellison said.

Persephone looked down at the mechanical man and thought of Dorian. Persephone wished she had the strength to go to him.

Ellison murmured words so low Persephone could not make them out. The room warmed, the light softened. She brought Persephone a cup of tea and set it beside her. The mug was huge, and looked like something a caffeine addict would buy in a novelty shop.

"I don't want to be here," Persephone said, before she knocked the cup over. She set the automaton in the chair and looked down at the puddle spreading across the hardwood floor. "I'm sorry," Persephone said, to Ellison, to Deandra.

The mechanical man's eyes opened. They whirred green and Persephone leaned closer. Space shifted around her, the man's eyes raking over her, his face frozen with fear.

The knowledge slammed into her like a train off its track. Something was very wrong with Dorian.

Persephone gasped and reached a hand out, slipping from Wile Isle into the web of space.

▸ ▸ ▸

THE LIBRARY WAS dark when Persephone fell into it. Its usual scent of musk and fire cinders and pine was replaced with the sickly sweet smell of pink childhood medicine that tasted of bubble gum. It was the whiff of a memory, hers or someone else's she did not know, but it made her shudder.

"Dorian?"

She called for him as she walked carefully along the perimeter of the library, fighting back fear. She knew she had reached the perimeter for an invisible wall brushed her shoulder, blocking her from the books. Persephone needed light, she needed to see to find him—and yet a small part of her found the dark comforting.

She wondered if she could hide here, swathed in it forever like a wound freshly bandaged.

"Dorian, this isn't funny. Where are you?" Persephone took three steps forward and stumbled over a rolled-up rug. She reached down to roll it out, and her hand closed around a broad, still shoulder.

The remaining exhaustion fell away like a bride's veil thrown back from her face. Persephone's blood spiked. She held up a hand and summoned aether, threw it into the air. A thousand sparks glittered, tiny floating lights with the sparkle of stars. They illuminated the unmoving form laying before her.

"*Dorian.*" Persephone bent over him, her breath coming fast, and felt for a pulse. She couldn't be certain, for she did not know how alive or dead Dorian was to begin with, but she thought she felt his life force still inside him.

He was frozen. Bespelled.

"Who did this?" Persephone asked, calling out to the library.

The voices of the Many were silent as though they were afraid of this world. She surveyed the room. It was much changed. The walls had widened and the room was now a large rectangle with walls of books stacked in rows. A cold marble floor rested beneath her feet. It looked like a library in a university might.

Persephone stood, looked around for a blanket, and saw a throw over a leather chair next to a small pillow. She took it and covered the unmoving form of the guardian, and slid the pillow under his head. Then Persephone walked quietly into the stacks. *Someone* had done this. Dorian had said nothing she did could harm him within the walls of the library, and yet someone had.

"Did you do this?" Persephone asked, her voice as low as poison. "You're a being—did you do this to him?"

The library chilled so fast that Persephone's breath puffed out in a small burst from her lips. "I'll take that as a no."

The library warmed again, and she walked on. Finally, after passing countless rows, Persephone stopped in the center of the last aisle. An unbearably sweet scent prickled the edge of her nose. Fruity and light—the air was perfumed with it.

Persephone closed her eyes, and drank it in. She knew that smell, it was as familiar to her as the owner of its name.

"*Hyacinth.*"

The lights of the library flickered and Persephone held up both hands. Anger flooded her system, and she used it to push forward. Once more Persephone stepped into the veil.

▸ ▸ ▸

PERSEPHONE STEPPED BEYOND the veil and found the path distorted. If space were a sphere, like the earth, it would exist in three parts on Wile Isle. The outer crust would be the island, the inner crust the library, and the core behind the veil would lead to the hinterland. Persephone could, she'd come to understand, feel the paths of each when she was in the in-between state— except this time the roads ran together. It was impossible to decipher which way to go.

As she'd stepped through, Persephone had been thinking of Dorian and Hyacinth and Amara. Now as Persephone studied the light around her, she cleared her mind, and focused on the island, on the cobblestone path outside Ever House, and the witch who had struck down her friend.

Persephone's lips tasted bitter like mustard greens as she licked them, and her hands moved deftly as she parted space. She'd make a new road, damn it.

When Persephone stepped from the veil, she realized she was not alone.

"Finally," a rich, sultry voice said, just over Persephone's shoulder.

Persephone turned to face the voice, and blinked in surprise. A beautiful woman with striking eyebrows and inquisitive eyes smiled at her. The woman had auburn curls that cascaded down her back, and wore a gown the color of emeralds. Her hands were covered in rings featuring the phases of the moon, and around her neck she wore an hourglass locket that matched the one Persephone carried tucked under her shirt.

"Who—?" Persephone started, before the woman reached for her. At her touch, the answer to the unspoken question crystallized in her mind.

"Hello, daughter of my daughters," the woman said.

Then Amara Mayfair waved a hand over the air, parted the threads of space, and pulled Persephone in after her.

HYACINTH EVER'S JOURNAL

Ten years ago, August 1st

I can't stop dreaming about Stevie. I don't know how it started, not really. One day I was wishing her away on every shooting star I saw, my eyes squeezed tight and teeth gnashed together. The next day, she was like an itch between my shoulder blades.

I kept reaching to scratch it, but the itch moved.

Up a centimeter, over a millimeter, down an inch. Until it settled in all its persistent glory smack between her eyes. I didn't want to stop staring, or give up looking at her anymore—at least . . . not in my dreams.

In my dreams, she walked onto Wile Isle wearing

a crown. Her words were a lullaby she sang to scare all my nightmares away.

> *Swish swish*
> *A siren's wish*
> *I've come*
> *I've come*
> *Welcome me*
> *I'm home*

FOURTEEN

HYACINTH EVER GASPED AWAKE, and found herself being studied like a termite who'd found its way into a newly renovated teak kitchen. Her sister's face was drawn, and to her right Ariel Way stared down like she could pry apart all the layers of Hyacinth and happily shred each one before setting the remains on fire.

"What did you do?" Moira asked, her hand shaking as she raised one to reach out and touch her sister on the arm, as if to reassure herself she was really there.

"You know what she did," Ariel said, curling her lip, something close to concern in her eyes. "Those new streaks of gray are clearer than any crystal ball. You don't get that sort of highlighting from a salon."

"You walked with the dead," Moira said, her lips thinning. "Why on earth would you do such a thing?"

Hyacinth groaned—her headache from being in between worlds for so long was no small thing. "Water, please."

Moira handed her a glass and Ariel pulled a vial from the basket she'd set on the bed.

"I'll skip your brand of poison, thanks," Hyacinth said, propping herself up on her elbows.

"It's lotus, wormwood, and a few herbs I've pollinated in my own garden," Ariel said, not blinking. If anyone could give a statue a run for its money, it was Ariel Way. "If I wanted you dead, I'd stand you in front of the mirror to slit your throat so you could watch. Which, after all you've done, has crossed my mind."

Hyacinth sighed, and bit back a smile. She couldn't help the hope that fluttered up at seeing her old friend wearing worry's face. "Always so dramatic."

Ariel added a drop to the water and Moira nodded at her sister. Hyacinth drank it down, and closed her eyes as heat rushed in. Her skin tingled as the tonic worked its magic. Hyacinth's pores opened and closed, her chakras bloomed and realigned. Five minutes later, Hyacinth's neck and cheeks were flushed, and she felt almost back to normal. Almost. Hyacinth studied the strands of hair in the mirror, frowning at the silver streaks woven among her dark locks.

"I can't undo what you have done," Ariel said, studying her hair. "But maybe the silver will keep the negativity you breed to a minimum."

"I'm not a damn house spirit," Hyacinth snapped.

"No, you're a devil."

"Enough." Moira pressed a hand to her forehead.

"Not even," Ariel said, crossing to Hyacinth. "She needs to explain herself, starting with teaming up with that evil witch, and her fake Persephone attacks on Ellison and me, and ending with wherever in Hades she's just traveled."

"Hades isn't far off," Hyacinth said, rolling out her shoulders.

"Then you should have stayed where you belong."

Hyacinth avoided meeting Ariel's eyes, as the blow landed. She cleared her throat and reminded herself to put one foot after the other. What other choice did she have at this point?

"It was bad enough when you were children that you barked and spit at each other, but I thought we'd lost you, Hyacinth,"

Moira said, rubbing a temple as she turned to Ariel. "I thank you for your assistance, but you may go now. I need to speak with my sister."

Ariel snorted. "Fuck that."

At Moira's narrowed expression, Ariel smiled. "As I said, I'm not going anywhere until she tells us what the hell she was doing. You had Amara in your home, she nearly killed Persephone."

"I would never hurt Persephone," Hyacinth said, her eyes flashing. "The castings were supposed to be harmless. Do you really think this little of me?"

"Bullshit."

"Ariel," Moira warned.

Hyacinth shook her head, reached a hand for the edge of the bed.

"What?" Ariel asked, leaning close enough that Hyacinth could smell the mint of her breath. "That demented witch you conjured clearly wanted to do Persephone, and us, damage."

"She wasn't supposed to hurt anyone," Hyacinth said, rubbing her forehead. "It got out of hand."

"Oh, a possessed witch did something evil? Surprise, surprise."

Hyacinth ignored Ariel's accusations, turning to rummage through her closet. It was easier when she didn't have to look upon her old friend's face. She chose a lilac gown to change into, tucked her curls on top of her head, and hissed when Ariel used her powers to tug on the strands of silver hair.

Hyacinth ran her fingers over her face. She pulled on her dress and looked back at Ariel. "*Without a key, there is no world. Without a lock, there is no key. When the key turns, we will all be free,*" she said, words she and Ariel had written ten years before when looking to bend magic.

"You lost your key when you brought Amara over," Ariel said.

"You know nothing," Hyacinth said with a small sigh. "Same as you ever were."

"Oh I know plenty. I know who you are and what you've done." Ariel took a step forward, her fingers curling into claws. "Try me, witch."

"Get over yourself." Hyacinth glared at Ariel. She tried to swallow, failed. She needed out of the room, out of the house. She needed, most of all, Ariel out of her way. "Stevie certainly did." Ariel's nostrils flared and Hyacinth blew out a breath. "You think you're such a victim, Ari. All the bad things happen to you. Nothing's ever on *you*. You couldn't get the girl, weren't able to keep her, and it's all *my* fault. Bullshit. I may not have your magic, but I didn't need it to show her who the better woman was."

The mirror on the wall trembled as Ariel's copper eyes turned black.

"That's *enough*," Moira said, clapping her hands together like an irritated schoolteacher and looking like she wanted to strangle them both. "Hyacinth, tell us where you were, and please explain that you're *not* working with Amara. Goddess help us."

"I would never work with that witch," Hyacinth said, before turning around. This, at least, was true.

"We saw her," Ariel said.

"You saw *someone*, I never said it was Amara." Hyacinth said, and held up a hand. "I was beyond this land, tying up a loose end. Now, I've a garden to tend to and a recipe for a particularly tricky spell to perfect."

"Hyacinth—" Moira tried to interject, but her sister waved her off.

She offered Moira an apologetic look. "I am sorry I gave you a fright. I'm perfectly fine." Hyacinth slipped her feet into her slippers.

"Yeah, we're not done, witch," Ariel said. "Who the hell are you working with, then?"

"It's funny you mention hell," Hyacinth said, and dusted off her sleeve. "Poor Persephone," she said, her eyes flashing as she stared at Ariel. The clock ticked from inside the room. From outside in the hall, Opal scratched at the door opposite the one the witches stood in.

"The truest witch wears many faces," Hyacinth said as she gave a slow smile. "Right now, she's prepared for checkmate, because, *dear cousin*, the queen just took your pawn."

▸ ▸ ▸

Amara Mayfair held Persephone's wrist like you'd hold on to a baby colt as she pulled her along through the veil. There was nothing threatening in the action, or to the woman. Whoever she was, within moments Persephone knew this was not who she had faced at Ever House. Which left a very large question.

Who was the witch who had possessed Deandra?

Persephone could not ask the question, for speaking was not something permissible within the sands between space. Each time Persephone tried, the words puffed out in a sprinkle of white-blue light before being absorbed into the fabric of the world around them.

Amara crossed through the threads and parted them with one foot in front of the other. She didn't so much as follow the paths as command them. Light and aether danced around Amara as she walked.

They stepped through and out of the veil, onto a cliff much like the one through the Arch to Anywhere in Ever House.

Amara released Persephone and walked on, throwing her arms back and looking up at the morning sun. Dawn was breaking here, while it was night on the island.

Persephone stepped back to study the witch, who couldn't seem to wipe the grin from her face.

"It's beautiful, isn't it?" Amara asked, an odd cadence to her voice, her face basking in the rising warmth of the sun. "This day was the most glorious of all days, and by the end of it everything had fallen apart." She turned to look at Persephone. "We are one hundred years past, because it is necessary to remember the beginning when you reach the end. I have been waiting for you, Persephone Mayfair, for a very long time."

"I don't understand," Persephone said. "If you're Amara Mayfair . . ."

"I am."

"Then who the hell tried to kill me?" The answer floated up like a mined speck of copper. "It was your sister, wasn't it?"

Amara looked out to the ocean, seemed to draw strength from

it. She stood taller, her shoulders shifted down her back, the natural arch giving her the air of a queen. "That's a layered question to answer."

Amara stretched, and crossed to one of the giant boulders down from the overlook. Amara settled herself, her green gown glowing against the gray of the rock. The witch herself seemed to glow, as though she were lit up from inside.

"There have been many times since coming to Wile Isle you have been threatened," Amara said, offering Persephone an apologetic smile. "I'm afraid a few of those times were at my hand. The way between worlds has been breaking down, so I thought it was safe—but each time I tried to contact you, I created a chasm. It drained you. When a witch is drained, she is brought to a painful brink of death. I only meant to warn you, I never meant to channel your power. I was a fool, and I am sorry."

Persephone blinked, crossed her arms over her chest. "A painful brink of death?" Persephone thought about what it had felt like before, when the shadows and darkness pooled over her. "That . . . darkness trying to consume me wasn't Hyacinth?"

"No. Hyacinth made a bad bargain for a hill of beans."

Persephone could only blink at her. "I don't understand."

"It wasn't meant to be an attack at all," Amara said. "Magic isn't cooperative, and it's especially tricky for someone like me trying to reach you across the worlds."

"Someone like you?"

"Who has limited power, and whose power is so unpredictable."

"So the spell you cast worked and rid you of your dark magic?"

"The spell worked," Amara said. "Though I wish to the Goddess it hadn't. I no longer have dark magic, and I barely have any of the light."

Persephone rubbed at her arms. "Where did your magic go?"

"To my sister. At least, that which she can hold. The rest, she has stored. The Menagerie of Magic is a treasure trove of magically infused objects, and it has grown beyond measure in power."

"But it's frozen, right?"

"Yes. The menagerie is frozen."

"Then how are you here now?"

And how were they . . . wherever they were? The air on the cliffs was warm, salty, and clean. The grass under Persephone's feet was soft and bending. There wasn't so much as a threatening ripple coming off the woman who should be trapped beyond the veil, but that did not mean Persephone trusted her.

"The menagerie is frozen but magic has been breaking down inside the hinterland. Cracks forming. Whatever happened with you and my sister True, who was trying to bend you to her will, your battle unspooled the strongest threads locking the hinterland completely away. I played my part in the spell, and my bargain allowed me this freedom to travel here." She turned her head up to the sky again. "For a price of course."

"A price?" Persephone said.

"Not one worth worrying over." Amara waved the question away. "Nothing like what your cousin might owe."

"Because of Hyacinth's bargain for a hill of beans?"

Amara nodded. "She's being, what is the modern phrase? Worked over by True."

Persephone sat down on a cushy patch of grass, pulling her knees to her and slipping her chin onto the back of her hand. She wanted to ask more about Hyacinth, but there was a more pressing question. "Deandra asked me what kind of monster I was. Before I came here. It's . . . it's part of what drove me to leave Greenville. Why would she want me to bend to her, why have me here at all if I'm meant to break the curse?"

"True's more powerful on her own land. She has a stronghold here, has for the last decade. It's also here that you can cross to the hinterland. True needs you, she needs your magic, which is so like mine, so she can be free."

"What about the magic stored in the menagerie?"

"She can't hold it all. It's imbued in the objects of wonder she planned to send home with those who attended. That was how she planned to empower them, to share our magic. She needs you to be her conduit."

"It's just never-ending, is it?"

The responsibility, the power, the loss of control—all of it was too much. Persephone thought of Dorian bound at the library after Hyacinth's attack, and forced herself to take a centering breath. "Hyacinth brought me here knowing this?"

"True wears many faces, and they're all equally convincing," Amara said. "Hyacinth isn't the first to be fooled by her, but she kept her ability to mind travel hidden well. You couldn't have known."

Persephone thought of Deandra and ran a hand over her face. "There isn't any solace in that."

"It's a sorry thing to inherit a legacy such as this," Amara said.

"Today I killed my former co-worker," Persephone said. "True may have possessed her body, but I crushed it to drive her out. Sorry isn't even close to what this is."

"A curse is a promise of pain. You should have inherited a legacy of magic, and were given, instead, a legacy of loss. Your mother. Your grandmother." Amara stood and paced the perimeter of the cliff. "My sister has always desired power, and she will do nothing to stop at regaining it. You must stop her. If she succeeds, if you or the others do not, we are doomed."

Persephone held up a hand, watched the spark of aether try and flicker. "Why does it have to be me?" As angry as she was, Persephone very much wanted it not to be her.

"Because it must. You are my blood. Directly descended."

"What about Hyacinth and Moira, Ariel and Ellison? They're yours, too."

"The Ever sisters come from True, and your other cousins from our baby sister who was off fishing when the spells laid waste to Wile and sent the rest of us to the hinterland."

Persephone blinked at her. "What?"

"My sister and I weren't the only Mayfair of our generation," Amara said. "We had a younger sister Louisa, and she is the great-grandmother of your Ariel and Moira."

"Why don't they know this? Why do they think otherwise?"

"Because I took the knowledge with me, to keep Louisa safe, to protect her from True. You alone are mine."

Persephone shook her head in wonder. "You cursed your sister as surely as you cursed yourself."

"Under the blood moon, I gave up everything. The price we all paid," Amara said, her voice growing weak, "was to be lost. Louisa was safe. What's unforgivable was the loss of the mortal lives within the menagerie. They died as the curse was cast. One hundred innocent souls gone."

Persephone swallowed her horror. "I thought they were stranded with you in the hinterland."

"No. The magic True used turned greedy as it was being pulled back again. The witches were one thing, but mortal women had little to offer it, so it stole their souls as its price."

Persephone gave a slow shake of her head, her stomach rolling over at the thought. "My god."

"I live with them every day," Amara said, tears thick in her voice. "I wake with their death and I retire beside it. There is no escaping what we have done."

Persephone blew out a shaking breath. "What does she want? True?"

"Freedom. The same thing she has always desired. To be known, to see the world. To remake it for the better, as she believes it should be."

"How do we stop her?"

Amara came and sat beside Persephone. Persephone studied the witch's profile and something clicked in her mind. Amara didn't hold eye contact with her for more than a few seconds.

"Amara."

The witch turned her face and Persephone tried to catch her eye. "You won't like what you see, daughter of my daughters," Amara said.

"I saw True in Deandra, didn't I? Who don't you want me to see in you?"

Amara stilled. When she turned it was with slow precision. Inch by painful inch. As Amara's eyes found Persephone's, silver swirled behind the irises. Persephone stared, transfixed. Persephone saw not one soul staring back, but two, three, four, five, on and on and on.

"As I said," Amara told her. "I carry the dead with me."

Amara looked away, and Persephone tasted fear so potent it coated her tongue. "How do I stop her?"

"The way to the hinterland is no longer blocked as it was," Amara said, pushing to her feet. "True is regaining strength and will use the way to fully return. She wanted you here, it's why she possessed Deandra. Wanted to drive you to Wile, wanted you to set her free. We give her what she thinks she wants."

▸ ▸ ▸

ARIEL RETURNED TO Way House, releasing her rage as she navigated the roads. Time had taught her much, and Ariel knew her anger at Hyacinth wouldn't gain her anything.

The hard truth was simple. Hyacinth hadn't been entirely wrong. Stevie *had* chosen Hyacinth. She had seen it with her own eyes.

The other truth was time's reveal: Ariel didn't miss Stevie. She stopped missing her almost as soon as the girl was off island.

Who did she miss?

She missed Hyacinth. She missed her friend.

But Hyacinth was no longer that person. The witch she'd become was operating with a broken compass and quite a few loose screws.

Ariel parked the cart and walked into the house, her feet clipping softly on the side stairs. The screen door jangled its welcome as she creaked it open and let it clang close. The sounds of home were the best tonic she knew.

Ariel found her sister in the kitchen, at the little breakfast nook, her lost appendage (more commonly referred to as her laptop) open in front of her. A small scrying mirror sat at her elbow.

Ellison didn't look up. "What was Moira's emergency? Did the body of Persephone's co-worker go missing?"

Ariel pulled out a chair and thunked down into it. The day was catching up with her, and there were still so many miles to go before she could sleep.

"No, she has prepared it and will be ready for the send-off when the witching hour comes." Ariel removed her sweater. "Poor girl. She never had a chance."

"The possessed rarely do. If she had lived, she would likely have spent the rest of her life battling her mind. It's a near impossible thing to recover from having your body and mind violated. There's a reason possession is the darkest of arts."

"Speaking of dark magic, Hyacinth is playing at things she doesn't understand." Ariel said, as the cups in the cupboard jostled before her favorite mug in the shape of a whimsical owl floated down to the counter. The stove clicked on and the kettle began to heat. Her favorite lavender tea dropped into her mug, and when the kettle whistled Ariel got up to go pour the water. The house could do many things, but navigating the element of water was not one of them.

"No kidding. What was she thinking, channeling the spirit of a dead witch for more power?"

"Oh, it gets better. When I arrived, Hyacinth was dead on the bed."

Ellison, whose fingers had been clacking intermittently on her keyboard, stilled. "I'm sorry, what?"

Ariel added a dollop of honey into the tea, and stirred it three times, counterclockwise. "She used her power over life and death to take herself under."

"Her power has never been able to manifest that level of spell." Ellison said, looking over.

Ariel sighed. "It seems her powers are finally progressing."

"Or she's bartering for more." Ellison cocked her head. "Amara?"

"That wasn't Amara we saw." Ariel sipped her tea, raised a single brow. "That was True Mayfair."

Ellison leaned back. "How can you be so sure?"

"Hyacinth told me. She called her by the nickname Gran gave her when she'd tell us the story of Amara and True."

"The truest witch?"

Ariel nodded. "Because Gran thought she was the light and Amara was the dark. I forgot about that theory."

"Not the first time Gran would be wrong."

The corner of Ariel's mouth turned up for a moment.

"Which begs the question," Ariel said, leaning back. "Why would she tell me? Just to needle me? It's not adding up. Only stupid villains show their hand early."

"Hyacinth is many things, but stupid is not among them." Ellison pulled the looking glass closer, peered into it. "Why did Hyacinth cross over?"

Ariel shrugged, sniffed the air. She smelled change. "Where is Persephone?"

Ellison looked down at her computer, turned it so Ariel could see. "Hyacinth's not the only one playing in the realm of the dead."

Ariel studied the image as Ellison ran her hands through her hair. "The lost Mayfair locket?"

Ellison nodded. "After I made her a very fine cup of tea, which was a complete waste of my favorite cinnamon spice, Persephone walked through space." Ellison dropped her hands to massage the muscles on her neck. "She didn't leave all at once either."

Ariel looked up, her expression sharp.

"Her spirit went first, but her body followed a few minutes later," Ellison said.

"She did not astral project."

"No. Those haunting her, they slowed down her passage."

"Gran's Mayfair locket story?"

Ellison smiled. "The locket of power can provide safe passage to lost Mayfair witches and their souls." She tapped the mirror. "I thought the locket Persephone wore was familiar, and then there's the mirror. It was Gran's. It arrived on my pillow the night Persephone arrived. I thought it might show me where Persephone went, but instead all I see is a room full of books."

Ariel tilted her head. "You don't think?"

"The Library for the Lost really does exist? Yes, yes I do. I think the locket was waiting for her like the mirror was waiting for me."

"We spent years as kids trying to contact the library and never got anywhere. Hyacinth always said . . ."

Ellison lifted an elegant brow. "That you would have to be lost to find it."

"Lost," Ariel said, thinking of Hyacinth's form on the bed, of Persephone's spirit leaving her body. "Or dead."

HYACINTH EVER'S JOURNAL

September 2010

> *Stevie isn't who she says she is.*
> *She's been to the Great Mountain. The red dirt on the bottom of her feet tracked into the garden, suffocating my roses. I woke up unable to breathe. When I went to my window, I saw her dancing in the moonlight. She looked up and her eyes were not her own.*
> *I don't know who she is.*
> *Or how to tell Ariel.*
> *I don't know what to do at all.*

FIFTEEN

AMARA AND PERSEPHONE WALKED from beyond the veil into present day on Wile Isle. It was nine o'clock. The air was crisp, the sky a kaleidoscope of stars. Night had wrapped its arms around the moon. Persephone walked carrying the burden of wanting to be in multiple places at once—in the library, helping Dorian, at Ever House, with her hands around Hyacinth's neck as she shook answers from her, and then where she was, which was where she knew she needed to be.

Persephone and Amara went quietly up the beach and climbed the steps to the front entrance of Way House. Persephone wanted this to be a formal introduction. After all, Amara was not the side-door kind of welcome. Amara was an announcement, the gong you chimed before a royal supper, the trumpet you blared.

Persephone needn't have worried as the Way witches, being who they were, expected their arrival. Ariel and Ellison sat on the porch in their rocking chairs, drinking wine from oversized mugs as they studied the aggressive inrushing of the tide.

"You must be why the sea is so unruly," Ellison said to Amara, tucking one leg underneath. "But you didn't set off the alarms, so unless our gran failed at teaching us her wards, you're of the light."

"Beatrice Mayfair," Amara said, with a regal inclination of her head. "She was a marvelous witch. I am someone who remembers."

"Remembers *what* is the question," Ariel said, before throwing Persephone a searching look. "You appear unharmed." Her shoulders dropped a fraction in relief, and Ariel shifted her study to the stranger. "We doused our wine with a hearty dose of juniper leaf."

"Then you should know I am telling the truth. I bring you no harm."

The witch spoke with an unusual cadence, and Ariel studied her more closely.

"Your grandfather," the stranger said to Ariel, "was a Proctor. You have the look of him."

"Who are you?"

"You know who she is," Ellison said, after a sip of her drink.

"I know she's not the only one keeping secrets," Ariel said, her face turning to Persephone.

"Your cousins know where you've been traveling to when you cross worlds," Amara said, offering a small smile.

"You can't penetrate my mind," Ariel said, shooting Amara a glare. "So don't act like you know what I'm thinking."

"Of course I can," Amara said, bringing her palms together. "You are the daughter of my daughters, and I am not of this realm. If that weren't enough, the looks you two exchange are so loud they're practically screaming."

"Your name?" Ariel said, raising a brow. "For a name is a hard thing to steal, and one prefers to gather it freely."

"I am Amara Mayfair," the witch said. "You are Ariel and Ellison Way, formerly Mayfair."

Ellison set her mug down with a crack, while Ariel smiled.

"Can you prove it?" Ariel said.

"What do you have in mind?"

"May the Goddess greet you," Ellison whispered.

"And may she heal you, love you, and treat you well," Amara finished, with a deep bow.

"Gran's blessing," Ellison said, leaning back and picking up her mug. "Only witches of our line know it, only those who mean us no harm can say it."

"It was my blessing, crafted under a harvest moon so many years ago." Amara pointed to the mirror Ellison had brought out with her. "I was lucky to discover the mirrors on the island aren't shut off to me behind the veil. What little power I have retained, I used to imbue the looking glass with aether. Basic mirror magic allowed me to keep watch over you, my children, my children's children, and my children's children's children these many years. It has enabled me to keep my threads of humanity intact."

"You should have shared your mirrors with your witch of a sister," said Ariel.

Amara's smile did not reach her eyes. "Her humanity was bargained off the moment she struck the curse."

"I think we might go inside," Persephone said, rubbing the back of her neck. "There is much to ask, much to say, little time to plan, and I desperately need some of that wine."

▸ ▸ ▸

HYACINTH EVER CROUCHED in her garden, collecting herbs and talking to the trees. She did so to center herself, as her sister had taught her.

Nothing was going as expected, but she couldn't give up now.

Ten years ago, in this very garden, Ariel Way told her about a girl she had dreamed about, a girl Ariel believed might break the curse.

"The grans always said she was coming, that it was only a matter of time," Ari had said, her hands busy tugging at the weeping willow's limbs because she could never stay still.

"Yes, but you think she's some kind of Queen of the Underworld?"

"Sure. Who better to break the curse locking our kin in a kind of underworld than a queen?" Ariel had said, dropping the bony branches to blow bubbles out of thin air—showing off her magic without meaning to show it off at all. Magic, energy, was second nature to Ariel.

Hyacinth looked away, embarrassed that she could only enhance the soil, her magic a whisper to the shout of power coursing in Ari's veins.

It drove her to distraction some days.

"I don't know, Ari. Why would our moms try and break it if this mythological dream girl were coming?"

"Maybe they got tired of waiting," Ariel said, her palms stilling. She never spoke about what happened, even though she was desperate for Hyacinth to help her find a way to send a message to their mothers.

"Maybe," Hyacinth said, not sure she bought it. "But still. I think we have to be careful we don't screw up and get sent away from the island, too."

"We have something they don't." Ariel flashed her a grin. "The desire to not harm, and each other."

They spent weeks reading. Studying spells of a hundred different ways to break a curse. To pierce the veil, to call to lost spirits, to send a message of hope across the tides. They finally settled on calling a lost spirit home, but it didn't work. Hyacinth knew the reason it failed. It was because for any type of great magic they needed the stronger witch. Hyacinth was simply too weak.

Then Stevie arrived in town bringing secrets and change.

In this very garden, Hyacinth had slipped wormwood and yarrow into a tonic, for reversal of magic and a bit of good fortune, and asked the Goddess to remove Ariel's infatuation with Stevie. She wanted her friend back, and she didn't trust the strange girl who asked too many questions and stared at Hyacinth like she could read her soul.

After Hyacinth finished making her tonic, she'd heard it. A stir in the wind, an echo of a voice. It came down from the Great Mountain. Through the oaks, up from the roots, down from the sloped land carved from secrets.

The Great Mountain had not existed on Wile Isle until the menagerie took place. Until the night of the curse, when one world was frozen away. Island folklore told that the mountain grew overnight, though, to Hyacinth, the story had always felt like a bit of make-believe.

When she was a child, Hyacinth and Moira explored the caves into the mountain, trying to find the lost witches frozen in time. But there was nothing there beyond the usual stalactite and stalagmite. Neither witch was overly fond of tight places, so their spelunking adventures had only lasted the one season.

That evening ten long years ago, Hyacinth heard that whisper, heard it call her name. Spoken in a soft caress, with *yearning*. She'd felt the truth in her bones. Hyacinth was not alone.

The whisper carried with it a request for health, for healing. Hyacinth quickly learned the person on the other side of the voice was dying. The being was trapped between worlds, her power waning, her life fading.

Her name was True and she was stuck between worlds.

Hyacinth knew who she was, knew her story as well as she knew the tales of Santa or the tooth fairy or the eight Elvin priestesses.

True told Hyacinth her sister had trapped her outside the hinterland, lost in the veil—that she existed on the wind, and she needed help. She needed Hyacinth's magic.

That this great witch thought her a powerful one was its own potent tonic. That someone so renowned would have to live such a limited life was tragic. When True promised Hyacinth the power she'd always dreamed of in return for aid, it sounded like salvation.

All she had to do was give her tonic to Stevie, under the blood moon, underneath the old apple tree that never bloomed. True promised it would send the girl on her way, and provide an opening for True to escape.

Hyacinth did as she was asked without thinking through the angles. It was two birds and one stone. Get rid of Stevie, gain real magic, and become the witch she was meant to be. Then she could find their mothers and bring them both home.

The spell did not go wrong, but it certainly did not go right.

Stevie drank the glass of wine. She dropped the goblet. She fell to the earth.

"What's happening?" Hyacinth asked, her blood speeding up as the color in the girl's face faded from dusky rose to pale pink.

She bent down to shake her awake, and Stevie's eyes opened.

"Well met, darling girl," a voice that was not Stevie's said. Then she cupped Hyacinth's cheek, and kissed her long and hard on the mouth.

When she released her, Stevie laughed so loud the leaves on the apple tree shook. Hyacinth never saw Ariel watching them from the path. Didn't know her once bosom friend had witnessed the kiss between Hyacinth and the false witch under the moonlight.

It would be years before Hyacinth would realize True had used her power to find her way into Hyacinth's mind. Drawing on the spirit of her nearest blood connection, Hyacinth's weakness was what made her the perfect person to open the door for True.

Hyacinth's goal had been simple. Goodbye Stevie, hello friendship with Ariel. She would have grown her power. She would have been the hero.

In the end Hyacinth got rid of Stevie, but it cost her everything.

True needed Stevie as a way on and off the island. She left, saying she would free the girl once she reached the mainland. Stevie was gone and, after what she witnessed, Ariel never forgave Hyacinth for it. Hyacinth tried to explain many times the first year, but each time she opened her mouth she got the hiccups, then a coughing fit, then pneumonia. Eventually she accepted that magic had a price, and this spell a particularly high one.

She even tried to set Ariel up with Laurel. She'd known of Ariel's long-standing crush, and watched the way Laurel stared at Ariel when Ariel didn't know she was looking. But that backfired, too. She eventually stopped trying to find a way back into Ari's life.

Time has a way of carving new paths, and when Hyacinth finally found Persephone, she was ready to do what had to be done. She was prepared to right her old wrongs.

In the garden, Hyacinth rocked back onto her haunches and listened for her sister. Inside the house, Moira slammed cupboards, making tea and muttering to herself.

Moira had been as good as a mother to Hyacinth in many ways. But Moira had more magic than she'd ever cared to tame. Moira didn't know what it was like to spend your life in someone else's shadow, to spend your every minute making wishes that would never come true.

She wouldn't have made the choices Hyacinth had, but that didn't matter any longer.

Hyacinth finished the elixir, stirring it clockwise to counter-clockwise, before lighting the fire bowl. The time had come. Hyacinth had put all her faith in Persephone, and now she prayed to the Goddess that her cousin would find the way.

It was all up to her now.

Hyacinth took a breath, raised the athame, and struck it down.

► ► ►

INSIDE OF WAY House, Persephone watched how the home was responding to Amara's arrival by lighting a fire, dropping orange peels along the floor in blessings and good luck, and rose petals along the back of the chairs. It took an hour for her to tell her tale, and when she was done, she studied the room into which they had retreated.

"The wood in your walls came from Ever House," Amara said, running a hand along the floorboards. "It was our home—before. After the curse was cast"—she glanced to Ariel—"I watched from my new home in the hinterland as every witch left on the island set out to try and break it. For decades you all tried every spell you could, only to be thwarted again and again. Until your grand-mothers, Beatrice and Viola Mayfair, and Magnolia Ever, found three precious stones that disrupted the paths of space."

"Precious stones?" Ellison asked.

"The lost charms of Three Daughters. Astral stones, spirited from the moon by the Goddess herself. A ruby blessed in blood, a rose quartz born to true love, and a moonstone harvested during the blood moon."

"What did they do with the stones?" Persephone asked, her hand going to her hourglass, where Dorian's rose quartz and El-lison's ruby were tucked away in the false bottom.

"They tried to use them," Amara said. "They didn't know the three stones fit into a lone key, and the key fit into a singular lock. In their excitement, they cast a spell and nearly split Wile Isle in two. During the earthquake it caused, your gran, Persephone, had a vision. A few months later, during the spring equinox, your grandmother Viola met a traveler, fell into lust, and grew ripe with child—your mother, Artemis.

"That's always been our way," Ellison said, staring out the window to the rolling tide of the sea. "Mating with travelers from other lands, letting the sea bring them to us and then releasing them like a fish when we're done with them. I once asked Gran if it was part of the curse, that love never stayed. She said it was a gift that our line was varied and diverse and so were our talents. That our world was large, even if we could not leave it often."

"She was correct in part," Amara said. "Lust is fleeting, while our sisterhood is eternal. But true love stays—if your heart is open to it." Amara gave Ellison a small smile, before continuing. "Viola had a vision, and in this vision, she saw the dark magic's price."

"Which was?"

Amara shook her head. "I do not know. I cannot see the vision of another. She packed her things, wrote a letter to her sister, and left. Whatever the price, she feared it so greatly she left behind her home."

"She did it to protect me," Persephone said, remembering her vision of Hyacinth and Moira dead at her feet. Her voice cracked as her heart gave a painful thump in her chest.

Amara reached out a hand to brush Persephone's hair from her face.

"Our mother tried to break the curse," Ariel said. "She was sent off island. All magic connected to the curse carries a steep price."

Amara sat on the small navy stool, before looking over her shoulder at Ellison. Ariel narrowed her eyes.

"What was that?"

"What was what?" Amara asked.

"That look. What is *that look*?"

"Your mother was lost," Amara said.

"Was?"

Amara gave a helpless shrug as Persephone glanced over to Ellison's stricken face. Persephone forced herself to swallow, grateful she didn't gulp. She knew where lost things, lost witches went. The truth was in the details of everything Amara said.

"What of the stones?" Ellison asked. "Did Persephone's grandmother take them with her?"

"She threw the two she could find, including her rose quartz, into the sea. The third was here," Amara said, tapping her foot over one of the removable floorboards in Way House. "The house would not surrender it. But one is hardly a concern when two are missing."

"In her letter to Beatrice that I recovered, Viola said that we were the key," Persephone said. "Our generation."

"What letter?" Ariel asked, looking at her. "You never said anything about a letter. Why is everyone suddenly cryptic and frustrating?"

"I didn't know I was ever not frustrating," Persephone said. "There's been a lot to say and not say. I didn't get to mention the letter before everything *erupted*."

Ariel lifted a brow, and Amara spoke. "Viola was correct. They were too early to break the curse. Spells have rules, and while we can bend them, the consequences of breaking one are dire. One hundred years, a proper seal of time, needed to pass for the curse to be ready to break."

"You say that like the curse is a person," Persephone said.

"Magic is a part of the divine, the divine is a piece of the Goddess. Who's to say it isn't a being of a sort?"

Persephone thought of the library, of Dorian, and bit her lip to keep her focus.

"They also needed the right key for the lock," Ellison said, looking to the front door. "A physical and metaphorical key. Persephone and . . . something else."

"Yes." Amara tilted her head, studying Ellison. "You saw this."

Ellison shrugged. "I see many things. Not all come to pass."

"This something else?" Ariel asked. "Where is it?"

Amara's lips curved. "Lost."

"Oh, something else is lost? You're smiling at that, fantastic," Ariel said.

"It is," Amara said, "but I have a feeling what is lost can be found, when it's meant to be."

Ariel rolled her eyes and stomped off, but Persephone looked at Amara.

There was only one place she knew of where lost things would go.

▶ ▶ ▶

MOIRA WAS TIRED of having a dead body in her kitchen. It had only been a few hours, but after learning Hyacinth had given her life over to the astral realm to seek some level of darkness in assistance to an evil witch, Ever House felt like a land for death.

That Deandra Bishop's body was cloaked and ready only added a level of strife to this day of horror. It was a day for the most bizarre of realizations.

Hyacinth was in leagues with a dark witch. Persephone had killed her co-worker in a misguided effort to drive out the dark. The curse was no closer to being broken. The Way witches tried to help the Evers.

There were four corners of the earth, and four corners to this new predicament. Moira did not know who to trust. She did not know what to do. Moira would no sooner turn on her sister than she would carve out her own heart and try to go on living without it.

But she wasn't sure how deep Hyacinth was in the throes of dark magic, or how to extract her from it. This was not something Moira had been taught, had never thought to learn for herself.

On Wile Isle, the rules were clear and concise. Learn from the light, seek the Goddess, *and harm none*. When the time came, and the anniversary of the curse was upon them, look to the stranger who is not a stranger to break the curse. The prophecy was clear. Persephone had come, she was the key.

And yet Hyacinth had made a fucking mess of everything.

When Moira tried to confront her in the garden, her sister started humming and pruning her violets. With her *hair*. She refused to speak to Moira, and eventually Moira gave up to go inside and make a truth serum. If Hyacinth wouldn't volunteer answers, Moira would steal them. Fuck the rules.

Moira knew astral mania was a common side effect of leaving your body for too long. That spirits and darkness hid in the veil beyond this world, and could manipulate anyone who traveled without form. Moira feared what had happened to her sister, and wondered how long it had been happening. Mania was the only acceptable explanation for Hyacinth's behavior she could come up with.

Moira finished the serum, and pocketed it. She'd administer it once the bigger task at hand was complete. She washed her hands and went over to where Deandra Bishop's body lay. She prepared it with lavender, lemon balm, and eucalyptus. When the time came, Moira circled it with salt, called up her circle, and set the boundary spell. Then she stepped back and waited.

Before her eyes, the body wavered like a television channel flickering in and out. The air fizzled, there was a loud pop, and the body was gone. Ariel's efforts to pull the body through space had been successful.

With the body gone, the air cleared.

Moira took a deep breath, blew it out, and smelled the hint of iron and sulfur. Not inside, but coming from the garden.

Hyacinth.

Moira turned and ran from the room, dashing through the kitchen and bursting out the back door.

The ground where Hyacinth had sat only a half hour before was blackened. A circle the color of spilled ink ringed her once favorite part of the garden, the place where Hyacinth swore the fairies guarded. Rust tickled Moira's nose and she walked closer, studying the scarred earth.

Blood magic. Dark, poisonous magic. The earth was thick with it. The air curdling from it.

Moira turned and grabbed her cloak from where it was thrown over the rail, and sent out her power. Calling for a trace of her sister, for a flicker of Hyacinth's signature on the island.

The only thing to come back to her was the river of primordial ooze, as black as the circle, as marred as the earth, running somewhere deep inside the great mountain. With her heart hammering in her chest, and her palms slick with sweat and fear, Moira threw the cloak over her shoulders and ran for Way House.

▸ ▸ ▸

WHEN THE CLOCK struck eleven, Ariel used her ability to reach into space to transport the body of Deandra Bishop from one spot on the island to another. She told Persephone it was rudimentary magic, when you got down to it, but Persephone noted that even Amara looked impressed at the feat.

Persephone's grief was a shroud of sadness as she studied the body. As her tears flowed, the weight pressed out into the room. It was like sharing space with a rain cloud, and Ellison walked into the kitchen to try to seek shelter from it.

"Why now?" Ellison asked Amara as Ariel and Persephone said a blessing prayer over the body. "You've had the mirror, you've had motivation. Why not steal back some of your magic from your sister and come over like she did?"

"My sister stole magic from those she came in contact with by slipping into their minds. Possession is dirty magic. It's great power, but it comes with a great cost. I would not take from another like that. Nor would I give up my humanity for power," Amara said, her voice weary. "You know the price power bears. You know what it took from your mother."

Ellison let out a shaky breath, but did not respond for a long moment.

"Timing," Ellison said a while later, noting how Ariel wrapped an arm around Persephone as she elevated the body in the air. "It's always timing, isn't it?"

"When the Goddess wills it, yes."

"Does this mean I'm being possessed?" Persephone asked once Ariel went into the kitchen for a sachet of aster. She was finally able to voice the question that had been dancing in the back of her brain. "By the Many?"

"No," Amara said. "*You* are in control of them."

"How can you be sure?"

"There are many things I do not understand, but possession is not one of them," Amara said. "You are not a possessed being, Persephone May. You opened the door for the Many, and you can close it."

The front door shifted open, and all of the witches followed the body out of the house, down the steps, and to the raft waiting on the beach. Deandra Bishop would be laid to rest at sea, and her soul—they hoped—would return to where all souls that no longer wander go.

"You know who the Many are," Ariel said to Amara, while Persephone and Ellison stood some distance away at the water's edge.

"Of course." She smiled. "Don't you?"

Ariel looked to where Persephone kept the Mayfair locket tucked beneath her shirt.

"The library keeps the souls of the dead," Ariel said, remembering what her gran had said of it.

Amara slipped her hands into the pockets of her cloak. "And the dead keep watch over the key."

"And my mother? That's where she is, isn't it? That's what the look you shot Ellison was about. I'm not a fool, Amara Mayfair. I haven't had that luxury in some years."

Amara reached a hand out and gave Ariel's arm a soft squeeze. Ariel bowed her head for a moment, and when she raised her chin again her eyes flashed bright.

"So are they *all* trapped in her, in Persephone? The dead lost and bound to that place?"

Amara shook her head. "No, not all, and not trapped. The locket is portal magic, it's one way in and out. It's a certain kind of freedom."

Ariel gave a nod of understanding. "And the price that you want to pretend you don't know about for breaking this curse?"

"There is always a price, Ariel Way. You of all people know that now."

▸ ▸ ▸

AT MIDNIGHT THE four witches set the body of Deandra Bishop to rest. Prayers and song were called and sung. Persephone's tears fell into the ocean, one more loss added to her roster of many.

They did not have to set flames to the raft or wait for a storm to break it asunder. The witches clasped hands, and called to the four quarters.

> "We call upon the guardians of the East, South, West, and North
> and the elements of Air, Fire, Water, and Earth.
> We ask for strength and protection, peace and guidance.
> We ask you seek Deandra Bishop's spirit,
> So she may rest, and lead her home.
> As we will it, so mote it be."

The raft tipped up and back, and out to sea. There it sank slowly into the welcoming waters. Down went the little boat, down went the body of the girl who would never reach her potential.

The four women turned to walk back up the beach to the house, and Moira Ever appeared on the edge of the ocean.

Moira walked slowly toward them, her coat billowing out behind her. Her face was drawn, as though she had aged years instead of minutes.

When Moira reached the others, she paused to rest her gaze upon Amara.

"Hello, daughter," Amara said, her expression calm.

"Amara Mayfair. I should have known," Moira replied. "I need your help."

SIXTEEN

D ORIAN WAS IN THE dark. He knew it was the dark because
he could not see even a millimeter into space. He knew he
was alive, or as alive as he'd been for the past two hundred years,
because he could hear himself think.

Hello?

He said the word again and again, listening to his inner voice
greet him. It was, to put it mildly, a surreal feeling to be a consciousness without a body.

Dorian had read numerous books on dying, for the Library
for the Lost had a nearly endless supply on books of almost every
subject. He recalled a chapter where people discussed experiencing
weightlessness. He did not think that was right, though, because
to feel yourself float, or to feel as though you were weightless,
implied you had a body to lose its connection to gravity.

He simply existed. And also . . . he did not.

Dorian's mind grew hazy, thought slowed and slipped. He
forced himself to think, to remember. Where was he? Ah, yes.

Fucking Hyacinth.

It said rather a lot about the Mayfair and Ever witches that
he had been the guardian over the Library for the Lost for two

centuries and he had not been foiled once, not until this generation of Wile Isle witches came into his world.

He was irritated, but not completely lost to anger. Without Hyacinth tricking him, she would never have brought Persephone to the island. If Persephone had never come to Wile, she would never have come into her powers and come to find him. Finding Persephone was the one thing that made his unendurable time as guardian more worthwhile. Or had.

Still.

Love was not something Dorian knew in his mortal life. It was a surprise to him to discover it might be the most potent and powerful treasure he'd ever overlooked. Now he was lost to Persephone, and lost to time, and there was nothing to be done for it.

Dorian thought of the books in the library, the catalogue of content he memorized every few years. The library brought in new information like a stream brings in water. It was constantly being refreshed, as knowledge and story were lost every day, every hour.

Lost.

Like him, like the library.

Could it be that simple?

If Dorian was truly lost, then surely the library would find him. He only had to wait. A little longer.

His mind shuttered, the edges growing fuzzy once more.

There was something he needed to know. Something to hold on to.

If only Dorian could remember.

▸ ▸ ▸

MOIRA EVER WAS quick to fill the others in on her sister's disappearance, as well as the darkness she'd called to the garden at Ever House. Persephone felt a jolt of fear comingle with her anger. Hyacinth had put a spell on Dorian, and now she wouldn't be able to confront her, find out why, and force her to fix it.

Persephone would have to do it all on her own.

"Such dark magic," Moira said, looking up into the night sky.

"I can't understand what would drive her to this. Now there's no power of three, there's no plan. She's blown it all up."

"True has always had a deft hand at swaying those who are bending to the point where they break," Amara said, her hands slipped into her cloak.

"Hyacinth isn't weak," Ariel said, earning a grateful look from Moira.

"She . . ." Persephone hesitated, but the fear and worry on Moira's face had her speaking up. "She isn't weak. I felt her strength the moment I met her." She thought of her many conversations with Hyacinth, flipping through the pages of her memory. "She seemed lonely at times, perhaps."

"Lonely?" Moira asked.

Persephone nodded. "It's a feeling I knew well, and Hyacinth seemed to be waiting for someone, or something."

Ariel looked away, before she walked off.

"It takes time to mend a broken heart," Ellison said, before glancing at Moira.

Moira paced across the sand. "I have to find her. Before it's too late." She took a deep breath as if to compose herself. Even so, Persephone watched the tremble pass through Moira's hands as she clasped them together.

"True will have planned on us coming," Amara said, studying the clouds shifting across the navy sky. "I would gather, from the spell you've described Hyacinth casting, True has bound Hyacinth to her, and pulled her into the hinterland. She knew Persephone's being here would cause enough cracks in the spell for me to be able to cross over. My sister can't cross, even with the door cracked open, but if it's cracked wide enough, she can bring someone magical to her—if to her is truly where they wish to go."

"Hyacinth is only bound to me," Moira said, her cloak falling back to reveal the pain etched across her face, the fierce light in her eyes.

"Damn it, Hyacinth," Ariel said, marching back to the women. She reached down to pluck up a handful of sand and watch the grains fall unevenly. She scattered the remaining grains. "She's bound to all of us." Ariel dusted off her palms. "Amara is correct. The earth has marked her as here but not here."

"I'm going with you to stop True," Moira said. "I can fight. I can do anything if it will bring my sister safely back."

Amara tilted her head, studying the four women who stood in a square, each naturally drawn to their quarter: North, South, East, and West.

"We are family, yet," Ariel said, taking her sister's palm.

Ellison nodded. "We are. I've always dreamed we would find a way to fulfill the prophecy and set our family free. We have to help Hyacinth."

Moira reached for Ellison and the two clasped hands.

"We only have a few hours before sunrise," Persephone said, stepping closer and placing a hand on Moira's shoulder.

Amara studied the grains of sand dusting across Ariel's skirt, how they fell in a solid line. She gave a curt nod. "The way should hold."

Then Persephone May, Ariel and Ellison Way, Moira Ever, and Amara Mayfair locked hands over wrists under the blood moon. Pulling her hourglass locket from where she wore it around her neck, Amara withdrew a small needle from its heart. She pricked her thumb, and asked each of the women to swear their oath in kind.

Five thumbs, five drops of blood, each pearl of blood dropped into a chalice the size of a thimble.

The woman took turns dipping the tip of their finger in. Each drew out a single combined drop of blood, and pressed it to their third eye, down their lips, and across the skin and bone that covered their beating hearts.

For the first time in three generations, a new circle was formed.

Time would tell if it would hold, or like those who had come from the land before them, if it, too, would break.

▸ ▸ ▸

THE ROOM DORIAN found himself in looked like a closet that had acquired the temperament of a four-year-old, and been told it could no longer play with its favorite toy. Racks of clothing were strewn over the floor, across the bookshelves, and somehow stuffed into the ceiling vents and strung over the chandelier. To top it off, the clothing was *floral* and in shades of burgundy, lavender, and taupe.

"It's my idea of a garden party," the melodic if not raspy voice to his left said.

He looked down and realized he was wearing one of the floral-affronted frocks. Lace splayed out from the sleeves and pawed at his palms and fingers.

"What is happening?" he asked, looking over to see an older woman with a tired smile and Persephone's eyes.

"What *isn't*," she said, and kicked her feet up on a squat floral ottoman. "It's been a small forever where nothing has happened and now, here we are with the threads of space coming together through the cracks in time. It's like chaos's birthday party."

Dorian closed his eyes. His head was pounding out of his skull, the room smelled of wine and cigarettes, and Viola Mayfair was somehow talking to him.

"You can't be here."

"Honey, don't tell me what I can and can't do."

Dorian cracked an eye open. "I guess she got your attitude."

"If you mean my granddaughter, I'll take the compliment though you'd be wrong. Her pluck is her own. Hard won, too."

"Why am I here, Viola Mayfair?"

"I'm not a Magic Eight Ball, Dorian Moskito. Saying my name won't deliver a prediction, but at least you know enough not to be surprised."

"The library is made of surprises, which makes its surprises remarkably unshocking."

"Yes, well. I think there's time enough for surprises yet."

Dorian looked down, and realized Viola was shaking. He met her eyes.

"I need your help, boy, and we're short on time so I want you to listen and listen well. When my granddaughter comes to help you, because Goddess knows help is what she's going to try to do, you have to give her something for me, and pass along a message."

Dorian lifted a brow, opened his mouth to argue. Viola's hand snaked out, and it felt like ice wrapping around his wrist. "This is not a joke, guardian. She needs you, and I need to hear you promise."

Dorian swallowed as some of her fear climbed onto him and skittered up his arm. "All right. I promise."

"Just as your library needs a guardian, so, too, does the world beyond. Wile Isle is a world within a world. It's how the Goddess built it, and when Amara and True altered her design, the new world became part of the balance. The hinterland must exist for Wile Isle to exist, for the library to exist. If one does not, all will perish."

She held out a box to him. "Take this looking glass and give it to my Persephone. Give freely to her whatever she requires for help, but be certain to tell her—there is *always* a cost. The debt must be paid."

He grasped the small container, his heart plummeting to his stomach. "The cost is too great, you're asking her—"

A chime rung out, cutting him off, and Dorian looked over his shoulder at a new sound. A ripping, tearing, horrible sound.

Cracks broke through, running up the seams of the walls, down into the floorboard.

"What have you done, Viola Mayfair?"

The witch drew herself up, her shoulders back and chin raised. "What I must to help my grandchild." Her lip quivered and the smile she gave nearly broke his heart. "Now you do what you must, and help our girl."

The chimes sounded again. The room broke in two.

Dorian watched, helpless, as Viola Mayfair was sucked from the room, before he screamed and the world once again went black.

► ► ►

THE WITCHES RETURNED to Ever House. Amara took her time as she moved, letting her fingertips graze over the handrail and her eyes savor every inch of the rooms they passed over and through. Amara had said to Persephone that Ever House had once been hers, and it was clear that no matter how long you were away from it, home truly was where your heart would linger. Persephone hoped when this was over, Amara could return to her life inside the house. That Amara might find a certain kind of peace when the end finally came.

"The key to magic," Amara said, "is to understand where power is housed. It's in the heart and the mind. Two interlocking chambers divided by the body. If the mind believes, reality can bend. If the heart truly wants, then the way will appear. When the mind and heart work together, well, anything is possible."

Amara paused at the top of the stairs and drew the air to her. "It still smells of jasmine," she said, a hint of wonder in her voice. "It was our favorite scent, mine and True's."

"It's always here," said Moira. "Like nature's spritz of perfume."

"My room was just down here," Amara said, stopping outside what had been Persephone's door. Amara pressed her palm to the frame. "It's yours now," she said, looking over her shoulder at Persephone. "I'm glad."

Before Persephone could think of a reply, Amara crossed to the room where Hyacinth had lain dead only hours before and, without touching the handle, sent the door flying open. "This was True's room."

The room was cast in shadows. As Amara moved into it, the shadows receded like ink pooling from a page. The room looked ordinary. In it sat a wooden bedpost framing a full bed with a navy quilt, cream pillows, antique lampshades and tables, and a wide circle rug on the floor.

The room did not, however, feel ordinary. Dark magic left a trace. Like a sour taste lingering in one's mouth or a film coating one's skin, it clung.

"Hyacinth's been using this room," Amara said, running a fingertip along the quilt. She crossed to the wall, and pulled from her maroon cloak a red garnet. "The Arch to Anywhere is housed here for a reason. Magic begets magic when it's channeled properly, and if the Goddess wills it. The arch is one of the strongest conduits in this hemisphere. It was meant for greatness." She studied the garnet and then tucked it back into her cloak. "It's where we must go."

"Why the arch?" Persephone asked, as they turned and followed Amara back downstairs, through the living room into the kitchen, through the wall of clocks, to where the Arch waited.

"We are using the arch's magic as a portal. We draw the energy up, and channel it out. The key is to see where we aim to go. To see Hyacinth and travel to her."

Standing in front of the arch, the five women closed their eyes, and held their hands out, palms up. As they concentrated, the elements moved around them. Spirit flickered from Amara's fingertips, floated up from Persephone's palms. Water rose off Ellison's skin, while the air shifted around Ariel and Moira.

The stone arch shimmered, and as it did the door faded. In its place was a walkway made of light.

Persephone imagined Hyacinth, her flowing dark hair and clever eyes. She saw her and she saw beyond the veil, into the hinterland she had traveled before. She reached, and her hand brushed into the solid wood of the arch door.

"I don't . . . I don't understand this," said Amara, frustration making her voice echo.

Persephone opened her eyes and looked around. Each witch stood with one outstretched hand pressed against the door. The door was partially opened, and beyond it was nothing more than a regular-sized pantry.

"What in hades?" Moira said.

"It's . . . a cupboard," Ellison said, staring blankly.

"No," Ariel said. "It's nothing."

"The way in is shut," Amara said, running a hand over the wood. "I don't know how True could manage this."

"She didn't," Moira said, stepping to the side, and reaching down. She pulled up a thin chain with a dangling silver hyacinth attached to it from the floor. "This was Hyacinth's doing."

Ariel swallowed. "I gave that to her for her birthday ten years ago."

Moira met her eyes.

"What do we do now?" Persephone said, running a hand over her face. "Try a new variation of the power of three?"

"It won't be enough," Amara said.

"What?" Moira turned to look at her. "Why not?"

Amara gave an elegant shrug of one shoulder. "It was never about the power of three. Hyacinth had a good idea, but it wouldn't have worked."

"Are you kidding me?" Moira said, exchanging a look with Persephone. "All of this and you're saying it was for nothing?"

"Not nothing. It was everything. You three were just knocking on the wrong door."

"So what door should we knock down now?" Moira asked, waving her arms. "I'll kick it open, just show me the way."

"The land beyond the veil is locked," Amara said, her words slow, her eyes going to Persephone. "It only needs the right key."

"The right—oh." Persephone gave a firm nod. "Right. You mean me."

"Let's go then," Moira said, turning.

"No," Amara said. "You are hearing me but you are not listening. That particular door needs a key. *Only* the key."

"Alone?" Ellison asked, her tone sharp. "That's crazy."

"And what does she do by herself if she manages to get there?" Ariel asked. "Juggle? True's more powerful on her own land, that's what you said. Storing her magic in jugs or whatever and waiting for Persephone to arrive so she can use her for however she plans to as a conduit."

"Persephone's stronger than any witch I've met," Ellison said, running a nail against her teeth.

"This is about more than being strong," Ariel said.

"You would leave my sister trapped?" Moira asked.

"I wouldn't send Persephone off by herself to get trapped, too."

"Stop it," Persephone said. "Both of you. You're wasting time. Amara, what do I need?"

Amara took a deep breath. "If we can't go together, through

the arch, then you will need the original key. How many stones do you have?"

"Two."

"You'll need the location of the last stone, then," Amara said. "With it, you can unlock anything."

"And *we* can save my sister," Moira said. "I'm not letting anything happen to Persephone either."

Ariel gave a shake of her head, paused, let out a curse. "Hyacinth said the truest witch told her, '*the* queen just took your pawn.' I forgot about it in the chaos of Amara's return and Deandra's send-off."

"Queen takes pawn." Persephone's fingers twisted together. Dorian. Finally.

"The pawn isn't who you think it is." Persephone closed her eyes. "I have to go." Waving an arm through the air, Persephone reached out into space. "I'll get the other stone. I'll find the way. I promise."

Persephone stepped forward, and, setting her spirit free, Persephone's body dropped behind her, crumpling to the floor.

▸ ▸ ▸

THE LIBRARY FOR the Lost had once again changed its form. The room was filled with floating sheets of silk and linen draped down from the rafters. It was like being in a dream, or, Persephone realized, like being in the cabin of the boat in the memory the library had shown her. Inside Dorian's memory.

In the center of the room stood a raised dais. Above it, floated Persephone's family grimoire.

The library offered no books to her aside from the grimoire in front of her. In fact, the library's shelves were missing, the stacks gone. This was a room void of story, void of a guardian. Persephone reached for the grimoire and ran a hand over it. Spirit rained down like sparks flickering against the pages.

"Show me what I need."

The book shuffled its pages forward, stopping on a spell: To Call a Lost Soul.

Persephone skimmed over the words. Then she reached for her locket and closed her eyes.

The voices of the Many, who had been so quiet since Deandra Bishop's death, spoke up.

"Mind the spell.

You must give something up.

To gain something back."

"I've given up enough," Persephone said, but knew the fates would not care. This spell called for sacrifice.

She ran her hands over her pockets. "Haven't I given up enough?"

"What is enough?"

Persephone looked around the room. "I don't even know what to offer."

She felt as if eyes were roaming over her skin. She had her power. Had little doubt the library would accept it as sacrifice.

"That would never do. What else do you have?"

Persephone's hand went to her neck. The Mayfair locket. It was the first and only gift she'd ever received. But giving it up was giving up a part of the connection she'd formed to Dorian.

Persephone sighed. She had to try.

She pocketed the stones from the locket, sliced her palm with its edges for good measure, and threw the necklace into the air.

The hourglass hovered suspended in the air before exploding into a mass of shooting stars. They shimmered overhead. Persephone thought she saw her own face reflected back. The stars dropped from the sky and Persephone acted on instinct—she threw her arms out and caught them as they fell.

A warm rush of air flooded through her, threaded in her hair, and wrapped around her bones. She breathed deeply and looked down.

A form appeared on the floor, the same one she stumbled over the last time she was in the library.

"Dorian," she said, crossing to him.

He was shivering, but he was alive—or as alive as he could

be. His clothes were wet, his hair thickened with ice. Wherever he had come back from, he had brought a piece of that realm with him. The room around them shifted and changed, the silk fabrics yanked away to reveal the library as it had first appeared to Persephone.

The large stone fireplace was stacked with wood, the embers cold. She found matches and kindling and the fire roared to life. Persephone slipped her palms under Dorian's broad shoulders, tugging him by the armpits, one inch at a time, until she had him in front of the fire. Persephone tried to warm him with magic, but, as always, in the library the usual rules didn't apply.

Persephone grabbed every scrap of blanket she could find, cursing the library for not leaving the sheaths of silk and linen behind. Then she took the top layer of Dorian's clothes off and wrapped him as best she could. When that was done, she went back to the family grimoire.

She tried to concentrate, but her gaze and heart pulled her back to Dorian. Each sentence Persephone read shifted from words to symbols. For all intents and purposes, Persephone might have been reading Finnish.

"How do I help him?" she asked.

"Time."

"Time?"

Persephone looked around. There was no time here, or at least not time according to the laws of physics. Persephone walked back to Dorian, and settled next to him. She wrapped her arms around his sleeping form, and stared down at the strong brow, slope of his nose, and rise of his cheekbones. She brushed her fingers along his jaw, and thought of how he had seen her, truly seen her, from almost the very first moment.

Her heart had been hammering in her chest since she first entered the library, but now it slowed. Grief settled in next to Persephone like a loyal Labrador who knows its mistress has returned home.

She'd lost so much. Persephone couldn't lose him, too.

Even as she thought it, Persephone knew what a fool's hope

it was to think. Because Dorian was never hers. He belonged to the library. If she didn't lose him now, she would lose him later.

Her tears fell, quiet and urgent. Persephone bent her head over his. She wished with all her magic she had the answers the other witches needed, the strength to break the curse, and time to spend freely with the man beside her.

As the tears fell, the light in the room rose. The voices of the Many were quiet, but something shifted. Books on the lowest shelf shook and tumbled free. They scattered along the floor, making their own bridge across the marble.

Beneath her, Dorian stirred.

Hope filled Persephone as her hands gripped him tighter. "Dorian?" she whispered. "Can you hear me?"

He groaned in response, and his eyelids fluttered. He gave a slow blink.

"Persephone." He reached up, and pulled her mouth to his. It was a question and an answer. She responded by kissing him full of all she wished she could give, before gently easing back.

"Are you okay?" Persephone asked, as she helped him sit up. She adjusted the blankets more firmly around him.

"I've never been so looked after," he said, with a wry smile. "All this and I only had to lose the light for it to happen."

"The light?"

His half smile fell from his face. "Hyacinth found a way to remove me from my physical form. To separate the guardian from the library. Or at least, I think that was her plan. The library must have a guardian. It simply drove the light from me, sent my consciousness into the archives."

"Of the library?"

He nodded. "It's the only way I can cross into them." Dorian stared deep into her eyes, his gaze searching. His fingers tightened on Persephone's arms. "Viola Mayfair. I remember. She . . . found me. I was losing my grip on who I was. The archives have a way of deleting old information when it is no longer lost. Viola came." He looked around, saw the books scattered along the floor. He climbed onto his knees, still holding her, his tone urgent. "She said to give you what you need, but to tell you 'there is *always* a cost. The debt must be paid.' Viola told me to tell you, she was frantic. She'd have to be to seek me where souls should never go. She. She . . ." He trailed off, lost looking back to wherever he'd been.

"Magic always extracts its cost," Persephone said.

"She didn't mean magic," he said, looking back at her.

"Then what?"

Dorian shook his head. "I . . . I don't want to tell you."

"Dorian."

He closed his eyes. "The prophecy was incomplete." He pulled out a small box and opened it. Inside was a small looking glass. "You have the power to break the curse. To do so you must remake the world. Only you have the power to do so, but if you do . . ." He looked down at the box in his hands. "The world will need a guardian. If you break the curse, you must remain in the hinterland."

Persephone did not try to stop the shudder as it ran through her.

"And if you do not break the curse, the world will crumble and the souls in it will be lost forever. If you do not do this—" He licked his lips and shook his head.

"If I do not break the curse, True will go free," Persephone said, a chill burrowing into her bones as the meaning of her vision shifted into focus. "My cousins will die."

"*You* will die," Dorian said, his voice a low rasp. "The world of Wile Isle and beyond will be at True's mercy."

Persephone closed her eyes.

"I can shelter you here," he said, looking around, taking hold of her arms. "Time doesn't work the same in the library. We can stay right here. You don't have to go. You don't have to do anything."

Persephone let out a hysterical laugh, which turned into a shaken giggle that hiccupped into fear. "If I don't break the curse and stop the witch, my cousins and I die," she said. The tears clogged her throat and she rubbed at her neck, trying to force them away. "If I break the curse and stop the witch, I'm as good as dead, aren't I?"

He put his hands on her shoulders. "You're locked away, like me, only in a shell of the world with no way to set you free."

Persephone covered her mouth to keep the sob contained. It was too much.

She had spent her life searching for her family. Knowing she didn't belong, that the power she had was pain. Now she finally had family and friends. A man she was falling for, ridiculous as the circumstances were, and she was being told she had to give it all up.

The other shoe had dropped.

Dorian rose to standing. He looked rugged and ridiculous and he made her stomach flip even as she fought not to scream at the top of her lungs.

"I came because of the key," she said.

"You mean rescuing me wasn't your goal?"

"It was a side road."

"You don't have to stay on the road at all," he said. "Let's jump in the bushes, you and me."

Persephone had never been so tempted by an offer. She wanted, with every cell of her being, to say yes. To run away from the problem.

But she'd been running for too long, and the problems never stopped coming.

As tempted as she was to run away with Dorian for all of time, Persephone knew it would never work. While her heart was fast becoming his, she had also fallen in love with Moira, with Hyacinth—who she still wanted to strangle—with Amara, with Ariel and Ellison. She couldn't let her family die, wouldn't allow them to remain cursed when she could stop it.

She didn't want to leave Amara, who had spent one hundred years fighting to repair the damage she had helped cause, to try and face this battle on her own. Not when Persephone was the only way she could win.

"I would follow you into another world, Dorian," Persephone said, her heart in her eyes, "would it not lead to the end of the one for those I love."

It was his turn to close his eyes, to nod, as Persephone ran her hands up his arms to cup his face.

After a short forever, he asked, "What do you need?"

This time when Persephone spoke, it wasn't her voice, but those of the Many. *"She seeks a key that leads to everywhere and the final stone to unlock the veil."*

Dorian's eyes shot open. "Persephone."

Persephone blinked. "Yes?" This time her voice was hers.

"Just checking," he said, blowing out a breath. "Viola . . . she also said to give you what you need." He gave Persephone a smile, and it didn't reach his eyes.

"Why don't you lead?" he asked, waving her forward. "It's what you did so many weeks before, when you first came to the library. I think the library will heed your call."

Clasping hands, they walked to a door and through it. "Dorian?" Persephone asked him, leaning into him as they navigated the long hallway. Her whole body was shaking, but she did not stop, only picked up her pace. "Why did the library choose you?"

There was a rustle behind her, Dorian's blanket-toga brushing against the stone of the floor. "Because I was born to pirate goods. Because I set everything in motion when I lost the magical items I was hired to protect."

"It doesn't make sense though," Persephone said. "That the library won't let you go."

"It needs a guardian."

"Yes, but can't someone else do it?"

"I don't think it works that way."

"But couldn't it?" Persephone said, pausing to look back. "Do you ever wonder if change is what the library is afraid of?"

The lights in the hall flickered off.

A gong sounded from far off and a crack splintered into the wall of the library.

A sharp searing pain split Persephone nearly down the middle. Her hand was ripped from Dorian's before she could gasp a sound.

The shadows descended.

Wind whipped up from the floor, throwing Persephone into the air. An unforgiving gale wrapped itself around her, tangling her hair and clothes as it tossed her back and forth like a towel tangled in the spin cycle.

As she rose, Persephone glimpsed the determination on Dorian's face, the fear in his eyes. He reached for her, but it was no use.

The library split apart.

Persephone watched Dorian slam one hand into the wall, curse, and slam his hand again. On the third attempt, a small door opened. He yanked a box from out of nowhere, pulled a pouch from it, and threw it up to her. She caught it as an inhuman cry tore from her throat.

The voices of the Many called out, and Persephone was ripped into a thousand pieces.

Dorian shouted her name. Persephone thought she heard him beg the Goddess to take him instead. Persephone threw back her head, and screamed with all her might.

▸ ▸ ▸

WHEN THE PAIN consumed her, the wind deposited her into the void. Persephone wasn't entirely certain she was still alive. She struggled to grasp a tether of space. To stay on a path. Her arms shook and her head pounded with the beat of a thousand drums. The voices of the Many tripped over one another, speeding up, growing louder. Warning her of what was to come. Persephone couldn't make out anything beyond it, and she couldn't force a breath into her body.

It was like being stuck inside an overactive beehive while the queen revolted. Persephone lay on the floor and begged the Goddess to make it stop.

A very small part of Persephone thought maybe she shouldn't get up. That she could stay lost. Lost witches ended up at the library, and she didn't want to keep going. She didn't want to break the curse, and she didn't want to die.

After too long and not nearly long enough, Persephone found the right path to drag herself back to Wile Isle. She crawled off the arch and found herself beneath Moira and Hyacinth's tree, a few feet from the black circle that marred the earth.

Persephone rested her cheek on the bark, too weak to wrap her arms around it. Tears ran down her cheeks as Persephone tried to hug it with her mind, and would have laughed at herself if she weren't facing her imminent doom.

No manner of tree hugging would put her back together. Persephone thought of her grandmother finding a way to tell Dorian the choice Persephone would have to make. The answers she needed, they all needed, were hers. The problem was the price of magic wasn't high, it was absolute.

Could she do it? Forfeit her life?

For thirty-two years, Persephone had been shuffled from home to home. She had lived a life without love. One devoid of companionship, of hope even as she clung to the possibility that she would find her place in the world. She had finally found her place among these witches, among family who saw her, loved her, and had helped her figure out who she was. She was strong and fearless, and right in this moment, she was fucking terrified.

Persephone closed her eyes and wished she could make the curse, the pain—all of it—go away.

Ellison's voice reached her first.

"Breathe in blessings, breathe out fear," Ellison said, floating just outside her sight line. "One breath after the other."

Beyond her she could hear Moira arguing with Ariel. "We have hours, *hours*, until the one hundredth anniversary of the curse. If we don't break it by then, Hyacinth is lost forever."

Amara was singing, her soothing voice low and warm. Something about time and love, about dark honeysuckle and ice apple trees.

Amara and Ellison crossed to her, their hands laid over her.

"There she is," Ellison said.

Persephone's power flickered and flared. Warmth rushed into her body, like a desert stream being flooded, it filled her up. This power was permission. It was a door into not the minds, but the hearts of the witches who poured their magic into her. It carried love and hope. It was strength and it was faith.

It was . . . faltering.

Persephone sat up with a start, yanking her hands away. Amara's color was close to gray, and Ellison swayed where she sat.

"You let me drain you?" Persephone said, feeling a little like a homicidal vampire. "Don't either of you have *any* self-preservation?"

"No," Ariel called, answering for them. "I tried to argue you would take too much but no one listens to me."

"She wouldn't do so on purpose," Ellison said, wiping her brow.

"You shouldn't have taken off like that," Amara said, reaching a hand out to brush Persephone's cheek.

"I had to. We needed the stone, and I needed to . . ."

Find answers. Learn the cost of breaking the curse. Have her heart broken.

"Yes?" Amara said.

Persephone cleared her throat. Her family was looking at her with concern and compassion, with such unbridled loyalty. She weighed her words, chose a truth that was not the truth. "I had to save him."

"Save her pawn." Ellison nodded, her smile gentle.

"You ran off to the library without fair warning to save a man," Ariel said, rolling her eyes. "Don't *you* have any self-preservation?"

"Her mechanical man," Ellison murmured, color seeping back into her cheeks.

Persephone looked over at Amara, who somehow managed to look worse as the minutes ticked by. Persephone turned to Moira. "I think Hyacinth knew. She figured out she was being used, but she still knew I was the key. She tricked Dorian, but I think she had to in order for my grandmother to pass along a message through him."

Persephone held up the pouch clutched in her hands. She tipped it to the side, and a large hunk of obsidian tumbled out.

"Your mechanical man saw Viola?" Moira asked.

"Yes."

"What did she say?"

Persephone looked down at the rock. She could tell them. Everything. All that Viola said, what Dorian told her. She could tell

306 · PAIGE CRUTCHER

them the cost of the curse. They loved her, she knew that. They wouldn't want her to make this kind of sacrifice.

Persephone looked up, and saw the trust on their faces. It was in the tilt of their heads, the intensity of their gazes, the way they held their shoulders back, waiting. Each woman stood not by her, but with her.

Her family.

Like the people locked away in the arch. Those women were her family, too, and Persephone could feel into the marrow of her bones if she were able to know them, she would love them as much as she loved the sisters of her heart standing before her.

Persephone took a slow, measured breath, and lied.

"Viola told Dorian Hyacinth was trying to help. She said it was time to break the curse."

"Oh, Hyacinth," Moira said, staring at the stone.

Persephone shifted her own shoulders back, and reached a hand out to Moira. Amara and Ellison placed their hands on Persephone once more, and Ariel gave a slow nod.

"Then it is time. Give me the rock, cousin," Ariel said, reaching out.

▸ ▸ ▸

WHILE THE OTHER women sat on the porch, working on a spell to bind Persephone to them, and Persephone accepted the mission to end all missions, Ariel studied the obsidian hunk.

Ariel loved puzzles. As a child she spent hours solving various riddles, studying details to re-create thousand-piece puzzles, and as an adult her favorite rainy day pastime was three fingers of scotch and a fresh game of Sudoku. This rock was no different. She angled it to the light, and noticed a seam that should not exist. Surveying the Ever porch, Ariel walked to the small chest beside Moira's outdoor library shelf and rooted around until she found what she was after. Holding a pack of matches, Ariel walked back to the steps, scooped a handful of plotting soil, and sat down hard on the earth.

"What are you—" Moira started, but Ariel shushed her away.

Ariel dropped the dirt on top of the stone, lit a match, and held it underneath. She blew off the earth, turned the rock, and spit out the fire, and a loud thwack cut through the air. The stone splintered in two. The witches crept closer as Ariel turned the rock on its side, knocked against the obsidian three times, and a lone skeleton key tumbled out.

Persephone's mouth dropped open.

Amara's smile was a flicker of its usual self. "It would require great sacrifice to take this from the library." Amara plucked out the key and studied the oval head. She looked over to Persephone. "They both, Viola and your librarian, love you a great deal."

Persephone swallowed hard, and looked away.

Ariel snatched back the key.

"I've seen that before." Ellison crossed to her, tapping the triangle symbol over a rectangle housing a figure eight. "In a vision I had when Persephone cast her spell. I was in a dome standing in front of a door, and the figure eight marked the door."

"It is the symbol for the Curse of Nightmares," Amara said. "Three in one. Interlocked, ever locked, away in the hidden world."

Ariel rapped on the other side of the obsidian and a moonstone tumbled out. "We have the last stone of three." She took the key back. "The others please?"

Persephone pulled her two from her pocket and passed them to her cousin. Ariel hunched over, muttering to herself. "Interlocked, two full circles." She paused. "Two full circles." Ariel turned the key three times, and blew. "False teeth," she said. Ariel dropped the stones inside the rock and they clicked into place.

▸ ▸ ▸

"The key," Persephone said, borrowing a notebook and pen from Moira, and rubbing at the place where the Mayfair locket should have been. Persephone started to draw. "To reach beyond the veil, to break the curse . . . would be us coming full circle to where Amara began. When her power was stolen, the curse was cast and the world frozen." Persephone sketched it out as she thought. "Then there's my return home, to a place I've spent my whole life wishing for, and the family I've always wanted. It's the interlocking, the full circles. That means something." She looked down at her drawing.

⊙⊙

"Looks like a tiny pair of spectacles," Ellison said. "One for your mechanical man."

"That's the interlocking part," Persephone said. "There are three worlds we're inhabiting. Wile Isle, the Library for the Lost, and the realm of the lost witches frozen beyond the veil—the hinterland. I can't move things from the library, but maybe here . . . if I had enough power." Persephone looked to Amara. "Sacrifice. Cost. I need to bring it full circle." She looked at Amara, realized the witch knew exactly the price the curse would take to break it. "No, it was never the power of three."

Amara tilted her head in understanding. "No, my love. It is the power of all."

Moira looked at her cousin. "If we all give Persephone enough of our magic, will that mimic the binding of the original spell?"

"If the connection holds," Amara said.

"Then, once I'm over," Persephone said, her eyes on the circles. "I can pull you through."

"Yes, but if you fail you will be on your own on the other side," Amara said. "You could easily be as lost as I was."

"To break a curse is to break the magic of the witch holding it," Persephone said. "We use the power of all instead of the power of three. We find True, form our circle, cast her power out, save Hyacinth." She swallowed. "It's simple."

"Then once the spell is broken, you send everyone home?" Ariel asked, quirking a brow.

"Sure. Safe and sound. Easy peasy, nice and breezy," Persephone lied, not meeting the witches' eyes.

Ariel snorted.

"Magic always exacts its price," Amara said, her voice gentle.

Persephone thought of Dorian trapped in the library. She thought of Deandra, of her grandmother, of Hyacinth still trying to break the curse from inside it. She looked over the faces of the women who would walk through worlds with her to save those who came before them, and Persephone forced the corners of her mouth to curve. Words have power. These words would weigh the heaviest in their promise. "I will accept the cost."

With the plan set, the witches made quick work of forming and setting their circle. Persephone took the center with each woman stationed at a quarter.

With their permission, Persephone siphoned their power until the paths of space were glowing around her, each a vibrant color and living vibration.

The power she'd pulled hummed to life beneath her skin as she raised her arms. The cool air cascaded down her back, and wind rushed up, blowing her hair forward. She only had to think *breeze* to stir it. Persephone felt wild with power, her whole body pulsing as energy roared beneath the surface of her skin.

When she had pulled all she needed into herself, Persephone surveyed the witches to make sure enough of their strength remained. All looked well at ease. All except Amara, from whom Persephone had taken the least.

"I am fine," Amara said, flashing a brief smile at Persephone. "I can't recharge the same as you. When I'm across this land, back in the other world, I'll be stronger."

Persephone nodded in relief, and took the key from Ariel, who begrudgingly passed it over. Then Persephone wove her fingers through the threads of space and slipped them like a crown over her head. She tied more around her torso, through her legs, under her feet, and over her chest, binding herself to the others.

This time, Persephone did not leave her body behind.

All of Persephone May stepped through the void, and beyond the veil.

seventeen

Persephone did not step into the veil, as she normally would, to find her path. This time, she stepped *beyond* it. Into where the world of witches and magic, of frozen grains of time, and dreams made of shadow, waited.

As Persephone walked from the mist, she looked down to see the pristine cobblestone path beneath her feet once more. The world of Wile Isle was duplicated to near perfection. This time, though, Persephone recognized in the details something was off.

The truth was there, hidden in what Amara had sung to her. Dark honeysuckle and ice apple trees. They were everywhere. The apples made of frost, their bark so sharp that when she reached a finger out, it sliced at the tip. Hidden just off the path, oak trees hung too low, their limbs mossy with fur instead of foliage.

Blood magic. She could smell it all around her.

The sun itself was frozen on pause, white stratus clouds framing it in the sky. Persephone looked over her shoulder, and saw the moon sitting in juxtaposition to the sun. The two sides of time faced off, and it was impossible to tell who would win.

Persephone needed to call the others through, and she couldn't waste a moment. Couldn't give herself the opportunity to second-guess her choice. She cast her circle with the small vial of salt she had in her bag, completing it with a personal item from each of the witches. Ellison's scarf, Ariel's hat pin, Amara's locket, and Moira's ring. She placed each item at a corner, sat in the middle, and reached across space.

The vibration started in the tip of Persephone's pointer finger. It ran along her palm, under her elbow, and up to her shoulder. From there, a shock of pain ricocheted across her chest bone, down into her pelvis.

This was wrong. There should be no discomfort, there should only be a knowing.

The pain grew and Persephone curled in on herself, reaching for help and finding air.

"You cannot take without giving."

The voice of the Many siphoned into one. A lone voice, insistent in her mind.

"Give?" Persephone asked it back, her breath heaving in her chest. "I have nothing left to give."

"If you do not balance the scales, the same will happen to them that happened to the guardian."

"What do you mean?" Persephone fought to sit up. "What happened to Dorian?"

"Before. When you tried to take him without the balance. It split him apart."

The world reeled around Persephone, spinning as she lost control. Magic always came with a price. Of course it did. Why hadn't Dorian told her sooner what she'd done?

She thought of what Amara had said, about love. Love. It has a funny habit of messing everything up. Persephone knew that now.

She needed to pay the balance to pull her cousins across. But how? She'd given up the locket, given up her lone talisman to the library in proof of sacrifice. She tried to draw another breath. The library had wanted power.

What about this world—what did this world want?

More, what was it afraid of?

There was only one way to find out. She'd have to do whatever it took to keep going.

Persephone let go of the sole thread of space she kept wrapped around her finger tethering her across worlds. The pain fell away. So did her connection—the binding spell was broken. The way back to Wile Isle was gone.

She gasped as breath flooded back into her. Wiping her brow, she blew the line of salt free, and gathered the items, putting them back in her bag.

"How do I balance the scales?" Persephone asked, rubbing her side and looking up at the distance between the moon and the sky.

"*You cannot take without giving.*"

"Thanks," she said. "You're as helpful as a fortune cookie."

Persephone could have sworn she heard the voice laugh before it faded away. For now, Persephone would have to continue on alone, because the sun wasn't the only thing watching her. She could feel eyes in the mist, surveying her as she headed for town. True would know Persephone was here. Persephone was almost out of time.

When Persephone had first traveled beyond the veil by accident, she had landed in the center of town. She went there now, looking for the bakery in hopes that if she retraced her steps, the Goddess would help her find her way to Hyacinth.

The first thing she saw when she entered town was the veil breaking down. Time had been set. One hundred years given to house this land and these witches. The space created, this spelled nightmare, was running out. As it did, it would take the witches with it.

The earth was no longer a lush and vibrant green, but a dark primeval purple. The grass flopped over on its side like a fish gasping its dying breath. No breeze stirred, and no witches walked here either. They were fully frozen, like the apple trees. Persephone paused in front of a woman wearing a timepiece, her eyes gazing beyond her to the sky.

Unblinking, unseeing, unmoving. It was the woman from the

bakery. If Persephone failed, her world would continue to decimate. The witches, all of the witches, would be lost.

"*All these souls and no place to go.*"

There was a deep sadness in the voice speaking for the Many.

"Is this . . . is this how it is for you?" Persephone asked.

"*No, child. This is how it will be for us if you fail.*"

Persephone's hand shook as she brought it to her eyes to shade against the sun.

"I'm sorry," she said.

"*You did not make the bargain, but you must pay the price. It is the way, and it is we who are sorry.*"

Persephone tried to draw up her resolve. She knew the souls of the witches—her ancestors—wouldn't reach the land of the Goddess if she failed. She hadn't considered what would happen to the Many if she did not succeed.

You cannot take without giving.

And she could not win without losing. So be it. Persephone took a deep breath. If she didn't stop True, they would all be as good as ghosts.

The chimes rang through her mind much in the way a person wakes from a dream—a slow blink, a part of her consciousness stretching, a new alertness somehow on edge.

The bells chimed again and Persephone turned.

Thunder rumbled overhead, the call of an invisible storm. In the distance, Persephone saw a tall spire, reminiscent of a church steeple. Lightning splintered in the sky, the air electric for a moment before the ground rumbled beneath her. Time inside this world was speeding up.

Hyacinth screamed.

The Many cried out in alarm.

Persephone ran in the direction of her cousin's voice as fast as she could, down the cobblestones through the center of town, past the post office, the bakery, the houses and shops with their new stone and slate shingles. As she darted down the path, decay crept in, trailing after her.

Ice apples curdled and fell from the tree limbs. Persephone

sprinted, trying to pull space to her, finding it slipped through her fingers.

She turned a corner, and where the mountain should rise into view, stood an oversized tent. Persephone turned a full circle. When glanced from the corner of her eye, it had the look of a circus or revival tent. Faced straight on, the tent showed what it truly was—a large tree with spires of limbs wrapped around itself. Persephone ran a hand through the air and the vibration rumbled up from the ground, weaving the truth of the vision together.

The creation before her was a sea of branches interwoven. It was impossible to pin down where the roots began and the tips ended. Not quite oak, definitely not maple or sycamore or willow. It was a tree like nothing she'd ever seen.

At its base a dark arch rose up, creating a vicious-looking door.

"The Menagerie of Magic," Persephone whispered, watching color shimmer outside of it. All the threads of space spooled here, like rainbow ice cream running down the sink to the center of the drain. It was a swirl of shades, the largest of which were shadows pooling out from the edges.

"Space and magic do not follow rules inside."

"What?" Persephone asked, looking for the voice inside her head, realizing there was—of course—no one to see.

"Inside the Menagerie of Magic, space bends, magic waits, and whole worlds can take new shapes."

Persephone leaned into the voice. She knew the cadence. Somehow . . . from somewhere else.

"Can you say that again?"

Silence answered her.

Persephone reached into her pocket and pulled out the key Ariel had reconstructed. She thought of what she knew of magic. Your head and heart must agree. What you believe, you become. It sounded like a motivational saying you'd get from a calendar in a museum gift shop—and yet.

Persephone held up the key and at her will, it changed form into a circle. A full circle. She slipped the key onto her wrist, took one step, then another. As the shadows swam along the ground toward her, Persephone focused on the key and the door. She *needed* to get inside—she *would* reach the door.

A hiss rolled along her shoulders, thunder crackling against the sky.

Persephone thought of Dorian, and the faith she had in him and he in her. She took three more steps, and the wind blew harsh against her back. The wind tugged at strands of her hair like cat claws playing with their mark before taking the final swipe.

She thought of Deandra and her sacrifice, and the world around her went pitch-black.

The key wrapped around her wrist warmed, shifted, a new transfiguration taking place.

Light shot up from it, a flash in the dark.

"*Open the door,*" said the Many.

Persephone looked again and saw instead of a dark gaping arch, a large key-shaped hole stood before her. A keyhole the size of a person. She took a breath for courage, and walked forward.

▸ ▸ ▸

PERSEPHONE SLIPPED INSIDE the arch like any good key fits any strong lock. On the other side of the tree that was not a tree, the entrance to the Menagerie of Magic waited.

Its front hall was a sea of mirrors. Ovals, squares, diamonds, rectangles—looking glasses of all shapes and sizes stared from their perches down (or up) at Persephone. In the center of the room sat a small table with a lone purple candle wider than her hand and taller than her arm. The candle was not lit, and yet its light reflected onto the walls.

Persephone bit back a shiver. She did not claim a love of looking glasses and tried not to think of the one in the box in her pocket. She knew Amara had made use of that particular magic, but Moira had taught Persephone that mirrors once were used to trap restless spirits. Still, *these* mirrors were not ones Persephone could avoid.

They were also not the scariest thing in the room. Not by far.

Between the mirrors, crawling along the walls, roamed shadows. Shades of men, women, and children slithered and writhed along the walls like guard dogs waiting to strike. If Persephone had wondered what happened to the restless spirits when they were not housed in the mirrors, she now had her answer.

A sea of shadow monsters.

Leashed but not locked, these creatures could only travel so far. The bodies of the witches were frozen, separated from the souls True Mayfair had stolen and trapped. The souls oozed a bleak sorrow wrapped in need so strong it nearly stole Persephone's will to stand.

"Frozen souls. Bound witches."

Persephone shuddered as she grasped the truth in what the Many told her. The witches of Wile Isle were frozen on the island, but their souls weren't. Instead they were caged here, in the menagerie, by True.

"Trapped."

Persephone cocked her head. That voice. She knew it.

"Who are you?" she whispered to the Many, but was met by silence.

Persephone forced one foot in front of the other as the lost souls quilted the room around her, and walked the final steps to the candle. She ran her hand over the flame as Hyacinth had taught her. It flickered and jumped. The flame was alive. As it responded, the shadows' mournful cries swelled into the room before they were sucked back into the mirrors.

Persephone swallowed past the lump in her throat and turned to look for a door. Another arch stood in the far corner of the room. It was a near duplicate to the one inside Ever House.

No cuckoo clocks ticked here to remind her time was fleeting. Persephone wanted to call out for Hyacinth, to try and spell the air for a circle to pull the others over, but knew being so obvious was like going into a haunted house and setting off fireworks for the hiding serial killer to find your location. While Persephone did not believe she had the element of surprise, as long as she moved with cunning, she had an echo of one.

What had the Many told her outside? *"Space and magic."*

If the rules could be bent inside the menagerie, Persephone

would find her chance. She didn't dare try to find Hyacinth on her own. It was likely a trick, but if it wasn't it was definitely a trap. She couldn't bring her cousins over while outside the menagerie, that had been apparent from how the land had revolted when she tried to keep her tether to them intact.

No, Persephone would have to be smarter than the problem if she was going to bring her cousins to her.

Persephone didn't attempt to cast a traditional circle or follow any of the rules of magic as she had been taught these past few months. Instead Persephone did what she did best, and listened to her heart.

She cupped her arms around the candle and pulled her fingers through the flame. Taking in the light, she saw strands of aether bending space. She saw the witches on Wile Isle waiting.

Persephone wrapped her palms around the vision of the witches, called them each by name. She rooted her feet to the ground, took a determined breath, and *pulled them through.*

Persephone gagged as the air swirled around her, as the ground shook and the candle flickered. The witches walked *through her* to cross over. The pain stole her breath; sweat broke out along her spine. When all four stood at her side, Persephone squeezed her hands around the flame.

She dug deep and drew. The candle's power, the island's power, her own power. It flooded her system.

Persephone had never felt so charged, so full of life.

"Where the hell are we?" Ariel asked, as Amara pressed a palm to Persephone's back.

Persephone looked over, a quiver of unease rippling along the power in her veins at how Amara's shoulders caved in, how waxy her skin appeared.

"We are in the inner chamber of the Menagerie of Magic," Amara said, light flickering across her face. "You've brought us inside."

"It was the only way," Persephone said, her voice echoing out too loud into the chamber.

"Not the *only* way," Ellison said. "Whatever you tried to do when you crossed over nearly worked, but I much prefer this method. Before it felt like you were trying to rip our insides through to our outsides."

Persephone dropped her hands. Yes, that is what she had done to Dorian when she'd tried to call him to her from the library. Persephone closed her eyes for a brief moment to think his name, see his face, and pray to the Goddess he was somehow safe, while knowing she would never see him again.

She pushed the pain away as it tried to rush her. It would be a tidal wave if she let it. She would mourn him later, if she survived this.

"This world wouldn't permit me to pull you through when I first crossed," Persephone said. "Magic doesn't work the same inside the menagerie. Hyacinth is here, and we need to find her now."

"The rules of this world are crumbling," Amara said with a nod. "We need to find the heart, where the magic starts and ends, because that's where Hyacinth and True will be."

Moira gave a curt nod and started toward the arch. Amara locked eyes with Persephone for a moment before she turned and followed.

Persephone watched the light and dark comingle in the room. How foolish they had been. Persephone stood facing a room full of trapped souls, locked in shadow. She waited for the Many to whisper something, a hint, a promise for how to help. The voice was as quiet as a grave before the digger's shovel strikes.

Persephone walked forward and approached the arch. They couldn't go back. They had to save Hyacinth and the others. The only way out was through.

Moira flanked her left and leaned in to inspect the arch. "It looks like a twin to Ever House."

Amara nodded. "The wood for the Arch to Anywhere came from this tree's double. When we were first stuck here, True decided to replicate everything in this world to match what existed in yours. I thought the menagerie was a piece of home for her, at first."

"Instead it became a place where she could grow her power,"

Ariel said, with an eye cast back at the mirrors. "She wants to be free of this world, and return to overrun ours."

"I can't entirely say I blame her," Ellison said, shuddering a little as the pulse of the menagerie ticked faster beneath their feet. "This place is terrifying."

"True's magic," Amara said. "It's grown as corrupt as she is."

"We need to get Hyacinth, shut True down, and get the hell out of here," Ariel said.

"As with the other arch, this one must work off desire and determination," Amara said, tapping a finger against it.

"Must it?" Persephone asked. "Don't you know?"

Amara shook her head. "I haven't been allowed to enter this sanctum in over fifty years. I have a small home in town, or did. I suspect it's decaying."

"*Everything* is decaying," Persephone said. "Space is unwinding the threads that hold this world together."

"Yes. I can feel it. The world is urging for me to reach out and pluck them apart," Ellison said, her hands clasped together. "It's all I can do to keep from tugging one thread like a child swiping an edge of icing from a birthday cake."

"I can bind you," Moira said, "if you'd like."

"Try and I'll wipe the eyebrows from your face," Ariel said.

"She doesn't travel well," Ellison said, as a near apology.

Persephone tasted rust as she bit the tip of her tongue. Goddess, she would miss these women. "Let's move," she said. "We don't know what we're walking into, other than our desire to find True. Amara, you look like you could topple over any moment."

"I'll hold," Amara said, but took her place behind Persephone.

The other witches flanked into formation, and though they did not touch, their magic wove as ribbons from one to the other, a solid connection. They closed their eyes, reached hands to one another, and saw their desire to find True in their mind's eye.

This time, their efforts worked. One moment the witches stood in the hall of the menagerie, the next they were on a lake of glass, beneath a tree of lights. Beyond them the world was smudged, faded at the edges.

"We're in a memory," Amara said, wonder tingeing her voice.

It reminded Persephone of being whisked into the pages of Dorian's past, when she'd been at the Library for the Lost. Persephone hadn't realized then that books could hold memories. Persephone now knew they could hold a great deal more. They could hold souls. They could hold damn near anything.

"It's Hyacinth's memory," Moira whispered. She took a step forward, and Persephone reached out and caught Moira's wrist. Persephone pointed to the clearing ahead, where a table stood with a basket full of fruit.

Ariel froze. "Their offers should not charm us, their evil gifts would harm us," she said after a moment, her fingers to her lips.

"Cheek to cheek and breast to breast, locked together in one nest," Hyacinth's voice was a whisper inside the room as she finished the rhyme.

"*Save her, save her,*" the Many whispered.

Persephone spun in a circle, looking, but did not see Hyacinth anywhere.

"*Goblin Market,*" Ariel said, looking up at the glowing tree above them. Its branches of lights flickered. They burst open and fireflies dripped out of the casings, fluttering down to hover just above the group's shoulders and heads.

"Come out, True," Amara called, her voice barely stronger than the twitch at the edge of her mouth.

"Come and find me, sister," the voice, made of smoke, whispered back. "I've been waiting for you."

Amara held up a finger when Ellison moved to speak. Amara closed her eyes, and reached out a hand. She dragged it along the base of the tree and came away with a palm full of blood.

> "*Show me what I need to see,*
> *with my power you are free,*
> *as I will so mote it be.*"

The droplets pooled together onto the glass lake beneath them, and in the blood a room shifted into view.

It was not a terribly large room. Objects inside it were piled from wall to wall, some visible, others covered in sheets. Persephone had seen a similar room before. It was a room of lost treasure, treasure sunken to the bottom of the sea that should have been with souls of the other two islands of Three Daughters. This treasure was not lost, but stolen. Much like the souls from Wile Isle that were locked in this very tree.

"The poem," Ariel said. "Hyacinth's favorite. We used to send each other snippets of it during the endless winter months."

Moira nodded. "She and I did the same. We'd leave the pages in the arch, like bread crumbs to help us pass the time."

"Maybe it's a clue?" Ariel said.

They studied the tree, the endless vastness of the dark room.

"It's the Goblin Market," Amara said, leaning into Moira for support. "We must eat the fruit. To move past this place, we taste the wine, give in to temptation."

"Come buy our fruits, come buy. Great. Let me guess, this is the part where the evil gifts will harm us?" Ariel said, reaching one hand out and running it along a strand of space.

"Can you reach beyond the memory?" Persephone asked.

Ariel shook her head, letting her hand drop. "I could, maybe, reach back into our Wile Isle. But with how this world is shifting and stuttering, that would be risky. I could lose my arm . . . or worse."

"So we eat the fruit," Ellison said, pressing a hand to her belly. "Sure. Why not? I can eat."

They were slow to advance on the table, waiting for a new trap to be sprung, but the glass lake remained frozen, the world beneath their feet dark and cold. The lights on the tree shifted from twinkling casings that looked like pods to small beetle bugs. The bugs morphed into butterflies that flickered just out of reach.

Moira sniffed, reached to snatch up a luscious-looking purple plum, and Ariel took it from her.

"Tell her." She looked deep into Moira's eyes. "Tell her I love her. I forgive her, and I'm sorry, too, okay?"

Before she could bite deep into the fruit, Moira snatched it back. "Tell her yourself, Ariel Way." Then Moira bit into the plum. Juice ran down her lips and chin as she grabbed the goblet from the table and tossed its contents back. "The power is in you, my brilliant Persephone," she rasped, looking at Persephone. She licked her lips and managed to whisper, "Don't hesitate," before her expression of pure determination froze on her face.

Persephone's knees locked. She swallowed back her tears as the juices ran clear, and Moira's skin colored from a deep olive to pink to snow white. The freeze spread out from her lips and cheeks, depleting the color from her hair, hands, and body. Moira turned from witch to ice in a matter of moments.

A crack split the glass lake beneath their feet in half, and before so much as a scream could form on their lips, the witches—save Moira—plummeted through the crack.

▸ ▸ ▸

THEY TUMBLED LIKE Alice down the rabbit hole for ten excruciatingly long seconds. When they landed on the other side, a sea of fabric broke their fall.

Persephone was quick to untangle herself. She jumped up and called for Moira. But when she tried to step forward the fabric caught her around her ankles and she went down again.

A laugh from the center of the room had Persephone's fists coming up as she tried to shake off the restraining cloth.

"Really, True?" Amara's voice floated up from somewhere beneath the linens. "That old trick?"

A wave of magic crested through the room, pulsing into Persephone's solar plexus. The familiar tug, her old friend, yanked once more. This time, it only reacted in one direction.

The blankets dropped and pooled into the floor before dissolving completely.

As they fell, Persephone got her first clear look at the room.

It was a bit like a bird's nest. A magpie's in particular. Unlike the boat, this room's treasure was pile on top of pile, shoved along the edges in the crevices, items boxed and in baskets, oversized bags toppling over beds. It was everything stuffed everywhere.

"Moira?" Hyacinth asked, her voice timid and small, coming from the corner. Hyacinth's eyes were glazed.

The witch was drugged or dying.

A low curse came from Ariel. Ellison whispered something too low for Persephone to hear.

The Many whimpered.

"Someone had to eat the fruit," Persephone said to Hyacinth, a lump in the back of her throat as she studied her face.

Hyacinth's remaining color leached away. "She wouldn't have eaten it, the poem was a warning, she had to know, she couldn't—"

"Do whatever it took to save you?" Ariel said, her tone surprisingly kind. "You should know better than that."

Amara took a step forward, but it was too late.

Hyacinth was up and running. She reached the arch on the other side of the room and threw the door open. Through a hole the size of a plum, Hyacinth spied her sister. Frozen. Trapped in a moment beyond space.

Hyacinth's frame shuddered as she struggled to stay on her feet. Ariel's eyes filled with tears and it took everything in Persephone not to rush to Hyacinth. She knew from the look on Ellison's face the witch felt the same.

But True, who was a carbon copy of her twin sister Amara, had not turned her gaze from Amara and Persephone. True stood straighter than her sister with hair a shade darker, but it was nearly impossible to tell the two apart from first glance. Then True snarled and the two women couldn't have looked more different.

Persephone drew in a breath. The game was far from finished.

"Two keys in the palm of my hand," True said. "Which should I unlock first?"

Persephone couldn't look back at Moira, couldn't give in to the grief pooling under her skin. She spared a glance out of the corner of her eye at Amara, who held her chin high.

Ariel and Ellison, at the edge of the room, worked their way toward True.

True couldn't see how each sister had a thread of space thumbed around her finger, how they focused on where to go. They reached True, and Persephone saw her cousin's blank face take them in, and realize what they meant to do. Hyacinth let out a shout in warning, but it fell on deaf ears.

Ariel and Ellison wrapped their threads around True in an attempt to start the first phase of the spell and bind her, and their magic ricocheted back.

The Many whispered loudly in her ear.

> "*Inside the Menagerie of Magic*
> *space bends,*
> *magic waits,*
> *and whole worlds*
> *can take new shapes.*"

True's magic had been waiting for them.

Ariel and Ellison fell to the floor, shivering as power poured off them in waves. Persephone let out her own cry as Hyacinth staggered to where Ariel lay, running her hands over her cousin, trying to help her.

"Oh goody," True said, scooping up an urn and crossing to them. "This really will be easier than I thought."

Magic emptied from Ariel and Ellison into the urn, filling it up. The remnants slipped like shadows among the objects, before fading entirely.

"*Magic must go somewhere.*"

Persephone's heart raced in her chest, but she forced a slow breath out. She couldn't react, needed to remember why she was here. She studied the objects and thought of the library, thought of all Amara had told her about her sister and what True initially sought to do. The power she'd tried to hold.

Persephone was a conduit. She was *the* conduit. She snuck along the edge of the room to where True waited. She sniffed the air, ran a hand along the threads of space. Persephone didn't have long. As soon as True realized what Persephone was doing, she would likely shift into the element of air and pull the items to her.

The Menagerie of Magic was not a house of magical items; it was a house of *magical power*. Persephone was the conduit, she could draw power in a way no other witch could. She would take every. Last. Drop.

Ariel and Ellison, crumpled on the floor, turned their heads in the direction of Persephone as though they could hear her thoughts. Ariel's fingers slid into Hyacinth's and she squeezed once.

Persephone held out her hands, palms up. Then Ariel whispered a quiet apology to Hyacinth, took back her hand, exchanged a look with Ellison, and the two Way witches threw the last embers of their power into Persephone.

As their magic left them, True's magic froze Ariel and Ellison Way completely. Trapping them as it had trapped Moira.

Hyacinth let out an inhuman cry. She wrapped her arms around the frozen form of Ariel.

Persephone bit back heartbreak and fear and reached for the urn. She touched her third eye, ran a fingertip across her lips, slashed it across her chest over where her heart beat, and commanded . . .

Release.

Power did not need to be asked twice.

The magic poured forth like a hot spring. It left the housed objects and crested across the room.

Return.

On her command, the magic coursed into Persephone—it crested over and over, again and again.

Persephone gasped for more, for air, for light. When the magic shifted into dark . . . she welcomed it with opened arms.

The amount of power that pulsed into Persephone could tug the ocean from the shore; it could turn clouds into mountains and raindrops into caverns.

There was nothing in the elemental realm that Persephone could not touch or do.

Except.

"There is always a cost," True said, her voice tinny and smug. "Don't you know better by now?"

The magic *shifted*, and slugged in one direction before it sped up in reverse.

All the power, all the magic she'd gained, poured from Persephone.

Persephone tried to plug the hole, tried to find the leak and stop it. But it would not shut off.

Every last trickle of new magic bled from her, and when it was done, it took the rest.

All that she was, all she'd been born to be, was stolen out of Persephone.

"Blessed be," True said, coming to stand beside her sister, throwing an arm across Amara's shoulder.

Persephone looked up, gasping on a breath that shuddered into a wheeze, and stared into the face identical to Amara's.

▸ ▸ ▸

IT WAS ALMOST like looking into a mirror. Amara and True Mayfair. More than sisters, they were two sides of a coin.

Persephone lay on her side, her eyes shifting from the sisters to the urn that was full of her magic. Her magic and Ariel's and Ellison's, and who knew who else's. Persephone's hand gripped in an involuntary effort, but she could not summon the smallest inkling of aether.

"I knew you wouldn't turn on me," True said to Amara, who appeared like a watered-down version of her sister as the strength that bloomed in True wilted from Amara. "What were you thinking going after the key on your own?"

Amara took a seat on the small stool a few feet from Hyacinth, who had yet to let go of Ariel's marbleized form. It was unclear if True even took stock of the fact that Hyacinth was still in the room—her gaze was focused so intently on Amara.

"What good will this do you on the other side?" Amara asked, waving a hand, her voice tired. "You know you can't hold this much power on your own."

"I don't need to hold all of it," True said, reaching out to press a hand lovingly against her sister's cheek. "I only need to transport it. When we are home, I will use it to restore Three Daughters and you. Return the magic and the darkness, rebuild our people."

"Into what?"

True smiled, and her face transformed into an upside-down fun-house version of Amara's.

"Into everything I need."

Amara closed her eyes. "You don't have a plan, do you?"

True's spine straightened as she tossed her hair back. "I will take what is mine. No one will stop us this time. No fools of men or beasts of burden. We will be queens, and the islands will be the start of everything." Her hands clasped together. "It's just as it was before, only this time I'll get it right. You'll have your home and gardens, and I'll have all the power I've been unable to hold. I'll control the source and I'll control the islands."

Amara shook her head. "I cannot follow you."

"Of course you can," True said, picking up a small looking glass and holding it out to better admire herself.

"No," Amara said, "I can't."

Amara shifted in her seat, just an inch, but an inch was all it took. Her element, aether, spirit, slipped out of her and into Persephone.

I cannot give you all the answers. I am sorry for that, but we grow short on time.

Persephone blinked and saw the vision Amara had shifted into her mind: Amara growing weaker day by day.

Amara's magic leaching the life from her in this world, and in any other.

Amara would not live to see Wile Isle again, or outside of this room. And yet her power, the last of it, she'd held back.

Amara had been holding back for years.

This was always the only way, Persephone. When it is time, you must strike, Amara whispered into Persephone's mind.

Hyacinth turned, and the connection between Persephone

and Amara was broken. Her cousin looked at her, then at Amara, before dragging her gaze to True.

"What of Moira?" Hyacinth asked, her words soaked in pain. "And Ariel and Ellison?"

True pasted on a clown's sadness. Exaggerated and plastic, her frown spread across her face. It was miles from reaching her eyes. "Sacrifices must be made, Hyacinth. There is always a price. This is what it takes for you to be truly free. I have kept my word; your well of magic will be filled when we return. You will be able to go anywhere, be anything. We will all be freed."

Hyacinth shifted in the direction of Persephone, and opened her mind. Persephone saw how True had tricked Hyacinth, how Hyacinth had worked for the past ten years trying to find a way to break the bond to the witch. How she'd tried to mend fences with Ariel, showing her the last of the memory Persephone glimpsed — Hyacinth telling Laurel to ask Ariel out, to take a chance on love, only to have Ariel misunderstand and the cracks between them widen into a gulf. Hyacinth's heart was in her memories, and it was as broken as Persephone's.

Persephone saw herself sitting on the couch in front of Hyacinth as they drank tea, and her cousin's love swam into her.

Hyacinth's eyes filled in one second as they stared at Persephone, and when she turned to True, they emptied. Persephone had never seen grief shift into power before, but Hyacinth reached out, snatched hers up, and staked her claim inside it.

Before True knew what was happening, Hyacinth sliced her palm, threw her hands out, and tackled True. She took down both the witch and the urn, which upended onto the floor.

"*Save her, save her,*" chanted the Many.

Hyacinth poured the magic spilling from the urn into herself, until the darkness of it hollowed out the irises of her eyes and turned her dark hair crimson red.

As Persephone watched the magic devour her cousin she tried to move, to scream, but she was frozen to the spot. Hyacinth's will held her where she stood.

Blood poured from Hyacinth's mouth, as her body wilted from immediate decay.

As Hyacinth held the magic, she turned and took more from the last waiting source.

True screamed. Her hands rising to her face as she raked nails down her cheeks. Hyacinth clung on, even as she was engulfed by the dark magic she embraced.

Now, Persephone.

Amara stood up, as calm as the sea after a storm, and reached for Persephone. She pulled her to her feet and met her eyes.

Change may be inevitable, but it can lead to a new, a better way.

Persephone stared into the depths of Amara's soul and saw the past flood forward: Amara and True swinging beneath a giant oak tree, picking carrots in their garden, singing songs and casting spells.

Amara and True holding each other during violent autumn storms, and clasping hands when they learned to control the ocean and turn the tide.

Amara's power taking over, manifesting into a darkness that would consume her and the land.

True devising a plan to save them both, Amara failing to stop her, and the plan turning as dark as the magic.

Magic always enacts its price.

"I am sorry," Persephone said, her eyes flicking to Hyacinth, her heart squeezing painfully in her chest.

She looked back at Amara and the witch smiled.

I will miss you, daughter of my daughters.

Persephone felt Amara's smile in the marrow of her bones. Then Amara cracked open her soul and poured every ounce of her being, pure and bright and light, into her great-great-granddaughter.

When it was done, Amara Mayfair fell to the earth. A husk of who she once was.

True screamed again, the sound so shrill it burst the mirrors, splintered all the glass in the room and in the chambers surrounding them.

Persephone was free to move, and the faces of the Many flashed before her eyes. As they did, she heard the lines from Christina Rossetti's poem.

> "*One had a cat's face,*
> *one whisked a tail,*
> *one tramped at a rat's pace,*
> *one crawled like a snail,*
> *one like a wombat prowled obtuse and furry,*
> *one like a ratel tumbled hurry skurry,*
> *she heard a voice like voice of doves, cooing all together:*
> *they sounded kind and full of loves in the pleasant*
> *weather.*"

They weren't just any voices—the Many were her family. They were the women who'd gone before her, lost and locked in the library, until Persephone came along and offered them a new way. First through the locket, and then at the last when she'd welcomed them home into her.

The last two faces paused before her. The first nodded, her eyes the same as Ariel's, her mouth as generous as Ellison's. Persephone bit back the grief as she nodded back to Ellison and Ariel's mother. Then came the next face, and this one was as familiar as Moira's and Hyacinth's. It was the face of *their* mother.

You have always had the power in you. It was her voice that she had recognized, so like her eldest daughter's. *Please save her.*

The walls rattled from the force. The floor fragmented into pieces. The land beyond the veil, and the Menagerie of Magic, was toppling in on itself.

Persephone blinked and the vision dissolved. This time she did not hesitate. She reached for Hyacinth and closed her fingers around her cousin.

"Let go," Persephone whispered, knowing what to do, no longer afraid. "Like you taught me, Hyacinth. I love you. Just let go."

Blood pearls dripped from Hyacinth's eyes. She looked at Persephone and her grief ran ragged through them both.

Hyacinth's tears fell faster, the blood shifting to ice, the ice to water. Hyacinth's system ran clean of the magic. As it ebbed clean from her it ran into Persephone, and Persephone fought to hold control.

She turned to True, and the temptation rose inside her.

It would only take one time. Spirit, the element of Persephone and within Persephone, could obliterate the dark witch. She could have vengeance. Revenge.

Change may be inevitable, but it can lead to a new, a better way.

Amara's words wove around her heart.

Persephone felt the Many. They were knitting her together, infusing her with the rawest of faith.

A new way.

She reached out and pressed a hand against True's cheek.

"Let go," Persephone said, her eyes reflecting back far more than her own soul.

Then Persephone drained every single last drop of magic from the witch.

Eighteen

T RUE CRUMPLED TO THE earth. Alive but frozen. A husk not yet depleted.

The outer world beyond the veil penetrated the menagerie now that it was no longer made by magic. The far wall of the menagerie crumpled, bringing down bark and vines and ice apples. They rolled across the floor, decaying as they scattered.

Persephone's control over so much magic was frail, tenuous at best even with the Many helping her. The power rose up, ready to claim her.

Hyacinth clamored, struggling to stand. She stumbled forward and embraced Persephone.

"I knew you'd figure it out," she said, a sob choking her words. "I screwed up so bad. I was only trying to fix it."

"Viola filled in the blanks," Persephone said, hugging her cousin, trying to stay focused. All around her the threads of time were unraveling and reworking themselves. "Dorian gave me the stone. You did fix it in the end."

Hyacinth shook her head. "I was only trying to protect you and Moira, and now . . ."

"Get your sister," Persephone told Hyacinth, as threads of aether exhaled around them. "All is not lost."

Persephone forced herself to breathe. Steady in and out like Moira had shown her. Persephone needed control. Her life and those around her depended on it.

Persephone could see now, with fresh eyes of the Many and the freedom of so much magic, what she was destined to do. The power had always been hers. It was nothing to fear.

With Amara gone, the souls she had carried would be lost among the witches on this forsaken island, trapped in the mirrors as shades of themselves. You have to give up something to gain something. There is always a great cost.

The Many must have known that, much as they must have known how Persephone would need them to harvest and contain so much magic for even a short window of time.

Persephone thought of Dorian and the library. She reached into her pocket and pulled out the pen Dorian gave her so many days ago. For emergencies, he'd said. She studied it, and knew how to use it.

Biting the cap off, she wrote on the air.

Dorian?

The word faded and, after a long pause, new handwriting replaced it.

It was quick to scrawl:

You are not alone, Persephone. You could never be.

Inside the Menagerie of Magic, space bends, magic waits, and whole worlds can take new shapes.

Persephone smiled and studied his words, turned them over.

Magic waits. Whole worlds can take new shapes. Persephone's element was spirit. As lonely as she'd been in her life, it was startling to realize she could never really be alone.

She thought of the two roads interlocking, two sides of one coin. The full circles. Change. Change could be its own magic, one of creating new possibility and a better future.

Persephone knew what to do.

She waited for Hyacinth to return, carrying her sister's frozen form. Persephone grabbed the shards of mirror off the floor, and pulled a thread of aether from the shadows.

Persephone wove it around the mirror pieces. As the mirror reformed, the shades—the trapped spirits of the witches frozen beyond the veil and the mortal souls Amara carried and had released when she died—crossed into the looking glass. Their shadows moved in and out of the frame, stretching beyond its borders.

"Break this when you're home," Persephone told Hyacinth. "The bad luck will be yours for a time, I can't do anything about that, but they—all the lost and trapped souls beyond the veil, mortal and witch alike—will be free." She hesitated. "There is always a cost."

"I will gladly pay it," Hyacinth said, squeezing Persephone's hand. "I'm so sorry. I—"

"It's okay, cousin," Persephone said. "I understand." She pulled Hyacinth to her and squeezed tight, counting to twenty, inhaling her floral scent, breathing her in, hoping the memory would last.

Persephone released Hyacinth and reached a hand to Moira. She brushed her hands across her cousin's nose and mouth, remembering the set of it as Moira practiced her Tai Chi, seeing the laugh on her lips as she taught Persephone how to sift flour. Persephone pressed her lips to Moira's and sent as much of the light as she dared into the frozen form. Then, Persephone whispered in her ear the final stanza from *Goblin Market*.

> *"For there is no friend like a sister*
> *In calm or stormy weather;*
> *To cheer one on the tedious way,*
> *To fetch one if one goes astray,*
> *To lift one if one totters down,*
> *To strengthen whilst one stands."*

When she was fully revived, Moira would understand Persephone's message. Moira would be strong enough for all of them.

Persephone tugged on the threads of space once more, and wrapped them around Ellison, Ariel, Moira, and Hyacinth. Persephone saw Ever House in her mind, saw the garden as it was before the scorch marks marred the earth. Saw the little gnome that guarded the land for the fairies and the fates with its single eye.

"Blessed be my sisters," Persephone whispered to the frozen forms of the Way witches, and to the Evers.

With love in her heart, Persephone recalled the words in her mother's letter.

"Love is giving up the whole world for the people you love. I gave up mine for you, and I would do it again in a heartbeat. The only way to keep you safe was to give you a fresh start. I may not have been beside you, but I have always been with you."

She understood the sacrifices love could demand now, and she was willing to make them for the women before her.

Persephone gave Hyacinth one last smile, and sent them forward across the realm, home to Wile Isle.

▸ ▸ ▸

WIND FLUTTERED THROUGH the menagerie, a cold chill cutting across Persephone's cheeks as loss ripped through her.

Persephone's strength wavered as she turned and crossed to True Mayfair's huddled form.

True was a witch no more; her power siphoned away, her magic leaving behind a husk of a woman with sad eyes and fear in her heart.

"Your sister gave me a gift," Persephone said, crouching beside True. "Now it's my turn to give you one, and restore a balance in the process."

Persephone placed her thumb on True's third eye, and saw beyond this land to the Library for the Lost. Knew what the library sought.

Persephone smiled her most secret of smiles, and made a wish for change.

She snapped her fingers, and the threads Persephone released wrapped around True's wrists and ankles.

Persephone reached out a hand, and pushed.

True toppled from this world into the next, and dropped down into the Library for the Lost.

Persephone wrote on the air with the pen.

The library needs a guardian. This one has no magic, but has a debt to pay. Perhaps now the library will consider your debt served.

The ground beneath Persephone's feet rumbled and stilled. There was a pause in the decay. The land beyond the veil waited.

Persephone's heart had made its greatest wish, and this time Persephone held out her own hand.

She counted slowly down from ten, and when Persephone opened her eyes, she laughed as warm fingers intertwined with hers.

▶ ▶ ▶

"How are you here?"

Dorian's eyes were smiling. "Isn't that my line?"

He looked around the room, at the once powerful objects that were now regular items housed in the fractured menagerie. "What did you do, Persephone May?"

She squeezed his hand and waved her other palm at the wall. The cracks formed into man-sized holes. "I'm restoring the balance, all the balances," Persephone said. "Come and see?"

Breaking a curse follows the same rules as breaking anything. A break needs to heal. The seductive nature of magic itself can cause a break. More begets more and as True Mayfair learned, once you have a little of a good thing, it's a short jump into *why not have a lot*? Persephone didn't have the same desire as True. Or even Hyacinth or any of her cousins. Persephone had only ever wanted one thing: to belong. To have family who loved and supported her, and to find her place in the world.

So it was, perhaps, in the end, almost easy for Persephone to do what needed to be done for the worlds to heal. To sacrifice herself.

Sacrifice meant the people she'd come to love could return home. Knowing they would be safe, that Moira would understand why she'd done what she had to do, Persephone could be at peace.

Persephone knew her place in the world. She was the balance. The key.

She understood it all now.

Her grandmother and mother had given her one of the greatest gifts. From them, Persephone had learned a powerful lesson. You sacrifice whatever it takes for the ones you love, especially when it's the right thing.

Amara had echoed this sentiment, as had her cousins. And so, this was always her path. To be sacrificed for, and to sacrifice for in return.

That, Persephone decided, was the heart of love, and she knew the heart of it was good.

The world beyond the veil was no longer crumbling. Its ties to the realm beyond were holding, connected to Persephone and the spell she wove even now as she walked Dorian to the center of town. It was the Spell of Dreams, as it should have always been.

"What are we doing here?" Dorian asked, his hand warm in hers, his faced tipped up to drink in the sun. It was the first time he'd been out of the library in two hundred years, and he appeared half afraid to blink and miss a single tree or brook or branch or cloud.

The air smelled of a thousand things, unmanufactured and pure. It was a delightful assault on the senses. Dorian's shoes clipped against the cobblestones. Everything was real here. Everything was out from behind doors and covers and the cloak of oppressing magic.

"I wanted to say goodbye," Persephone said, careful to keep her voice light even as her heart tripped over itself in her chest.

Dorian stopped walking. "Goodbye? Why do you have to say goodbye?" He stepped closer to Persephone, staring deep into her eyes and the Many who dwelled there. "You did it, Persephone. You saved everyone. You saved me. I wouldn't be here, freed from the library, if that weren't true. How did you do it?"

"It was the final step in the spell. The balance had to be reset in the library and back on Wile Isle. True Mayfair is now drained of her power. She'll wander for an eternity if the library deems it, guarding the stacks and living just a whisper away from the power she so craves. She won't be able to harm anyone again."

Persephone pulled out the box her grandmother gave to Dorian, opened it, and showed him the mirror inside. "My cousins are back where they belong, guarding and keeping the island." Reflected in the mirror were the four women. Moira sat in the garden with her arms around the blessing tree, Hyacinth behind her, with arms around her sister, and the Way sisters with their arms around Hyacinth. "They will finally be free to come and go from Beltane to Michaelmas to the spring equinox and every time in between." Persephone breathed deeply as she closed the lid on the box. "This world needs its guardian, and the souls from the Library for the Lost deserve a way out of purgatory. I can give them that here."

Persephone pulled him further down the cobblestone path to a clearing that had not existed hours before. Dorian could not know it, but it was a replica of the exact spot Amara had taken Persephone to when they met. A mirror image of the land of their family's birth on the cliffs of Scotland.

The rest of the land on this world Persephone continued to make. She shifted each surface to feature places that reminded her of Ariel and Ellison, Moira, and even Hyacinth. Persephone only had to see it with her heart and head for it to rise. Pieces of other worlds woven into one fabric to make a tapestry.

Here on the cliffside, Persephone paused at a stone cottage with a chuffing chimney and a small creek running beside it. There was a hammock in the yard and a swing attached to a large oak tree. Two jade Adirondack chairs sat on the small porch, a little bookshelf in between them. In the yard, beside the small garden, sat a gnarly little gnome with a bemused expression tugging on his elfin face. He was missing an eye.

Persephone smiled at the scene before them. "You know, I've never had a proper home before."

▸ ▸ ▸

IN ALL HIS time in and out of port, Dorian lived only for and on the sea. A boat was no home, not really. The library had been a cage, an occasionally gilded one, but a cage nevertheless.

He looked at Persephone's profile. At the strength in how she studied the land, the way her shoulders rolled back and down, like a soldier preparing herself. Was it any wonder, he thought, that the one treasure he'd never expected turned out to be a witch who could snow him under with the lift of her finger?

"That's all well," Dorian said. "I won't try to stop you, but I'll be damned if I'm going anywhere."

Persephone swiveled to face him, her stalwart gaze and warrior's posture dropping in a flash. "What?"

"You brought me here to say goodbye?" He shook his head. "You saved me, and thought what? You would push me away?"

"I'm giving you a chance to have the life you never had," she said, her voice tinged with exasperation, her eyes going dark.

"Not if it's not with you."

"This isn't a vacation, Dorian. You just got out of purgatory, are you so willing to trade it for another one?"

"It's not purgatory," he said. "It was a temporary stopover, maybe, but you said you're restoring the balance, and I can't imagine the balance means you sacrificing everything to never get what you desire."

"You know that's not how magic works."

"I know there's always a way, a loophole, if you're clever enough to search. For too long I wasn't. I accepted my fate, pitied myself. I didn't fight hard enough, but you, you have done nothing but fight and you've done more than move mountains, you've unmade and remade worlds." He reached out, took her face in his hands. "I shouldn't be here at all, and I won't leave you now."

Persephone's breath froze. This wasn't going how she planned, and the offer was too big.

"This is what I want," Dorian said. "All I want."

He brought his lips to hers, and poured everything he couldn't say into the action. Persephone's arms went up and around him, and some of the magic she carried couldn't help but slip into him. The light that bound her bound itself to him, and Persephone finally gave in to her heart's greatest hope.

They kissed the stars down into the sky and the lightning bugs into the air. They kissed the waters warm and the air into mist.

When they finally unwove themselves from each other, Dorian reached into his pocket and pulled out a book with the final page unwritten.

"I think it's time," he said.

Persephone smoothed a hand down her hair, and let out a laugh. She passed him the pen he'd given her and called into the wind, pulling the stars up from inside her and sending them out.

Dorian wrote the words Persephone spoke.

The Many were finally free . . .

Two by two, the Many ghosted from Persephone. They shifted and formed as they walked from shadow to shade to solid being.

A strong wave of gratitude and love crested over Persephone as the lost souls from the library and from Three Daughters islands were lost no more.

Persephone and Dorian watched them walk into town, into their new life, safe in the knowledge that they were guarded and they were loved.

Dorian stared at Persephone, his heart in his eyes. "For the first time in two hundred years, I know what it is to feel free."

Persephone looked up at Dorian. Safe in the knowledge that she was neither alone nor lonely. Those she loved were safe and the curse was broken.

She was guarded and she was loved.

Persephone May was finally free.

ACKNOWLEDGMENTS

THIS BOOK OF MAGIC would not exist were it not for the truly amazing people who assisted me in the journey of this novel.

Ashley Blake, you are more than a fearless champion of my work, and agent extraordinaire. You're one hell of a friend. Your guidance and support have meant more than I can say. Rebecca Podos, thank you for going above and beyond, and for your help in making it all happen.

My spectacular editor, Monique Patterson, who believed in the magic of the women of Wile Isle. I am so grateful for you and your vision for this book, and damn lucky to work with you. A huge thanks to Mara Delgado Sánchez, as well as DJ DeSmyter, Rivka Holler, Sara LaCotti, Jessica Zimmerman, and all the wonderful people at St. Martin's Press.

I belong to an extraordinary sisterhood of writers. The Porch— JT Ellison, Ariel Lawhon, Laura Benedict, Helen Ellis, Patti Callahan Henry, Lisa Patton, and Anne Bogel. You each inspire me in a thousand and one ways. JT and Ari, thank you for holding me up (sometimes literally) and cheering me on during even the hardest of days.

My Goonies, who are truly the only people I would willingly

follow underground for a quest anywhere at any time: Lauren Thoman, Sarah Brown, Myra McEntire, Court Stevens, Carla Lafontaine, Kristin Tubb, Erica Rodgers, Alisha Klapheke, and Ashley Blake. You make everything better.

Alisha, this book would not exist if not for you. You told me to write it, you read it as it was written, and you never doubted me or it for a single millisecond.

Myra, thank you for getting down on the floor with me, and always having my six.

Special thanks to Lauren Roedy, Rae Ann Parker, Victoria Schwab, Dana Carpenter, River Jordan, Joy Jordan Lake, Bren McClain, Kerry Madden, Alissa Moreno, Jolina Petersheim, Blake Leyers, and Brent Taylor, whose encouragement and thoughtful words I carry in my heart. You have made a difference.

Rachel Sullivan, thank you for always cheering me on, you are a true goddess like your queen of a mother before you. Lynne Street and Jenn Fitzgerald, thank you for being the best early readers ever and constant supporters. Amelia McNeese, thank you for never doubting I would get here.

Dallas Starke, Katy Melcher, Sara Cornwell, and Julia Sullivan, huge love and thanks to each of you for keeping me sane over our twenty- and thirty-year friendships, being excited with me for each step of this publishing journey, and accepting and celebrating me for being exactly who I am.

A bushel of hugs to my brother Josh McNeese, for putting up with all the books and teaching me the poetry of really good music.

A huge hat tip of gratitude to Marilyn Weaver and Ken McNeese, and Mel and Mack Weaver, my parents and grandparents, who encouraged me to celebrate my overactive imagination, championed my ability to read and, well, do pretty much everything else at the same time so long as I didn't have to put the books down, and allowed me to be as weird as I wanted to be.

Marcus, your love and support have changed my life and shown me what true magic is. You, Rivers, and Isla are my everything.

Reader, this book is for you. May it be a light if you need one, or simply a reminder that there is blindingly brilliant light in you.

Author's Note

Dear Reader,

For me, there is truth in magic and magic in truth. When I sat down to write *The Orphan Witch*, I was six months' pregnant with my daughter and unable to visualize what the future would be. In my mind, I was holding a scrapbook of the past, flipping through losses and miracles and promising mistakes that are the story of my own life. As I looked back in order to dream forward, I knew a few things to be certain: women are badasses, magic is real (though the varying forms of what magic *is* are debatable), and books are the best portal to another world.

    The Orphan Witch is a story I always wanted to write but spent years too scared to put pen to page. It is a story of sisterhood and sacrifice, of the high cost of living a life of courage, and the beauty and curse of great power. It is a story of powerful women whose stories (like the stories of all the magnificent women I know) don't have linear plot lines. We carry worlds inside of us, and those worlds are layered and nuanced. I wanted to illuminate this strength, and how it amplifies in the face of true sisterhood.

    I also couldn't stop thinking about how shadows don't run from the light—they're an echo of it. We don't have to be afraid of the darkness when we know how to use it. I thought a lot about the incredible women I know, how strong these women are. How flawed they are. How they don't let the wounds they carry stop them from being the people they want and are meant to be. How no matter where they come from, who they've been, or what they've had to overcome, when they are accepted and encouraged to be who they are, well, *anything* is possible. Much like our shadows, magic is there, even if we can't always see it.

Sincerely,
Paige Crutcher

DISCUSSION QUESTIONS

- What was your favorite part of *The Orphan Witch*?
- What was your least favorite?
- Did you race to the end, or was it more of a slow burn?
- Which scene has stuck with you the most? Why?
- Did reading *The Orphan Witch* make you want to learn more about the history of magic?
- Of all the information presented in the book, what has stayed with you the most?
- What feelings did this book evoke for you?
- If you got the chance to ask the author of this book one question, what would it be?
- Which character in the book would you most like to meet?
- Which places in the book would you most like to visit?
- What do you think of the book's title and cover? How does each relate to the book's content?
- How well do you think the author built the world in the book?
- What would you have done differently if you were Persephone?
- What would you be willing to sacrifice for those you love?
- Do you think the author made it clear why Hyacinth made the choices she made? Would you have made the same choices?
- What do you think the author's purpose was in writing this book? What ideas was she trying to get across?
- If you could hear this same story from another person's point of view, who would you choose?
- If you could read a continuation of the story, whose point of view would you choose to read?
- What do you think happens to each of these characters after the end of the book?

ABOUT THE AUTHOR

Paige Crutcher

PAIGE CRUTCHER is a former southern correspondent for *Publishers Weekly*, an artist and yogi, and co-owner of the online marketing company Hatchery.